RED BELL

by brandon spacey

RED BELL

by brandon spacey

First Edition

Cover art by brandon spacey.

Also by brandon spacey:

Callie Simmons Novels

Midnight's Park
Resurrecting Mars
Into the Darkness

Standalone Novels

Shedding Sadness
Chasing Comets

Shawn Stedwin Novels

A Flutter in the Window
Hello, World

For Melody

Thank you for all the support and encouragement.

PART ONE

PROLOGUE

The black sky was almost glowing with hidden stars, and the air was crisp with moisture. It had stopped raining within the last few hours but the invisible clouds still lurked, seeming to mute everything a few notches. As Callie stood outside the front doors of the airport, she realized that back home it was winter weather. But here it was in the mid-eighties. She took a deep breath and ran her hair back behind her ears as she looked around. She would have to get used to the warmth. She could already feel sweat forming on her back.

Callie fingered her phone open and checked the time. The service indicator on the top of the phone was spinning. It still thought she was in the States, and had not yet updated the time. With a sigh, the phone disappeared into her jacket pocket. The jacket, she realized, would itself have to disappear pretty quickly. A cabbie stepped forward and raised his eyebrows at her as he waved. She nodded and stepped away from her rolling suitcase, then opened the back door and got in. The driver loaded the suitcase in the trunk then got in and rolled away from the airport. He offered her a bottle of water, which she gratefully accepted, then he asked where she wanted to go.

"Suva, please," said Callie.

The cabbie nodded and pulled onto Queens Road. Callie began to settle in for the long ride and pulled her phone out again. Still spinning. "Excuse me," she said, leaning forward. "Could you tell me what time it is?"

"Twenty-one-fifteen," he said over his shoulder.

"Thank you," she said, and leaned back. Callie was supposed to meet her contact at the heliport in Suva at zero hundred hours, or midnight. She would have plenty of time for figuring out her plan on the ride.

Before she had left, she had worked with a woman named Kimmie or Cammie or something, in the HR department. Kimmie or Cammie had set her up with a temporary Royal ID badge for her visit to Fiji. It did not give her any special authority or restricted access, but it would at least tell them she was company official. Any special access permissions for the Fiji location would have to be granted and given by someone who worked in the Fiji location. They maintained their own security access lists.

Her plan was sketchy, at best. Callie knew she would be welcomed into the building, but wasn't worried about that part of it very much. She figured she would be able to talk her way into the right parts of the building once inside, but wasn't sure what the right parts even were. Maybe she would just ask to see Brian Bradley. If he had an office here, maybe he would take her visit. It wasn't a high-tech plan, but it was one she felt deserved some merit. He would surely have to see that she had the tenacity to get here at the very least. If nothing else, that deserved a pat on the back, didn't it? And what would it hurt to go ahead and see her? Of course, she was playing with an all-green deck. Nothing but positives. Callie was trying to keep from her mind the possibility that he would turn her away. Or, worse yet, that he wasn't even here. But if everything resolved down to Fiji, surely she would learn something while in Fiji.

After two-and-a-half hours in the car, they finally pulled onto a dirt road that ended abruptly at a chain-link fence surrounding a small cinder-block building. A weather-beaten Fijian flag waved atop the squat building in the light breeze. Callie looked around and frowned, then stretched as the cabbie got out and opened her door.

"You're sure this is it?" she asked.

"Is *it*, yes, is *it*," he replied, nodding emphatically. He looked like he was in a rush to get out of town. He quickly unloaded her suitcase and set it on the dirt of the parking lot, then he stood nervously awaiting payment. Callie reached down for her purse, and that's when she realized it wasn't there. She looked around, then spun in circles quickly, trying to envision the last time she had seen her purse. Had she brought it into the cab? She could not remember. She dove back into the backseat, searching thoroughly for something that clearly wasn't in there. It was one of those things that was so natural to feel by her side. It was so alien *not* to feel it that she couldn't recall with any real clarity the last time she had even seen it. "Oh dear God," she called to no one.

"Lady, I must be going," the cabbie said, sounding urgent.

"Okay, okay!" she cried. "I'm trying to find my purse."

"Are you serious? Good God, woman! I just drove you three hours!"

"I know!" she shouted, hands in the air. "I'm sorry! Just hang on!" She dropped to her knees in front of the suitcase and ran the zipper, flopping the large half open into the dust, immediately scanning the insides for anything resembling a purse. Silly, she knew, because she had never ever carried her purse in her suitcase. The tote bag she had used as a carry-on told the same frightful story. She opened her makeup bag where she always kept a couple of hundred-dollar bills stashed when she traveled. She stood up and handed the man two hundred dollars. "Here. Keep the change. I'm sorry," she said. The man looked at it, then at her, then he was back in the car and peeling away.

"Wait!" she shouted, turning to try to make some sense of his action. But he already had the car in drive and was pulling out onto the dirt road. "Wait, dude! You can't leave me here!" she said, waving her arms. She gave chase, but it only lasted two steps before the futility made itself obvious. *Why did you speed away?*

Callie Simmons was standing alone in a foreign country with no identification. No wallet, no money, no credit cards, and no idea what to do next. In the dark. She held her hands up for a moment, jaw dropped and breathing deeply. She felt suddenly and hopelessly lost. She had just spent seventeen hours in a plane, followed by almost three in the taxi, and now stood here in a deserted parking lot. She whipped around to have a look at the flag again. It did look old, but what did she know? Did that mean anything? Her phone still had no service, so she could only guess at the time. She found herself twirling in circles, searching the sky for a helicopter, shaking her head in disappointment and a bit of fear. If her contact failed to show, what would she do? What could she do? All she had was a paperweight for a phone, and a half-empty bottle of water. Though she stood in possibly the widest of open spaces, Callie began to understand that claustrophobia could still reach her.

CHAPTER 1

Jennifer Cambria sat at her desk with her head in her hands. Her hair hung around and between her fingers, resting on her blotter. She took a few deep breaths. Walter Watson sat across from her. It had been four weeks since his arraignment, and the hours had blown by like race cars, peppering them with bits of tire rubber and debris. He wondered if his head would ever stop spinning from it. Things had moved so quickly through the court system, he had scarcely had the time to consider that this level of efficiency was completely out of character for the government.

The criminal trial had been scheduled only two weeks after his arraignment. In the courtroom, Walter, having been standing with his head hung low had snapped his neck up and looked his attorney in the eyes, asking *What the hell?* non-verbally. She had bit her lip and shaken her head ever so slightly. The judge's schedule was uncommonly vacant due to some missed vacation or some other shit Walter had not quite caught. What it boiled down to was that the judge had planned to be gone, and then suddenly wasn't. So his schedule was not crammed full of trials and hearings like the other judges in the court. Walter wasn't sure if this was good or bad luck for him. He guessed the not-having-to-wait part of it would be less stressful in the end.

So jury selection had happened almost immediately, and the trial only lasted an hour. After seeing so much courtroom drama on television for his whole life, Walter had expected it to drag on for weeks, attorneys pacing in front of the witnesses, pointing at people on the other side, leaning on the judge's stand... None of this happened. In fact, the opposing counsel asked most of his questions without even standing up. It was very anti-dramatic. But somehow, the magic of Jennifer Cambria and her incredible knack for jury selection had won through and found him smiling when the gavel closed the book on his case.

Cambria's modus operandi had been not to pretend the assault hadn't happened – but rather, to ask the jury to agree with her that the world needed more men like him. He was the true hero here. And the jury, being a majority of middle-aged white women, had been seen nodding in all the appropriate places. Some jerk assaults a poor, defenseless blind girl, and rapes her while she's unconscious. Instead of calling the cops, Walter had handled the man himself. Cambria had plead the case of Codi Cohl right alongside Walter's own. She had told of the negative results of the rape kit; the fact that it wasn't necessarily a far stretch to find Tim's semen in the girl because they lived together, and were lovers up until just about that very moment. And Codi, having been unconscious at the time of the supposed rape, could not even recall the event in the least. There were no bruises or scars to prove she had been assaulted, either. But somehow, a beautiful woman sitting on the stand testifying these very things had found favor with the jury. It certainly did not hurt that she was blind either. The jury were visibly moved by her testimony, no doubt having put themselves into her shoes in their minds. It was a scary place to be.

With almost no real – or at least usable – evidence, what would the police do to Tim? The police could talk all day about putting bad guys away, but Walter had handled it within an hour of it happening. That was service. That was protection. And the jury saw that. It also probably did not hurt that Walter looked like a movie star sitting calmly in his sand-colored linen suit, leaning back in his chair, hands clasped casually in his lap. Big hands. The ladies of the jury were probably looking at him in ways their husbands would not have approved of. But that was the way the system worked, Cambria had told him. People like to look at attractive people.

"Look at Ted Bundy!" she had said, lifting her shoulders and holding her hands up. "He wasn't really gorgeous, but he had charm for miles. Most of the women they interviewed at that time just refused to believe he was guilty. Just because of his looks!" she said, jabbing a finger at Walter, who had sat in her guest chair with one elbow on the chair arm, scratching his chin.

"And you're good in the looks department," she had said. "If I get the right set of jurors up there, you'll walk. Community service at most."

And so it had been. The prosecution had overshot their egos by going for the full Monty. They wanted felony assault and battery, first degree. The DA's attorney had presented the 911 call as a key piece of evidence. But it was so muffled and overrun with noise as to be almost completely unusable. A man could be heard telling Tim to avoid Codi Cohl. But it was impossible to positively identify the man as Walter. And since the location was unknown due to the call having been made on a cell phone, the evidence had not gone over nearly as well as the DA had hoped.

The police had shown up and arrested Walter just as he was coming out of Tim's apartment, and had seen the blood on his hands and the condition of Tim himself. It was obvious there had been a fight. But that was all. No premeditation could be established. No planning or hatred or evil like he had wanted to show. It just wasn't there in Walter's eyes. He had given the jury his best Ted Bundy smile and performance. And Cambria had looked like an absolute pro in her sleek black trousers and navy sport coat. She was attractive too. The other side wasn't. And maybe that mattered in the eyes of the jury. *Silly humans,* Walter thought.

So as it rested, he was not guilty of first degree felony assault. The jury just wasn't able to find it in their collective heart to put this guy away for that. And so he walked. No probation; no community service; no jail time beyond time already served.

He wasn't, however, so lucky in the civil suit. Of course he was guilty of wrecking this man's face. Should he serve time for it? Well, that had been decided against in the criminal trial. But he was certainly responsible. Now they sat in Cambria's office preparing for the final verdict. Cambria had told him he would likely be responsible for all Tim's medical bills, which would no doubt be pretty hefty.

"What kind of shit is that?" Walter asked. "I mean, they found me not guilty of kicking this guy's ass. But I have to pay to have his face fixed?"

Cambria looked at him with her hard brown eyes for a long moment. "Walter you were found not guilty of felony assault. They know you beat him up. They just didn't find intent behind it beyond reasonable brotherly protective offense."

Walter nodded, chewing his fingertip. "Still."

Cambria breathed in and made a face. It was the face of a mother trying to maintain patience with a loud child at the grocer. "Walter, I told you to prepare for this. You should have seen the civil coming. Now, we can't go crying over spilled milk. It's over." She ran her hair back behind her ear and turned to pick up her briefcase. "Start thinking about what you can afford as payments to this guy."

"Payments?" he said, frowning. He looked at his fingertip then wiped it on his shirt. "Why can I not just pay it all off at once?"

She shrugged and threw him an apathetic smirk. "I suppose you can. But typically people don't like paying for their enemies' hospital bills. So they want to setup a payment plan and drag it out as long as they can."

Walter nodded, no emotion visible on his face. "Whatever's clever. I just want to be done with this shit."

Jennifer Cambria leaned against the corner of her desk with one hand, the other holding the strap of her briefcase over her shoulder, and stared at him for a long moment. She pursed her lips and took in a breath, then said, "Let's go."

Callie had started to walk down the dirt road, giving up all hope of meeting her contact, when she finally heard the *whump-whump* of a helicopter in the distance. Then she suddenly felt alight with a sense of excitement and fear. She turned and started jogging back to the squat little building where she had left her suitcase hidden in a bramble. She reached the small outpost as the lights of the helo came visible over the forest to the north.

North? Was that the north? Callie spun around looking for the moon. She thought she was oriented properly, but realized she had no way of knowing. She was operating completely on her knowledge of the map, wherein they flew into the left side of the island, and now she was somewhere near the bottom. But beyond that, there was no real way of knowing if she was right. Instinct told her she was facing north. Who was Callie to argue with instinct? She rolled her eyes at that.

The helicopter set down in the road about fifty yards from her, and Callie had to cover her ears and squint her eyes. The dirt was hitting her like tiny shards of glass, and it seemed to last a long time before someone finally came out of the fog and grabbed her by the arm. It was a woman. She had goggles and earphones on and her hair was pulled back into a tight ponytail.

The woman gave her a thumbs-up and Callie, pushing her own thumb up, noticed peripherally that someone was taking her suitcase. She turned quickly but the woman squeezed her arm, almost forcing Callie to turn back to her. The woman shook her head and gave Callie another thumbs-up, then Callie saw it was the pilot, or at least another person from the helicopter. He heaved the suitcase into the open side door of the helo, then hopped in the open front door. Callie followed the woman, ducking appropriately and squinting her eyes the whole time. When they got to the back door, the woman helped her hop up into the belly of the aircraft, then shortly the door closed.

The woman tapped Callie on the shoulder and offered her a set of earphones. She put them over her ears and was immediately rewarded with a break from the loud wind outside. The woman adjusted the mic in front of her face, then spoke to Callie, clear as day.

"It's much easier to communicate in here with tech then out there." She smiled at Callie.

"Yes, it is," Callie said, returning the smile.

"Are you Callie?"

Callie felt a mischievous smile dart across her lips. "I guess it would be pretty crazy if I wasn't..." she said.

The woman nodded. "I'd have to push you out mid-flight."

Callie smiled again, then shook her head. "Please don't do that. But I left my stupid purse on the airplane, so I have no badge, no wallet, no cash..."

The woman cut her off, closing her eyes and shaking her head. "It won't be a problem. I know what you're supposed to look like. I can get you a new badge."

Callie exhaled loudly. "Oh, thank God." She looked around her, catching her bearings as the pilot looked back at them. The woman nodded and he pulled back on the yoke. She felt her stomach drop as the rotary hopped into the night sky.

"I'm Cardna," the woman said, extending her hand to Callie.

Callie took her hand, but leaned forward widening her eyes. "I'm sorry, what did you say?"

"Cardna," she repeated. Then she stared at Callie, awaiting the obvious incoming.

Callie nodded. "Callie Simmons. Nice to meet you, Cardna." She put her hand against her own heart and added, "Well, hopefully I won't be a Simmons much longer."

Cardna tilted her head inquisitively, and Callie wondered why she had blurted that out. Not only was it totally irrelevant to her task at hand, but it meant she had thoughts of her relationship with Jack Carpenter that she had not even yet admitted to herself. The last she had checked with herself, she still wasn't even sure he was the right one. But being that this was her first time to spend any real time away from Jack since they had gotten serious, Callie would have liked to be able to send him a text letting him know she was okay.

"Well, I'm a little embarrassed now. I'm not sure why I said that," Callie said.

"No need for that. What's his name?"

Callie, thinking of her new friend Rebecca, decided to be daring, and shot back with, "How do you know it's a him?"

"Please, honey. I can see it in your eyes. You're not the type," Cardna observed.

Callie lifted her chin. "Wow, that's a powerful trick," she said.

"No trick. You just wear it where I can see it," said Cardna.

Callie opened her mouth to speak, then closed it. She thought maybe she had better keep it closed for a little bit. What the hell was she trying to do with this woman, anyway? Why was she trying to be like Rebecca? She had no practice at it, and had no idea where she would go with it if even she succeeded. Now she had made a fool of herself.

"So… about that name?" Cardna finally said.

"Oh. His name is Jack," Callie said and nodded, feeling confident about that at least.

Cardna patted Callie's hand across the legroom between their seats. They sat facing each other in the dark for a moment. "You ever think about how smell travels?" Cardna asked.

Callie pulled her head back on her neck, frowning. "What?"

"Seriously. We know how sound travels. We know about light." She looked out the window momentarily. "A little bit, anyway. We know how touch works. Nerves and all that," she said, flicking her fingers at the darkness like she was flinging water off her fingertips. She had Callie's full attention. "But do you have any idea how smell travels?"

Callie smiled, almost giggling, then stopped herself. Was Cardna being serious? After a moment, Callie realized she had been asked a question, and was now beginning to wonder if it had not been rhetorical. She cleared her throat and tried to subtly dip her nose to see if she could smell herself. Cardna was looking at her though. "Uh, why, do I stink?" Callie finally asked.

"Not that I've noticed. Just making small-talk," said Cardna.

This was her idea of small-talk? Wow. She was probably the star of the parties she attended, full of useless trivia. Callie cleared her throat again and said, "Well, I suppose it's the way molecules bounce off each other, and-"

"You're fun at parties aren't you?" Cardna said.

Callie didn't know whether to laugh or be insulted. She decided on both. She allowed herself a laugh but secretly decided she didn't like this woman very much. She would definitely be holding her cards a little closer to her chest from now on. At least around 'Cardna'. Whatever the hell kind of name that was. What the hell kind of name was it, come to that? Did her mother not know how to spell blue jay?

"It's originally a surname," Cardna said, breaking the silence.

"Excuse me?" Callie said, shocked that this woman could apparently read her thoughts. What was going on here?

"My name. My great-grandfather was Canadian. I'm apparently named after him."

"How about that?" Callie said, nodding slowly. "Did you get made fun of in school?"

Cardna looked out the window again. "Not any more than any other kid. Never bothered me much. I guess I was born without that embarrassment gene. I've never cared much about what people thought of me."

"And yet you wear makeup," Callie said. She took a deep breath and tried to steel herself.

"You can tell in the dark?" Cardna said, shooting her eyes at Callie.

Callie shrugged.

"Well, I think I meant negatives. If someone says or thinks something negative I kind of just move on. I have no time for that. Or them."

"That's a good policy," Callie agreed.

"Did you know your great-grandfather?" Cardna asked her.

How much did Callie need to tell her? How long would their acquaintance last? Was she a necessary component in the success of Callie's little personal mission here, or would she just show her to the receptionist and walk out of Callie's life forever? She decided it didn't hurt to be friendly.

"No. My mom died when I was little. I never really knew my dad," Callie said.

"Really?" Cardna asked.

"Yeah."

"No. You said 'really'. You never *really* knew your dad. What did you mean by really?"

"Oh," Callie said. *Wow, this woman was sharp.* "I mean he was in an out of my life through childhood. I don't remember much of him. He was mostly away. Had nothing to do with me." As Callie's thoughts returned to this sore subject, she found her chest shuddering a little like she was going to cry again. And she had thought she was all cried out. Why was she even still tender about this? She had not seen her father in almost twenty years. This was no fresh wound.

"I reconnected with him in my early twenties, but it didn't take," she added.

Cardna nodded slowly, looking straight into Callie's eyes. "I like that."

Callie swallowed and almost talked. She almost said a cuss word, in fact. "Come again?"

"I like how you said it didn't take. That's a clever way of phrasing it."

Callie lifted her chin, feeling a little relief. Maybe this woman wasn't that much of a bitch after all. But boy, was she hard to read, or what?

"Okay, grab onto something," Cardna said, looking out the window.

Callie grabbed the buckles around her waist and looked out the window herself. She wondered how Cardna could tell anything was about to change. It was darker than pitch out the window, and Callie could see no visibly discerning characteristics in her line of view. She did hear the rotor on top of the bird change its dynamic though, and it felt as though their descent was slowing a little. Shortly, there was a bump, and immediately the rotors began whirring down.

Cardna popped her seat belt and took her earphones off, then grabbed the door handle. Callie reached out and stopped her, putting her hand on Cardna's on the door handle. Cardna looked at her without changing her bland expression. The lights came on in the cabin. Suddenly, Callie could see what this strange woman looked like.

"I wanted to thank you for coming out and picking me up. All of you. That's, what, three of you?" Callie said, turning her head toward the front. Cardna nodded somberly. "Well, thank you. That's a lot of trouble for a lot of people."

Cardna smiled a little number at her, narrowing her eyes, and said, "Don't mention it. We take care of our own." Then she opened the door.

Callie hopped down behind her and noticed Cardna had taken her hair out of the ponytail it had been in earlier. She reckoned that might have been a necessary step against the manufactured wind of the propeller. As they made their way across the concrete, Callie realized she could see for miles. It was a dark landscape, almost certainly wooded, but just visible. And on that realization, she stumbled. They were on top of a building.

She had to stand still for a moment, hands out away from her hips as she caught her balance. It wasn't necessarily that she was afraid of heights – and certainly not when on the middle of a large rooftop. But the sudden realization and perspective shift of seeing the world back away slightly, revealing itself to be a lot lower than she had previously thought... that had scattered her nerve momentarily. Her blonde hair flicked in the light breeze and she turned on her heels looking for the moon. Still no luck on that front, and Callie was beginning to lose her bearings entirely. She simply had no idea which direction she was facing. And somewhere in the back of her mind, that mattered. She had always dedicated at least a small part of her conscious thought to knowing what direction was what, and when she was unsure, she could begin to feel uneasy if she let it rise to the surface. And here it was beginning to sweep up on her.

After a long moment of letting the cool breeze dry the sweat on her face, she began to feel a little better. She stood still a moment longer with her eyes closed before she finally opened them and took a deep breath. "Cardna?" she called.

"Yes?" Cardna answered, turning back to face her. She was several meters ahead now.

"Which direction am I facing right now? I'm sorry, I just need to know."

"Northeast," Cardna said, matter-of-fact.

Callie raised her left hand toward what would be north. The world spun and snapped into place as suddenly as a final puzzle piece hitting home. And just as suddenly, the tension disappeared from her stomach. "Thank you," she said, and carried on toward Cardna and the door beyond her.

"You okay?"

"Yeah. Just sort of lost my bearing for a moment."

"You're one of those, huh?" Cardna asked, not with any detectable condescension.

Callie frowned. "What's that?"

"One of those people who feels uncomfortable unless you're facing north."

"Not quite. But uncomfortable when I don't know what direction I'm facing," Callie said, tilting her head slightly. Was this woman onto something here?

Cardna nodded. "That entorhinal part of your brain actually activates when you face north. It's a homing signal humans have built in to their brains."

Callie smiled. After a moment of staring at Cardna's unchanging face, the smile faded. "You're serious," she said.

Cardna nodded again. "Yes." She reached up and tapped the left side of Callie's head lightly. "It's not uncommon. Are you good at navigating?"

Callie thought for a moment and screwed up her mouth. "Yeah. I think so."

"Good. We go," Cardna said, turning back toward the door.

"So what is your superpower then?" Callie said, trying to feel as normal as Cardna was trying to make her seem.

Cardna shrugged, not turning to look at her. "Well, I can call a coin flip before it hits the ground with up to fifty-percent accuracy."

Callie laughed out loud. She noticed Cardna had not waited for the pilot and the other passenger – nor had she said anything to them since they landed. Callie guessed they were close enough not to need the formalities. Cardna stopped at the door and put her hand on the handle, then pulled a badge from her shirt. It was on a lanyard that ran under her hair, around her neck. She held the badge up to the door and waited a moment, looking Callie in the eyes as she waited. Then the door clicked open. A subtle buzz resounded from the badge reader. She pushed the door open and swept her hand in, allowing Callie to go first into the darkness of the stairwell.

"It freaks some people out," Cardna said, and actually let a half-smile show itself this time.

Callie laughed out loud again, and put her hand on the strange woman's shoulder as she passed. She had a sudden dawning realization that she was now in the building where it all happened. Through the corridors of this hidden building ran the blood that fed the evil empire she had hated for so long. The very guts of the world ran through the floors beneath her feet. And just like that, the tension returned to her stomach.

CHAPTER 2

As she pulled to a stop in the parking garage of the courthouse, Jennifer Cambria put the car in park and reached up, adjusting her rear view mirror so she could have a look at her lip-liner. She made a few pops with her lips and touched the corner of her mouth, then popped open the console and retrieved a small silver flask wrapped in dark gray elephant skin. Still looking in the mirror and moving her head slightly from side to side, she unscrewed the cap and put the tiny hole to her mouth. She then held it out, again without looking away from the mirror. Walter took it from her and took a long sip of the spirit within.

He sighed and held his breath for a long moment, staring out the window at the leafless trees in the courtyard. A woman was standing by a picnic table, face buried in her phone while her kids ran around hollering like little banshees. Walter looked back at his attorney as she was readjusting the mirror. She took the proffered flask and took another short swig. She held it out to him again but he waved it away. Cambria screwed the cap back on and made it disappear. The console snapped shut and she turned in her seat to look at him.

"You're gonna do fine in there, hoss," she said.

He raised one eyebrow and returned his gaze to the lady in the park. Her kids were now trying to climb the tree. "I'm not nervous."

Cambria shrugged. "It's okay if you are. I just don't want you to be surprised."

Walter snorted. "Nothing surprises me anymore."

It only took ten minutes. Once the judge entered the room and the crowd found their seats again, it seemed like the Cliff's Notes version of a hearing had been read rather than the real thing. Walter stood there long after the judge had exited from the same door he had entered ten minutes before, while the opposing counsel stood talking to her client. Jennifer Cambria sat patiently with her legs crossed behind the table, staring at him, waiting for him to say something. Walter finally turned toward the other table and slipped his wallet out of his inner coat pocket. Cambria was up on her feet quickly, and grabbing him by the arm, but Walter shrugged her off. Despite repeated attempts to dissuade him verbally, Cambria had no luck. Walter wrote a check and slid it onto the table and walked out the half-height door.

"Walter, what the hell are you doing?" Cambria said, following him out the courtroom door. He finally stopped and turned to look at her once they were out in the hallway.

"There," he said, pointing back toward the door whence they had come. "It's over! I don't have to think about it ever again. Aside from this bullshit don't-leave-town order, I'm done!"

She stood there panting, her purse strap dangling from both hands. "Walter, why do you even pay me?" Cambria shook her head slowly.

"Because you're damned good at what you do. And you're always there for me," Walter said. He took her by the arm this time and pulled her in, kissing her on the cheek. "You're a killer, Jennifer."

He was out the front door lighting up a cigarette before she even started moving.

Outside, she joined him by the pillar that stood towering over them at twenty-five feet tall. She looked up at it casually, squinting against the brightness of the daylight. "I used to love coming here because of these pillars. The pillars of justice."

Walter took a thick drag of his smoke, then turned his head toward her. He had one hand in his pocket. "And now?"

"Well when you do shit like that, it makes me hate my job."

Walter chuckled. "Why? What the hell does what I did have to do with what you did?"

She sighed and tilted her head at him pleadingly. "Really? I fought hard to get you a payment plan that was both comfortable and insulting to opposing party at the same time. And you go and write him a fuckin' check?"

"Wow, Jennifer, I don't think I've ever heard you curse."

She reiterated her posture with a head movement. He finally turned toward her, dropping his cigarette onto the concrete and crushing it out with his loafer. "Look, I didn't mean to make a mockery of anything you did. I just didn't want to be thinking about this shit every month for the next seven years. That's like a damn car payment."

She breathed in and Walter could see her licking her teeth behind her closed lips.

"Seriously. Thank you for what you did. But I'm sure you can understand my position," Walter said.

Cambria stood staring at him for the better part of a minute before finally nodding. "Okay. Fine. Just let me leave the room first next time." Then she walked off.

"I hope there won't be a next time," Walter answered.

As they slipped into the leather seats of her Mercedes, he said, "But come to that, I need to refill your retainer."

She waved her hand in the air dismissively as she put the car in reverse. "Please. You know we're good. Consider me retained."

Walter smiled. "Now, that, I like the sound of."

Callie quickly realized that she had been wrong about the building. They had landed atop a sort of apartment for the company. It was a living quarters for the dedicated and visiting employees of Royal, and was next door to where all the action actually took place. This relieved her somewhat, but only delayed the tension, pushing it back to another day. Tomorrow, she would have to relive the stomach-churning anxiety of entering the enemy's headquarters with no real agenda. For tonight, she would be comfortable at least. Cardna had shown her to a guest apartment and keyed the door to Callie's thumbprint, thus eliminating any need for key or card.

As the door closed behind her, the lights came on in the hallway, softly illuminating the dark wooden floor, and spilling into the living area. Callie crept slowly toward the end of the hall and into the living room, where there stood expensive furniture on a soft shag rug. She ran her hand across the back of the couch and oohed at the sensation of the soft suede, then rounded to the other side past the coffee table, and pulled back the curtains that covered a window that took up an entire wall. Through the glass, she could see nothing but trees, dense and dark, but beautiful in their stark coldness.

After staring into the forest outside her window for a long time, she turned and entered the kitchen, where again, an automated light welcomed her. On the counter stood a bottle of red wine, a tall wineglass, and a note. Callie read the note as she poured herself a glass of the sweet red.

> *Callie… I look forward to hosting you on your visit, and hopefully getting to know you a little bit. I've heard so much about you – it's great to finally be meeting the legend. Enjoy the wine. Be well. ~ Cardna Darwyn*

Callie smiled and tossed the note on the counter top as she put the glass to her lips. She had not realized she had made such a global impression with her legacy. As she made her way out of the kitchen and into the bedroom, indirect lighting came on underneath the bed. The carpet in here was very thick and soft. She slipped her sneakers off and ran her toes deep into the carpet as she walked. The room was spacious but not arrogant. The bed was tall, but not wide. A queen, piled high with pillows and extra blankets. She frowned at the utility of such comfort in a country where it never got below 70 degrees.

As she walked slowly toward the dresser, relishing the thick rug under her aching feet, she held the wine glass tight against her chest with both hands wrapped round it. She might have appeared to be protecting it against theft. On the dresser stood a wood-grained stereo speaker. Apparently it had a stereo built in, for when she pressed the triangle button on top it began playing soft music. Callie breathed in deeply, smiling from her lips to her warming belly. The wine was working on her like the kneading hands of a massage therapist – dissolving the stress of travel. She knew that as soon as her head hit the pillow, she would be deep asleep. But before that, she sure needed a shower.

She made her way into the bathroom to discover a large Japanese soaking tub awaiting her in all its glistening white glory. No shower for her tonight. She smiled again and turned the handle on the tub tap. As the water began spilling into the round tub she undressed and refilled her wine, then lit a candle on the counter top. The tub was gigantic – maybe four feet across and perfectly round. It was probably half as deep. She reckoned three people could fit in it comfortably together, and definitely two. That made her think of Jack. Had that been her heart speaking in the helicopter earlier? Was she ready to marry him? Well, there was plenty of time to think about that, wasn't there?

She stepped into the bath and unwrapped a bath bomb from a collection that filled a good-sized bronze bowl on the counter. As it dropped into the water and began fizzing, Callie had a crazy thought. If Brian Bradley officed out of this location, he might well know she was here already. After all, there had been a welcoming committee in that helicopter. Three Royal employees had come to collect her. She had seen the pilot. They had made eye-contact, in fact. And of course, there had been Cardna, with whom Callie had had much conversation. But who was the third body in that chopper? Callie had not gotten a look at his face. She'd only known it was a man because of the shape of the shoulder and the obvious body movements that only men make. He had never turned around to welcome her or engage her at all. What if…

The bed was soft and cool and inviting after having been awake for so many contiguous hours. Callie fumbled with her phone for a few minutes before finally letting it slide unceremoniously out of her hand onto the nightstand with a loud thunk. What good was it if she couldn't even tell the time with it? She had planned to set an alarm, then reconsidered, then realized it was pointless. She had also planned to sit in the bath until the water got cold, but that plan was foiled after about forty minutes when she realized the water had not even begun to cool. That acrylic tub must have been severely insulated from within, because it retained heat like nuclear fission. She had climbed out sweating and red and accepted her defeat.

But even with the overwhelming exhaustion and the near-perfect comfort the bed provided, she lay awake long into the morning. Callie's eyes finally began to grow heavy as the sun was coming up through the large glass window she had forgotten to pull the curtains on. Well, at least that told her which direction her room faced. And with that, she was out.

Walter let himself in to his front door with the key and was immediately welcomed by the squeaks of excitement from Fotchie, his Jack Russell terrier. He had to sit down on the tile floor of the entry hall and let the little doggy lick his face and run circles around him. Thevi leaned against the wall with her arms crossed, watching from the end of the hall. When his eyes finally caught her, Walter smiled at her. She did not return the smile, but instead held her arms out and let her robe fall open.

His face fell, and he was instantly hopping to his feet, dusting his rump, and closing the short distance to his exquisite wife. "Hello, Candy Cane," he said, and covered her mouth with a kiss. Her arms wrapped round him and he shortly felt her fingers in his hair.

When Thevi pulled away, looking him in the eyes, he took a deep breath. "You're home," she said, simply.

Walter nodded.

"Is it finally over?"

He nodded again. She was staring at his mouth, chewing her lip. Concentrating. Clearly, she wanted to ask him something. "I can't leave town for a while, but yeah, it's over."

"Why can't you leave town?" she asked, stroking his shoulder.

"They're monitoring him? Monitoring me? Monitoring something. I don't exactly know. I didn't precisely pay attention."

"So you don't know how long you can't leave town for?"

Walter shrugged. *Doesn't matter.* "Where the fuck am I going?"

Thevi shrugged, then made a face. Then she did that thing where she was crossing her arms and lightly running her fingers up and down the outside of each opposite arm, staring at the floor.

"What is it, darling?" Walter finally said.

She breathed in deeply before answering. "You're not going to pull that shit again, are you?"

Walter frowned. "What shit? Breaking that rapist piece-of-shit's face?"

She pulled her head back and frowned herself. "No. Getting caught."

Walter had to smile. Then they were kissing again.

The phone rang four times before there was an answer. Callie pulled the heavy receiver away from her face and frowned at it when he answered. "Walter? Am I waking you up?"

"Huh? What the fuck?" he said.

She frowned again. "Sorry, I didn't know if you slept in."

"Slept in 'til three?" he replied. "What is this about?"

"Three?" Callie said. She shook her head, closing her eyes, then pulled her hair and sighed. "I need more coffee. You're in a different time zone aren't you," she said.

"I don't think I've ever slept until three pm," Walter said. "No matter the time zone." After a brief pause, he asked, "What's up?"

She was running a hand through her unkempt hair. "This is so crazy down here, Walter. I so wish you were here."

"Where, Fiji?" There was a slight delay in his responses. She reckoned it was from her being on the other side of the globe from him. "Have you called Jack? What time is it there?" he asked.

Callie looked at the clock on the nightstand, then closed her eyes again. "Seven in the morning. Yes, I called Jack. He must be at work. He didn't answer."

"Ah. So we're at least on the same day."

Callie had to process this for a long moment. "Yeah, I guess so. Look, I don't know what to do here, Walter." She sat patiently, awaiting a response. But all she heard was the artificial line noise phone companies added to digital calls. After a long pause, she said, "Walter?"

"Yeah, I'm here. I'm just having a little trouble understanding the logic of flying halfway around the goddamn globe without any kind of plan."

"Walter, don't you dare cuss at me right now. I need some moral support. I'm a little claustrophobic right now."

"I'm not sure you're using the right word, honey."

She opened her eyes and looked at the bright yellow disc that was beginning to creep up over the trees. "Why? It's exactly how I feel," she said. "Trapped in a box I can't get out of."

"Okay," Walter said, sighing. "Let's break this down. Have you made contact with the guy yet?"

"No. But I have a weird suspicion he might have been on the helicopter that picked me up last night."

"You're going to have to explain that to me," Walter said and cleared his throat.

"Well, three people were on the copter. A woman and two men. I didn't get a good look at the third person, but I'm having this weird feeling that it was him."

"Well, Callie, your gut feelings are usually right. So you know he's at least there. That's a good thing, right?"

"Well, one would think, but this place is huge. They have a completely separate barracks for the employees. It's a whole building with the helipad on top," Callie said. "So I was thinking I might just-" she started, but was interrupted by a soft knock at the door.

"Hey, I gotta go," she said, and dropped the phone onto its cradle. Callie stood up and tied the thick robe around her waist, sliding her feet along the carpet on the way to the door. She considered asking who it was, but quickly snuffed the thought. She knew who it would be.

So when she opened the door with a sweet, welcoming smile for her new friend, she was not only shocked, but disappointed to see it was not Cardna. The smile slid off her face, and she worried she might now look inhospitable. "Yes?" she managed, trying not to show her confusion.

"Good morning, ma'am. Miss Darwyn said you would be up. She would like you to meet her in the cafe."

Callie straightened her head and pulled her robe tighter across her chest. She cleared her throat. "Okay, can you tell me how to get there?"

"No, I'm sorry. You can't get there. I'm here to escort you."

"Excuse me?" Callie said, frowning.

"You need a badge to get there. I'll wait while you get dressed," the short woman said.

"Okay. Okay, let me do that, then," Callie said, finally. "Would you like to come in?"

"No, thank you." The woman turned away and swiped her phone open. *Awkward.*

Fifteen minutes later, Callie was being shown into a modest but not tiny cafe that was completely lit by the morning light spilling through the huge windows on the east wall. The tables were all at floor-level, surrounded by round benches that one had to step down into. Callie thought she recognized the concept, but couldn't place it.

Cardna was waiting at one such table with a steaming mug of coffee in front of her, and a tablet in her left hand. Callie could see as she stepped down into the booth that Cardna was reading some news story on the tablet. She spoke as Callie found her seat, not quite directly across the table from Cardna.

"Good morning, Ms. Simmons. Sleep well?"

Callie nodded and smiled, then said, "Yes. Not much, but yes, well."

"Good. I'm sure you'll make up for the lost time tonight," Cardna said. "Coffee?"

"Yes, please," Callie said, looking around the cafe. There were several other people scattered about the other floor booths, but no one was paying any attention to the newcomer. And none of them was familiar to her. All of them were busy reading something or other on phones or tablets.

Cardna looked up at someone out of Callie's vision and shortly a mug was delivered. Cardna slid the carafe across the table to her. "Thank you," she said, and poured herself some black coffee, of which she immediately began trying to change the color. She sipped from the mug and had to frown suddenly at the goodness – the freshness – of the brew. It was bold and wonderful. She suddenly regretted decorating it with so much cream and sugar. After a few minutes of long but not awkward silence, Cardna finally set the tablet down and pulled her own mug in front of her.

"Sorry. Had to finish that column."

Callie waved away the apology.

"So. Tell me, Ms. Simmons, why are you here?"

Callie squinted and smiled a sour number, like she had sucked a lemon. "Cardna? May I call you that?"

Cardna widened her eyes as she sipped from her mug, and nodded briefly.

"Will you please call me Callie?"

"Of course."

"Thank you," she said. "Well, I'm here to make some acquaintances, to ask some questions. A sort of general get-to-know-how-all-this-works thing."

Cardna looked bored. "Uh huh."

Callie raised her own eyebrows. "What?"

"Let's cut the bullshit, darling. No one flies halfway around the planet to see how it all works."

They stared at each other for a long moment. Callie felt her will dissolving. Confrontation was never her strong suit. Intimidation somewhere in that same neighborhood. Callie swallowed. "Look," she started.

Cardna smiled and reached her hand across the short section of table between them, covering Callie's hand with her own. "Honey, you can be honest with me. I have suspicions, but I need to hear you say it."

Callie was shaking her head slowly. But she wasn't pulling her hand away from Cardna's either. "I'm sorry, I don't follow."

"I thought we agreed to cut the bullshit."

Callie giggled and pulled her hand away this time. She tried to hide the obvious fiddly nature of the gesture by wrapping her hand around the back of her mug. It didn't go over well. Cardna was smirking. "Well," Callie sighed, "I didn't really agree yet." And Cardna smiled. A real smile. This eased the tension in Callie's stomach a little.

"Look," Cardna said, and reached out for Callie's hand again. Callie actually allowed her to take it from the mug. Was this a power move? A proving ground for Cardna's ascendancy? Showing Callie just exactly who was in control here? Well, whatever it was, it was working. "The simple truth," Cardna continued, "is that you're not going to get very far here without my help."

Callie frowned again. "I thought I would be getting my own badge…"

Cardna reached into a bag beside her with the free hand and pulled a badge out, sliding it across the table. "Here's your badge. But you're not going to get through any doors I don't think you should get through. That's not just a figurative statement."

Callie swallowed, pulled her hand away from Cardna's, and swept the badge up off the table. The move was both utilitarian and assertive in its intentions, yet still carefully decorous. "Okay, I'm not sure what you're asking. Are you asking what my motives are?"

Cardna sat up straight, collecting the carafe and refilling her own mug with the steaming coffee. "Yes. Very simply put, I need to know what the main reason is for your visit here."

Again, they stared at each other in silence for a bit. Callie found it unsettling that she felt like she might be getting better at this. Maybe the intimidation was dissipating. Maybe she was just getting stronger. Either way, she did not feel near the embarrassment of staring into a stranger's eyes as she had before.

Cardna was the first to look away. Callie felt a small victory in this. Cardna had looked down at her mug to watch herself twist it on the table to put the handle in line with her other hand. It was a smooth move, but Callie had caught it. "Here's the other thing, Callie," she said, finally meeting Callie's eyes again. This time with not only the strength and confidence that her gaze had previously possessed, but with a slight tinge of that boredom again. Like this could all go this way or that, and it didn't make a shit to Cardna which way that was. If Callie didn't want to talk, Cardna wouldn't force it. But then Callie also wouldn't get anywhere. Cardna was fine with whatever. And this might just be wasting her time.

"I'm not necessarily your enemy here. I might actually be your friend," Cardna finished.

Callie tilted her head thoughtfully. Now this was an angle she hadn't considered. But the underlying truth was very obvious. If she didn't show some of her cards to this woman, she wouldn't get to finish the hand. So, finally accepting of her fate, Callie decided it was useless to go on with her previous plan – which, she had to remind herself, wasn't a plan at all. She sighed and dropped her own eyes to the mug in front of her. She used this opportunity to refill her own coffee. This time she left it black. When she once again met Cardna's gaze, there was a new look on the other's face. It wasn't so much a confidence as a comfort. A soft look that betrayed a little sympathy. *I'm here for you, friend. Whatever it is you have to say, I'm ready to listen.*

Callie stared a second longer, and finally decided to lay it all out. "I'm here to find someone. Several years ago now, I worked for the Oliver Company." Cardna was nodding, Callie noted. "They sent a crew on a trip to Mars and never came back."

This time it was Cardna who tilted her head thoughtfully. She took a small sip of her coffee and leaned forward, both hands hidden under the table. She was listening intently now.

"One of the men on that mission was Brian Bradley," Callie said, and waited to see if there was any reaction in Cardna's eyes. There wasn't. The other woman did, however, furl her lips and begin chewing on the bottom one. Not nervously, necessarily, but maybe in unconscious concentration.

"I didn't know at the time, but apparently there was another ship out there at the same time. Somewhere in the vicinity of Mars. A ship that belonged to your company." Callie got a chill up her spine as she said the word *Mars*, suddenly feeling spooked that it was even possible to get out that far. Worlds of progress had been made toward the goal of being a space-faring civilization!

Cardna squinted slightly, and said, softly interrupting with a touch on Callie's knee under the table, "My company?"

Callie nodded. "Royal Research apparently had a ship out there, waiting to rescue him."

Cardna shook her head skeptically, frowning at the ridiculousness of this statement. "Rescue him? From what?"

Callie took a deep breath and looked around the cafe again. Several people had left without her noticing. "I don't know why the Oliver mission failed. Well, I think I do, actually. But that's not the point. My question is, why were they able to rescue that one man from a doomed mission, but not the rest of the crew?"

Cardna's eyes were wide now. She was shaking her head slowly, and probably unconsciously.

"I mean," Callie said, and noticed her hands were trembling slightly. She allowed Cardna to take her left hand again when the other woman again reached out for it. "I mean… that's not just wrong. It's diabolical."

Cardna was looking at Callie with the eyes of someone who was trying to empathize with the loss of her friend. If nothing else, Callie at least had her attention now. All of it.

Callie breathed in deeply again and continued. "Somehow, Bradley made it back here to Earth. Unnoticed. You see, he used to work for Oliver as well. But maybe that was a farce."

"You're thinking the Oliver badge he wore was covering a Royal one."

Callie thought about this analogy for a moment. Then she nodded. "Yeah, maybe. But we didn't know he made it back. I only found out a few months ago. We all had thought he perished with the rest of the Oliver crew."

Cardna pulled her hand away and looked about the cafe herself. She was chewing her lip a little more intensely now. She took a deep breath and then a large gulp from her coffee. "Let's get out of here, Callie," she said.

CHAPTER 3

As they pulled out of the garage the sunlight greeted them and Callie had to shield her eyes. Of course, her sunglasses – like everything else she seemed to be needing – were in her room. Probably still in her suitcase. Or maybe they were in her purse. *I have no idea where anything is.* They slowed to a stop momentarily at the gate. A man leaned down and made a gesture with his hand. Callie peripherally saw Cardna make a gesture in return and the man nodded. She had not seen the gesture well enough to describe it, but it had started like a cheerleader's wave, then moved to a fist before her hand had moved out of Callie's vision, blocked by Cardna's shoulder. "What was all that about?" she asked.

"Duress signals."

Callie frowned and nodded. Neat.

They spoke very little as Cardna drove them to wherever they were going. Callie had tried to ask her where they were headed as they left the cafe. Conversationally. Like she wasn't a little nervous about it. True, she was comfortable enough in the presence of this strange woman. She had, it seemed, gotten Cardna to find sympathy for her plight very quickly. But that only went so far. She, Callie, was still trapped on this island with no power of her own. She was at the mercy of everyone's hospitality. If they turned on her, she could be vanished like a mobster in the sands outside of Las Vegas. She knew her own vulnerability. But Cardna did seem interested, at least, in hearing what Callie had to say. Would she believe? She looked as though she did already. And why not? There had been no opinions spoken yet. Only Callie's verdict of the actions as being evil. But surely, any human in her right mind would agree with that assessment, would she not? All moral beings can see evil the same way. Can't they? Or was this naivety?

The trees formed a tunnel over and around the road, letting only sparse light in. Light that had a green hue to it. It was a peaceful and beautiful sight, if not a little eerie. A little… claustrophobic. That word again. How could Walter not understand her claustrophobia? She was now in the passenger seat of Cardna's Mercedes Benz, comfortable in the cool leather, but a little more aware of this feeling of enclosure. Trapped in this car, held in by a strap of seat belt. In this tunnel of forestry. On this island on the other side of the world. Briefly, she wondered if that part of the brain Cardna had mentioned that felt good facing north had any counterparts to it. Were people born in the southern hemisphere the same way about facing South?

Callie had asked where they were going while they were still inside the building, but she had been shushed. She caught on quickly that Cardna thought anything said within the walls of the compound were subject to monitoring. But now that they were traveling, Callie thought it might be okay to talk about *something*. Maybe not her mission, but *something*. Right?

Cardna reached up and touched the car's control panel screen just above the gear shift knob, and Callie had a thought. "I figured you would all be driving Teslas down here."

Cardna looked over at her in the semi-darkness of the car's interior. Both of her hands were at the top of the steering wheel. "Come again?"

"Teslas. Electric cars. I figured they would prevail down here."

"Why would you think that?" Cardna said.

Callie looked out the window again. It had just been conversational. Maybe even rhetorical. She just wanted to know they could still talk. "Not many gas stations out here, I guess. High-tech company, all that."

Cardna nodded. "Yeah, I like Mr. Musk. I love his enormous sense of entrepreneurship. His ingenuity. But the world's just not ready for electric cars yet."

"Why is that?" Callie said, almost chuckling. Cardna made eye contact with her. The stare lingered a moment.

"Well, the batteries only last five or six years. And then they have to be replaced. The old ones have to be buried somewhere. They're not recyclable. And they're enormous. Gigantic bio-hazardous shit they have to bury somewhere – presumably the ocean. And there are going to be millions of them."

Callie's smile disappeared quickly. She had never considered the waste side of the argument. Everything produces waste, of course, but…

"And let's not pretend we don't know where we get the power – the electricity – to charge those batteries," Cardna said, cutting off her thoughts. After a moment, she added, "It actually takes more fossil fuel to charge those batteries throughout their life than a combustion-engine car would use in the same lifespan."

"Holy shit," Callie said, and suddenly clapped her hand to her mouth. She felt her cheeks turn red, and looked at Cardna, who was staring awkwardly at her.

"What? What's wrong?"

"I'm sorry," Callie said. "I just swore."

Cardna giggled. "I'm not offended, Callie. I might even have said such things before, myself." She patted Callie's leg then looked back at the road ahead of them. "Though I haven't since I was a teenager."

Callie's embarrassment grew thicker. "Oh, I'm sorry," Callie said again.

"I'm kidding, darling. Let it go."

Callie looked back out the window, then quickly turned back to Cardna. "Are you serious though?"

"No. I probably cursed this morning when my alarm dragged me out of a pleasant dream I was having."

"No, I mean about the batteries."

"Oh, absolutely. I wasn't opining, sweetie. This is well published data. These cars look like the saviors of the planet, but they're actually going to create a lot more problems than they pretend to solve."

"That is insane," Callie said, shaking her head. And suddenly, they were decelerating. They had only been driving for about twenty minutes, she reckoned. She heard the soft click of the blinker and then they were turning right, into a driveway off the tunnel of trees. In Callie's estimation, they were now heading east. And shortly, they pulled up to a modest house, set alone against a backdrop of trees and more trees. There were no other houses on the road. The roof was covered in a mossy-green layer that spoke of years of existence shaded from the harsh sun above.

They walked up a cobbled path to the front door, which stuck when Cardna turned the knob. She leaned against it and it gave, swinging inward to reveal a dimly lit, rustic room, cozy in its simplicity, and completely devoid of technology. This appeared, at least to Callie's first glance, to include electricity.

"Wow!" she whispered as they stepped into the coolness of the interior.

"You don't have to whisper here," Cardna said. Callie almost started, but caught herself and giggled.

"This is amazing! Beautiful!" she said.

"Yeah, it's a nice retreat," Cardna said, tossing her keys on a small coffee table that sat in front of an overstuffed cloth sofa piled high with pillows. Beside the couch stood a basket full of soft blankets. And the only other furniture in the room, which was a large matching chair. "Go ahead and make yourself comfortable. Would you like something to drink?"

"No, thank you," Callie said, and looked around the sparse room. "Actually, that coffee is starting to cry for a way out."

"There's a nice bush out back you can squat beside," Cardna said as she settled onto the sofa, staring Callie in the eyes.

Callie almost smiled, but didn't want to be rude. "Oh. Okay."

"I'm kidding, darling. You need to relax a little. There's a bathroom in the room behind me. It's not probably as modern as you're used to, but it works."

Callie felt relieved and let a weak smile play her lips. *Thank God.* The bathroom was indeed primitive. There was a porcelain bowl on the floor. But there was no tank behind it. Just a round seat in the middle of the floor. Beside the can was a large bucket full of brackish water with a plastic pitcher floating in it. She got the idea pretty quickly, and relieved herself in short order. The pitcher held enough to raise the water level above the trap, sending the waste water out the bottom, almost like a normal toilet. *What the hell is this place?*

As she came back into the den, she didn't immediately see Cardna, and a flash of fear poured through her. Worried she had been abandoned here, Callie almost cried out, but then she saw Cardna on her hands and knees in front of the small sofa.

Back in the den, Callie found herself again wondering about the technology that powered this place. There were some lantern sconces on the walls, but during the daylight hours, there seemed to be enough light creeping through the windows that they weren't needed. There were no fixtures in the ceiling. A potbelly stove stood in one corner, with a neat pile of logs stacked beside it. But no other modern amenities were visible. When she sat down, she noticed Cardna had curled her legs up under her on the sofa and was half-covered with a thick blanket. Callie took the cue and curled her own legs up on the big chair, reaching for a woolen blanket to mimic what she was seeing.

"Well, I guess you had better start from the beginning," Cardna said.

Callie nodded deliberately, but looked around the room before she spoke. "What is this place, Cardna?"

"They have these cabins strewn about throughout the surrounding area of the suburbs. There are regular homes too. But these cabins are completely primitive. Just a nice little escape when I need a day or two to unwind from work."

Callie nodded again, a little more comfortably. "I would love to know what exactly you do, sometime."

"We'll get there. For now, talk."

"Okay. Right to the point," Callie said, chuckling. Then straightened herself and met the other woman's gaze. She looked ready to be convinced. There was that, at least. She took a deep breath and started. "When I worked at Oliver Company, I started sensing something was wrong with the mission. And I was in communication with Donnie, who was on the mission itself. He kind of spurred me into an investigation of sorts. I started looking into Mr. Bradley. I eventually found a stack of receipts he had hidden under his filing cabinet that betrayed what he had really been doing there for the past two years or so.

"While they were preparing for this mission to Mars, he was ordering parts for the ship from some backyard company. Not from Lockheed or Boeing. This stuff he was ordering was not space-hardened. But he was creating fake invoices, showing he had paid full price for the parts." She breathed in and looked down at her hands, trying to wring out the coldness from them. Cardna was staring at her intently, obviously very interested in what Callie was saying. This made her feel a little better.

"Anyway, I later found out that this money he was embezzling was sent back to Royal to fund the purchase of one of Oliver's satellites."

"No effing way," Cardna said, her first real injection of excitement since the conversation had begun in the cafe earlier that morning.

Callie was nodding. "Yeah. They bought an Oliver satellite, presumably to steal the proprietary communications technology the company used. Obviously, they had assumed it was used company-wide. The assumption was correct. So they, I guess, used this communications chip to listen in on, and even follow, the Atlas ship as it made its way out to Mars."

Cardna's hand was now over her mouth, a look of utter fascination in her eyes. Either she was completely enthralled, or she was a very good actor. It was too late to matter at this point. Callie had stepped in with both feet. She had to take this thing to the end, now. And – as Cardna had so eloquently pointed out earlier – you had to trust someone. If not, she would never get past the first door. She had to have an ally. And that meant getting someone to listen to the story, and believe it. And not only believe it, but want to be a party to its resolution.

She continued, "No one knows why. Was it a spy mission?" She shrugged, in answer to her own question. "I don't know. No one who was on that mission is alive anymore. I lost some really close friends," Callie said. She breathed in and out, feeling like her breathing was not bringing in as much oxygen as she was used to. Her head felt light.

"We all know," she said, making eye contact with Cardna, "Royal has better tech than any other company out there. They didn't need our communications tech. But for whatever the reason, they had it. They bought it with our money too." Callie shook her head quickly, closing her eyes against the apparent absurdity of that statement. Or angry with it. "It's psychotic."

She saw Cardna nodding slightly. Was this a point in her favor? Was she being swayed?

"Anyway, a few months before the mission happened, one of the crew developed a heart condition. He couldn't go. So Donnie assigned Brian Bradley as the replacement. Well, in a mad rush to get the ship to be actually space-worthy, he started ordering and having these crap parts he had previously put on replaced with good ones. He spent a fortune. And didn't get done in time.

"But there's kind of a theory I and a friend of mine have developed – that Royal told him not to worry. They were going to follow along, so if the ship failed in mid-flight, they would be there to rescue him."

"This is insane," Cardna said. She put both hands on her forehead, widening her eyes. Then she pulled her hair back and left her hands on top of her head. "This is absolutely crazy."

Callie nodded soberly. "Yeah. So, well, I'm not on a company-funded mission. This is personal. I want to ask Bradley why he did all this. Why my friends had to die. Why did they have to die at all?" Callie said, and her voice cracked. Her eyes filled with tears suddenly, and the saltwater burned. She quickly reached up and tried to wipe them dry, but it was useless. And then she felt the hard corner of a tissue box tapping against her forearm.

She took the proffered box from Cardna and said a quiet thank-you as she wiped her eyes dry. Callie took a few moments to compose herself. Cardna waited patiently. And then she finally asked a question when she felt the mines had been cleared. "And you're absolutely sure of his involvement with this?"

Callie nodded soberly, again. "Yes. There were several other factors that indicted him, but yeah, those invoices under the file cabinet were the deal-sealer. We found pictures on his computer of Donnie in a – well, in an embarrassing situation. Phone calls. Whatever. Yeah, we know. I know. Everyone else is gone. But I know."

"So what then?" Cardna said, spreading her hands in front of her.

"What do you mean, *'what then'*?" Callie asked.

"I mean, what if you get your reckoning. Let's say you talk to Mr. Bradley and he admits to it all. What then? Are you happy? Do you just go home? Do you try to prosecute him? What do you do?"

Callie nodded. "Well, I don't know." She suddenly felt like she needed to keep this part secret. She sure was pouring an awful lot of trust in to Ms. Darwyn, without really knowing her.

"Oh, come on, Callie," Cardna said, grinning. "You don't expect me to believe that – once again – you flew halfway across the pl-"

"I don't know, Cardna!" Callie almost shouted, cutting her off. Cardna flinched. "I don't know," she repeated, a little more in control of her emotions. "I really hadn't thought that far ahead."

Chewing her bottom lip again, Cardna nodded, staring at the rug between the couches. "I see. So you came all the way out to Fiji – on your own dime, as you said – to confront someone and give him a good finger-wagging. And then you'll go home."

They sat there for a moment, in complete silence. And again, Callie was reminded of her vulnerability. She was in the literal middle of nowhere out here in the woods, in a cabin she could not locate on a map. With a woman she was trusting with no good intuition to do so. On a strange island in a foreign country. Alone. She shivered. What if she was wrong about Cardna?

"How much did your plane ticket cost, Callie?" Cardna said, breaking an eerie silence.

"Excuse me?" Callie said, looking up at her.

But Cardna didn't answer. She only subtly hiked her chin an inch.

Callie sighed and looked back down at her hands. "Listen. I'm not here to assassinate him or anything. I just want to know why. What? To what end?"

Cardna stared at her for a very long time in silence. And then she surprised Callie by saying, "What if I told you why? What if I cut out the middle man, and I, myself, told you why they went out there?"

Callie was so shocked she must have looked like a deer on railroad tracks, staring into the face of an oncoming train. She could only stare as the seconds ticked by on a clock that wasn't there. And then she finally found her tongue. "You mean... You mean you know?"

Cardna was looking at her through squinted eyes. Those nearly closed eyelids held back some of the most vivid green Callie had ever seen. Fitting with their current environs, she thought. And then she finally nodded. "I do know, Callie." She shook the blanket off of her and stood up, tossing it over the arm of the sofa. And as she walked past Callie, disappearing behind her, Cardna's fingers dragged softly across Callie's right shoulder. "But I'm not sure you would believe me if I told you."

CHAPTER 4

Walter stood in the doorway of the back door. He was smoking a cigarette, staring out at the swimming pool. It was still covered from the winter. There were leaves everywhere. He always dreaded the coming swim season, having to uncover the pool and get rid of all the leaves. It was an all-day affair. But that was not truly what was on his mind at the moment. He was trying to replay his conversation with Callie in his mind.

He knew she had said something about the buildings being separate. And that it was big. But why had she had to go so suddenly? She had not been hiding from anyone. At least not that he was aware. She was over there on a company badge. So she shouldn't need to worry about her little mission being discovered. Even if it were, wouldn't there be some people there who were in their right minds? *Clearly they would see that she was right, and...* But it wouldn't wash. This was the company that had sabotaged the Mars mission. If they were capable of that, it meant they were made up of people were like-minded to the cause. Whatever cause would allow an entire ship full of people to perish in space.

He blew the last of the smoke out and pinched the cherry off and dropped the butt in a dirt-filled flower pot by the door. Walter ran his hand through his hair, then crossed his arms. Fotchie was standing on the pool deck staring up at him expectantly. "What about it, Fotch?" he asked the dog. "Is Callie okay?" But the dog only tilted his head in that curious way that could mean everything, or nothing.

Walter's position at Royal was in a state of rest. He could go back to work now that the hearing and punishment had finished in his assault case, but he would have to undergo review first. He and his boss, Roland, had had a rather unpleasant exchange the last time Walter had been in. During that presentation, Walter's head had been elsewhere. And Roland had told him to take some time off and get his head in order. The words he had used had not pleased Walter, and Walter had made sure the other man knew it, with some choice words. There was a greater-than-zero chance the scabs from those words were still fresh. Still, he couldn't help but feeling it might be beneficial to have access to company resources right about now. It would take two weeks to review his situation and determine if he was suitable to return to work. A whole lot could happen in two weeks.

But he could not just let Callie down if she needed him. It wasn't that Walter cared much about the money. Though it was an expensive trip to Fiji, he wasn't concerned about the cost. He had the money. And Callie's welfare was more important. But he didn't know anyone who worked in Fiji. At least he didn't think he did. Who knew who had ended up down there? People were shuffled around all the time. The point though, was if he were to fly down there, he wouldn't know where to go. He could find the compound, he thought.

But what then? He would have to smile his way in. Somehow he didn't think that would work at Royal, Fiji.

Walter lit another cigarette, then slid his finger across the lock pattern on his phone. Scrolled through his contacts. Clicked a name. Hit the green phone icon. After a brief moment of ringing, a familiar, sandpaper voice answered on the other end. "Yes, master."

"How is my little kitten?" he said.

"Oh, you know. Same day, different thing."

"What is today?" Walter asked, taking a drag from his cigarette. He could hear Rebecca taking a drag of her own.

"Ah, let's see. Today is May eleventh. It's Eat What You Want Day, Walt!"

"Oh, well, I guess you're in luck then," he scoffed, and wiped his upper lip with the back of his sleeve.

"It's a lifestyle I cannot regret, my dear Watson."

"Hey, you'll get no lip from me about it. I'm a lesbian trapped in a man's body."

"Yes, but you see, I've had the other before. And yet I lean this way. You are, in fact, the one who doesn't know what you're missing. You might actually like it," Rebecca said in a sigh.

"There's a greater-than-zero chance you're right. But there are so many zeroes before the first real number after the decimal that it's basically nil."

"Well, sexuality is at least something we can see eye-to-eye on."

"Amen to that, sister," he replied.

"So to what do I owe the pleasure of this conversation? It sounds like you're out," she said. It sounded as though she was watering her plants.

"I'm out," he agreed, nodding. He took another pull from his cigarette, then blew the smoke out sideways. "Been out for a minute, actually. So, hey, look, I have a favor to ask."

"This won't be another plea to observe my bedroom habits, will it?"

"Well, if it's going to take more than just the one…"

"Long way to go, baby."

"Okay. Well, then. In that case, onward," he said, holding his cigarette high up. "So, our friend, Callie, might be trapped down in Fiji."

"Oh to be so lucky. How does one get trapped in the most beautiful place on Earth?"

"By walking into the wrong party."

They had moved to the kitchen area. That is to say, if this were a regular house, this would be where the kitchen was. As it were, there was a long wooden block with a couple of bowls on it, and some cases of water stacked in the corner. There were no appliances. Cardna's hand was wrapped round a bottle of water, leaning on the counter top. Callie stood facing her, arms crossed and digging in with her mind. Cardna was about to let go a little secret, at least it seemed. That would concrete it in Callie's mind that she had made the right decision about trusting her. Again, though, she had to remind herself that there had been no real options. *You can bet on the number 8 horse.* Why? *Because that's the only one left.*

"Look," Cardna had said, after she had made her way across the room, leaving Callie in the large seat with her shoulder tingling from a touch. "If I tell you this, it has to be absolutely sworn that you will never share me as the source."

Callie had stared straight ahead at the window, wondering what kind of face Cardna was making behind her. Was she smirking? Was she wide-eyed and serious looking? Hands trembling in front of her chest, like Callie herself felt like doing? Or was she leaning against the counter and looking smug, rolling her eyes? All she could do was leap now.

"You have my word," Callie had said simply.

"Come stand with me, please," Cardna said. And Callie had complied.

Now, here she stood, looking this woman in the eyes and wondering what was about to come out of her mouth. There wasn't much that would surprise Callie. She had seen some insipidly out-of-bounds things in her recent years. Things that should not be allowed to exist within the laws of physics. But still, she felt she was about to be shaken. For some reason, the gravity of Cardna's words was more than the weight of the letters that made them up. She rolled her neck, stretching some circulation back into it, trying to mask the apprehension that now wrapped tightly around her stomach.

Cardna straightened her head as if she were just settling an argument with a toddler. *There, now. Isn't that better?* She stared at Callie, then ran her eyes up and down her body, unnecessarily. What was that all about? Was she sizing Callie up for a physical altercation if Callie didn't respond appropriately? "Okay. Royal has been doing their own research regarding the Red Planet."

Callie widened her eyes. Was that it? Wow. Researching Mars? That was about as deep as the puddle left in a Frisbee after a hard rain. She furled her mouth, but maintained her serious look at Cardna, eyes still wide. And perhaps Cardna read that reaction properly, because she giggled, then smirked.

"Years, Callie. They've been doing it for years. I think…" she started, then blew her cheeks out and stared at Callie for a moment. Pondering. After a long moment, she sighed and said, "I *know*… There are some serious research implements down in the basement. Like some really heavy equipment that might do some really crazy shit."

Callie frowned. *Heavy?* She was about to speak up when Cardna held a hand up, closed her eyes, and shook her head.

"Listen. I'm playing these cards as I draw them. I'm trying to decide how to tell you certain things without completely fucking myself."

"I gave you my word. So you might as well spell it out, because I'm not very good with metaphor."

Cardna stared at her for another long moment, those narrow slits that passed as eyes still right there on display. After a long silence, she finally said, "Okay, try this. I've heard in whispers and quiet conversations," she said in almost a whisper – as if she were trying to recreate the rumor mill herself – "that there might be something earth-shattering down there."

"Wow," said Callie.

Cardna gave her a disappointed smile and shook her head. "Still warming up. Bear with me."

Callie stood up straight, putting both hands flat on the table top. She took in Cardna's posture and body language. The woman looked like she was truly on the fence about divulging something incriminating about… about who? *The company? Brian Bradley? Herself?* Callie decided to be patient. To see if waiting would draw out the final words, like a hot match draws out a tick.

"In the basement there are pallets full of equipment and machinery," Cardna finally said. "From the whispers I've heard, some of this equipment *might have* capabilities that could potentially answer some of your questions about Mars."

Callie shook her head. This was getting ridiculous, and it was beginning to feel a little like a game. Only she wasn't sure of the rules. Hell, she wasn't even sure what color she was supposed to be playing.

Cardna smiled at her. "Let's take our time. I'll tell you everything I know in time. Let me develop a little more trust. Come. Let's ride," she said. And with that, she was turning on her heel, opening the front door. Callie looked around the place, unbelieving and annoyed. *What the hell is going on here?* The image of playing a game she didn't understand returned. Like playing Chess on a Chinese Checkers board. Or Yahtzee with nothing but an Uno deck. She finally held her hands up in a *what now?* gesture and followed the other woman into the dooryard.

In the car, there was again a lot more silence, and not much else. Callie wondered how many radio stations they got out here, and how well they even received them. Pretty quickly though, Callie realized they were heading right back to the Royal compound. She frowned at the absurdity of such an unnecessary trek, only to turn around and go right back.

"I had to take you somewhere I knew they wouldn't be listening," Cardna said, again seeming to read Callie's thoughts.

"Well, I appreciate your time and discretion in this matter."

"In this matter?" Cardna said, laughing out loud. "Why did you get so formal all of a sudden?"

Callie had to laugh herself. When the laughter died though, she said, "Seriously though. I wasn't sure how you would take it. It's a little frightening to fly halfway around the globe, as you put it, and have no one I can trust."

"Well, you can trust me," Cardna said, putting a hand on Callie's knee. It was then that the alarm bells went off in Callie's head. That was one of the only mantras she remembered from her mother, hearing it as a child. *If anyone ever tells you that you can trust them, don't.* Callie's stomach tensed up and she might have grabbed the door handle a little harder. Fortunately, the other woman had not seemed to notice it. But if she were indeed reading Callie's mind...

"When we get back, I'll have you wait in my office, and I'll go get him for you. We can talk to him together."

"Who, Bradley?" Callie asked, frowning.

"Yes. That's what you want, right?" Cardna said.

"Well," Callie started, then stopped. She lifted a hand to her mouth and started biting her knuckle. A nervous tic she had been trying to shake, but had not had much luck lately. It had only recently reappeared, and she scarcely even recognized when she started doing it.

"Callie?" Cardna said, interrupting her thoughts. "You okay?"

"No. I'm fine," she said, and put her hands in her lap, finally realizing the tic for what it was. "I just… Well, I guess that's what I want. Though I'm not sure what I'll say to him."

"Well, I might can help with that," Cardna said, sounding very motherly. And then that subdued blinker was clicking, only barely audible above the air coming through the vents. And like that, they were back. The car slowed at the gate where the same man from earlier looked into the car through the windshield, then waved at Cardna. She waved back with two fingers on top of the wheel. Then they were pulling back into the parking garage, down a level or two, and then out and across the brightly lit corridor to the elevator. It blew by like a dream to Callie, who was gnawing on her inner thoughts. What *would* she say to him? She realized her heart was beating heavily in her chest. Was this a new excitement or just nervousness? At least one thing seemed certain: Callie had been right that he was down here. And now, here she was about to go meet with him. This is exactly what she had wanted! This was what she had flown halfway around the planet to make happen. And here it was, actually happening! Shouldn't she feel a little more confident? Boy, she could sure use a quick puff or two from a joint. *Ding*

The elevator doors opened and Cardna almost physically pulled Callie out into the hallway. She was guiding Callie by the arm down the carpeted walkway that butted right up to a long row of windows. Through those windows was paradise. One could literally see miles of treetops stretching out toward the ocean. Strikingly gorgeous. Callie would be taking a picture right now, had she had her phone. Her phone, she recalled, was on the nightstand next to her borrowed bed.

What if Bradley did admit to everything? What if he said he was sorry? Leaned over in his chair, only inches between his knees and hers, and took both of her hands in his own, and said he was truly sorry. Dreadfully, unabashedly sorry. Maybe he even has a tear in his eye. Because at the end of the day, she had to admit that it was at least possible he didn't have any part of the planning that went into that disaster. Maybe he was a pawn just like the rest of them had been. Maybe he was innocent. Maybe he had no control over what happened out there. What if Brian Bradley had been manipulated just like the rest of them? Well, she saw as they entered a door off the main hallway, she was about to find out. Here was her office. The office of the esteemed Cardna Darwyn. Complete with a chair and a table. A nice framed picture on one wall. And that was it.

Callie stopped with her knees against the ugly orange fabric of a chrome-framed chair and stared at the blank white wall in front of her. As she was about to inquire as to what kind of work someone could get done in an office with no desk – no computer, no phone – she heard Cardna say very simply, "Wait here," and then the door closed behind her.

She turned so quickly it almost made her lose her balance. "Wait..." But Cardna was gone. There was no window in the door. There was no window *by* the door. There was no window at all. Just that stupid fucking picture of an elephant sitting on a tree branch. Callie looked at it again. Elephant. Why was that triggering a memory? What role did... *Wait!*

She grabbed the door handle with every intention of slinging it open and storming out into the hall. Only it didn't quite go like that. For there was no actual door handle to grab. Just a flat brushed-nickel disk where a knob should be. And that was when the alarm bells in her head stopped ringing. They were taken over by the *imminent nuclear-war* klaxons. They filled her head with hot fear and panic as quickly as light fills a white room.

You can trust me!

And she had. Callie had trusted Cardna. What the hell else could she do? She had trusted her. And now she was locked in a windowless room in a strange building belonging to arguably one of the most secure companies in the world, halfway across the planet from the comfort of her home. And she had walked right into it. Willfully, she had walked right into it.

CHAPTER 5

"I'm not trying to sit here and tell you we had some secret code or anything. Like whenever she says 'fire hydrant' or 'eggshell', I spring into action, knowing exactly what to do. We don't really have a protocol," Walter said, shaking his hands. He was leaning forward in his chair, his forearms resting on his knees as he spoke. Rebecca, meanwhile, maintained her normal stoic posture. Astute, complacent, aware. In control. Her hands were clasped in her lap, her legs crossed. One foot bounced ever so slightly up and down. That might have been her pulse causing it.

"But I do know her, Bec. I mean, I really *know* her. Like in a really intimate way. When she says, 'I gotta go', then I know she will be calling back. It's been almost eight hours."

Rebecca took a visible breath in. A deep one. Her head tilted while she took it. Millions of pupils throughout the course of human history had watched teachers make the same gesture in the midst of trying to maintain patience. Now she was looking at her hands, twisting a ring on her right index finger. Over and over. Round and round.

"Walter, I trust you. You know I do. That's why I let you crash here sometimes."

"Thank you, Bec," he said, and then he shut up. Sometimes common sense prevailed.

"If you say she's in danger, I want to trust that. I really do."

"But?"

"But…" she said. She took another long breath, then stopped twisting the ring. She straightened her skirt and looked him in the eyes, deliberately taking her time. "But eight hours?" she finished, twisting her face up in an advertisement of near mockery. *Don't cha think you might be overreacting here, sweetie?*

"Look, Walt. Even the police make you wait a few days before you can file a missing persons report. And she's not even missing. She just didn't call you back after an interruption."

"Hey," he said, sitting up straight and pointing his whole right hand at her. "It's more than that. I've called repeatedly but it rings and rings. Voice mail. But not straight to it." He took his own deep breath and tried to recompose himself. "That's not like her. She never walks away from her phone."

Rebecca furled her lips, then looked at the clock. An obvious gesture that Walter caught. "Okay. Let's say we go with that. She's been abducted. Or… or ran away," she said, waving a hand in the air, "whatever you're saying happened. Let's go with it. What do we do?" Rebecca waited a moment, looking him solemnly in the eyes. "Fly down to Fiji?" she added after a long moment, smiling while she said it.

Walter looked up at her and met her eyes for a long moment. And her smile disappeared like a bird at a magic show. "Fly down to Fiji," she said, returning to her previous gesture of impatience, twisting the ring on her right hand. "You want to fly down to Fiji."

Again, they met eyes and stared at each other for a long while. Rebecca was shaking her head slowly. Walter was still not answering, so she spoke again. "And what will you do when you get there?"

"Well," he said, holding a hand up again, "I think we should just go bang on the doors."

Rebecca was smiling mildly at him. Then suddenly she stopped. "Wait. We? You want me to go to fucking Fiji with you?"

Walter pulled his head back making a face. "Well, yeah."

"What the fuck, Walter? What the hell am I going to do down in Fiji?"

"Look, I need a partner, okay?"

"Why me? Aren't you married?" Rebecca said, pointing her own hand this time.

"Dude, come on," he said, leaning back, putting his hands back on his thighs. He stretched his back and looked around the room. He could find nothing interesting to stare at, so he returned his eyes to the hard gaze of Rebecca Judas. "Thevi is bad ass as a wife. But she's not an adventurer. And certainly not an investigator."

Rebecca snorted loudly. "And I am? I'm a fuckin' optics tech, Walter!"

"I'm paying for your ticket. Just come. Please."

CHAPTER 6

The corridors were damp-smelling. It wasn't an unpleasant smell. Like a rain fresh-fallen, or the smell of a lumberyard. It was the unnatural smell of wet concrete. Something primal was awakened by such smells. Like sitting by a campfire, when the animal was awakened, this was an energizing kind of smell.

The floor was slightly concave, allowing water to pool and stand. When the rains came, it would rush like a river, and make its mark far up the walls. But for now, there was only a slight reminder of its utility – because even the underground gutter tunnels couldn't be continuously sloped. There were graduations of descent all the way to the basin, wherein all the sewage tunnels ran together. But each on its own could hold a fair amount of water. It was enough to get your shoes wet if you didn't come dressed in the proper urban-ex apparel.

And it wasn't as if it were completely dark. No, there was some fair amount of light coming in from the storm drains. Sometimes one had to go several hundred yards between those drains – those reminders of the real world outside – those potential escapes. But their light was still evident.

There was also the persistent and comforting sound of dripping water. One could never quite trace its origin, as it seemed ubiquitous. The temperature was not unpleasant either. In fact, the only thing unpleasant was the incessant, nagging thought that she might not get out of here alive. A child's nightmare, it was. Surely, she could squeeze through one of the many rain gutters, were it to come to that. But finding her way back to the surface through the tunnel whence she originally entered – well, that was another thing.

These were the stakes. And there were always stakes. Every war has its roses. This tunnel *had to be* explored. Duh. Many people had spent probably many years designing and constructing these underworld labyrinthine tunnels. Who was she not to appreciate them? Not to explore them would be much like turning one's nose up at them. A blatant disrespect for the ingenuity and craftsmanship of such a remarkable wonder. Why weren't there tours of these things? Someone could sell cotton candy at the entrance. Hell, she could sell lemonade! She had done it before, and that was on a curbside. She wasn't even representing an exhibit!

The little girl lifted her nose and closed her eyes. She was gripping the lapels of her jacket with both hands, a very slight smile belying her current predicament. She had been lost in the tunnels for hours. Well, that's what mom would say. Lost. Such a subjective word, wasn't it? Nah. She wasn't lost. She was enjoying herself. The scent of abandonment. The sound of neglect. The light of the forlorn. These were things she treasured.

Her friends had come in here a few times, back in the day. That was a long time ago now. Back when they were sub-ten. That seemed like years ago, now. She was about to be twelve. Heck, she was even starting to grow breasts! Her school counselor had pulled her into the office and encouraged her to start wearing a training bra. Had her mother not thought to buy her one? Well, no! Duh! *I don't need one yet!* Oh, but you do, sweet heart.

Yeah. She was almost twelve. She didn't have time for those sub-tens anymore. Of course, they weren't sub-ten anymore. They were the same age as she. But that's when they had stopped coming here, you see. It was the day Daisy thought she was a leader. Oh, she had led them all right. She'd led them right into trouble. They got lost and couldn't find their way out. It had taken the fire department being called. Dumbos. Seriously. How do you get lost in a concrete tunnel?

Not her. Not Callie. You see, Callie carried a stub of chalk in her pocket. She had marked a little arrow on each tunnel she came out of. When there was a fork in the path, she marked whence she had come. Duh! She couldn't believe everyone hadn't thought of that. It was so simple!

And now here she stood, smelling the cool, damp air, and full of nothing but calm. She couldn't even remember how many times she had come here now. Now that she came alone, she could take her time. She could enjoy herself without the annoyance of all the girls who were scared to be here in the first place. She wouldn't be rushed. Heck, she didn't even need the chalk anymore. She had been here enough times to know the maze by heart. Now she just came here for pleasure. To be alone. To get away from the craziness that seemed ever incessant banging on her door. And it was peaceful. There was no longer any danger of those girls coming here, throwing mud and rocks at her. She turned something bad into a peaceful retreat.

The dripping water was also comforting. It sounded so beautiful down here, right at this spot – coming through in stereo. Quadraphonic! It was coming from all four sides. And – what was that? She opened her eyes and twisted her head around. It had sounded like a loud *CLANG!* Callie looked at her Swatch. It was six-forty-six. Wait. That's the same time it had been the last time she looked. And that had to have been over an hour ago! Holy cow!

Well, no need to freak out. That's what the sub-tens did. Not the nearly-twelves. There was nothing to panic about down here. But even still, it might be time to start back. Since she didn't know what time it was, that meant she could be late for dinner. And if that happened...

She would rather not think about what that meant. She knew. She just liked to avoid tinkering with the thought. She turned on her heel to leave, and stopped cold. There was a man standing there, blocking her path.

Sitting here alone in this room felt a lot like being in that tunnel junction so many years ago. She was almost forty now, and had not thought of those sewage tunnels in many, many years. But suddenly, here it was, present with her.

Another memory that hovered nearby was her getting stuck on the elevator in the Royal building. She had at least not been alone there; she had been with Walter. Walter had ended up getting knocked unconscious when his chin collided with the top of her head. But at least he was there. Callie had not fared too well that day. She had completely lost her mind with fear and anxiety in that tiny boxcar. That same abject terror was threatening to revisit, if only she would succumb. It's like she was surrounded by a chain-link fence with concertina wire around the top. And it was surrounded by an angry mob. They were banging their torches and pitchforks against the fence. How long would the links hold up to that siege? How long would *she* last, knowing they were there?

She stood in the middle of the floor, her hands clasped in front of her, facing the door. She closed her eyes and tried to concentrate on her breathing. She literally had no other option. Banging on the door or the walls would be a lot like banging on the bars in a jail cell. They're not going to let you out. The guards are all used to hearing that. In fact, that's when they start coming by with their batons, isn't it?

But this was not a jail. She was *not* in a cell. Maybe someone out there *would* care and react to the banging on the walls! Maybe there was a sane person in this building! So she decided that was the route she would take. Until the first bangs revealed that the wall was painted cinder. It made only muted thumps inside the room – let alone outside the walls, she reckoned. And it hurt like hell. Maybe the best thing to do was to get comfortable. Assuming she was going to be here for a while was probably the smartest line of thinking. If she accepted that, maybe she wouldn't lose her head again.

So she turned to look at the elephant picture on the wall. Only it wasn't an elephant. Now it was an isthmus with a lighthouse on it. In her panic and haste, she had failed to notice that it was not a print, but a screen. It was even recessed into the wall like a window pane. Fascinating. Well, it would be fascinating under other circumstances. Right now she didn't have time to… Wait. Yes, she did. Time was, in fact, all she had. It would give her something to do, and maybe help keep her mind off the impending riot within. Those fences were gradually closing in.

Lost. Alone. Scared. Trying to be a big girl. Trying to suck it up and not embarrass herself. Trying to think logically. Just like in those storm tunnels when she was twelve, all those years ago. It all circles back around, doesn't it?

The man never had a chance. Callie didn't know if rape or abduction or just plain crookedness was in his game plan –

she didn't care – because she didn't stick around to find out. She had instantly turned on her heel and run off screaming bloody murder. And not only did she have the advantage of knowing the tunnels, but she also had her chalk.

She ran until her legs were aching, her hands were trembling and her lungs were on fire. And she screamed until she was hoarse. She never even saw a glimpse of that man again. She had escaped. And that was the last time she ever went into those tunnels. Twelve-year-old girls don't need to be spending time in tunnels where grown men hung out, she reckoned.

Callie was prepared to take her punishment when she got home. Punishment for being late for dinner and worrying her mother sick. But the punishment never came. Somehow, coming home screaming and red in the face with a wicked fear in her eyes was enough to advertise that she would not be making that trip again. She had learned her lesson. She didn't even go out front after that for nearly six months. Every car that drove down the road was a kidnapper. A rapist. A serial child-killer. Callie Simmons didn't have time for all that. She just stayed inside.

Way points and decisions in her life all seemed to refer back to those tunnels for self-evaluation. Like an autobiographical desk reference. Any time she thought she might be considering a wrong decision, all she had to do was be reminded of that frightful evening in the tunnels. It might have kept her out of many bad situations, but it also had undoubtedly caused her to miss out on many opportunities as well. There were years of therapy after that. Those fifty-five-minute sessions in the cold counselor's office twice a week also stole from her childhood. Her mother, for the few remaining years she had with Callie, lauded her efforts. She praised Callie's ingenuity for having and using that chalk. For being wily enough to escape certain violence. And to this, Callie would always shrug.

She also had many nights ruined by the night terrors that came afterward. Her mind would venture to those places where she would not allow it to roam in her waking hours.

Those *what-if* places. Like, what if the man had caught her? What if his intentions were sex? He would have had complete privacy. *What if* he had tied her up down there and kept her there for months? Ball-gagged and shivering in a puddle of almost-cold rainwater. He would visit her every day to bring her food and water. Among other things.

The night terrors were rare now. Very rare. But Callie did find that when anything traumatic happened in her life, they would resurface. And it was always the same scenario: the preteen girl in the tunnel, facing the man she never saw again. She still remembered his awful face. It never left her. He still haunted her, if only in memory and dream. Being trapped in the elevator had summoned the return of the dreams. And she had the feeling that being trapped in this room – if she were to walk out of here alive – would be bringing them back too.

The picture on the wall changed again. It was not a quick flash to another image. Instead, it was a slow, fading disintegration of the pixels until they were all replaced with the ones from the new image. Kind of a cheesy transition, if she were being honest. It seemed like a high-tech company would be more-

Suddenly, the screen was replaced with a live-camera view of an office desk. There was a man sitting behind the desk with his hands on the blotter. He had spectacles on his nose and his hair was thinning. He was rugged looking in an almost handsome sort of way, but not quite as much as he maybe used to be. Like maybe he used to be good looking. Now he was just a middle-aged man who needed a shave and a good grooming. It took Callie a few moments to finally realize who it was she was looking at. And he looked nothing like the Brian Bradley she remembered from the Oliver Company.

CHAPTER 7

I t was not until they were being pushed back from the gate that it happened. Walter and Rebecca were buckled into their seats in first class. Rebecca had already kicked off her sandals and was staring out the window at the dark concrete of the apron below. Walter had fished out his wired earphones and was holding the cord up in front of his face, trying to let it dangle itself into some semblance of sense. The plane was in motion, going backwards. It suddenly – and Rebecca would later say violently – came to a stop. Decelerating abruptly from a couple of miles per hour to flat still was jolting. But probably not violent. Everything else about the episode, though – she would swear – was.

They had only been pushed back ten or twelve feet, Rebecca guessed, when they stopped suddenly. A few passengers expressed opinions of the sudden stop. One woman cursed after spilling her mimosa on her blouse.

Rebecca caught Walter out of the corner of her eye looking up. She looked at him. He had a better view of the aisle, as he was on the aisle. She could not see what was going on up there unless she raised up to a squat on her seat. And why the hell would she do that? Shortly, she returned her attention to the apron. Then the announcement from the cockpit got her attention again.

Something about a brief interruption, wouldn't take long then they'd be on their way, blah blah, blah. Rebecca didn't pay much attention. Until, that was, Walter was pinching her elbow and leaning in to talk to her privately. Walter was worried because the cockpit door had actually opened. They weren't supposed to do that once the plane had backed up, he thought. He said someone very captain-looking appeared in the doorway and made eye contact with him before turning to engage the stew who was standing there next to the door.

Rebecca finally did lean way over against him, trying for a better vantage. And indeed, someone with epaulets on his shoulder was definitely looking at Walter. Then there was light on the man's shoulder. Someone had opened the front door – the very door they had entered only half an hour before. There was a bit of commotion, then the captain disappeared into that short corridor, presumably to look out the door.

Within a few minutes, he was back in sight, and there were two marshals coming into the aisle of the plane. And it only took a few steps before they were right there in front of Walter. The one with the mustache squatted and put his hand on Walter's forearm. "Sir, you need to come with me."

Rebecca quickly sat up straight, eyes widening. "What the fuck's going on?" she asked to no one in particular. No one seemed to want to answer her though. Walter looked over at her and made a face. But he was standing up. He was complying. *What the hell, Walt?*

"Uh, excuse me," Rebecca said, trying to stand, then realizing she was restrained by her seat belt. She unbuckled herself and stood, grabbing the back of the seat Walter had lately been occupying. "Uh, sir, can you please tell me where you're taking him?"

Walter turned to look at her. "Call Cambria," he whispered loudly.

"What?" she said. Rebecca wasn't looking at him, but rather at the man who was apprehending him. "Hey!" she said. She reached out and tapped the man hard on the badge sewn onto the man's upper arm. "Hey!" she repeated. When the man finally turned his gaze toward her, she added, "Where are you taking him?" Her eyes were wide. She did not look frightened. She looked like an angry Karen. Like someone had just rattled the wrong cage. Like she wasn't asking a question, but rather, making a statement.

"Call Cambria!" Walter said again, this time with some vocal force.

"Yeah, okay, Walt," Rebecca said, almost sidelong. Like she was trying to get an annoying toddler to stop tugging on her pant leg.

"Hey!" she tried again. Walter had succeeded in getting his satchel from under the seat in front of him and was now actually out in the aisle. She didn't have much time. "Hey, asshole!" she said, maybe a little too loudly.

The man behind Walter finally gave her the attention she had summoned. "Ma'am," he said, holding a hand out, palm down, patting the air, "please take your seat. This does not concern you."

"The fuck it doesn't!" she might have actually shouted. When the man didn't respond, but rather, turned back to face the front and was moving away from her, she changed her tone. "Hey! Sir! Can I come then?"

Rebecca started trying to rope in her own bag and move toward the center aisle. "Sir? Can I come? I can't go to Fiji alone! I need…"

The man was now back in her row, using that same hand to hold her in place. Though there was no physical contact, she could feel its weight, several inches in front of her chest. "Ma'am, you need to take your seat. This does not concern you. You may not leave with us."

And just like that, she was alone on a flight to a small country halfway around the planet.

Annoyingly, Cardna Darwyn was standing just off Bradley's right shoulder, but was too tall for her head to be captured by the camera. She stood with her arms crossed, like a bouncer at a shitty jiggle shack where all the men continually got too handsy. It was almost as much a statement of power as locking Callie in this room had been.

In the brief instant it had taken Callie to recognize whom it was she was facing on the screen, she had experienced a chill that washed down her spine and then felt that cold stone-like presence known as dread in her stomach.

"Hello there, Miss Simmons," Bradley said finally. He had a smug smile on his face. Callie never wanted to punch someone as badly as she did right now.

She crossed her own arms in an effort to at least not look shaken. And by God, she felt like she was doing a good job of *not* being shaken. She had maintained her composure. She had not lost it like she had done in that elevator. How many months ago was that now?

"Ms. Darwyn here tells me you had something you wanted to ask me?" the man said, lifting his chin. His mouth was slightly open, showing his teeth. Like he was just so interested in hearing what she had to say. This was not the forum she had envisioned when she had bought her expensive plane ticket.

Callie could not clearly remember meeting Brian Bradley. She only knew that she had. She had also spent many unremarkable hours in his presence at company meetings: breakfasts, conferences, all the other insignificant interactions that would not force his memory on her. He was forgettable. It was only after he had left and she had begun to suspect something was awry that she had started thinking he was more important than originally conceived.

Callie cleared her throat. Composure was hard to come by in this state, but she was giving it her best effort. "Well, I was… I was hoping we could have this meeting face-to-face," she said.

An oh-face. Wide-eyed. "Oh, is that not what this is?"

Though she had never technically had a negative interaction with the man in real life, she still associated him with everything bad that had happened to the Atlas crew. It was a subconscious thing, beyond her control. Instinctive. Intuition. Like hearing the voice of your childhood captor, years after the incident occurred. She knew this could play against her, if she were to allow him to see her visibly shaken over the ordeal. Here he was confronting her behind the security of a Zoom meeting, and she was worried about being intimidated. Clearly, he was not a man who had much in the way of a backbone.

Callie smirked and shook her head, disappointment raining from her visage. "Come on. I'm locked in a cell and you're there in your comfortable leather office chair. What is this? Really."

The man nodded, and then looked to the woman at his right as if for confirmation. Then he spread his hands. "I'm sorry, I don't follow. I thought you wanted to have a conversation. Apparently, I was wrong!" He then frowned, chin hiked, and looked like he was looking for something on his computer screen. Momentarily, it blinked off, then went back to the image of the elephant on a tree limb.

"WHAT!" Callie screamed, striding forward and banging her fists on the glass in front of the screen. "WHAT THE FUCK ARE YOU DOING TO ME!??!"

And in the next instant, those same aggressive fists were balled up and screwing into her eye sockets as she crumbled to the floor in tears and humility.

Rebecca sat in Walter's seat for long after he had been removed from the flight, hands tight on the armrests, and staring at the door through which he had disappeared, wide-eyed and full of flight. Only she had nowhere to flee. She was literally trapped on the plane now, and heading for a foreign country. She had been out of the country many times. She had never been to Fiji, but that didn't matter. She had been to Australia. She had been to Japan. It wasn't necessarily the distance. Hell, it wasn't even the seclusive nature of the place. It was the ridiculousness of the situation that had her worked up. This wasn't her mission. She barely even knew Callie. She had reluctantly agreed to accompany Walter on this mission of his because she trusted him and loved him as a friend. To go rescue this dumb bow-headed girl who got herself wrapped up in some shit she didn't need to be poking her cute little nose into. An agreement was an agreement, though. Maybe that wasn't entirely fair. She had liked Callie quite a bit. A completely different personality, right? But opposites attract. Callie had, after all, been the one Rebecca had called to come give her some company when Codi was in the hospital and Walter was in jail. Of course, she had not had many others to choose from...

But now the stakes had changed. Right? Now Walt had been dragged off the flight – God knows why – and she was alone. She wasn't the one who had the blueprints for the plan. She didn't know where they were going, how to get there, how to get in, or even what to do when they got there. Furthermore, if they actually got to the point where they came face-to-face with Callie, she didn't even know what to do then! She was completely in the dark here. Company for the man on the mission. A moral support figure… That's all she was! Rebecca didn't even know the full story!

When she looked around at the other first-class passengers, none of them were looking at her. None of them looked like they *hadn't been* looking at her either. But at least she was not currently the center of attention. She took a moment to try and gather her thoughts. Rebecca caught herself chewing her thumb, and looked around again. The plane made a turn toward the sun, and the harsh rays fell back away from the windows on the left side of the craft.

She had to take inventory of her situation. What the fuck happened to Walter? Well, she couldn't worry about that right now. She did not know, and there was no way she *could* know. So she had to drop that. Stewing on things that weren't explicable were not productive. What *did* she know? Well, she knew she was alone on a flight to Fiji. She knew the woman she was trying to 'rescue' was named Callie Simmons, and that she was likely at the Royal Research Corporation compound, outside Suva. She knew she would not be let in on her good looks alone. It would take a badge that she didn't have. Hell, she didn't think Walter even had that badge. But at least he had a company badge. He did work for Royal. Rebecca didn't.

Rebecca Judas was trapped on a flight she could not stop. She could not ask the flight attendants to stop it and let her off. She could not tap the captain on the shoulder and say, 'Excuse me, but that man you let those guys escort off earlier, well, I should be with him.' She was in this thing until it touched the ground in Nadi. So she had better start figuring out what the hell she would do when she got there.

Leaning her head against the headrest and closing her eyes, she gripped the ends of the armrests tightly and concentrated on her breathing. Think. She felt the landing gear clunk into closed position beneath the plane. Think, Rebecca. A billion thoughts raced around her head, playing chase. Usually they would fall out as they realized their insignificance. But these thoughts were all in it for the long-haul. They all felt like they were important. She would have to weed through them one at at time.

Fortunately, she had plenty of time to do just that before they landed.

It had not taken long for Callie to lose her composure, after all. Almost instantly, when the camera had turned off, that steel composure she had felt dissolved. But that was okay, right? Was it not okay to crumble and cry like a baby when they weren't looking? As long as she presented a strong front for them to see, it didn't matter how much it cost her in private, did it? For she *had* stayed strong – at least in appearance – when the camera was on. And for that, she was proud of herself. Unless…

Unless… What if the camera in here was always on? They could, in theory, be watching her right now. They could have been watching her the entire time. And in fact, it was probably likely that they had been. It was more likely than not, now that she thought about it. Callie's back was against the wall. She sat hugging her knees. She stifled her cries and tried to regain some of that composure. She had to stay strong. Not knowing whether the camera was on or not meant she had to assume that it was. She had to live like it was. Without moving her head, she looked up at the corners where the wall met the ceiling across the room from her. It was taller than it was wide. There were no visible cameras. And in fact, nothing to differentiate one square inch of wall from any other in the room. It was ridiculously plain. She had to crank her neck to look at the two corners above and behind her. No cameras visible there either. So it would seem the only eyes they had on the room were in the TV screen somewhere. As long as Callie sat with her back against that wall – or otherwise stood facing away from it – she could be emotional, if needed. With this small respite, she crossed her arms on her knees and buried her face in the V formed between body and thighs. She closed her eyes and allowed herself a quiet cry.

It was an indeterminable time later that Callie was startled awake. Awake. That meant that she had dozed! Indeed, there was a line of drool on her chin. She quickly wiped it off and stood up, turning around to face the screen.

The light house again. How long had it been, she wondered? Well, it had been long enough to realize she needed to pee.

"What's your plan here, ass holes? Are you going to feed me, ass holes? Are you going to let me use the restroom, or will I have to do it in the corner, ass holes?" she said. She was speaking loudly and slowly. She looked around the room and spread her arms to illustrate. "As you can see, there are not many places for me to keep my dignity in here, ass holes!"

Callie dropped her arms to her side and stood there panting, staring at the screen. Somehow it seemed as though the nap she had inadvertently slipped into had steeled her resolve again. She felt powerful all of a sudden. Careless. Strong and bold. What else could they do to her? Hell, it couldn't get much worse than this, could it? She caught herself shrugging.

After a moment of nothing happening, she shook her head and rolled her eyes. Then a thought occurred to her. The two chairs in the room had steel legs on them. That TV was behind a thick pane of glass. Probably bulletproof, but she had nothing else to do. Callie scooted her feet lazily over to the closest chair and bent over, putting one hand on each side of the cushion. She stayed like that for over a minute. After catching her breath and talking herself up, she stood up straight. The chair came with her. Slowly, she turned to face the glass wall, chair to her chest, legs sticking out in front of her. She walked up to the glass and lifted the chair – without changing its orientation – above her head. Then, using all her might, she swung the steel feet down into the glass. At the moment just before impact, she crunched her eyes and face up, anticipating a hard rebound. Instead, what she got was an explosion. Her momentum actually carried her forward so hard she lost her balance and fell into the shattering glass as the chair continued its forward motion.

Callie realized at the last possible second that she was going with it, into the room behind the glass. And she was likely going to suffer major trauma to the abdomen from the shards of glass sticking up from the bottom. It was too late to stop the fall, as she had already swung beyond her center of gravity, and her arms were still way out in front of her. Her eyes got really wide as she fell. She might even have screamed. She slammed forward into the opening, her upper half falling into the dark room beyond the wall. The force of her landing expelled a giant breath from her as her stomach hit the glass-rimmed opening. The chair fell forward beyond the short shelf that was just below the glass on the other side of the wall, clanging and bouncing loudly off into the darkness. Instinctively, Callie pulled her hands back just before the fall ended, and ended up scraping them backward across the jagged row of glass shards. But otherwise, she realized, it had not cut her up too badly. She raised up off the shards, looking down at her stomach. There were no puncture marks in her blouse, and no visible blood spots. After her quick assessment, she scanned what she could see in the next room and saw no one standing there waiting for her. What she found interesting, when she finally had a chance to reflect on it, was that there had not been a TV there at all. Which meant that had been a very expensive piece of glass she had just shattered. She could see wires draping down onto the wall below the opening. Tiny, thin things that looked like shimmers of copper. They had not been visible in the glass before. Of course, she had not stood there studying it close-up.

Callie approached the opening, and this time, leaned way into it by placing her hands on the narrow shelf just on the other side. She looked both directions, but was disappointed to see the room was only a narrow closet-like space, only a third as wide as the room she had spent the last several hours in. And there was nothing else in it. Certainly no desk with her enemies behind it. That had all been piped in on wire and the magic of technology. There did not even appear to be a door in the tiny room. How odd. That meant they had sealed off the small room during the building of it. Well that couldn't be right…

Callie carefully lifted her leg over the shards and tried to rake her shoe across the glass, knocking out any loose pieces and hopefully flattening out the obstacle a little bit. It did knock a few pieces loose, but not enough to matter. She would have to brave it. And brave it she did. She swung the leg full over the wall and left her right foot dangling about a foot above the floor on the other side. Then, placing her hands carefully on the safest looking spot on the shards, Callie hopped, transferring the weight to the right side, and came down on the other side, off-balance and staggering. Quickly, she lost balance entirely and fell into the far wall, dragging the inside of her left leg across the shards and tearing a pretty good swath out of the calf of her left pant leg. Still, though, no blood. She bent over to examine her leg and found some red scrapes. Maybe a little skin coming apart – but no blood. She stood back up and turned to examine the room more closely. But she had been right in her initial assessment. But wait! What was this? There seemed to be a seam in the shape and size of an average door, at the end of the length of the room, adjacent to the broken glass wall. If she could just…

That was when the door in the other room swung open violently and two men came storming in. They stopped quickly, and now stood face to face with Callie, silent but intimidating. Callie stupidly raised her hands. "Unarmed, guys." When she thought about the concept of their needing to know that, she almost giggled. Even armed to the teeth, she would not be a threat to these two commandos.

One of them approached the glass and pulled a large knife out of its sheath, which he carried on his belt. Callie took a step back. He flipped the knife over deftly and raked the thick back of the blade across the glass, effectively accomplishing what Callie had tried to do with the back of her expensive shoe. After a few rakes, the glass was almost flush with its surrounding metal edging. It would now be a lot safer to cross. The man looked up at Callie as he sheathed his knife. He held a hand out toward her. "Come on, ma'am. You need to come with us."

Callie took a deep breath, and realizing she had no other options, took the man's hand. She stepped forward and raised her foot to straddle the wall again. The man stopped her foot with his hand though, and spoke again. "It's easier if you sit on it, then swing your legs over together."

"I'll manage, thank you," Callie responded, a little too smartly. She did it her way. There were no scrapes this time, but she did realize the man had been right and it would have been easier his way. She saw him shrug as she stood up, then let go of her hand and guided her out in front of him. The other man led the way. In the hallway, Cardna stood with her arms crossed, staring at Callie bemusedly.

"Well, that was dramatic," Callie said.

"What, breaking out our twelve-thousand-dollar plasma screen or your daring ballet over the wall?"

Callie stopped and looked down at her pants, brushing off some glass dust from her rump as she did so. She sighed and met Cardna's eyes again. "No. Sending two Rambos in there to collect me."

Cardna Darwyn furled her mouth. She was chewing her bottom lip. She did not look happy with Callie. Good. Eff her.

"You don't expect me to apologize, do you?" Callie said.

"I don't know. Would it matter if you did?" said Cardna.

"I suspect not." She stood for a moment in silence, then said, "You locked me in a flippin' room with no doorknob and expected me not to freak out?"

Cardna raised her eyebrows. "Freak out? You looked like you held it together pretty well to me."

"Glad to know you were watching," Callie said. "So. Do I get to talk to the ass hole yet?"

Cardna scoffed under her breath. She was still chewing her lip. "Oh, no, Callie. You lost your chance at that. Brian's gone."

"Gone. What do you mean, 'gone'?" Callie asked, frowning. She crossed her arms. There didn't seem to be anything else to do with them. There was no escape from this. At least not yet. Not here. The two bozos were standing right behind her, watching to make sure she was a good little girl. Behaving.

"Oh, he took off," Cardna responded. She finally changed her posture. She reached up with her left hand and twirled a lock of hair hanging by her cheek, then ran it behind her ear. "He got the idea you didn't really want to talk after you mocked him."

Callie sagged her shoulders, tilted her head and looked disbelievingly at Cardna. "Boy, did you turn out to be a b-word, or what? I trusted you!" she said, jabbing a finger toward Cardna. The other woman didn't flinch. "You were so nice to me earlier. Then suddenly, you lock me in this stupid room? What the heck, Cardna?" Callie could feel tears threatening to come forward. Her eyes were stinging a little bit. She was just so damn frustrated. None of this made sense. She could understand if when they came to get her at the little outpost on the road last night, someone had just said, 'We can't let you in!' or 'You're not going to get to talk to Brian Bradley.' But this? To take her to some cabin in the deep woods… to treat her like a friend? To be nice to her? Why make her believe she had a chance? Why go through all this rigmarole only to shut her down like this? "I truly don't understand what you're doing here, Cardna."

For the briefest instant – for just a tiny flash of an instant – she thought she saw something in Cardna's eyes. A refocusing of sorts. Like she almost flinched… Cardna's demeanor changed just slightly. The way she straightened her head, the way she breathed in and shuffled her foot right at that second… it all seemed meaningful. But the words she spoke didn't match. "Sorry, Callie. You have been deemed a threat to the security of our operation here. I cannot let you meet face to face with Mr. Bradley."

Callie held up her hands, palms up, and leaned forward, saying, "Fine! I don't even freakin' care anymore! But why lock me in a room for hours! I'm starving! I'm thirsty!" she said, shaking her hands in the air. "I have to…" she started. After the briefest of pauses, she changed direction, and finished, "use the ladies' room!" She had almost said she had to pee, in front of these two men.

"I can take you to the restroom. We'll get you a snack and some water," Cardna said. She reached out to touch Callie's arm, but Callie pulled away, frowning. The other woman straightened and sighed inwardly, clearly not liking the loss of control that move had betrayed. "I'm sorry, Callie. That was the safest way for you to meet with him."

Callie suddenly felt rage explode in her chest. It blew up into her head instantly, and before she knew what was happening, she flung forward and shoved Cardna hard in the shoulders, sending her back into the wall with a yelp of surprise. Before Callie could move forward, or start her shout, the two men had her by the arms – one on each side. Meanwhile, Cardna stumbled, having lost her footing, and fell awkwardly at an angle, landing hard on her rear.

"You stupid idiot! Why didn't you guys just search me for weapons or something? Like I'm a threat?" Callie shouted. "Like I could be a threat to anyone?"

Cardna was still on the ground, staring up at Callie. Her body was at an odd angle, one hand behind her, holding her up, while the other was trembling in front of her. She was not trying to get up. "Callie, you don't understand. Mr. Bradley takes his security ver-"

"I'm not a threat to anyone!" Callie shouted, jarring forward again, trying to break free of her human restraints. Cardna was breathing heavily, staring Callie in the eyes. She finally shook her head and gave Callie an angry, disappointed look.

"Take her to the other holding room," she said with a dismissive wave of her hand. She finally started getting up as the two men obediently whisked her down the hall. It was not a long trek though, as the other room was only a few meters away.

"How many of these rooms do you have here?" Callie said, scoffing. "And why?" she said loudly, trying to laugh. It sounded forced and fake though. She was under duress. She really did not want to be thrown into another room. This time, when they shoved her into the room, one of the men followed her in and collected the two chairs. Her only potential weapons had just been confiscated. But right before the door slammed, she heard Cardna shout from the hallway, "Take her to the jane first."

Thank heavens for that. The men even waited patiently outside for her, with only a minor admonition that she not try anything funny. She did not feel very comical. She just wanted to pee in peace and private. When she finished, she opened the taps and stared into the mirror for a long moment, staring at the puffy redness in her cheeks and eyes. Callie splashed some warm water on her face and then shut off the hot tap and let it run cool. She put her mouth to the faucet and drank down some of the cool water, not trusting that Cardna would keep the other part of her promise. The water was crisp and tasted rich with nutrients. She stood and swallowed a few times, then dried her hands and met the two men in the hallway.

"Okay, boys. Lock me up again so I don't hurt anyone else."

When the door slammed behind her, Callie collapsed, immediately overcome with stress and emotion. Before she could even take inventory of the room, she was curled up on the floor and sobbing.

CHAPTER 8

It must have been several hours later, because Callie actually felt like she might have had a good nap. Good being a relative term, as she was lying on the hardwood floor using her arm as a pillow. She felt worn out and beat up, aching all over and tired to the soul – but a little refreshed in the mind. She sat up and scooted so that her back was against the wall. After rubbing her eyes and combing her hair with her fingers, she breathed in deeply and took her first real look around the room. It was almost identical to the first one she had been in, sans the chairs. The table was there. The illusion of a TV was there. Showing the same several pictures in a long, repetitive loop.

Callie leaned her head back against the wall and continued to breathe deeply, trying to clear her mind. When would that stupid TV come to life and startle her? Based on the comment Cardna had made in the hallway, she now thought they were *not* constantly monitoring her. Maybe they only saw her when she could see them on the screen. She moved her tongue around in her mouth and counted her options. She did not even get to one.

She would have to sit and watch the pictures on the screen change. Maybe she could study them for clues. Clues to use for what purpose, she could not imagine. But what else did she have to do? There was literally nothing else to do in the room. How had it gone so wrong? So comically and ridiculously wrong! This company that seemed so much like an evil empire – the dark corporation in novels and movies – was turning out to be even more sinister than that. Locking a visitor in one of these *holding rooms* as Cardna had called them… How sickeningly and unbelievably twisted could a company be? Well, it had to be made of individuals who believed in that mission statement. *We promise to treat every visitor like an inmate at Alcatraz. We're not happy until you're not happy.* She was rocking her head slightly and slowly back and forth on the wall when the screen changed, and there was Cardna's pretty face. Just as suddenly as a Florida rain, it had appeared out of nowhere. She was staring straight into the camera. Callie briefly had time to consider what that meant. That meant she was looking at the camera. Not at the image of the captive in the middle of the screen. Unless somehow the camera was mounted in the *middle* of the screen…

"Hello, Callie," the voice said softly. There was no real humanity in it. It could have been Hitler saying it. Or Gandhi. No betrayal of emotional alignment was evident whatever.

"Hello, Cardna," Callie returned with a sour face. She spoke with a tone sweet as salt.

Cardna did that thing where she twisted her head a little, then started chewing her lip again. This was a tell, Callie realized. Like in a poker game when people made a certain face, or tapped their fingers on the table unconsciously, or chewed on a thumbnail without knowing… This was a weakness that Cardna herself wasn't aware of. Callie made a quick mental note to search her memory catalog of every instance she could remember when Cardna had done it. She needed to figure out what she was telling by it.

"Well, I thought you would be happy to know that I was able to get Mr. Bradley to change his mind. He has agreed to give you another chance."

"Ooh, how exciting! His exalted has allowed me an audience?"

"Knock it off, Callie."

Callie held her hands up. "Why? What's the point? This is so backwards – so *inhumane* – that I can't even imagine it being real. By now I don't even expect to be let out of here alive."

Cardna lowered her gaze. Yeah, the camera must be in the middle of the viewing screen. Neat trick. "Who do you think we are, Callie? We're not murderers."

"HA!" Callie said, pointing at the screen. "THAT is priceless! That's precisely what you are!" She lowered her finger and put both hands on the cold hardwood. "Well, maybe not you personally, but your company," she said, making a sour face again. "You guys are definitely that."

Cardna almost rolled her eyes. Callie had to give her credit for that restraint. She had been able to catch herself at the last possible instant. But Callie had caught it. It was definitely *going to be* an eye-roll. "I'm not going to sit here and bicker with you about what you think we are. Would you like to speak to Mr. Bradley or not?"

"Sure!" Callie said, throwing her hands up. "This is stupider than a flippin' cartoon. No one could write this crap. Not even…" she started, lifting a hand out like she was about to offer Cardna a slice of pie through the screen. Or a nice brooch. "Not even…" she repeated. But her mind had gone blank. She could not think of any authors. She had been prepared to deliver a nice one about some great writer who suddenly…

"Okay then, I will let him know you've declined his meeting," Cardna said, interrupting Callie's thoughts. And suddenly, she was looking up toward the upper left corner of the screen.

Callie was up on her feet faster than a flash of lightning. "NO!" she shouted, her hand reaching toward the screen in a pleading gesture. "Wait! Please! I'm sorry. Don't go," she said. She took a step forward and folded her hands together in front of her chest. Tears were stinging her eyes again. She was wringing her hands together, and probably didn't realize it. "Please don't leave. I'll speak to him." Just like that. Her tough-guy act fizzled away so suddenly. And it had taken her whole life to summon that steel!

It had worked though. Callie's pleas had stopped Cardna's move toward closing the session. She was once again staring at Callie in the eyes, virtually at least. They stared at each other across this digital chasm for several long moments before Cardna finally turned away, turning bodily in her chair and pushing away from the desk at which she sat. And from the shadows behind her, a man materialized. As Cardna stood up, he scooted over and took her place in the seat, finally lowering enough to bring his face into view of the camera. It was only then that Callie could actually confirm it was Brian Bradley.

He rolled the chair up to the desk, looking down to the left and then the right before leveling his gaze at her through the camera. And then he stared at her for a long period just as Cardna had done. Why the hell was that woman protecting this man so much? For what reason? Why would anyone do anything for this slime-ball? A man who would get a woman to fight his battles for him! Callie imagined if someone broke into his house, Bradley would pick up one of his children and use the kid as a shield before he faced the attacker himself. What a coward!

"Hello, Mr. Bradley," Callie said, trying to smash down all her insubordinate thoughts and ideals. No way in reality should this man ever be called sir, or addressed with any kind of respect. But she had to admit she was at his advantage. In that game of poker, he had all the cards. All she had was the joker.

"It's my understanding," he said, "you think I had something to do with the…" He took in a breath and thought carefully for a moment before continuing. "Something to do with the *failure* of the Atlas mission."

Callie had to dig deep into the reserves of her willpower to find the strength required not to roll her eyes at that. She felt she absolutely *had to* show this man respect, or he would click out of the conference faster than she could blink her eyes. She decided to go with the honest approach. Blunt, but honest. She breathed in deeply and said it carefully when she finally spoke. "Yes. You fuck. I do. I know it." Her face was squeezed into a madness she could feel flowing into her body like a vat of hot pitch had spilled from her head and was draining slowly but surely into the rest of her. The anger must have been more than just a feeling. She must have been wearing it like a mask, because she saw Bradley sit up straight, leaning away from the screen – probably unconsciously. His face straightened. He looked like he had… *sobered*. That was the best way she could describe it, were she asked. He had suddenly *sobered*. At least now she had his real attention.

Bradley cleared his throat, then furled his mouth before talking. "I see you feel very passionately about this, Callie. But let me assure you, I was not in control of any of it." Before she could retort, he held his hands up, tilted his head and said, "I'm not saying I wasn't there; that I wasn't part of it. I'm just saying I wasn't in control of it."

"Okay," Callie said, nodding. "So you weren't the one who dropped the match. I get it. But nor did you reach for the extinguisher. But you're not to blame," she said in a ridiculous hyperbole of her anger. A caricature of the rage, holding her hands up in front of her, exaggerating her body movements. "No, no! You're innocent of all charges."

Bradley, surprisingly, tolerated it all. When she was done, he finally said, "I think you oversimplify things you could not possibly understand."

Callie interrupted, "Oh, yeah, I have a hard time understanding things. My 200-IQ is just below stupid," she added, holding her thumb and finger a quarter-inch apart. "I was so close to being smart."

Brian Bradley sighed. "You know that's not what I mean. I mean, you were not there to witness it. Imagine trying to explain to a blind person what a sunset looks like," he said, obviously thinking he could play the simile game like she had.

Callie was shaking her head though. "Uh-uh. Not working, dude." She crossed her arms.

"Callie, you were not there. You can't possibly understand what it was like. I had no control of anything. I didn't even know what was going on."

Callie took a deep breath, the let it out with an exasperated sigh. "Okay. Cool. You're forgiven. Can I please leave now?"

Bradley frowned. Clearly he had not expected this. "Uh…" he started, and turned to look at someone off-screen. When he turned back, he said, "Are you serious? You want to leave?"

"No, I want to stay locked in this cell for the next short forever. Yes, you ass hole! I want to *leeeeeeeeeeeave!*"

"Well, there are some complications involved in that," Bradley said.

"Complications? Like what?" she said, rolling her eyes.

"Well, number one, you destroyed a twelve-thousand-dollar imaging glass," he said, holding up a hand as if offering her a deal.

"I'll write you a check. Next?"

"Well," Bradley said, and tried a careful little smile, "there's the part about your potential for disclosing my continued existence."

"I'm sorry," Callie said, "I don't follow." She shook her head.

Bradley smirked. So he was smarter than her after all. "What I meant was that there's a danger in your *telling someone* that I'm extant."

"I know what the words mean, butt hole," Callie shouted, squinting and leaning toward him. "I just don't see what the problem is. You don't want people to know you're alive?"

"Well, not certain people, maybe," he offered.

Callie turned and walked toward the opposite wall, trying to figure out what he was saying here. If he was worried she would tell someone about his being alive, that meant two things. Number one, it was someone she knew – otherwise, he would not have the worry. And number two, it meant it was probably detrimental in a major way for him to be alive – at least to this person. Thirdly, it meant he was going to find a way to keep her silent. Okay, so there were three things.

She was still pacing when he spoke again, but she held up her hand toward the screen and he fell silent. Callie had to finish thinking about what this meant. Maybe there were four things. Or even five. What if she told someone? Would that someone – assuming it was the right someone to tell – fly down to Fiji and come looking for, and potentially hurt Brian Bradley? Or even kill him? Or was it more like a tax-evasion thing? Maybe that was it. And she didn't give a flip about that. Quickly, she turned on her heel and faced the screen.

"Hey. I think you need to tell me why you don't want someone to know you're alive."

Bradley tilted his head and frowned. He started shaking his head slightly.

"Listen," she said, pointing at the screen, "hear me out. We might not be at odds here. Like if it's a tax thing or something, I could care less… I *couldn't* care less about that. Your secret is safe."

He stared at her for a long moment. "Okay. And if it's not a tax thing?" he asked, making quotes in the air.

"Well," she said, and shrugged. "I don't know. That's what I mean! If you tell me, we can decide right here and now if I'm actually a danger to your continued existence."

Brian Bradley pulled his head ever so slightly back. He was nodding slowly. Ever so slowly and subtly. "You see,

Callie, I trust you about as far as I can throw you. So that's why we're in this predicament."

"Okay. Well, then consider this." She stood with her hands behind her back, staring at the floor. "You are extant, and that's apparently a worry for you. Well, it is for me, too. As well as *every single person* who knows where I am right now. If my existence doesn't continue, or even if it doesn't get *confirmed,*" she said, holding her two index fingers up together, "then you won't be extant for very long."

Again, he did the slow-flinch thing. He leaned back in his chair and took a deep breath. Man, what was with all these people and their tells? Callie was getting good at reading people. "You know, I'm actually really surprised a smart guy like you didn't consider that aspect, Brian."

"Well, of course I figured someone knows you're here," Bradley started. But Callie interrupted him.

"BUT!" she shouted. "BUT, but, but, Brian. You didn't figure that I told them *why* I came here. They all know I'm here to see you. Many, many people already know you're alive." Callie stood still then, and stared at him through the screen.

And he returned the stare. It was almost like…

Callie shuffled her feet. Lifted her chin a little.

Kind of like maybe he was…

She lowered her gaze and looked levelly at him. She wasn't smiling. But she also wasn't *not* smiling. It might have been her evil look.

Like maybe he was considering that she might be…

Cardna leaned into view from Bradley's right side. She was whispering something in his ear. He was looking away from the camera, taking in what she said. Then suddenly, he turned and looked hard at Cardna. Like he was shocked. Callie might have lifted her chin again. Her hands were behind her back again. She felt a little empowered, even though she didn't quite know what was going on. She knew something had shocked that man. And that couldn't be anything but good for Callie. She was feeling a little more confident now. That was for sure. She was getting good at reading body language. And she had just seen him flinch from what Cardna had said. And now, presently, he gulped! *Holy cow!*

When Bradley turned back to the camera, Cardna leaned down on her fists on the desk and stared into the camera – into Callie's eyes – herself. "Uh, Callie, you have someone here who came to see you."

CHAPTER 9

The fact that there was no formal reception area was at first jarring, but it quickly started making sense. And it might have worked in Rebecca's favor. Walking into the reception area, had there been one, would likely have netted her zero favor. The receptionist could easily have disavowed all knowledge that Callie was visiting. Or, even more likely, might not have had to disavow anything. It might have been absolute truth. No idea she was even here. Either way, Rebecca might not have made it past the desk. Either Callie isn't here, or someone has let the receptionist know not to let anyone through for her.

But being that there was no formal reception area, Rebecca did not have the same options for entry. She found herself in the parking garage, having rented herself a car when she arrived at the airport, and instead of trying to find a non-existent area, she had started trying to figure out how to get in. She had been walking slowly toward the elevator, staring at her phone, sending a text that would never leave her phone in this environment. This attention deficit had made her look unsuspicious. So when the elevator happened to open just as she approached, Rebecca just walked right on, past the woman who was heading out. And right under the hard arm of a multi-million-dollar security system. When the elevator opened on the ground floor of the building, the doors had opened and deposited a wandering Rebecca right into the heart of a cube farm.

She had looked up then, realizing her phone just wasn't going to be of any use down here on this island – let alone in this concrete Faraday cage. And when she saw that there was no formal reception, Rebecca went about trying to find someone who might know something. She had begun by looking for offices. Someone in charge. Maybe not an executive, but a manager. A shift super. Someone low, but with a little more self-worth than a cube rat.

The funny thing to Rebecca, in retrospect, was that she had not even known this was a highly secure facility. Not being a Royal employee herself, she did not know that this was their headquarters – their mecca. So, in not treating it as a most-holy sanctuary, she was able to act completely normal. Unimpressed and unimposing. She had learned that if you look like you belong somewhere, no one questions you. A clipboard or a ladder gets most people through most security stops. Walk in like you belong there, and people assume you do.

Rebecca had quickly discovered that she had to go up a floor to find a single office. The entire first floor was cubes – at least the part of the first floor she had seen. When she got to the second floor, she popped out of the elevator, readjusting her purse on her shoulder, and reached up to push the thick glasses back up her nose. This, somehow, had made her look important and official. So when the woman coming out of her office almost bumped into Rebecca, she immediately stepped back and took the role of the underling.

"Ooh, I'm sorry, ma'am."

Rebecca had looked at her and smiled. "Oh, that's okay. I'm looking for Callie Simmons. She around?"

The woman had raised her eyebrows and said, "Oh, is she an employee here?" And when Rebecca nodded, the woman added, "Here? I'm sorry, I just don't recognize the name."

Rebecca had reached out and softly grasped the woman's arm, just above the elbow – another assertive gesture that tells people subconsciously that you're the one in charge – and smiled again. "Oh, no, she's from state-side. Just visiting."

"Oh, okay. And…" the woman started, and turned toward her office, then turned right back to Rebecca, looking a little confused. "And you are?"

"From state-side, too. Just trying to find Callie." And that was how she had completely busted the security at the most security-driven company on the planet. Well, she would have to check that statistic when she got time. This had just been too easy. The addition of the second sentence had made it seem hurried and urgent. All techniques she had learned in another life. A life she didn't much talk about these days. In fact, never. She never talked about it.

The woman had taken Rebecca into her office and not only started dialing numbers, but had also offered the visitor some coffee from her pod-puncher. Rebecca gratefully accepted, and was now holding a steaming cup of Donut Shop blend. It smelled better than it tasted. What the hell, it was more instant than instant coffee.

She stood looking at the woman's pictures, but only held her coffee cup with one hand, and close to her mouth – another sign of dominance and authority. Managers keep it close to the mouth – where it's needed and quick. No time wasted in taking a sip. Not worried about looking good. And not warming her hands with the mug. She had inner warmth already. Didn't need coffee for that.

Today, Rebecca wore her hair down instead of her typical braid. It looked more managerial. More professional. Though she had opted to leave her nose ring in. When the woman asked her name so she could relay it, Rebecca turned only her head to the woman and said over her shoulder, "Piper." Then she deliberately took a sip of the coffee. "Piper Beck." Then she listened, uninterested, as the woman said the name into the phone.

After a few moments and some affirmatives from the woman, she hung up the phone and said, "Okay, Ms. Beck, if you'll just follow me…"

As Rebecca, escorted by a middling manager, came down the hallway, one hand securing the purse strap on her shoulder, marching with a confidence Callie could never have managed on her greatest day, Cardna Darwyn approached from the opposite direction. Brian Bradley was behind Cardna, but he was clearly not escorting her. No one with any perceptive abilities would have mistaken him as being in charge of anything. Cardna walked with her arms swinging, her fingers and thumbs together, as if about to snap, chin held high and in perfect calm.

Rebecca, though she walked a pace behind the woman escorting her, was clearly not intimidated by the building, the atmosphere, or the approaching woman. She walked with a stride commonly seen in people of great power – and Cardna saw it immediately. As they neared the dynamic stopping point determined by the laws of physics and the lengths of their respective strides, they both slowed perceptibly. And then they stopped. Rebecca still stood a meter or so behind the woman escorting her, and had a very subtle smile on her face. Completely unafraid.

"Ms. Darwyn, this is Ms. Beck," the woman said, swinging a hand out, offering her as if she were a dish. And the way Cardna was looking at her, maybe that wasn't far from it.

"Hello, Ms. Beck," Cardna said. "Thank you, Stephanie."

Stephanie bowed slightly, and turned demurely away, retreating down the corridor between the offices and the windows that looked out upon the forestry below.

"Greetings. I'm sorry, you have the advantage of me," she said, reaching forward for a handshake.

"Darwyn. Cardna Darwyn."

Rebecca did not so much as twitch an eyelash at the name. Instead, she shook the hand as it came toward her, and then returned her own to her purse strap. She then stood awaiting the next bit of action.

"Right. So Stephanie tells me you're here to see Callie Simmons."

Rebecca nodded and smiled at Cardna, then looked out the windows on her left, almost as though she were uninterested in the conversation. Almost as if she *knew* Cardna would have to comply with her demands.

"Okay, well, she's not currently available at the moment," Cardna said with a marked hesitation.

"Redundant. Hmm. Okay, well, I'll wait. Where shall I setup then?" Rebecca said, finally returning her attention to the woman in front of her.

"I'm sorry?" said Cardna.

"For what?" asked Rebecca. Her eyes did not widen. She just smirked a little.

"Ahuh." Cardna said. "You, uh… you said redundant."

"Oh," Rebecca said, and reached out to touch Cardna's wrist, "yes. You said 'currently' and then added 'at the moment'." Now she was staring Cardna directly in the eyes. Rebecca could tell the other woman was beginning to lose her sense of control here. Maybe a little intimidation.

"Ah! Right," Cardna said, smiling. "I just meant that…"

"That she can't come to the phone right now. But if I'll leave my name and number… Right? Well, I'll be happy to wait." She straightened the purse strap and smiled again and made a little show of taking in her surroundings. Then suddenly, Rebecca reached out and touched Cardna's wrist again. "Oh, do you know how long she'll be, though? Just curious." She noticed the man standing behind Cardna had not only remained completely silent so far, but had also completely failed to make any kind of eye-contact with Rebecca. He had, in fact, been on his phone the entire time. This not only advertised his disinterest, but painted a sign on his forehead that screamed 'SUBORDINATE!' Likely, Rebecca figured, he was here to play the part of the muscle. He was the quickest thing she could find under the circumstances, and was not quite moving the needle on Rebecca's intimidation dial.

Cardna stared Rebecca in the eyes for a long moment. A moment in which Rebecca did not even blink, but rather continued her polite semi-smile of confidence as she waited to hear what she wanted to hear. Then Cardna finally relented. "Right. Yeah, sure. It'll only be a few minutes. She was just, uh… She was -" she said, then turned to the man behind her. "Hey, go check on her, will you? See what's taking so long."

The man looked like he had no clue what was going on, though. He frowned momentarily, then looked up at Rebecca, finally making brief eye contact, then looked back at Cardna, frowning.

"Just go find out what the fuck is going on, please," Cardna said in a forceful whisper that was not lost on Rebecca. Then she turned back to Rebecca. Rebecca smiled a little welcoming smile at her. Cardna said, "Sorry. She was just freshening up a little bit. She'll be right out." She reached down to her belt and pulled the badge that hung there on a retractable line. She held it against the badge reader on the door by which they had happened to stop. "You can wait in here, Ms. Beck," Cardna said. "I'll be back to check on you in a moment. Can I get you anything?"

"No, I'll be fine, thank you," Rebecca said. She waited until Cardna had turned nervously away before she herself turned and entered the conference room.

"Brian! Wait up," Cardna said, walking as quickly as possible without actually jogging, to catch up with the man. He turned to look at her. "God damn that woman," she said.

"What? Who is she?" Bradley asked.

"I don't know. I think she's an executive. I need you to go get Callie and put her in that conference room. I'm going to go check the intranet and find out who she is."

"You think she's a Royal exec, you mean?" Bradley asked. "I don't recognize her."

"Yeah, well that doesn't mean much. I already made that mistake once. I refuse to look a fool again. Just go get her please."

That one-time mistake to which she referred had been about a year ago, when a strange man had wandered in to Cardna's office. A lot of visitors were in the building that day, and she had not gotten around to meeting many of them. The man had come in with his hands in his pockets and started looking at the pictures Cardna had hung on her office wall – all while she was on a private phone call.

After a minute of uncomfortable fumbling on the phone, she had finally put her hand over the mouthpiece and asked, "I'm sorry, can I help you find something?"

The man had turned toward her, smiling. He looked frumpy, were she to call a spade a spade. Yellow tie. Brown tweed jacket. Very Dwight Schrute. "Ah. No rush. I was just waiting for you to finish your call. Go ahead."

Cardna had scoffed and said, shaking her head, "Well, would you mind waiting in another fuckin' room? I'm on a call here."

The man had raised his chin and said, "No, I think I'll wait here. Seeing as how I own the building. And since I own the phone too, I'm guessing I'm paying for the personal call you're making. So I'll stay."

The man she had sworn at was Kim Coyin, the C.E.O. of Royal Research Corporation. Cardna had not recognized him because she had never paid attention to the upper echelons of the company hierarchy. It had been a stupid day all around, meeting and greeting a bunch of people whose names she would never remember. And the craziest part about it was that Cardna had known Mr. Coyin was in the building. And she had still made the greatest career-limiting-move of her life. Thence on, she had sworn never to make the same mistake. There was no way she would put herself in that position again. So either this Piper Beck – again, another name she did not recognize – was a fraud here to help Callie pull off whatever stunt she had come to pull, or she was someone who had true authority. If she were a fraud, she was the best actor Cardna had ever seen. That was why she was taking no chances.

Cardna would just get on the company intranet and scan the names of the executives real quick. If Piper Beck did not show up in her search, she was sure there would be no penalties for kicking this woman's ass.

The sad part about it all, in her mind at least, was that they were *supposed* to be security-conscious. They were *supposed* to check badges. No piggy-backing through the badge readers. Keep an eye out for suspicious persons and behavior. They all heard about it at least once a year in the safety briefings. But God forbid you ask an exec for his or her badge. You were liable to get chewed out for not knowing your company. Forget that one exec – a president of something or other, if Cardna recalled correctly – had been fired, and then the next week had walked *back into* the branch with no badge. And the receptionist had buzzed him in. All he had to tell her was he had left his badge in the car. Oh, heads rolled for that one. And there had been a week's worth of meetings about checking badges following the incident.

Still, no one really did it. And to the person standing in the elevator, watching a fellow employee run toward the door – *'Hold the door, please!'* – you were supposed to let the door close. Let that person use his own badge to reopen it. No one did that. So, there existed a double-edged sword. You ask the wrong executive to show his badge, or let a door slam in his face, you were likely to be chewed out or written up. But if you did the polite thing – hold the door, or ignored the fact that there was no badge showing – you could bet you would be chewed out *and* written up. Possibly fired. Definitely fired if you let the wrong person in and you were being tested. It was a ridiculous catch-22.

So her own personal solution had been to let someone in, make sure he or she was comfortable, then go verify. Take action privately, in other words. Cardna had told her entire team to act in this manner. Put the suspect in a conference room and come get her. She was not about to lose her job, or be demoted again for some bullshit test.

But here was a peculiar situation. Obviously, Cardna could not – and could never – know whether Callie had called a friend before she showed up. What Cardna *did* know, was that Callie's phone was basically a brick here in this country. She also knew it had been on the bedside table back in the woman's room. Either way, if this were a rescue mission, it was an incredibly quick response. Hell, the flight from New Jersey – where Callie had come from – was almost twenty hours alone. Now admittedly, Cardna had forgotten the poor girl was in the holding room over night last night. She had not seemed to notice. At least Callie had not said anything. She acted like she thought she had only had a nap. If she did know, then that could be a serious bit of trouble for Cardna on its own. And she did feel terrible about it, really. She was not trying to be *that* inhumane.

Even more peculiar than that scenario, though, was that if this woman was *not* here to rescue Callie. What the hell did she want to see her for? Well, it could be that she heard there was a woman in the holding room, and flew out to have a look at how she was being treated. Not likely, Cardna had to admit. But in weighing the options, she had to consider every possibility.

The third, and perhaps the most likely along the lines of Piper Beck being an executive, was that they were to rendezvous here. An executive meeting another employee for a meeting, as they would both be in town. An employee from a field office. An emp-... *Wait!*

What if Callie isn't even an employee? That was where she had to start. She opened a new tab in her browser and typed Callie Simmons into the intranet. Instantly there was a result. Her face and employee ID popped up on the screen. Only... only, she was no longer an employee.

Cardna shoved back from the desk, suddenly getting angry. *What the fuck is going on here?* Her arms extended straight out in front of her, gripping the front edge of the desk, and she began to tap the fingernails of her index fingers on the wooden veneer in front of the blotter. She scooted back up to the desk and squinted at the employee data file on Callie Elaine Simmons. There was, of course, some data that she did not have access to. This was just a company intranet page for employees, after all. Not a human resources file.

It did say she used to be an employee, several years ago. And then there was another set of dates more recently, where she was listed as a private contractor, working for Andrew Matthew Minus, in the New Jersey field office. Cardna pursed her lips and tilted her head. She clicked on Minus's name and looked at his profile. Current! What time was it there in New Jersey? She looked at the time zone map. Holy shit, it's the past there. New Jersey was a day behind. Sixteen hours in the past. She looked at her watch. Yeah, there was no way Minus would still be at the office at 20:00 hours. Even still...

The phone rang only once before someone answered. "Yello," the gruff voice on the other end said. It shocked her so badly that she shot up out of her chair, knocking it backward into the wall with her legs.

A pleasant but timid woman named Stephanie had shown Callie into the conference room, and then pulled the door closed and disappeared. The door, Callie had noted with absolute lack of hesitation, had a door handle on it. As soon as Callie was in the room, and able to pay attention to its only other occupant, the other woman stood up and Callie embraced her, both arms around the neck.

"Hey, baby," Rebecca said softly. One hand was on Callie's shoulder, by way of the back. The other was rubbing Callie's back from shoulder blades to lumbar. Up and down, slowly, calmly. Callie was sobbing, but holding back. She was thankful that Rebecca allowed her this cry. They didn't know each other very well, so this itself was a powerful gesture of magnanimity. After as brief a time as she could make it, Callie pulled away and wiped her eyes. Then she turned and found a chair behind her and pulled it up to meet her.

Once she was seated, Rebecca followed suit. But she kept a hand on the table, holding Callie's own. "Walter said you were in trouble."

Callie nodded.

Rebecca shook her head.

Callie frowned and tilted her head.

"Nothing. I just don't get it. I told him he was being paranoid. How could he have known?"

"We sort of have a language," Callie said. She was dabbing her eyes with a tissue she had pulled from a box on the table.

"Technically," Rebecca said, holding a finger up, "that's a lack of language. Apparently he got this idea based on the fact that you *didn't* answer your phone for a series of hours."

Callie allowed herself a genuine smile. "Well, thank you for coming. I'm not sure what we do now, though."

Rebecca nodded slowly, a look of knowing on her face. "Yeah, I didn't figure, if you really were in captivity, that you would have all the answers. I will allow, however," she said, again holding that finger up, "that I did fantasize about your coming up with some grand plan while I sat on the plane."

"That's a twenty-hour flight, Rebecca. How did you make it so fast?"

"Yeah, that was a tough one. I'm likely not to wake at all tomorrow. Whatever 'tomorrow' means," she added, looking around the room and making quotes with her fingers for effect. After a brief moment of their staring at each other, Rebecca said, "Any ideas at all? I don't suppose they're just going to let you walk out of here, are they?"

"No. Not at all. I just really didn't have any kind of plan when I came here." And when she saw Rebecca's look of surprise and fear, Callie held up her hands defensively. "I know, I know! But in captivity, I've not had the clearest state of mind to work with."

"Okay," Rebecca sighed, squeezing Callie's hand on the table again, "I guess I can understand that." She leaned back and rolled her head around, stretching her neck. "It would be nice if you had found the self-destruct button or something," she said.

"I know, right? I wish I did know some secr-" Callie started, and then suddenly straightened up. Her face fell as she stared at the floor behind Rebecca. "Holy cow, I just remembered something!"

"Yeah? What's that, sugar?" Rebecca said, crossing her legs. She still looked so damn relaxed. Callie wondered how she could be so stress-free in this environment. She also wondered how the heck Rebecca had gotten here so fast. How she'd even gotten *in* so fast.

Callie was now sitting bolt-upright, and gripping the ends of the armrests with knuckles turned white with tension. "I think I know a way out. We have to get out of this room though."

"Mr. Minus?" Cardna said hopefully into the phone. She was staring at nothing, trying to imagine him in his office. She was twirling a lock of hair in her left hand.

"This is Minus. Who's this?"

"Hello there. May I call you Andrew?"

A chortle came through the receiver. "No, you sure as hell may not," he said. She lost her hopeful smile, but then he added, "Call me Matt."

"Oh. Ha! Okay, Matt. My name is Cardna. I work in the Fiji office."

"Ah. Okay, hello Cardna. What can I do for you?"

"Well, I was just calling to verify employment. Do you have a Callie Simmons working for you?"

There was a click on the line. *There must be something wrong with the connection*, Cardna thought. She pulled the phone away from her face and frowned at it. That always seemed to help. "Hello? Mr. Minus?" she said, returning the mouthpiece to her chin. "Hello?"

After a long moment, she held the receiver against her shoulder to ponder what had just happened. What did it mean? Should she call him back? Did he *mean* to disconnect? Had he hung up on her? She furled her lips and shook her head. Well, this was suspicious.

They were walking down the corridor, but Callie kept wanting to jog. To skip a step or two every three or four. Rebecca, however, was still walking behind her, checking her surroundings occasionally, and trying to calm Callie back down. "Callie!" she would whisper. "Chill the fuck out, darlin!"

Callie was walking with her arms down at her sides, but her hands out, fingers splayed. Like some ballet move. She looked nothing *but* suspicious. Rebecca kept rolling her eyes and shaking her head. But she also couldn't keep from cracking a smile. If nothing else, it was endearing. "Callie!"

But Callie was more nervous than she had ever been. She kept feeling like if she got caught – *captured* – she would be killed. Like a prisoner of war. Well, that couldn't be too far off, could it? *I mean, come on! They already locked me in a room with no doorknob for like – like...* How long had it been? Hours, obviously. But how many? Three? Four?

They had come to the end of the aisle of windows. The building had widened out a few paces back, and now they were in a walkway between cubes on the left and offices on the right. Not all of them were offices though. Some seemed to be conference rooms or break rooms. She even thought she saw a bean bag in one of them. What the heck was that? A recreation room? A relaxation room? Maybe she needed to work here, after all.

Finally, she had to stop. She was almost at the end of her rope. About to admit defeat. Her hands were tingling. She turned around and faced Rebecca, who still looked calm as ever. Pretty even. After a twenty-hour flight and who knew what else, she looked fresh and pretty. Smiling lightly. Her hand on her purse strap up by her shoulder. She could have been on a tour of the Queen Mary. Just following the tour guide. Oh, no thank you, I don't need a cocktail. Yes, I'm fine. I'm enjoying the exhibits. Thank you.

"Dangit, Bec, I can't find the room I was in. I know we're on the right floor though," Callie said.

Rebecca stepped forward, a motherly look of concern on her face, and took Callie's arms just above the elbows. She was close enough to kiss. Callie could smell peppermint on her breath. *Of course she has fresh breath. Roll eyes.*

"Calm down, sweet heart. Let's think through this. What was the configuration of the room?"

Callie dropped her panic and stood still for a moment. She let the stress drain away. Somehow, it felt like Bec would protect her. She did not, however, want to try to dissect that thought. About why she felt safe. About *how*

Rebecca would protect her. Her mind flashed back to the first thought she had had when she saw it was Rebecca who was waiting in that room for her. *How had she even gotten in?*

Cardna finally, thoughtfully, dropped the handset back into its cradle, then put her hands on her hips. Had she actually believed the disconnection had been accidental, she would have called back instantly. Instead, she was standing here acting like there might be a question. Maybe because she did not want to face reality. Or maybe because she was trying to convince herself it was even possible. The ridiculous coincidence of a disconnection on a digital line at that perfect instant. Mention the name Callie Simmons and the line goes blank. Right.

Sitting down and scooting back up to the desk, Cardna rested her elbow on the surface and her chin in her hand, tapping her teeth with her fingernails. What was her next move here? Brian Bradley wandered into her office at that moment, leaning on the doorjamb. She looked up at him. "What you got?"

"Well, I took them to the conference room. Well, I didn't. I had Stephanie do it," he said.

"Good call. I'm trying to figure this gal out. Callie used to be an employee. And then a stint as a private contractor, working for a guy named…" Cardna said and paused as she turned to click on the original tab in her browser. "Named Andrew Minus."

Brian stared at her, emotionless.

Cardna leaned back in her chair. "Who do you think this Piper woman is?"

He twisted his mouth and raised an eyebrow. "No idea. But she obviously had credentials to get in the building."

Cardna nodded. "Guess so. But I searched the employee directory and that name doesn't show up at all. There's a Becky Pope, but no Piper Beck." She turned back to her computer and closed the current tab. This left the tab with Callie's info open in front of her. Something sparked in the back of her mind, but it was too quick to latch onto. It was gone as fast as it had come.

Callie turned slowly around, taking in the surrounding structure. A woman walked by with a stack of folders in her arm, but was staring at her phone as she walked. Then Callie looked at Rebecca. "The door was on this side of a hallway. There were windows over here," Callie said, pointing to her left.

Rebecca lifted her chin in understanding. "Well, okay, that means we need to be on the south side of the building."

Callie frowned. "How the heck do you know that?"

"Because," Rebecca said, taking her arm and gently guiding her to turn around and walk, "we are on the north side of the building. And looking out the windows, I don't see another part of the building facing us."

So they proceeded to the end of the corridor and turned right, then right again after about twenty meters. Aha! Now there was a row of windows, presumably facing south, and doors on the right. A group of people had congregated about thirty meters down the hallway, and were talking quietly. Most of them had coffee cups in their hands. In short order, Callie had found the door. She knew it was the right one. But the handle wouldn't budge when she tried it.

"Locked?" asked Rebecca. Callie nodded, feeling the nervousness creep back into her blood and body. "Wait here," Bec said, touching her arm. "It'll be okay."

Rebecca walked toward the group of people confidently. In less than a minute, she was coming back with one of the women at her side. And they were laughing together. *What the hell had she said?*

The woman flipped her badge out and slapped it against the reader mounted next to the doorjamb. The light turned green, it beeped, and she pushed the door open.

"Thank you so much, Candace," Rebecca said, smiling and touching the woman's arm. *Holy cow* Callie thought. *She's good.*

When they went inside, Rebecca turned to shut the door behind them. Callie whipped around, suddenly remembering, but she was too late. It had already clicked closed.

"Oh, shit," Rebecca said when she realized there was no door handle. "I hope you're right about that secret passage, Callie."

Callie stared into her eyes for a long moment. "Me, too."

△　　　△　　　△

"So, nothing on the intranet?" Brian Bradley asked, crossing his arms.

"Nope. Well, she could be new. Or she could look different than one of the pictures. Who knows? A nondescript husky woman with brown hair and – what color eyes does she have?"

"How the hell should I know?" Bradley said, holding his hands out without uncrossing his arms. "I didn't even notice her hair color."

"Great. Brilliant. Glad to have such a keen observer of detail on the team," Cardna said, rolling her eyes. "Which conference room are they in?" she asked, moving her mouse to another application on the screen.

"The Sundown," he responded.

Cardna opened the app and scrolled down to the room he had mentioned. When she clicked on the name, the right side of the screen opened a camera view of the room, from one of the corners by the ceiling. It was instantly obvious that there were no occupants. "You sure?" she said, and started clicking on the other conference rooms on the same floor.

"Yeah. Why?" Bradley said, coming around behind her desk so he could view the screen with her.

"Because no one's in the Sundown." Click. Click. Click. A conference room called The Strand had a full house. Fourteen people sat around the large table. Click. Click. Every other conference room on the floor was empty. Cardna twirled her chair around and looked at Bradley. "Where the fuck did they go?" Her heart was suddenly beating hard and fast in her chest.

Bradley was already out the door. Instead of his turning left though, as Cardna would have figured, he had turned right. Toward his own office. That chicken shit was going to lock himself back in his office! *Oh my God!*

Cardna hurried out the door and down the hall into the main office area, looking through windows as she maintained a fast gait through the floor. She walked right by the original holding room where Callie had broken the glass yesterday. It did not even cross her mind that Callie would go back in there. There was, of course, the thought that the women had just gone down the elevator to the parking garage and left in Piper's car. Why she had not thought of that before, she couldn't begin to imagine. She pulled her cell phone out of her back pocket and scrolled contacts as she walked, occasionally looking up, or through a window.

She pressed dial for the contact she had saved called front gate. When she got an answer, Cardna said, "Hey George. Did anyone leave in the last few minutes? A visitor woman with another woman passenger?"

"No, ma'am. No one has left in a couple of hours," said George.

"Will you stop them if they try to leave, please?" Cardna asked.

"What are they driving?"

"I don't know. But it would be someone you gave a guest pass to earlier this morning." She could hear the gears turning in his head for a moment.

"Ma'am, I didn't pass any visitors this morning. I'll check the tape though and see if I find who you're looking for."

"Okay, great. Her name is Piper Beck."

"Ah, Miss Piper! Yes. I remember her. She's not a guest. She said she was from the Maui office," George said.

Cardna slapped her forehead. Hard. "Fuck sake, George. We don't even have an office in all of Hawaii. How do you still have a job?" Angry, she hung up the phone. Well, at least they were still on site. She called Brian Bradley next. She was getting ready to chew someone's ass. This was getting ridiculous.

"Callie, I hate to be the asker of stupid questions, but why don't we just leave? We can take my car," Rebecca said as they hurried to the back of the room where the broken glass still framed an opening.

"Because I don't think they'll let us leave. There's a security guard at the gate. I think he lets people in easier than out," Callie said.

Rebecca put a hand on her shoulder as Callie was swinging her leg over the opening. "Wait. Callie. What does that mean?"

Callie looked back at Rebecca. "They have some sort of hand signal you have to make to be able to leave. It's a duress signal. If you don't make the right gesture, they'll apparently stop you."

Rebecca, keeping her hand on Callie's shoulder, stood staring at the floor, thinking about this for a long moment. "Hmm."

"Wait. How did you get in?"

Rebecca looked up. "I told him I was from the Maui office. He just let me right in."

"Maui?" Callie frowned. "Like, as in Hawaii?"

"No. Upper east Boston," Rebecca said. Her face was still serious.

"Do they even have an office there?"

"I don't know, babe. But it worked."

Callie pursed her lips, impressed, and nodded. "Okay, well let's proceed. Because, might I remind you, we ain't getting back out that door," she said, pointing at the door that had no knob.

"Right you are," Rebecca agreed, nodding. "On you go, then."

Callie twisted and swung her left leg over the opening, then turned to help Rebecca. Rebecca ignored the gesture and put a foot up on the opening, grabbed the inner edge and just stood up with both feet on the ledge. She was having to crouch way over to avoid hitting the top, but she was just standing on the threshold instead of trying to scoot through on her rear like Callie had done. Then she simply hopped down. Callie shook her head, rolled her eyes, then turned toward the far wall, hidden in relative darkness.

"It's over here," she said as they scooted into the end of the hallway-like room. After their eyes adjusted, they could both see the seam around a perfect door-shaped rectangle in the wall adjacent to the glass opening.

"No door knob here either," Rebecca pointed out. Callie put her hands on her hips and looked high out the top of her eyes. An incomplete eye-roll. Rebecca slapped her shoulder. "How does it open?"

"I don't know. I hadn't gotten that far yet when they came in and got me earlier," Callie responded.

"I find this fascinating. A secret panel. Well, assuming it opens. I want to work for the kind of company that builds these kind of secret passages," Rebecca said.

Callie had dropped to a squat and was running her finger along the seam from the ground all the way up. Rebecca reached forward and pushed on the left side of the panel. Nothing happened. Then the right. It clicked back a few millimeters, then clicked again, and swung toward them. Callie stood up. They looked at each other for a minute. Rebecca was smirking, maybe a little proud of herself. Callie furled her lips, drew in a breath through her flared nostrils and pulled up on her pants. "Okay, hot shot."

Then they were on the other side of the door. Quickly, Rebecca turned and pulled the door back to its closed position using the handle someone had conveniently installed on this side of it. It clicked closed. Callie looked up at the ceiling. There were dim blue lights all along the ceiling, very high up, about every six feet. Just enough to see by. The ceilings were a lot higher in here than out in that room. "What the heck is this place?" she said, mainly to herself. She was whispering.

"It looks like we're inside the walls," Rebecca said, following Callie's gaze up to the ceiling. "Where now, trailmaster?"

Callie shook her head then looked back and forth down the hallways. She had a sudden chill up her spine and onto her arms. This was a little spooky. "I don't know. But something tells me we should head toward the garage, generally," she said finally. And off they went, down toward what Rebecca called the west. Very quickly, they came to end of the corridor. There was a ladder running up and down in a large tube, but they could go no farther without climbing. She looked back at Rebecca in the dim, blue light. Rebecca shrugged at her. Her skin looked like it had a luminescence to it, and was sky blue, like the indigenous beings in James Cameron's movie, Avatar. And her teeth were incredibly white. *Wait! These were black lights!*

She mentioned this to Rebecca, but the other just prodded her, looking down. "Let's go!"

Callie took hold of the rungs and began descending into the darkness below.

CHAPTER 10

Cardna's frustration finally boiled over and got the best of her. She began shouting as she walked through the cube farm. "Listen up! Everyone, may I have your attention! There are two women somewhere on this floor who do not belong here. Has anyone seen anyone they don't know? Anyone suspicious?"

It did not take long before someone stood up and made eye-contact with her. It was Candace. She was on the phone but covered the mouthpiece. "I let two women into the holding room about fifteen minutes ago," she said.

Cardna stopped dead in her tracks, then waved at Candace and turned on her heel. Back the other way. As she strode down the corridor, people instinctively moved out of her way. She looked like a woman on a mission – someone not to be bothered with. She was almost jogging when she got to the holding room. Badge. Beep. Click.

She threw the door open and glanced around the room. No sign. Quickly, she trotted up to the broken glass window and peeked in the anteroom beyond. Not there either. Did Callie know about the hidden door? Cardna didn't know if the woman had had time to discover it before they had come in and gotten her earlier. It was still flush with the wall, closed. Chances were, she thought, they would not flee into the wall passage. Those passages didn't go all over the building.

There were, of course, structural limitations to a secret passageway. For one, they could not cross a wall where there were windows. They also could not cross empty spaces like hallways. The passages were all inside interior walls, and ran along until they reached a point where a regular room or hallway, or window, would be, and then they ran into ladders that ran up and down, where the same pattern ran on the next floors.

Cardna did not know why they were built into the walls; they weren't used very often, to her knowledge. She certainly had no use for them. And as far as she knew, there were only two entrances to the passages that opened into regular spaces where people could see them. They were protected with simple badge readers at these two doors, and completely conspicuous. Hidden out in the open, they attracted no real attention or curiosity. Those who did not have access did not care. It was just another door through which their badge would not take them.

She also couldn't imagine *why* Callie would have gone into the passages as a means of escape or egress. Number one, Callie did not – presumably, at least – know the layout of the routes. Number two, well, it would only take her to places she could not reasonably expect to escape from. There was one door in the basement level that Cardna's badge wouldn't even get her in. There were only a few people in the building who could get through that one. She had never seen beyond it. She had never even asked about it. It was one of those things for which she knew she would not get an answer. Need-to-know basis, and she didn't need to know.

Cardna stood with her hands on her hips, pursing her lips, waiting for inspiration. Quite probably, she reckoned, they had taken the elevator down to the parking garage, and were going to try to drive off the premises. George would stop them for sure, now knowing he had screwed up royally earlier. And all would be well. She would have them both arrested for trespassing. And Callie, well, maybe she could also pin destruction of private property on her as well. Cardna did not like being taken advantage of by strangers. And this Piper Beck woman had made a fool of her all around.

When they reached the level below, Callie quickly caught on to that which Rebecca had considered a floor above her not two minutes ago: these passages were limited in their utility. They couldn't go across hallways or windowed walls. So what *were* they for? Why have them at all? Surely they served some kind of purpose. When Rebecca dropped onto the walkway next to Callie, she shared this idea.

Rebecca agreed, "Yeah. I thought of that too. But I bet they're used for control of some sort. Like hidden controls, or access to secret rooms that don't show up on the floor plan."

"Yeah, that would make sense. That would mean there could be an entire floor, even, that could be accessed."

Rebecca shrugged. "Yes, but you would see it from the outside of the building then. Unless no one has ever bothered to count the floors by windows."

Callie's eyes got wide. "Basement!"

"The elevator takes you to the basement."

"Yeah, but you would never know if the elevator went to the *same* basement. Or if it skipped a floor. Or didn't go down as far as our tunnels here," she said, spreading her hands.

Rebecca shook a finger at her. "Good thinking, Callie. But what do we do when we're in the basement? I mean, why aren't we just trying to escape?"

Callie let go a large sigh. "I'm not trying to escape. I'm trying to find the secrets. I know Brian Bradley is up to something, and this building holds all the clues."

"Blackmail?" Rebecca asked, eyebrows raised.

"Maybe," Callie said, shrugging. "Maybe we can get ourselves into some real trouble, anyway."

Rebecca smiled. "You're fuckin' crazy, you know that?"

"Yeah! Let's go!" she responded, and they were off again, going down the ladder as far as it would take them.

When they finally dropped off the very bottom rung of the ladder, Callie's shoulders were burning. They had come down as many as twelve or thirteen floors. She had lost count at some point. But it was, she saw very quickly, different down here. It was wide open and well lit. It almost looked like a normal floor, but there were no interior walls. Just large concrete pillars. In the middle of the floor was the elevator column, but there were no doors visible on it. At least not from this perspective. Callie pointed at it, then they headed that way.

Callie went one way around it, Rebecca went the other. They met at the other side, shaking their heads. "Well, you were right," Rebecca said. "It goes straight through this floor."

"Yeah, or that's the bottom where all the springs and stuff are," Callie said. They both looked at the wide concrete column, as if to imagine what lay within.

"Hmm," Rebecca hummed thoughtfully. She began browsing toward the direction they had been moving before, and lights began coming on, sensing the occupant. As they flickered to life, they revealed row upon row of large clunky shapes covered in thick canvas tarps of ecru and olive drab.

Callie realized with a near start that this must be the very equipment to which Cardna had been referring at the safe house. A chill of excitement ran through her arms as this opened her mind to two separate realities: one, it meant Cardna had told Callie something that was now verified. There was definitely equipment down here. And two, it might just be that Callie was getting closer to resolving her life's greatest mystery.

She and Rebecca strolled slowly through the neatly organized aisles of these monstrosities – some of them as much as eight feel tall, and every bit as wide and long. She was on one aisle and Rebecca on the next, walking about the same speed. They would see each other between each piece of mystery, but they were not speaking. Just observing. It seemed to go on interminably. And further, Callie noticed, the lights were going off behind them. They were not on timers, but completely controlled by motion. *Strange.*

They finally passed one large piece and turned toward each other. "Not much point in going on like this, I guess," Rebecca suggested. She looked up at the canvas-covered mound and reached out, touching the edge of the hard shape beneath. Callie did the same.

"Yeah, I guess not." She crossed her arms and looked back the way they had come. A light came on at the end of the long corridor between shapes. They had both seen it, and dived behind the piece of equipment they had just touched.

"Be still!" Rebecca whispered harshly. "God damn lights."

Callie looked up with her eyes without moving her head. How long had it taken each light to go out? She didn't remember – she hadn't really counted. It had just been something she had noticed peripherally. And after a few more seconds, they clicked off. A sigh escaped her tightened chest, and she could feel Rebecca take her hand in the dark, squeezing her fingers.

"Fuck sake, that was close," the other woman said. Callie almost giggled. It came out as a gasp expelled through her nose, and made her head come forward. "Be still!" Bec repeated quietly. They could not see around the box they were hiding behind, but would be able to tell shortly if the lights began coming on. They could not hear any voices, and Callie reckoned it was due to the sound-proofing qualities of so much canvas.

After a very long time, during which Callie and Rebecca sat still in the dark, they heard a loud bang. It had sounded like a door slamming. Callie raised her eyebrows. Rebecca squeezed her hand again. The sound had represented some sort of finality. Callie did not know why she believed that, but likened it to looking into a house through a window. It was just a feeling, you knew when the house was empty. Even saving for the occupants being in another room not visible from the window, the house just had a dead feel to it.

"Hey," Callie whispered. "Do you think they're gone?" She could feel Bec nod.

"It sure is dark in here."

"Yeah. I was thinking that."

"I guess now's as good a time as any," Rebecca suggested.

Callie nodded, and they instinctively stood up together. The lights did not come on.

Cardna Darwyn had considered making an intercom announcement telling everyone to watch out for these two women. But that was stupid, and for multiple reasons. One, it would be belying her outward facade of control. She did not want anyone to know she was freaking the fuck out on the inside. Not only that, but the outward control. It would advertise to the whole building that she had literally lost her charge. Physically. Of course, ninety percent of the occupants of the building did not know there were even two strange women on the campus. Nor that Cardna was holding them. But to advertise it...

Another reason was that she could not be sure the two fugitives would not hear the announcement. Obviously this Callie woman knew the security protocols that would keep them pretty much confined to the building – or at least the premises. Just like a European bank that locked its would-be robbers inside when the alarm was triggered, there was nowhere to go. Eventually, she would find them.

They walked slowly down the manufactured corridor, holding hands. Rebecca had taken the lead. Why the lights were not coming on they could only guess. But both had reckoned it might actually be a good thing. Moving was slow, but relatively safe. The pathways formed between the large crates and lumps in the dark were around eight feet wide. Everything was nicely spaced out in here – likely to allow access to each package with a forklift.

When they finally got to the end of the makeshift corridors, they could see again. There were lights coming from an alcove across the large empty space they had originally been standing in. There was a long cinder block wall, and on the left end of it was a set of double-doors. They looked very sturdy, with the sheen of painted steel and windowless. There was a large red sign on each of them with white lettering, but neither woman could make out what they said from here. The row of lights that were on ran all the way across the open space, only a few feet from that solid wall.

They sat against the last crate in the line, crouched and waiting for an idea. They did not have to wait long. There was a sudden and loud *clunk,* and then one of the two doors opened. A man came out wearing what looked like a space suit. He began popping seals and taking the suit off, hanging the components on a hook by the doors. Callie frowned and looked at Rebecca.

"What the hell?" Rebecca said. "Must be some serious bio-hazard shit back there."

"You know, that would not surprise me in the least," Callie said, shaking her head.

The man took the face covering off, and Callie immediately recognized him. "Oh my God!" she whispered, "It's Brian Bradley!"

Rebecca's face shot toward Callie's, a look of seriousness in her eyes that Callie had not seen yet. And with no further warning, she bolted up and was walking quickly across the open floor toward the man who was still fumbling with his boots. Callie was so much in shock she didn't even know how to react. Should she wait here? Should she chase down that crazy woman? *What the heck!?*

Rebecca startled the man, very obviously. He flinched heavily as he looked up at her, still ten meters away from him, then looked around quickly to see if anyone was there to help him, presumably. Or maybe to see if there was a place to run and hide. There wasn't.

"Excuse me!" the woman said loudly. Callie could hear her words clearly from her hiding spot. They must have been thirty meters away.

"Who are you?" Bradley said. "What are you doing down here?"

"I'm checking inventory. Didn't you get the memo?"

Bradley was standing still, dumbfounded, his hands stilled from their recent task of buckling a dress belt. He stared with concerned eyes at the approaching woman who certainly looked official, but he obviously didn't recognize. The fact that he had asked who she was told Callie all she needed to know.

And Rebecca's gait did not slow as she closed the final few meters between them. And at the last instant, just before she ran right into the poor idiot, she raised a fist and swung *through* the man's head with the intensity of a cannonball, finishing her last step afterwards.

Callie yelped in surprise and revulsion, but simultaneously felt a heat in her stomach that might have been excitement. Rebecca had stepped *through* her punch, and the man had collapsed like a sack of something very heavy. Callie's hand was unconsciously over her own mouth now, her eyes wide and her heart slamming in her chest. Now Rebecca was bent over the man, searching his pockets. She finally stood up and turned back toward Callie. She stood with her legs spread about shoulder-width apart, her fists hanging by her sides holding a cell phone in one and a badge in the other. And she was panting, catching her breath. She looked sinister, staring at Callie through the tops of her eyes. Lustily. That was the stance of victory. Holy God, this woman was bad ass.

CHAPTER 11

The two women had dragged Brian Bradley by his clothes to the place where they had hidden only a few minutes before. The man was out like a sack of coal. Initially, as Callie had run to her new friend, she had heard him snoring an evil-sounding deep-chested rasp that sounded as if he were about to die. Rebecca had informed her that it was the sound of unconscious aspiration, and he would be fine in a few minutes.

Now they stood here with a man slung between them like a hammock. Rebecca had him under the arms, and Callie had his socked feet. She stared at Rebecca with a mix of fascination and awe, and perhaps a wee bit of attraction. Rebecca was looking back down the aisle they had explored earlier, evidently wondering how far they should drag him into the cityscape of dark shapes.

Callie was catching her breath, and felt sweat cooling in her armpits. "What now?"

Rebecca looked back at Callie. "Take his belt off."

Callie instantly dropped his feet and dropped to her knees. The thought of being in a position to take the man's belt off repulsed her, but she did as she was bid. It slid out easily and she handed it to Rebecca, who pulled up on Bradley's arms, leaning him forward to a sitting position. She then pulled his arms behind his back and looped the belt around his wrists. After three complete circuits, she pulled tightly and hooked the belt on its catch.

Callie stared, fascinated. She tried to put her hand over her mouth again, but quickly caught herself and decided to fidget, wringing her hands together instead. She didn't want to look too off-kilter. This was completely new territory for her, but she didn't want to advertise her awe.

Once the belt was safely cinched, Rebecca stood and turned toward the large hulk of hidden whatever behind her and squatted to grab the corner of the canvas. "Help me grab this," she said.

Again, Callie immediately complied. It was nice to have someone to follow, who knew what the hell she was doing, or at least had some semblance of a plan. She took the other corner on the back, and together, they lifted the cape up to expose a stack of wooden crates. They whipped it up to rest across the tallest part, and Rebecca begin heaving against one of the crates that sat atop another. Shortly, she had it twisted to the point where a corner was hanging off. Whatever was inside was obviously heavy, as Rebecca was now out of breath herself, and leaning on her fists, which were on the crate. She looked at Callie. "What do you reckon they keep in these damn things?"

Callie chuckled silently. She was shaking her head. She was wondering what the plan was here, but it was beginning to look like maybe Rebecca wanted to put Bradley *inside* one of these things. Shortly, Rebecca heaved again, twisting the crate back and forth, creating minuscule forward motions that brought it closer and closer to the edge. The cantilever it formed was growing unstable.

"Watch your feet," she finally said, and made one more twist. The crate teetered, then crashed down on the concrete floor thirty-some inches below. It landed right on the corner, exploding in a wreck of splintering boards and revealing what was inside. Which was a… Well, Callie could clearly see what had been inside the crate, but she had no idea what it was. Apparently, neither did Rebecca, who stood opposite her, staring at it with her hands on her hips, breathing heavily. When their eyes finally met, Rebecca grinned.

The object that had come tumbling out of the crate was the color of an old army tank. OD Green and dull in luster. There were no obvious markings on it. It had a large section roughly rectangular-shaped and thick, like maybe twelve inches. This was up on one end, but it was obvious it was supposed to sit flat. She could, therefore, see the bottom of it. There were four small appendages that screwed into the thing's body. Adjustable feet.

The secondary portion of the object, which her mind wanted to call a *thorax* for some reason, was almost the same shape, but more egged in the middle, and attached to the bottom piece with a hidden turret of some sort. It had twisted when it first landed, coming to rest with the heaviest side facing toward the ground. The top part was a perfect cube of about twelve inches each side. And on each side there were panels held on with many tiny, color-matched screw heads. The top side of the bottom section had a large handle on it, but Callie didn't need to touch it to know she wouldn't be able to lift it.

"So, uh…" Callie said, rubbing the side of her head, then pulling her hair back. She guessed it was probably a wreck. "What is your plan here?"

Rebecca grinned again, then said, "Right. Well, I just needed a flat spot for him. Help me lift him."

They struggled for several minutes, lifting the man up onto the first set of crates, that formed an approximated table, roughly seven feet across. Once he was in place and they were both neatly out of breath, Callie followed Rebecca's gesture and they pulled the tarp back down into place, effectively locking him in. Callie shivered with the memory of all her claustrophobic experiences. Were she to be the one to wake up in such a place, having *no earthly idea* where she was, well, it would be bad.

They had laid the man on his back, so his weight was on his tied wrists, which would make it take even longer for him to escape. All they were doing, Rebecca had informed her, was buying time. Time for what? Who knew. But he was the bad guy, right? They looked at each other again, then Rebecca picked up her purse and said, "Let's go!"

They moved quickly across the floor to the set of double-doors, and Rebecca held the badge up to the reader. It was then they noticed there was more to it than that. There was a keypad next to the reader and now the perimeter of each key was illuminated with a green light. It was breathing on and off. "I don't guess you have any idea what his code would have been, do you?" Rebecca said.

Callie shook her head.

"Well, never mind on that, then," she said, and turned to the door that stood on the wall that ran perpendicular to the double-doors. There stood a single door by itself. It was the one they had come through to get into this room. She looked back at Callie again, then said, "You ready?"

Callie shook her head quickly. "For what? You want to go back out of here? To where?"

"Well, I don't know," Rebecca responded, holding her hands out to illustrate the situation. "But this seems like a dead-end. You have any other ideas?"

"Is he going to be okay?" Callie asked, tilting her head in the direction of the man in the canvas terror-tent thirty meters away.

"He'll be fine. Maybe a little shaken, but fine otherwise," she said. Clearly, Rebecca had no remorse about the actions they'd taken.

Callie nodded. "Okay. Then no, I don't have any ideas. How long do you think we have?"

Rebecca was taking a deep breath, shaking her head, and eyes wide, staring at Callie. "I don't know, dear. But he's probably likely to be loud when he wakes up."

"Right. Okay," Callie said. She turned to look behind her. "What about that door over there?"

Rebecca followed her gaze. "Storage closet."

"How can you possibly know that?" Callie said. She was walking toward the door that had previously been hidden from view by a large stack of boxes. It was almost invisible even from this angle, as it was tucked away in a makeshift hallway formed by those boxes, and the lighting was bad back there.

"It doesn't fit the schema of the overall room. It's on the same wall as our bio-hazard doors here, yet it's not secured," Rebecca said, as if she were listing off all the obvious reasons Callie should believe her.

She reached the doors quickly and saw everything she had said falling into place. Indeed, there were no badge readers on the door, and no lock. The handle twisted easily. Immediately, the dank smell of an old cellar rushed out to greet her. It was a storage room. And there was nothing much of interest within it. Callie turned back to Rebecca, walking like a woman defeated.

"Okay, you were right. But I don't know how you knew that."

"Doesn't matter. What matters is *that* door," she said, pointing at the two mystery doors from which the now unconscious man had emerged. The red signs were clearly visible from here. And they read the obvious, NO ADMITTANCE, Authorized Personnel Only, and so on.

Callie looked at the double-doors, then whipped around toward all the crates across the empty space of the large room. The hundreds upon hundreds of hulking masses hidden under thick canvas tarps. Surely, not all of them were stacks of wooden crates. And some were massive. Gigantic lurking things whose identity could never be known to her. She turned to look at Rebecca again.

"Hey. How do you reckon they got all those in here?"

Rebecca was almost squinting as she looked at Callie. Head tilted, arms crossed. She twisted her neck to look down the length of the room where Callie had just looked. She had caught Callie's drift.

"Yeah, you're right," she finally said. Not all of it would fit through these double-doors. That was an assumption they had both made, but it was a fair and conservative guess, almost certainly based in reality. And all that aside, the forklift itself wouldn't fit through them.

"Good call. So what are you thinking?"

Callie felt affirmed and proud to be of some use to this woman. "I think there's a big door down there somewhere," she said, pointing into the darkness.

Rebecca, arms still folded across her chest, was nodding slowly. "Okay. Yeah. Let's go find that fucking door." She casually reached over and flipped up a bank of light switches, without looking at them. Suddenly, the lights in the dark part of the room started blinking to life. Some took longer than others, and the effect was like a chain of dominoes falling, the farthest coming in line after the nearest.

As they started walking toward the aisle they had left not half an hour before, they both heard it simultaneously. A faint beep, and then the handle of the door they had come through twisted. And they were off, running without need of a further cue. The door swung open behind them as they made the first corner, putting them in the aisle they had been in before.

"Hey!" a woman shouted. She had seen them, but they had a head-start. And the most curious thing happened. Coincidence, or just plain luck, Callie couldn't say. But it seemed these things always happened in time with some inexplicable clock not visible to humans. Brian Bradley woke up and started shouting.

His shouts had actually startled Callie with a hard set of chills, as she had run by his resting spot under the tarp. She was only a few feet past it when he started wailing. It might have spurred her to run faster. She said, "Oh dear God!" and heard Rebecca start laughing. It was good timing though, because as soon as Cardna came around the corner, she was sliding – literally *sliding* – to a stop in her loafers. She had to stop to free her partner. That gave them time to get far enough ahead to potentially lose their tail entirely. Not realistic, maybe, but Callie could hope.

Being able to see in this part of the building was a different sensation. There was a real beauty to the organization of the covered lumps of whatever-they-weres. Callie reckoned there were seven or eight columns of the neat rows of unidentifiable relics. And the rows were innumerable. Hundreds? How effing big was this building? It seemed like they had run a quarter-mile already. And there was no end in sight. In fact, she noticed the floor sloped down to where the ceiling actually blocked their view of what was coming. Much like a large cruise-liner. *Holy cow.* And then they were running back uphill, gradually.

Not long after that, though, it finally came to an end. The rows of tarp-covered components dropped off suddenly, and about fifty meters beyond was the wall. They could suddenly see the entire width of the wall, only broken once, a little left of the middle, by a roll-up door. Right next to that was a pedestrian door. The roll-up went nearly all the way to the ceiling, which was close to twenty feet high. It was giant. *Please, God, don't let that door be locked!* Callie was repeating this in her head as she ran. Her hands were sweating. She was a good runner. She ran four miles a day back home, but not typically wearing dress pants and a blouse. She was, and she could tell that Rebecca was as well, aiming for that human door just to the right of the overhead door.

When they finally got up to it, Rebecca bet everything on the odds of being right, and twisted her shoulder toward it to be ready for the hit. She blasted through the door, hitting the break-bar with both hands, and her shoulder slammed it open so hard it banged against the wall outside and swung back at her, whereupon she hit it *again*. Callie was swift on her heels, and said, "Go, go, go!" at the last second. She too banged through the door, now laughing, and let it slam behind her. She might run four miles a day, but she didn't sprint them. As they came to a slow stop outside, she had a moment to reflect on how much it actually took out of someone when they ran flat-out like that.

They were on a loading dock of sorts – sheltered by the building above – on a ramp that led the forty or so feet up to ground level. There was a wrought-iron fence stretching across the entire width of the ramp, but a human-sized door stood open to the right. That's where they aimed. There were two men standing near it, smoking cigarettes and staring at the two women. As they approached, not running, but also not necessarily walking, one of the men straightened up and said, "Holy shit, you scared the Christ out of me."

"Yeah, sorry about that. Saw a rat in there," Rebecca said. "Can I get one of those smokes, boys?" she added, and slowed to a walk to close the last few meters between them. The man who had spoken widened his eyes and nodded, holding out the pack toward her. A cigarette was sticking out the opening in the pack. Rebecca deftly swiped the butt and put it in her mouth, then leaned in and let the man light it. "Thank you, Sam," she said.

"Hey, don't mention it," he said, frowning. "I'm sorry, do I know you?"

Rebecca laughed easily. "Really? Come on, don't play," she said, and kept walking. Callie played a weak smile as she followed Rebecca out the gate, where the other stood waiting for her. Rebecca swung the gate closed, where it clanged shut.

"Whoa," the other man said. "Hey, lady, did you know your pants are ripped?"

The two ladies kept walking though, and soon enough, rounded the end of the dock area and were out in the sunlight. "How did you know his name?" Callie asked, genuinely surprised. She looked down at her leg where a large portion of her thigh was showing. She made sure that's all the man had been able to see. Not that it would change anything either way.

"He was wearing a badge," Rebecca said in a snarky tone, then took a drag from the cigarette. They finally stopped and faced each other, hidden from view by the edge of the building. She had a slight sheen of sweat on her face, and her lips were bright red. Callie thought she looked amazing. Having never thought Rebecca was *that* pretty before, just sort of attractive, this threatened to change her mind.

"Well, we're out!" Callie said. "Now what?"

"Well, I suppose we get lost in the woods."

CHAPTER 12

Callie had initially thought Rebecca was serious, but when the other had grabbed her arm and started guiding her around the end of the building, she was quickly relieved. It seemed that Rebecca had come up with a plan while they had been running. How was this woman's mind working in directions Callie had not even thought of?

Rebecca was speaking softly as they walked, still holding Callie's arm just above the elbow. "I'm going to get in my car. I want you to try to get as close to the guard house as you can get and watch the on-comers."

Callie was nodding slowly as she began to catch onto the plan. Though she did not know how close she could actually get to the guard shack, or even if she would be able to catch the signal through the windshield, she could see it might be the only way out.

"What if I can't get the signal?" Callie finally asked.

"Well, do you want me to have a go at it and you drive the car?" Rebecca asked. They had stopped and were now staring at each other. They were on a side of the building where there were no windows on this floor. It might have been part of the parking garage.

"I don't know. I think it might be easier to strike up a conversation with the guy at the shack. Just stand there and talk to him and see if anyone drives up at that point. You seem to be a little better at starting conversations with strangers than I," Callie offered.

Rebecca was nodding slowly, staring at nothing, chewing her bottom lip. Callie frowned at the sudden recollection of Cardna doing the exact same thing. Rebecca made eye-contact and Callie shook her head. *Never mind.*

"Okay. I also think it might be wise to hide you in the trunk, or…" Rebecca started, but immediately saw Callie go white and start shaking her head, and redirected. "Or duck down in the backseat, even. Just so you're not visible in the car. Number one, they probably know better what you look like, and number two, they might have been told to look for two women in a car together."

"Good point," Callie said.

Rebecca finished her cigarette and crushed it out on the brick wall of the building. Looking around for a good place to toss the butt, she finally shrugged and dropped it on the grass, then crushed it in with the toe of her boot.

Callie was standing there watching her, arms crossed on her chest, just waiting for the next thing to happen, when a thought suddenly occurred to her. "Hey. Why are you here, by the way?"

Rebecca looked up at her and smirked. "You mean, *instead of* Walter?"

Callie shrugged. "I guess. I mean, I wouldn't have even thought you would come at all. But – well, yeah. You *without* him seems a little weird," she said. Then added, "I mean, no offense."

Rebecca shook her head, making a face. *Nonsense.* "Well, I was going to tell you all about it, but we haven't had much time to talk. Come on, let's walk as we talk," she said, taking Callie's arm again. They were headed in the general direction of the opposite end of the building from which they had come – assuming it was the front. They were also assuming there would be an entrance to the parking garage as well.

"See, here's the thing," Rebecca said as they walked. The sky was beginning to get dark. Callie wondered if that meant a potential shift change at the guard shack. Were they armed with that information, she reckoned it might be useful. "Walter was on the plane with me. He basically begged me to come with him. Not that I didn't want to see you. I mean, I feel like we sort of bonded after what happened to Codi. But anyway, beside the point. I just thought it was a little strange for him to be trying to recruit me. Watch your step," she said, and they moved around a sprinkler valve box.

"He had said you were in a bad spot and needed someone to come get you out. Hell, I don't know. Maybe he was just looking for an excuse to come down to Fiji for a bit."

Callie laughed at that. "That sounds like Walter. Spontaneous as a Florida rain."

"Indeed. Anyway, he talked me into it, appealing finally to my sense of adventure, and the thought that I needed a little getaway. But I asked him how the hell I would be useful at all. One, I don't know you very well, and number two, I don't work for the company, and would have no idea what to do or where to go." She shrugged.

"Well, you seem to have figured it out," Callie said, smiling widely. She was actually extremely impressed with how resourceful and ingenious Rebecca had been. The woman was quick on her feet, and even quicker with her tongue. She had known exactly what to say the instant it had needed to be said, on the several occasions where Callie had witnessed her verbal interactions. It looked to Callie as if the woman had been prepared very efficiently and professionally for this operation. She allowed herself a snicker at that. *Operation! HA!*

But was it funny? Was she not in at least some fair amount of danger here? She had certainly felt like she was. Being locked in a *holding room* for hours on end? Held against her will? What kind of company did that crap? Evil people! She was getting mad all over again, thinking about the way she had been treated – all in the name of protecting that damn Brian Bradley! Then on the tail of that thought, she recalled Rebecca laying him out like a mat, and had to giggle again.

"What's so funny, blondie?"

"I was just thinking of how you knocked that man out with one punch. Incredible!" Callie said, shaking a fist with excitement. "He so deserved it."

"Ah. Yeah, well, I couldn't see much option, so I had to think fast. I won't last long against a man, come to that. So I have to take a sucker punch here and there to get the upper hand."

"Here and there?" Callie said, head forward and eyes wide. "How the heck often is this a tactic you find yourself having to employ?"

Rebecca waved it off. They approached the end of the building and she held out her hand in front of Callie's chest, slowing her before they popped out into the view of a potential waiting crowd. Or a camera. There were – surprisingly – none on this side of the building. She peered around the corner, then carried on. They both leaned forward then as they dug in for an uphill climb, to where the large entrance to the parking garage awaited them.

"Anyway, you can imagine my surprise when Walter was snatched off the plane right in front of me," Rebecca said.

"What the cow?" Callie almost shouted.

Rebecca burst out in hard laughter. "Callie, you kill me with your little sayings," she said, shaking her head. Her eyes were watering. When she had finally regained her composure, she said, "He was escorted off the plane by two marshals."

"Like… arrested?" Callie asked. This was shocking, to say the least. She thought all that crap was over with. They reached the top of the hill and sneaked into the side of the garage entrance, back into the relative darkness of the overhang.

"Yeah, I suppose so," Rebecca answered. "I can think of no other instance in which police would just come in and take someone off a plane. I was *completely* unprepared for that," she said, stressing the long Es of the word with exaggerated exasperation. She even held her hands out like she was stopping a crowd of oncoming bulls with the power of suggestion.

"I can imagine," Callie said. She was frowning, trying to imagine what the scene must have looked like.

"So yeah, before we even had a chance to talk about a plan of action – which we were going to spend the twenty-hour flight doing – *vwoop!*" she said, flinging her fingertips at the air in front of them. "He was gone. I was in a total state of panic. I was asking if I could get off the flight with him, because, like, seriously! What the fuck, right?" Rebecca said, turning to Callie and holding her right hand up like she was asking for a handout. "I mean, what do you do? And now I'm on this plane, trapped in a twenty-hour trek to somewhere I've never been, to rescue I woman I hardly know, from a company I have only heard horror stories about, in a building I didn't know existed, that I have no credentials to get into."

"My God," Callie said, "when you put it like that…"

"Yeah!" Rebecca said with a scoff. "Like that was how it was! Fucking crazy, man! I've never been so intimidated in my life."

"So did you ever find out why he was arrested?" Callie asked. They were approaching a car that had no others near it. Like it had gotten here too late to get a good spot, and all the others had left.

"This is me," Rebecca said, fingering the fob that unlocked the doors with an audible beep. "No. I didn't," she said as they naturally came to a stop in front of the vehicle. "I have no idea, still. Though it must be pretty serious if they came onto a fucking *plane* and got him."

"Okay," Rebecca had said when they got in the car, "try to get down in the floorboard as best you can. You can use that blanket to try to hide yourself." And Callie had complied. Her knees rode the hump between the two wells of the rear floorboard and her head was up against the door, but the blanket should do the trick. Rebecca had bought it at the airport before she had boarded the flight with Walter, and the color had been serendipitous, as it matched the carpet of the floorboard almost perfectly.

And now they were moving. Callie could feel the incline of the ramp against her left side as the rear of the car was downhill. Rebecca had spoken to her as she drove, but the sound was very muffled under the blanket. She had told Callie she was just going to approach the guard shack and see if she could get through, and – failing that – just park and go in and do some sweet-talking.

After several minutes of driving though, Callie was getting hot. And she was just about to maybe pull the blanket down *just a hair* to get a little breath of cooler air when Rebecca suddenly reached back and pulled the blanket off her.

"Okay, come on. We're through," she said.

For several miles, Callie just sat staring at Rebecca in the now darkening car. The sun had officially set on Fiji, and the instrument panel lights were illuminating the sweaty skin of the woman Callie had only just gotten to know. "I seriously don't get it. How are you so amazing?"

"Ha!" Rebecca scoffed loudly. "You should have seen it, Callie. It was a beautiful thing. As I approached the gate, I could see the guard take notice of me and make a hand-gesture. But I had prepped myself, accordingly," she said, picking up the Styrofoam cup that had been sitting in the cup holder on the console. She used it to illustrate the next part, when she said, "As I got to where I was supposed to respond, I just did this, like *oops!* and raised my eyebrows and smiled. Like, 'sorry, my hand is full!' and he just smiled and waved me through."

"What the complete eff," Callie said, shaking her head. "That is so amazing," she added. She reached over and boldly took Rebecca's hand for a moment, squeezing.

After a few minutes of staring out the window at the dark landscape beyond the roadside, she finally said, "You know, I don't know how I'll ever repay you."

"Have a drink with me, Callie Simmons."

Callie gulped. She had the sudden image of being seduced by this woman, suddenly remembering that she was gay. Callie was about as promiscuous as a nun, herself. The idea of being with a woman was almost completely foreign to her. She did not, however, want to insult her new friend with the wrong comment. Or by making the wrong assumption.

"A drink?" she finally managed, dumbly.

"Yes. A drink," Rebecca said, turning her head to look at Callie, a faint smile painting her lips. She looked amused. "Callie, I know you're not gay. I'm not trying to pick you up. I am happy with my lover at home. Though I will admit you are fun to look at..."

Callie blushed and had to take a deep breath. She turned to look out the window again. She was grinning now and chewing on the back of her thumb.

"Seriously, Callie, relax," Rebecca said, reaching across the console and taking a firm grip of Callie's upper thigh, much like a doting mother might do to her child. There was no sex in it.

Callie met her gaze again and nodded slowly. "Okay. I'm sorry if I..."

"Knock it off," Rebecca interrupted. "No need for apologies." She squeezed Callie's thigh again, then returned her hand to the wheel. "It's funny how awkward people get around gay people. They think they can't say certain words or make certain jokes. Not saying you're like that. But in general. It's like they just don't know how to act."

"Yeah, I guess I am kind of that way. I just don't hang around too many gay people, you know?"

Rebecca squinted her eyes closed and wrinkled her face as she nodded. "Yeah. I could tell."

An uneventful three-hour trip later brought them to the airport. Callie breathed a huge sigh of relief, even though her suitcase and phone were still in the suite she had spent less than a full night in. An old George Carlin joke occurred to her, in which he said something like, "Now you've got shit all over the world!" and she had to giggle. She had left her purse on the plane getting to Fiji. Now her suitcase was being held captive in a sort of billeting room she would likely never see again. She highly doubted she would get a surprise knock on her door one Friday morning, *'Special delivery for Ms. Simmons from Cardna Darwyn, et al.'* Oh well.

"So here's the deal," she said, turning to Rebecca when they pulled into the rental return lot. "I know it always goes in the movies or whatever, that someone says, 'I forgot my wallet, but if you cover me here, I'll catch you on the flip side,' or whatever. But I don't have anything. I don't have my ID. I don't have my passport or my wallet or my credit cards or anything. I don't even have a phone."

"It's all right, darlin'," Rebecca responded. "We'll see if we can get you back to the states, then we can worry about all that." She rooted around in her own purse for a moment, then came out with a thin wallet and slid a card out, handing it to Callie. "Take this. Go in and get yourself some clothes, a toothbrush, whatever you need. We'll square up on the 'flip side'," she said, making quotes in the air with one hand.

"Thank you, Rebecca. You truly are the best. A savior in the flesh."

"Well, I don't know about all that. But yeah, I happen to be an independent woman who has her own money, so you're in good hands."

The flight was pretty rough in the beginning, due to a lot of turbulence. The winds aloft, the pilot had said, whatever the heck that meant. But once they got high enough, and *away* enough, it smoothed out. Getting through the ticket counter had not been a problem at all. They told her the worry would be when she arrived back in the States. If there were going to be a problem, that's where it would take place. If only she had not left her damn purse on that plane. Had she just checked around her seat, she would have seen that her purse was right there, waiting to be found. It wasn't even hard to miss. It was bright yellow, for God's sake. Anyway, that was gone now. Unless some good Samarian were to return it. *Samarian? That didn't sound right. Samurai?*

"I love this part," Rebecca said a little too loudly, popping an olive from her martini into her mouth. She was watching the little seat-back telly in front of her and enjoying the heck out of it. Callie glanced at the screen in time to see Michael Caine whip Steve Martin across the bare shins with a switch he pulled from a flower pot. Bec had her earphones on, so everything she said was over-amplified. Callie giggled and rolled her eyes, then went back to staring out the window.

What had happened to Walter? She was so nervous for him. What could have possibly happened now? Something bad enough for them to pull him off a plane? Did they have to land first, or had they not taken off first? Why would they wait until they were airborne, if the former. That wouldn't make sense. She wondered what kind of crime qualified for forceful airliner removals. She was chewing on her fingernails, without biting them off. It was an old tic beginning to show itself again.

That was one of the first things she intended to do when she got off the plane. Well, as soon as she got another phone. First things first. And what was his number? Wasn't that the joke of it all? No one knew anyone's phone numbers anymore. At least she didn't. Heck, she didn't even know Jack's. In case of emergency, shouldn't she know her boyfriend's number? With that thought, she felt a sudden pang in her chest. She had forgotten she was supposed to be missing him. She had been too busy on this adventure crap to think about her beloved Jack.

"Owwww!" Rebecca said, cringing in her seat. Her shoulder pressed up against Callie's as she twisted bodily, reacting to the whip-crack across Steve Martin's shins after a running start from across the room. Callie giggled again and leaned her head against the top of Rebecca's for a moment, glancing at the screen, then returning to her thoughts.

Walter's phone number, which Callie had only ever asked for once and had never memorized, was programmed into Callie's phone. That was the future. You tap someone's contact and press the call button. No need to memorize anything anymore. Heck, she didn't even have to remember anyone's birthd- she suddenly had a thought. She reached over and pulled up on Rebecca's earphone. "Hey!" Callie whispered as quietly as she could. Rebecca had almost turned sideways in the seat, almost leaning against Callie with the armrest in the upward position. She turned her head slightly. "What day is it today?"

"May twentieth. It's Be a Millionaire Day."

"What does that mean?" Callie said, frowning.

"I guess we're supposed to imagine being a millionaire," said Rebecca, holding her hands up.

"Oh. Okay. Well, I had this stupid check for a million dollars that I left in my purse. Had I not left my purse on the *plane*, I *would* be a millionaire," Callie said with a resigned sigh, then let the earphone pop back onto Rebecca's ear. Rebecca returned with a 'what can ya do?' face, having never pulled her attention away from the screen in front of her.

May twentieth. Why did that date seem important? Well, it was probably nothing. Absently, her eyes fell onto the screen in front of Rebecca's seat and her eyes focused. Steve Martin was now crawling down the beach toward the water, hoping to be stopped. Rebecca was chuckling, shaking in the seat. Callie smiled and leaned her cheek against the top of Bec's head again. Out the window, there was nothing but stars. She could see a swath of the Milky Way cutting across the sky. It was frightening to think that most of the trip would be over the ocean. Hundreds of miles from anything resembling land.

Maybe she should try to get a little sleep. She looked toward the aisle as a flight attendant made her way up to the front, touching the seat backs as she went. Then she looked up at the ceiling in front of her, leaning her head against the headrest. And that, without any further fanfare, was the last thing Callie remembered.

CHAPTER 13

Callie felt free as a dove as they strolled through the customs area. For Callie had no baggage. Wasn't that a funny statement? She had nothing to declare, either. At least not that any of these people would want to hear. She was given special attention, too, since she didn't even have a passport.

She felt Rebecca squeeze her hand and saw the reassuring smile as they took Callie to a little room, where she would spend the next sizable portion of her life, it seemed. And there, she waited. If she had a phone she could at least crush some candy. Or play snake. Or text Rebecca and let her know not to bother waiting up. There didn't seem to be any point. Callie had a few friends out here on the west coast, but again, what was the point of having friends if you didn't have a phone? She could not possibly remember their phone numbers, and it wasn't like you could look them up in a phone book anymore. So she sat waiting alone in the room until someone finally came in to work her case.

She was clearly American, for what that was worth. Most people in the airport *weren't* American. So why should she be special? She answered all the woman's questions and was able to recite her driver license number – *hey, there was one number she remembered* – and her home address and everything else she could think of that might link her to a life in the states. And, surprisingly, it worked.

They had not, she learned, found her purse. No good Somalian had turned it in after all. *Was that right?* She thought maybe she still didn't have that right. Maybe she was just exhausted. After only two hours, she was allowed out of the room with a temporary pass that actually had her picture on it. It was amazing how quickly the government could get stuff done when they really wanted to.

Out in the waiting area, she found Rebecca watching a video on her phone. "Any word from Thevi?" Callie said as she approached the bench. Rebecca took her earphones off and shook her head.

"No. Still isn't picking up. I left a message, and have texted her a few times. They're still unread."

Callie nodded. She was really beginning to worry about Walter. This was not like him. It was not like him to get arrested and be out of touch for days. She had to giggle, in spite of the ridiculous nature of the reality she was apparently living in. In a reality where Walter was the bad guy, things were definitely screwed up.

"Did they get you squared away?" Rebecca asked.

"Yes. I can fly. I still have no way to get money yet," said Callie.

Rebecca held up her hand, a clear and formidable stop sign. She was not going to let Callie worry about this part of the excursion. There were plenty of things Callie had to worry about, and Rebecca was just being an amazing friend, taking as much off her plate as she could. And it was not lost on Callie how much money they were actually talking about here. A planned trip to Fiji would cost well over a thousand dollars one-way. Walking up to a counter and saying you wanted to fly to Fiji, right now, was probably double that. Or coming home, for that matter. It was with this thought that she realized how thankful she was to have friends who actually had money. She had never known Rebecca's financial status, but assumed that if she was friends with Walter, then she was probably not poor. It was comforting to know she wasn't going broke just to get Callie home. And Callie would certainly pay her back when they got home. Callie needed a glass of wine and a long bath when she got home. Long, like, as in a whole day.

On the plane back to New Jersey, it was much the same thing. Rebecca was again enjoying the in-flight entertainment, earphones over her ears, giggling and eating the free peanuts. She had stopped drinking martinis though, and this time around had switched to vodka tonics. After she finished her first drink, she turned to Callie, pulling her earphones off. "Hey, did you know Royal Research acquired Gray Horse Intel?"

Callie frowned. "What in the world brought that up? No, I didn't know that."

"I was just thinking about it because I saw an office as I was making my way up to find you in that building, and it had a very familiar name on the outside of it. This woman I went to school with had a little sister with that name. And it's kind of a unique name, so I was wondering if it was her." Rebecca looked around for the flight attendant, shaking her plastic cup in a way that said she was hoping to get another vodka. She popped another handful of peanuts into her mouth and crunched. She held up a finger while she chewed, then finally swallowed. Callie giggled. Rebecca was acting like a starving child, having to eat between sentences to avoid passing out from hunger.

"Anyway, when I saw her name on that sign, I decided to look up Gray Horse. Apparently Royal acquired them a few years ago."

"That's strange," Callie said, glancing at the television screen in front of Rebecca. "In Manhattan they're still in separate buildings. I thought they were still separate entities."

"Well, they may be," Rebecca said, holding that finger out and waving it around. "Maybe it's just the international conglomerate thing."

"Yeah, I guess maybe it's different overseas than in the States. 'Cause up there, they're their own company," Callie said. Rebecca's finger froze in midair.

"I'm sorry, what the fuck. Did you just use all three 'there's in a row?" Rebecca said, twisting her head to look at Callie. "You did, you little tramp! That was awesome," she said, slapping Callie's leg.

"Huh. I didn't even realize I did," Callie said. She was blushing a little from the sudden attention.

"Can you do that with your, yore, you're too?" Rebecca said.

Callie squinted, shaking her head, trying to unravel the verbal ball of yarn she'd just been tossed. She was not in a state of mind to think clearly, apparently.

"So anyway, I think we might have a friend in the building there," Rebecca said.

"Well why didn't you stop in and say hi?" Callie asked.

"Door was shut. Hell, she might not have even gotten there yet. I think it was dark."

"Wait," Callie suddenly said, waving her hands in front of her, squinting her eyes, "you lost me. You had a friend who had a little sister. You saw little sister's name on an office inside… *Royal*. Right? So what does that have to do with Gray Horse?"

"Well her name placard said Gray Horse Intel right below the name. Just interesting."

"Ah. Well, do you think we could use her?"

Rebecca laughed out loud, leaning forward and kicking the seat in front of her. A woman peered between the seat backs, clearly not amused. Rebecca held a hand up and managed a laughing 'sorry' to the woman, which got her to turn back around. Callie was giggling too, but she didn't quite know what had been so funny.

"What?" she finally said, when Rebecca was still laughing ten seconds later.

She grabbed Callie's leg just above the knee, and was using it for life-support. Rebecca finally leaned back and pressed her head against the headrest and breathed out slowly, trying to catch her breath. The air smelled of peanuts. It was not an unpleasant smell. Even with the hint of vodka right on its heels.

"God, girl, you're gonna give me a stroke." Rebecca wiped her eyes with the napkin on her tray and then said, "Use her. I don't know why that was so funny. But it sure fuckin' was." And she was off laughing again.

Callie widened her eyes, holding up her hands, exasperated. *Whatever!* And when Rebecca had finally gotten hold of herself again, Callie said, "You must be drunk. See, this is why I don't drink at altitude."

"Oh, darling," Rebecca said, returning her hand to Callie's thigh. Callie looked down at that hand as it squeezed. Rebecca must have a thing for thighs, she thought. "This is why I *do* drink at altitude. I get drunk on half as much and it lasts twice as long."

"Okay. So…"

"So," Rebecca said with a fresh squeeze, then released Callie's thigh and pulled her braid over her shoulder and flattened it against her chest. She had braided it herself on the flight in from Fiji. She'd said at the time it was nice to feel normal again. "So anyway, yes, I think we might be able to *use her* as you said. I will call her when we get home."

Callie nodded.

The flight attendant leaned in, hands on knees. "You ladies doing okay?"

Rebecca looked at Callie, smirking, then back to the woman. "Well, I am," she said, putting her hand on her chest. "I don't know about her. She hates alcohol, so I'm not sure she can ever be 'okay'."

"I do not!" Callie exclaimed.

The woman giggled. "Want me to bring you another vodka then?"

"Oh, that would be very okay," Rebecca said, touching the woman's hand.

When the flight attendant had disappeared, Callie said, "I notice you get pretty touchy when you drink at altitude."

"Yeah. You're lucky we're not napping together," she responded.

After five-and-a-half hours in the sky, they finally touched down on home soil. Or at least close-to-home. Callie would now have to catch an Uber home, which would take yet another hour. And it would require payment, which she could do if she had a phone. So again, she decided, she would have to rely on Rebecca.

"I hate to ask, Rebecca, because you've been so generous, but," Callie started.

"Why would that make you hate to ask?" she responded, slinging her purse up on her shoulder. They were waiting by the baggage carousel. "Wouldn't my generosity make it *easier* for you to ask for the next thing?" she said. But at least she was smiling.

"Come on! Don't make me feel worse about it. I just don't have a way home."

"Nonsense," Rebecca said. "I have Walter's keys."

Callie, pumped full of exhaustion and relief at the same time, walked with her shoulders slumped. It had been a long few days. Hell, she didn't even know what day it was. It had seemed like a week. She had asked why the heck Rebecca had Walter's car keys. But she had not been surprised by the answer, and in fact, rather, had found she had already known it. Walter did not like to carry a lot of things in his pockets. So when they had passed through security at the airport, he had asked Bec to put them in her purse. She had. And now they had his car. Where he was would have to take second fiddle to the comfort of this convenience for now.

On the way back into Neptune City, Callie had gotten a bad feeling. Rebecca was all ears, too. She had been nothing but accommodating and kind over the last few days, and Callie was beginning to count her among her true friends. They had only started bonding when Rebecca had called on Callie after Codi's assault a couple of months ago. Short-lived so far, maybe, but damned if Rebecca wasn't a true friend.

"Rebecca."

"Callie."

Callie sighed. She was trembling. Her hands wringing together and just over all fidgeting. It was obvious she was in severe discomfort.

"What are you about to ask me for this time?"

Callie looked over at her in the darkness of the car. Two days wasted on flying. Ridiculous. Her life was passing right before her eyes. She sighed loudly. "I have asked you for so-"

"Stop, Callie," Rebecca said. Again with the thigh-grabbing.

"Okay, okay, I'm sorry. Okay. I just have a bad feeling."

"About Walter." It was a statement. Not a question.

"Yes. About Walter."

"Well," Rebecca said, shrugging. Her fingers extended out from the steering wheel. "I guess I do, too." She drove for a long moment in silence. They were both pondering the thickness that had developed between them in the car.

Callie finally looked over at her. "I was going to ask if we could go by the house and see Thevi."

Rebecca met her gaze and smiled a wily number. Then she winked and squeezed her thigh. "Already on our way, babe."

When Thevi answered the door, she looked like a lost child. Her eyes were wide. Her red hair was in a weak excuse for a ponytail that had escaped and was exploding on the top of her head. She looked as though she had been crying for a long time. Her cheeks bore the weight of all those tears. At first she focused in on Rebecca, holding out her arms, then slowly turned and noticed Callie, then turned toward her, then went somewhere in the middle and embraced them both at the same time. And she let it all loose.

Eventually they made it past the doorstep, where Thevi had collapsed into tears and anguish, her heart pouring out into the starlit night. They helped her inside and closed the door, finding the nearest couch, and sat on either side of her. She was bawling freely and having trouble catching her breath in between. Rebecca and Callie let her cry for a long time, just rubbing shoulders and holding her close, until she was finally able to sit up straight and face them.

Callie was filled with a nervousness that had begun to blossom on the doorstep, and was now turning into a real fear that Walter might have died or something.

Thevi was finally able to start talking. She talked for over an hour without so much as a breath of an interruption from the other two ladies. And when Callie left, that nervousness had grown into a full tree of despair.

The next day, after Callie had gone through the ridiculous headache of buying a new phone and trying to get all her life back to normal, she stopped in to Charles Lancey's office. The old man had been her boss for her entire tenure at Bohr Enterprises. He was sitting upright in his desk chair with his hands, one atop the other, on top of his cane. He had made his pleasantries and welcomed her back, and – the poor old man – assumed she was back for good. Finally. Callie had been gallivanting around the planet for the last six months, and barely shown up to work. If this man wasn't the portrait of patience, Callie didn't know who was. But here she was, about to tell him she was in fact, *not* ready to come back. And on top of that, maybe even ask him for advice.

"Mr. Lancey, I need to ask a favor," Callie said. Her hands were trembling a little, out in front of her.

He nodded at her. The light smile had not yet left his face. Maybe that was a good sign. She was standing there wringing her hands and just staring at him when he finally reached out with an old hand and offered her the chair across the desk from him. She had known she was welcome to sit, but had just not thought of it. Now she sat.

Callie was spinning the ring on her finger, nervously trying to put words together in her head. "Listen. Sir, my friend has been arrested. I lost my purse. I just got back from Fiji, where I lost my purse on the plane. On the way *down there*, in fact," she added, tilting her head. Then she waved her hands. "I guess none of that really matters. I'm just…"

Mr. Lancey held out that strong old hand over the desk, in her general direction, and at first she didn't know whether to take it, or just look at it. But soon, her question was answered when he started softly patting the air over the desk. "Calm. Calm, dear heart. You need more time."

Callie did not nod. But her wide eyes and stoic posture told it all. She swallowed and her eyes got glassy. "I've got so much going on that… that…"

"I know," he said, nodding and closing his eyes. "I trust you. I know you'll be back when you're ready. I know you don't need the job at all. The fact that you so reverently keep me in your loop illustrates your dedication to that effect. I support, and strongly, any endeavor that might find you in the grasp of its wanderlust."

"Thank you, Mr. Lancey. You've been so kind and generous. Can I ask you something though? On a personal level?"

He turned his hand over on the top of the cane and held it out to her, as if in offer this time.

"Do you think it's a stupid endeavor to go after the Royal Research Corporation?"

Lancey's light smile faded a bit. Then he nodded very slowly. Like he was finally seeing what this was really about. After a long, pregnant pause, he finally said, "I think that if one human were to attempt such an endeavor, it would be you I would choose to lead the charge."

Callie almost smiled. It was a raw, stale feeling in her face. More like pain than pleasure. "Thank you, sir," she said, then took a deep breath. Happy to have his approval and encouragement, she rose and turned to leave.

"Ms. Simmons?" he said, stopping her before she got to the door. She turned to look at him. He was standing, leaning on his desk with one hand, the other stretched out toward her with a note in it. She returned to take it from him as he said, "Trixie said this gentleman has been trying to get in touch with you."

The approach to Matt Minus was a markedly different encounter. Upon Callie's knock upon his doorjamb, he had swiveled in his chair, then held out his hands, and stood up. "Callie Simmons! Already blew through that million bucks so you're back for more menial labor?" He was walking toward her with a big smile on his face, his hands still outstretched as if he would hug her. Which, Callie knew, he never would. Minus was not a hugger. They both stopped, still several feet from each other.

"I lost that check on the plane," Callie said, looking out the window, then back at the short man, who was now stuffing his hands in his pockets.

"Ah, that's fine. I'll have them cut you another one."

"What?" Callie said. "Put the company out two million bucks?"

He waved a hand in the air then leaned on his desk with it. "No one's going to cash a million-dollar check without some serious ID."

Callie raised her chin. "Ah, okay," she said. The million-dollar check was the last of her worries right now. "Listen, Minus, can I sit down?" she asked after a moment.

"Of course." He pulled a chair out for her before returning to the other side of his desk. "What'ya got? How was Fiji?"

Callie sighed, stretching her arms back over her head. It felt like it had been a million years since she last sat in this chair. "That was not the trip I expected it to be. Let's just say that."

"Where's your boy?" Minus said, holding his palms up.

"That's the thing, see. He's been arrested again."

"Again?!" Minus said, almost shouting. He was making a sour face. "What the hell did he do this time?"

Callie stared at her hands for a minute. She was beginning to fidget again. Twisting the ring on her finger like it needed winding. She cleared her throat, then said, "Nothing. That guy, Tim Blisk – the one he assaulted?" she said, making sure she saw Minus was on the same page before continuing. "Well, he apparently died from complications from the initial injury."

Minus was staring at her wide-eyed, mouth agape. Callie stared at him for a long moment.

"Yeah, he never quite recovered properly. So Walter has been arraigned on second-degree manslaughter."

Minus was now shaking his head. "Holy mother."

"I know, right? Apparently they pulled him off the plane when he was about to leave for Fiji."

"Wait. So he was going to Fiji too?" Matt Minus said, looking like he was about to play an imaginary piano in the air above his desk.

"Yeah. Long story. Anyway, the judge apparently decided to detain him until trial because he wrote a check right there and paid his debt to society off with one scrawl of a pen." Callie rolled her eyes. "I guess the impression the judge got was that Walter did not really think he owed anything, and since he's wealthy, the money was the easiest part. I don't know how that translates to flight risk or whatever, but he's not convinced Walter won't be violent again." She pulled her hair back with one hand and sighed nervously.

Minus looked intently at her, raising his eyebrows.

Callie shook her head before continuing. "You know, Minus, there's some awful shit going on down there in Fiji."

The man scoffed, then his face got serious and he leaned back in his chair. It looked like he had thought Callie was joking, then saw that her face didn't change. Now he was listening.

"This woman, Cardna Darwyn, tricked me into trusting her. Then she kept me locked up in a holding room – just like the ones they have at *police stations*," Callie said, jamming her fingertip onto the desk to underline the point, "for over twelve hours with no food or water."

"Wait, wait, wait," Minus said, trying to interrupt. Callie held her hand up though, cutting him off.

"No, Matt, let me finish please. I'm not worried about that now. But it's just incredible, the tactics they employ there. Like, why would they even have an interrogation room? But that's what it was. It had no door handle on the inside." She shook her head, eyes closed, trying to clear the junk that was trying to slow down her thoughts.

"Anyways, here's the thing. You know..." she said, leaning forward and looking him in the eyes, "You know how powerful this company is, Minus. Royal has their hands in so much stuff. They have so much more control over the things around us than anyone knows."

He was tilting his head thoughtfully, but not trying to interrupt.

"They've apparently been going to Mars for decades now."

"Decades," Minus said, seriously.

"Decades."

"Royal."

"Royal," Callie repeated, jamming her fingertip on the desk again.

"You have the whole temporal delineation experiments, the Mars thing, your little Bloop thing," she said, waving her hand again, and Minus finally did cut her off.

"My *little* Bloop thing. Let me remind you that my little Bloop thing paid you over a million dollars," Minus said.

"Whatever, Minus. That's not what I meant. I wasn't mocking it. I just couldn't think of the name of it right at the moment. But they're everywhere. They're in control of so much top-secret technology."

Minus finally leaned back and steepled his hands together under his chin. Then he spread the fingers apart, looking Callie in the eye. "All right, Callie. What are you after here? I thought you were going down there to talk to Brian Bradley."

"I did. And that... that..." she said, shaking her fingers beside her head, trying to come up with the diction. "That chicken shit wouldn't even see me. He Zoomed me."

Minus frowned. "Zoomed?" Then his face changed. "Oh. Like the meeting. Got ya."

"He wouldn't even face me, Minus!"

Minus grinned at this, then twitched his head. *Welp, no surprise there*, his face said. "I told you that you can be intimidating, Callie."

Callie took a deep breath, closing her eyes and shaking her head. She finally grabbed handfuls of her blonde hair and squeezed, then yelled out in exasperation. "God, Minus!"

"What would you like me to do for you? Why are you here?"

"I just need someone with some weight to do something down there. Someone with some pull. I need someone to care."

Minus began fiddling with a pen on his blotter, staring at it like it was a thousand miles away. Then he sighed and made eye-contact again. "Callie, I care. But I don't weigh anything here."

"Who does?" she asked, spreading her hands.

"You want someone with some pull down in Fiji?"

"Do you know anyone who works down there?"

Matt Minus sat staring at his blotter again for a few long moments, then said, "Well, yeah. Candace Hanning. Not sure she has the kind of pull you're looking for though," he said, flipping his hand over.

"I get on well with Candy. I just need someone to believe me."

"Well, believing you and going on a crusade with you against one of her fellow employees are two different things, Callie."

"Just let me have a shot. I just need a badge, Minus."

He wheeled back up to his desk and rested his elbows on it, rubbing his face with his fingertips. After a long enough moment where Callie started believing he wouldn't answer, he finally said, "Okay, Callie. You'll get your badge." After a moment though, he frowned and said, "Wait. What happened to the badge Camrie set you up with?"

Camrie! That was her name. "I don't have that anymore. Right before I got on the helicopter, I realized I had left my purse in the plane. Badge, wallet… all of it. Gone."

"Helicopter? What the fuck?" Minus said, screwing up his face.

"Yeah. The taxi from the airport took me to some little outpost thing. They had arranged to come get me from there with a company helicopter. Cardna was in it."

Minus was shaking and scratching his head at the same time, frowning at his desk. "Hold on, Callie. This doesn't make any fucking sense. Why didn't you just take the taxi directly to the building?"

Callie sighed and made a face of impatience. "Because you can't j-…" But she trailed off. Then her eyes got wide. "What in hell."

Minus was now nodding, eyebrows high again. He could see she was putting it together.

"Rebecca drove straight up to it. Why did I have to go the long way?"

As Callie pushed out the front door of the building and into the warm morning, she walked with a purpose. She wasn't quite jogging, but someone with a smaller stride would have to jog to keep up with her. She was sliding her thumb down the screen of her phone with her left hand, while her right slipped into her jacket pocket in search of her car keys. Her hand hit a sharp slip of paper first. Frowning, she pulled the note out. It was a missed call note that simply read 'TC for Callie Simmons x2' at the top. And as she walked, she glanced up at her car, quickly approaching. Then she read the bottom of the note. 'Says it's urgent. Thanks, Trixie.'

Callie stopped in her tracks and looked straight ahead, at nothing. *Trixie? There really is a Trixie there? What in hell...* She shook her head, trying to clear the brain bugs, then found her key fob in her pocket and unlocked the car.

As she slipped into the leather seat, she pulled the door closed and looked at the note again. "Who the heck is TC?" she said aloud. There was a phone number in the middle of the paper. Shrugging, she laid her phone against the magnetic mount on her dash and initiated the call routine with a voice command. "Hello, Robot," she said, then pushed the start button on her dashboard. The car started. The phone dinged at her. Ready for a command. She told it to dial the number on the note.

After a few rings, when she was about to hang up, a deep voice answered.

"Hello. Is this," Callie looked back at the note to be sure, "TC?"

"Yes'm. It sure is."

"Hello. This is Callie Simmons. I got a message to call you?"

"Ah, yeah! Hello Ms. Simmons! You probably don't remember me, but I worked with you a little bit at The Oliver Company."

Callie's heart skipped a beat. It wasn't that the voice *wasn't* familiar. But she still wasn't placing it. She didn't remember anyone who went by TC. That was for sure. She was frowning at the dash and grabbing a handful of her bangs, trying to wrack her brain.

"I'm sorry, sir, but I don't remember anyone by that name. Can you help me out a little bit? What department did you work in?"

"Ah, well, you might have known me as Thad back then. Thaddeus Cloys."

Callie's heart stopped in her chest. She had gone speechless.

CHAPTER 14

It took a long moment of Callie just sitting in silence with her hand over her mouth before she was able to find her voice again. She was smiling, shaking her head and speechless. Thaddeus had to ping her to make sure she had not hung up. This finally brought her around, and she stuttered into the phone. "Yeah, yes, Thad, I'm here. I'm sorry. You just took me by complete surprise. It's so good to hear from you! How are you?"

Why Callie had not thought to reach out to him before was beyond her. Of course, when the Atlas to Mars mission had gone south, the company had begun its quick descent into its own oblivion. Samson had sold off their assets and left camp within a year. Everyone left was given a decent-sized severance package and was forced to find somewhere else to work. Callie had not kept in touch with anyone else from the company, because all the people she cared about had gone on the mission. Save for Thaddeus and Samson himself.

Social networking made it possible to find anyone these days, and easily. She occasionally touched base with some old friends through OuterCircle but Thad had not been one of them. Callie had always appreciated his kindness and his easy-going nature though.

"I've been really good, Ms. Simmons. Really good."

"Okay, you're going to have to start calling me Callie. No more chain-of-command here, okay?"

"Yes ma'am, I will, Callie."

After a few minutes of pleasantries and catching up, Callie started getting the feeling he was waiting for something. The conversation started feeling like it was waning a little, so she finally just said, "So, Thad, what's up?"

"Oh, nothin' much," he said.

Callie rolled her eyes and giggled. "No, I mean, why did you need me to call you?"

"Oh. I uh, well, I didn't. I got an email saying you had been trying to reach me, and that I needed to call you."

Callie frowned. "That's strange. Who sent you the email?"

"That's the funny thing. I have no idea!" said Thad. "I tried to respond to it and the email bounced back."

Callie's eyes got wide now. "Was it an anonymous account? Like a disposable email account?"

"May be. I don't know much about that stuff. It just said it was urgent that I got in touch with you. I thought it was you sending it at first. But then I thought you would have an established email address somewhere."

Callie was scratching her chin, tapping her fingernails on the steering wheel. Yet another flipping mystery to unravel. Just what she needed. She sighed loudly, then said, "Okay, Thad. Where are you now?"

"Well, I'm at home just now," he said simply.

"Okay dork butt. Where is that? Where do you live?"

"Ah, I see. Sorry, ma'am. I live in Houston now," Thaddeus said.

"Houston? Why in the heck would you go there?"

"Well, for a while after Oliver, I was trying to get on with NASA down there. Now I'm working at a record warehouse."

"A record warehouse?" Callie asked.

"Yeah! It's really cool. Records. Like vinyl records? We distribute outta that warehouse and I'm really good at keeping inventory and stocking," Thad said, sounding proud but humble at the same time in his unique way.

"Well, I bet you are," Callie agreed. "My boyfriend would be consumed with jealousy. He loves his record collection." She twisted her mouth up, thinking again. Houston was too far away just to run out and see him. But she reckoned she might need to keep that option in her pocket. "Okay, Thad, here's what I'm thinking. Someone is trying to get us together."

"What do you mean by that, ma'am?" Thad asked.

"There's a reason someone wanted you to call me. And if you're not searching for any answers about the Atlas mission..." she said, then waited patiently to see if he would respond in the negative. "You're not looking into that mission are you, Thad?"

"Oh. No, I'm not. I don't know what happened to those boys, but it breaks my heart every time I think about it. I don't know how I could do anything to look into it. Maybe I don't know what you mean though, ma'am."

"THAD!" Callie said, a little too loudly. "Stop calling me ma'am! Let me be Callie to you!"

"Whoa! Okay. Sorry."

"It's okay. Okay. So think with me here. Let's work through this."

Thad laughed out loud on the other end of the line. "I don't know how much I can help with that, Callie! I wadn't born with a scientist brain like all you guys. But I'll try," he said.

"It's okay, hon. Let's see though. I am looking into it. So I'm the one that's searching for something. So if someone wanted you and I to make contact, that means someone must think you know something I want to know. That tells me two things: number one, you probably know this person. Number two, you probably *do* know something valuable to me, even if you don't *know* you know it. And number three, that tells me this person must be our friend."

Thad was speechless, but that was okay. He was for right now just a sounding board. Callie was thinking through her words, tapping her teeth with a long fingernail. She could hear him shift on the other end.

"Who do we both know that would be trying to do such a thing?" she finally asked. "And why do it anonymously?" Callie sighed again, then added, "Any thoughts on that, Mr. Cloys?"

"Well it sounds to me like someone don't wanna get in no trouble. But I don't know who we both know in common," he said. After a brief pause, he added, "No one that's alive no more, anyways."

Callie was nodding. "Yeah. Me neither. But maybe that's not what's important. Maybe we just need to download everything you might know about the mission, right into my notebook. Then I can determine what the heck I need to do." Again, she said tapping the steering wheel with her fingers, then finally looked at the clock on the stereo and said, "What is it, Wednesday? Hmm."

"Yes ma- uh, yes."

"What are you doing tomorrow night? Could I take you out to dinner?"

"Well, sure! I didn't know you were in the area, Callie!" he said, a definitive excitement in his tone.

"I'm not. But I plan to be."

"Rebecca?" Codi said, almost too quiet to be heard.

"Yes, hon?" Rebecca said, coming to the back of the couch. It was instantly obvious what she wanted. Natalie had fallen asleep with her head in Codi's lap, while Codi sat reading a book in Braille. She affectionately called them 'bumpy books'. She was also holding up a wine glass in her left hand. Rebecca smiled and took the empty glass from her hand.

"Do you want some more, sweets?"

"Does the pope shit in the woods?" Codi asked quietly.

Rebecca laughed out loud though, and ruined the effort. "God, girl, have you been hanging around Walter lately somehow?" she said, turning to the counter to refill the glass. Her laugh had startled Natalie in her slumber, but not enough to bring her back to the land of the living.

Codi Cohl had been out of the hospital for several weeks now. On her little stint out to the Fijian island, Rebecca had left Codi with Natalie. What perfect, serendipitous timing that had been, Natalie coming back when she had. She and Codi had taken to each other very quickly. Though Rebecca reckoned there weren't too many people who Codi *wouldn't* click with. Codi was incredibly kind and loving to everyone Rebecca had ever seen her interact with.

This reading and wine had become a nightly routine for Codi, and Natalie had latched onto it quickly, laying her head in the other's lap and listening to music on her mp3 player. This also usually involved Natalie getting high. Codi did not do much of that though. She had told Rebecca she didn't like the way it made her eyes act up. Apparently her brain's new interpretation of the signals coming in from the bionic implants did not agree with cannabis. It totally changed the way she saw everything, Codi had said.

Rebecca had been the one who had gotten Codi into the experimental surgery program that had given Codi the retinal implants. Codi could now see more than a totally blind person, but not like someone who had full range of vision. The implants produced blocky and discolored imagery that was sometimes hard for her brain to translate.

After *Operation: Monster Hunt,* Rebecca had applied for the licensing for one of the apparatuses that had temporarily given Codi almost-normal vision. The million-dollar crate-sized apparatus was not available for purchase though. She had tried to bargain with Matt Minus, who had been in charge of the monster hunt, but he said he just didn't have the authority. The optics package wasn't his project, and there was nothing he could do about it. She had wanted to at least have one at home where Codi could use it in the comfort of the apartment. It was obviously too unwieldy to use anywhere outside the home. Everything Rebecca had tried though, was instantly shut down. Royal Research just wasn't going to budge.

Codi did not have much in the way of personal belongings, but what little she did have was all here now. She had effectively moved in with the two lesbian women. Somehow, it wasn't crowded, either. The apartment wasn't small, but it was an apartment. The office, which was technically a bedroom, was converted back to a bedroom, though Codi spent most of her time in the den, as did the other two. And they all got along swimmingly. Sam Hakeen, Codi's blind love interest, came over quite often, and the four of them would listen to loud music, dance or play games. Sometimes Sam would walk to the apartment from his own place. Most of the time, though, Rebecca or Natalie would go get him. They were very accommodating to Codi, who called herself 'helpless' a lot. They both assured her that just having her around was as good as any rent money she could provide. And they didn't need the money.

Rebecca had wondered at first how Natalie would take the newcomer, as Natalie had been overseas for a long time when Rebecca first brought Codi around. When Natalie had come home unexpectedly one evening, they had all been there. Codi, Callie, Rebecca and Jack. But it had turned out – and quickly – to not be an issue. Codi just wasn't ever in the way. And now, she lived here.

Rebecca touched Codi's shoulder over the back of the couch, then guided her reaching fingers to the stem of the wineglass. When Codi took the glass, Rebecca put her fingers in Codi's hair, then started pulling it back, playing with it. Codi cooed and took a sip of the red wine. "Hey, Bec," Codi said after a moment of letting the wine – and probably, the soothing fingers in her hair – sink in a little. "I got a response today from *WhiskeyNeat*."

Rebecca breathed in deeply, audibly. "Oooh, tell me more!"

"Well, the lead editor doesn't do the hiring apparently, but they want to bring me in for an interview with him."

"I could see how that makes sense. The editor would be the best guy at the magazine to tell them whether or not you're a writer," Rebecca said, braiding Codi's hair and undoing it, over and over. Codi's hair was too short to hold more than three or four knots of braiding. It was a muscle-memory thing for Rebecca, who wore a long braid almost constantly, and played with Codi's hair almost subconsciously.

"Yeah, but that makes me like, super-fucking nervous. I mean, why do they need to meet me at all? Why can't I just send in some sample writing?"

Rebecca lightly slapped the top of Codi's head. It was more of a pat, really. "Don't be silly, special. Every company wants to meet a potential employee before they hire her."

Codi leaned her head back, face toward the ceiling now, though her eyes were closed. She had flipped the bumpy book closed over her thumb, but now took that hand out and held it out, palm up. "Okay, so…" she said, jiggling the wine glass a little as she spoke, "why meet with the editor then?"

"Really, Code. I think you're reading way too deep into this. This is probably completely normal protocol for a magazine. Especially for a mag like *WhiskeyNeat*. They sell more copies than *Rolling Stone*. And without all the liberal bias bullshit."

"Yeah. Maybe," Codi said, sighing. "I'm just nervous."

"How come? They know you're vision-impaired, right?"

Codi didn't answer verbally. Instead, she nodded, taking a sip of the wine.

"Okay, then don't sweat it. And once this guy lays eyes on you, you'll be hired on the spot."

Codi reached up and patted the hand that rested in her hair. "God, I hope not. I don't want to work for anyone that shallow."

"Well, I'm terribly and horrifyingly excited for you, darling. You're going to nail it. When's the interview?"

"Tomorrow at ten if I can make it," Codi responded, setting the wine glass on the arm of the couch. She kept her fingers on it though.

"Great! Well, I will take you then. I've been looking for a reason to take a day off. We'll grab pizza on the Square when you're done."

In the last week, Callie had checked off almost every item on her To-Do list, so when she awoke Thursday morning, it was with a pleasant, natural pace. Not the quick-start, heart-slamming type that popped her eyes open and started her day with a stressful outlook. She was asleep one minute, then she was just awake. And it felt so nice. She felt more refreshed by a single night of sleep than she had in a long time.

One of those check-boxes had been getting her driver's license replaced. She had also applied for a new passport, but that would take a while. Two of her credit cards had already arrived along with her license, and her bank debit card. When you pay for the expedited processing of a lost card, she mused, they really get to work.

As she slipped out of bed and picked up her phone, she had a startling thought. In a moment of almost perfect clarity, she thought she knew with an absolute certainty who had connected her with Thad Cloys. Slapping her phone down on the body-warmed sheet, she put her left hand to her forehead and closed her eyes, running over the thought. *Who could possibly want us to connect? And why?* Well, it had suddenly begun to seem obvious. Well, not the identity of the *who*, but the familiarity.

Callie believed with a sudden and ferocious passion that the person who had sent her the video of Atlas crashing into Mars was the same person who sent Thad the message to contact her. The anonymous sender of the video had used a 10-Minute-Mail account. She guessed Thad had gotten his from a very similar service. And maybe even the same account. Those accounts literally lasted ten minutes, then were auto-purged by the server. Someone could conceivably have sent multiple emails from the same account before it deleted itself. She would have to compare the auto-generated sender's name with the one Cloys had, *if* he still had it. If they did not match, that did not mean they weren't from the same sender. But if they *did* match, it was confirmed beyond all possible doubt.

She scooted her feet into her house slippers and opened the curtains, letting the weak glow of the sunlight pour into her room, then set about making coffee. While she ground the beans into fine powder, she stood with one hand on her hip, staring out the back sliding door at the dewy grass. What connection did the crash of Atlas into Mars have with Mr. Cloys? And furthermore, what connection did the person who sent the email have with him? Assuming, of course, it was the same sender. It was. It had to be. Callie could accept no other reality.

She opened her laptop and pulled up the video again, and re-watched it. There was nothing new to see. No details she had not caught before. There was no sound, and no view of any human beings in it. It looked like a dash cam clip on the most expensive car ever built, crashing into the mountains of Arizona. *Were there mountains in Arizona?* Nevada. Wherever. It was obviously authentic though. The video bore the Oliver Company's logo in the bottom right, and a fourteen-digit date and time readout that matched the window when it would have actually happened. The subtle, jittery image was very still for a while, the blackness of space just visible on the upper edge of the screen, and then it started moving quickly and expediently toward its sudden death a few seconds later. It was a haunting image in its statement of finality. Callie did not know where any of the passengers were at the time of the crash, but she could feel its impact in her soul. The sudden loss of so much life was horrific and palpable even absent in its visibility.

Shaking her head, she put the phone down and moved the coffee grounds from the grinder to her Presto coffee maker. Then she called Ascend Airlines and booked a ticket for the six-hour flight to Houston that afternoon.

Rebecca sat in the lush lobby of the *WhiskeyNeat* magazine headquarters, on Times Square, perusing a copy of the magazine. She had initially smirked at the clever marketing device – all of the magazines on the coffee table were *WhiskeyNeat*. And though she had never been a subscriber herself, she had read her share of their music columns. The magazine offered biased perspectives on whiskey, cigars and music, without the added political conservative-bashing of its closest competitor. She found it odd that it wasn't some parent company on the marquee outside. This building, these offices, were WhiskeyNeat. The magazine was big enough to move away from home and have its own emblem. There were hundreds of the magazines around the waiting room.

Codi had gone in, white cane clicking here and there, about thirty minutes prior. She had, Rebecca had noted, gotten quite good with the stick, and was using it a lot more confidently in public spaces. A woman had opened the waiting room door – much like a dentist's office – and welcomed Codi in, then offered her an arm to guide her to the desired office. This had made Rebecca happy – reaffirming that they had been expecting a blind woman, in spite of such obvious dichotomies as it presented. She didn't need to be able to read the magazine, which didn't offer a Braille edition. She only needed to write.

Codi's submission column had been the requested four thousand words on anything she liked that fit within the magazine's wheelhouse. Codi had opted for talking about the aggressive and radical changes music underwent from decade to decade and why it always seemed to fall on that ten-year dividing line. Rebecca had found the column insightful and interesting without it being obtuse or arrogant. And obviously, the magazine had liked her style.

The one paragraph of the column that had made Rebecca look up and rethink what she had just read seemed to sum up the entire argument:

> *One could almost believe there to be a palpable sense of duty to adapt with the flipping of a calendar page, whence comes a stylistic exodus from one decade to the next. As if dictated by the changing of our clocks from the last minute of one year to the first of the next. The detectable and historically dependable pattern of perfect distinction since the inception of recorded music is both real and realistic.*

Now Codi was thirty minutes into an interview with the hottest music mag on the planet, and Rebecca was feeling her own brand of excitement in the lobby. She sat, legs crossed and bouncing her foot, trying to focus on a column about the whiskey distillery the boys from High Rise Fire were opening. But focus, she could not. Her mind was so full of excitement for Codi that she found herself reading and rereading the same sentence several times, until she finally resigned to it and flipped the magazine closed. It was then that she looked up, seeing a shadow move across the wall to the left of the glass front door.

The door opened and a tallish woman stepped in, dressed in all black with a sparkly and iridescent black boa wrapped round her neck. Purple-streaked glossy black hair stood in a perfect pile atop the striking woman's head. She stopped and removed her large sunglasses and turned in Rebecca's direction, then smiled lightly. Rebecca's heart stopped momentarily when she realized who it was.

"Oh my God!" she said, little more than a whisper, slapping her hand over her suddenly huge smile. The woman looked back at her and smiled again, obviously used to such attention. Rebecca said, "Sorry, I just realized who you were." No one else was in the lobby though, and there was no fear of drawing unwanted attention to the superstar – who was standing here plain as day, alone. No bodyguards. No entourage. Just the singular woman, unprotected and completely spectacular.

"It's okay," the woman said, walking toward Rebecca with a hand coming up to shake. Rebecca stood as she approached. "What's your name?"

Rebecca shook her hand, but didn't let go. She covered it with the hand she wasn't shaking with, and looked up at the ceiling. "Oh my God. Codi is going to flip out," Rebecca said, then finally looked back down at the woman, who was about the same height as she. "I'm sorry, I've lost my manners. I'm just a little starstruck. My name is Rebecca Judas."

The woman tilted her head and looked thoughtfully at her. "What a pretty name!"

"I didn't mean to interrupt you. I just obviously couldn't control myself," said Rebecca.

"No, it's completely fine. I'm a little early, so there's no interruption at all. Who is Cody? Is he…"

"She," Rebecca said quickly, and squeezed the woman's hand again before realizing she had not yet let go – and nor had the woman tried to escape – and let go. "She's my dear friend. She's actually here for an interview right now, to be a columnist."

Tanis's eyes got wide. "Whoa! That is super cool!"

Rebecca made a *humble-but-proud* face. "Yeah. We're pretty excited. She's going to interview you someday, Tanis."

Tanis pulled her head back, looking a little speechless herself. "Wow. Love the enthusiasm." Then she put her hand over her heart and added, "Well, Rebecca, I would be honored!"

Rebecca was shaking her head lightly, still unable to believe what was happening here. The lead singer of One Last Orbit – her generation's Taylor Swift – was standing here talking to her like an old friend.

"Hey, have a seat!" Tanis said, sweeping her hand back toward the seat from which Rebecca had arisen. So she sat. And then Tanis sat on the bench next to her, knees swung toward Rebecca. "So tell me about Codi," she said, putting her hand on Rebecca's knee.

Rebecca, ever the personality, covered the woman's hand with her own and said, "Well, she's an amazing human being. But the reason I'm here, I suspect you're asking, is because I'm her ride. We're not related or anything. We do live together though."

Tanis was nodding in an exaggerated way that said she was really listening. Clever.

"Where are you girls from?"

"Just across the bridge. Neptune City," Rebecca said.

Tanis squeezed the knee she was holding. "Love it. Ever eat at the Anchor?"

Rebecca rolled her eyes. "Every chance I get. Amazing king crab."

Tanis smiled widely and nodded more quickly. "So you're just out for the interview, or are you going to slum around these parts for a while?"

"Yeah, we figured we'd grab a slice on the Square, then maybe hit the record store or something."

"Right on!" Tanis said.

"What are *you* doing here? An interview?"

"Photo shoot," Tanis said, making an *aw-shucks* face.

"Taxing, huh?"

Tanis shrugged. "Part of the job, I guess. Not my favorite part though. I'm in it for the music!"

They chatted for around ten minutes before Tanis looked at her watch. It felt to Rebecca like they were old friends reconnecting after a long hiatus. There was no shyness or arrogance to be felt. "Hey, I have to get in there. But let me get your number. I'll call you sometime. Maybe we can hang out."

Rebecca's eyes got wide again. "Serious?"

Tanis looked at her, matching her serious expression. "Sure. Why not? A rock star can't have girlfriends? Plus I'd like to meet Codi."

"Well, absolutely. That sounds amazing," Rebecca said, still in shock. She rattled off her number as Tanis typed it in, wondering if she would really ever call. She smiled. Then the damnedest thing happened. As she slipped her hand into her purse to retrieve her phone, with which she planned on taking a selfie with the One Last Orbit singer, the other woman beat her to the punch.

"Do you mind if I take a shot of us, Rebecca?" said Tanis, raising her phone. It was some late-model Android wrapped in purple sparkly rubber to match the woman's hair and fingernails.

"Do I mind? Do bears wear funny hats?" she said and scooted close to Tanis, who smelled of lavender – of course she did – and clove.

Tanis giggled and put her arm around Rebecca's back, then they put their cheeks together and smiled while Tanis thumbed the shutter button on the screen and snapped a beautiful picture of their faces.

As they separated, Tanis opened the image, showed it to Rebecca, then said, "There's one for the Insta!"

Rebecca found herself smiling from ear to ear, and willed herself to shake loose from the ensnarement this magical woman had her in. *What a ridiculous aura she has! She's like a fucking tractor beam.*

"Thank you for the picture, Rebecca. It was so nice to meet you. I can't wait for that interview with Codi," Tanis said, holding a thumb up and winking. Then she disappeared through the door marked STAFF.

"Holy fuck," said Rebecca, staring wide-eyed at the floor with her hand over her chest.

CHAPTER 15

As Callie stepped out of the taxi, she was immediately reminded of why she hated Houston, Texas. She looked both ways and crossed the busy street, and quickly got under the shady awning of Owen's Steakhouse. And standing right by the door was the giant of a man she had almost completely forgotten about. He had a wide, beautiful smile on his face. He spread his large hands as Callie approached and pulled her in for a hug. Her face disappeared somewhere in his chest. Thaddeus stood about a foot taller than she, and Callie had not thought of herself as short, at about five-six.

She had worn an all-white dress that showed a lot of legs and arms, but completely covered everything else. She had on short pumps and had actually straightened her hair this morning, which was never necessary. She had straight hair anyway. But now it stuck straight down like daggers and swept her bare shoulders.

Thad was wearing a dark gray suit with a wine-colored tie that looked like an entire paycheck and complemented his black skin. He had tiny silver studs in both ears, and large silver rings on both of his massive hands.

He rocked her back and forth as they embraced. "Thad, Thad, Thad. How you doing, big buddy?"

"I missed, you little lady!" He finally pushed her away, holding her shoulders, and just stared down at her. "You look great, Callie Simmons! You haven't aged a day!"

"Well, you're right about that," she said, taking her shades off and slipping them in her purse. Her new purse. "I've aged about twenty years."

They stood there for a few minutes under the restaurant's awning, while the Maître d' stood, hands behind his back, just waiting. Frank and Nancy Sinatra sang *Something Stupid* through the little speaker above the door at a medial volume while they caught up. Callie was swinging her hips and snapping lightly by the time they decided to go inside.

Thad held his hand out and Callie turned toward the door where a Maître d' stood holding it open. Callie saw her reflection in a thousand tiny mirrors just inside the door and the air instantly felt warmer. The inner dining area was lit by candlelight and sconces with actual gas-lit lanterns. It felt busy and bustling, though there weren't but twenty or twenty-five tables in the main area. In one corner, on a ridiculously small stage, a band was playing big-band versions of fifties tunes like Peggy Lee, The Ronettes and Louis Armstrong, and somehow it wasn't too loud. A man and woman dressed to the nines were singing and smiling at each other amidst the backdrop of heavy brass. It was wonderful.

As they pulled their chairs up to the table, the host handed Callie a red rose stub, which Thad took and slipped behind her ear for her. She was all smiles. Surely, they had places like this in every state, didn't they? In a sudden rush of emotion, Callie realized that places like this were what she lived for. The wine and steak she planned to consume were part of that equation. But the romance, the big band sound, the dancing on crowded floors and candle-lit tables with soft tablecloths… these made her feel young in the soul again. And without realizing she was subconsciously associating Houston with the experience of Owen's, Callie said, "I'm sorry I haven't kept in touch, Thad. You must think I'm a terrible friend."

Thad smiled broadly, showing a lot of teeth, shaking his head. He was leaning back, his hands on his thighs under the table. "Nah, don't say that! We were never what I would call *friends*. Don't feel guilty. I *am* glad to see you though!"

Callie shook her head and put her left hand around his right wrist. It didn't make it much more than half way around. "Thad, is anyone else still around?"

He shrugged and looked around the dimly lit restaurant. He was still smiling. "Yeah, I guess the line crew and some of the warehouse crew probably are. I kept in touch with Mary for a while, but even that eventually just faded away."

Callie leaned in a little closer, taking interest in the prospect of a new lead. "Now who was Mary, again?"

"Sam's assistant," Thad said. He was still smiling, and Callie had to remind herself that he had the type of face that naturally smiled. He probably had to make a concentrated effort just to *stop* smiling.

She nodded, remembering, but silently a little bummed, knowing Mary wouldn't be much help. "That was so sad when I heard about Samson."

Thad nodded, shrugging again. "Yeah, but I didn't know him too well. I didn't find out until after the funeral had already happened, so I didn't go."

A waiter appeared and took their drink order and handed them each a menu, then bowed away gracefully. Callie looked about the place and saw she was not the only one wearing white. She had worried momentarily that she would be. When the drinks came – Callie's chardonnay and Thad's Old-Fashioned – she took a sip then leaned in again, putting her elbows on the table, almost facing Thaddeus. He held up his glass and peered into it, then took the orange peel out and took a bite out of it. The fireplace behind her reflected in the smooth glass of his cocktail.

"I do love a good old-fashioned," Thad said. I've never been here, so I haven't had this one. But I collect 'em," he said proudly.

Callie giggled. "So, Thad, you know why I wanted to meet with you. I'm investigating what happened to the Atlas."

Thad made a sour face. "Well, ma'am, I can tell you what happened to the Atlas," he said, looking like he was telling a bad joke.

"No, honey, I know. I know what happened. And I know why. I'm trying to find out the secret stuff."

"What secret stuff?" he said, frowning. There it was. He was capable of not smiling after all.

Callie took a deep breath and looked back at the band in the corner. The woman was now singing *Cry Me A River*. Callie breathed out and took a big swig of her wine. She placed both her hands flat on the table and pushed her chair a little closer to Thad, then twisted in her seat and leaned over. "Okay. This is gonna take a minute."

△   △   △

"Hello?" Natalie said.

"Dommie. You're not gonna fuckin' believe this," said Rebecca.

"You're goddamn right I'm not!" Natalie said, almost shouting. "I'm looking at my social feed now. What the living fuck, Judas?"

"I know, right?" Rebecca said, hand on her chest. She was pacing in the waiting room. Playing with her hair, twisting her rings, and inventing several other fidgets along the way as well. She had an earbud in her ear, and her phone was down at waist level where she could continually look down at the screen, where Tanis's Instagram feed showed her latest post. She already had several thousand likes and comments on it. "I am in serious shock here. She came in to do a photo shoot, and we were the only two in the lobby for like ten minutes. But get this, Dommie."

"What else? Holy shit, I'm gonna come."

Rebecca squealed with laughter. "I know! She asked for my number!"

"Oh my God. I'm dying. If she calls you, I will die. I will literally fucking die."

Rebecca shook her fist in the air, closing her eyes. "I know. Coolest day of my life."

Shortly after they rang off, the staff door reopened and the woman who had escorted Codi back earlier reappeared with Codi in tow. "Rebecca?" she asked, raising her eyebrows. Funny thing, that, as Rebecca was the only one in the waiting room. But she was already standing, so she sort of skipped a step toward the door, the excitement still not having drained from her system.

"How'd it go, Codes?" she said, leaning in and taking Codi by the hand.

"Uh, well, do you have a few more minutes, or are we in a rush?" Codi asked seriously.

Rebecca tilted her head, frowning. This effect would be lost on the sightless Codi, though. The other woman was smiling politely in the door. Maybe it was for her. Who knew? For that matter, *who cared*? Rebecca was having trouble putting two thoughts together in her head.

"No rush, baby, what's going on? Is anything wrong?"

"No, no, nothing's wrong. I got the job, but Tanis Ransom is back there and wanted to know if we would join her for the photo shoot."

When Callie had finished laying everything out for Thad, he widened his eyes and shook his head. "Damn!" was all he said. His hands were on his hips again. Callie had spent only a small portion of the speech talking around her steak as she chewed with her hand in front of her mouth, just trying to spill everything as quickly as possible. For some reason, she felt like Thad Cloys would believe she was trying to recruit him into helping her. And while that wasn't her intention, she had begun, somewhere in the middle of the exposition, to think it might not be a bad idea to let him believe that. Maybe even to lean into it a little bit. And what if he flat out said something like, *'Boy, I sure wish I could be on the team!'* That would be a welcome blessing. And if he couldn't be, she had plausible deniability. *Oh, honey, I wasn't asking you to join me.*

The band had moved into something Callie didn't recognize, but thought it was something folksy like Bob, or maybe Joni. The candles, the wine, the music, and now the satiation from her New York strip steak were all working together to build the perfect night. Callie slipped her credit card into the leather folder the waiter had set down and put her elbows on the table, fists together, to look at Thad.

"What do you think? Think I have something?"

"Well, yeah, you have something," Cloys said, nodding and looking about their general area. A woman walked by and looked a little too long at Thad. She was wearing a very low-cut blouse and no bra, and her big boobs were swinging around like balloons full of water. Callie had to fight back the urge to roll her eyes. She noticed that Thaddeus did not feel the same objection though. He smiled politely at the woman and returned his attention to the altogether less balloony Callie Simmons. She did not feel inadequate, but was suddenly very aware of her own chest. Did men look at every woman's chest, or just the ones on vulgar display?

"Okay. Do you have some more time, Thad?" she said finally, just as she was beginning to blush.

"Yeah, sure. I have all night for you, Ms. Simmons," he said, holding up a hand.

"Do you have a favorite coffee shop?"

He didn't. Thad did not drink coffee, apparently. So they opted for a bench in a small park a few blocks away from their vehicles. Callie had never actually felt safer in the presence of a man than now. Jack was great; he was no lightweight. But Thaddeus Cloys was like a He-man. The kind of guy that changed men's mind about fighting, when they saw him step out of the car.

"So do you think you know anything that might help me, now that you know what I'm looking for?" Callie said, as they settled into the bench. The bench was separated into three segments by steel armrests. All in an effort to keep the homeless from sleeping on them.

"Well, something you said earlier caught my attention," Thad said, adjusting his trousers and trying to get comfortable. Callie felt bad that she didn't know the city any better, wishing she could offer him somewhere a little less metallic and windy. "Those two crates we were going to take up, then they ended up on the mission bird."

Callie nodded. "Yes. The urn shells from ETIS. Right." ETIS was Extra-Terrestrial Interment Services, the company run by Pablo Phoenix out in LA somewhere. Donnie Oliver's name had been forged on some contract saying they would take a couple of crates of these remains and bury them on Mars.

"No, ma'am. That's not what they were."

"I beg pardon," Callie said, leaning in a little.

"You might have been mistaken about that. Those urn shells were little," Cloys said, holding a large hand up with his finger and thumb spread about six inches apart. "Like the size of a magic marker."

Callie frowned and pulled her head back. "What the heck were they then? Maybe I need to recheck my notes."

Thad shrugged. "I think they ended up taking the shells up, but there were only a couple boxes of 'em, and they didn't take up much room on the ship. Them boxes were like the size of shoe boxes. They wadn't that big," Thad said. He crossed his arms and took a glance around the park, then said, "Those crates they were talkin' bout, they had these big egg-like things in 'em."

Callie made a face. "What the heck? Eggs?"

He shrugged again. "Yeah. Bradley had said they were extremely important to the mission. Like mission critical or somethin'. And they had these black like shiny things in 'em. They just looked like…" Thad said, holding his hands up and trying to make the shape with them.

"That's okay," Callie said, reaching out and touching his shoulder. "What about them?"

"Come again?"

"You said I mentioned them earlier and it got you thinking. What did they make you think about?"

"Oh. Yeah," he said, and snapped his fingers, "Bradley said somethin' like 'You know people's died for these things' or some shit." Thad got wide-eyed. "I'm sorry, that just slipped out."

"It's fine," she said, looking impatient. "What do you think that meant?"

"I think he meant that someone'd been killed over 'em. Like for real," Thad said, a weak smile on his lips. Callie thought it looked like the kind of smile one displayed when you should already know what he's talking about.

Callie was shaking her head though. "You mean, like someone had actually died?"

Thad nodded patiently. Softly.

"Who could he have meant?"

He shrugged and smiled, looking around like he was scared to name names. This giant of a man, scared by the weaselly little man Brian Bradley. Bradley, who had seemed to be afraid of Callie herself. It was endearing to Callie. But she did respect his sense of propriety.

"Well, I don't want to sound rude or anything, ma'am. But I figured that was pretty obvious, if you ask me," Thad said.

"Well, then you might have to consider me a dumb-dumb, babe. I have no idea what you're talking about," Callie said. She was beginning to get a little impatient. What the heck was he talking about? Brian Bradley wasn't going to kill anyone!

"You 'member that crew chief, Robert Keith who died in his apartment?"

Callie's face fell. Her heart stopped momentarily. She did remember that. Donnie Oliver and Mike Thurman had gone to find him and had achieved that much. Only the man had been dead in his apartment for apparently a couple of weeks, if she recalled correctly. At the time, she had thought it had been considered suicide or something.

"You think Bradley killed that man? Over these egg things?" Callie said.

"Lemme put it like this, Ms. Callie," Thaddeus said, holding his hands up in front of him as if he were holding an invisible football. "There's some things you just know. And I heard lots a stuff when I worked there. I was like the maid. Always in the room when the important people was talkin'. And I heard all the stuff they didn't think I heard. But thing is, I was friends with 'em too. So they didn't worry 'bout me knowin'. 'Cause they knew they could trust me."

"Okay," Callie said. "So you heard some stuff."

He was nodding again. The wind had picked up a little and the detritus of a Houston evening blew across the park. Callie saw Thad tracing a paper plate with his big eyes. When he finally made eye-contact with Callie again, he looked a little embarrassed. He grinned and saw that she was waiting for him to say something. He said it all. "Yeah. Bradley had that man killed because he had threatened to tell Donnie about them two crates."

Callie was tilting her head thoughtfully toward the bench while she watched the big man fidget. Why was she surprised by this news? She had completely forgotten about the dead man found in his apartment. But she couldn't imagine ever having thought it was Bradley who did it.

"He worked for some powerful people, Ms. Callie," Thad said, answering the rest of her question.

CHAPTER 16

All the way home, Codi was a chatterbox. Rebecca let her talk it out. It wasn't that Rebecca herself didn't want to be chatty as well, but she was enjoying hearing the excitement pour out of Codi's mouth, like a never-ending train. It was nice to see her this excited about something. Since the terrible experience she had barely lived through on Minus's monster-chasing waste of time, Codi had been victim to many sudden cries and bouts of depression and fear. Rebecca could not imagine the level of sheer will it would take to pull oneself through such a traumatic experience. Not only being stuck in a submarine in the deepest part of the ocean in the world, but being newly blind at the time… *Good God.*

It was almost immediately obvious that Codi was not nearly as excited about the new job as she was the chance encounter they had happened upon with the majestic and wonderful Tanis Ransom. Not only was she Codi's favorite singer, but she was so down-to-earth, which was oddly poetic as well. The woman only wrote celestial love songs and songs full of space and the cosmos.

Rebecca, ever the lover of music, had been stunned to see the rock star as well. But Codi was bouncing and squealing and Oh-my-Godding over and over in the studio. It had been adorable to Rebecca. *But come on! You have a new job, girl!* After letting the electrified Codi Cohl get it out of her system, Rebecca finally put her hand on the girl's arm and said, "Okay, baby."

Codi, sensing she had maybe gotten a little carried away, put her hands on her face and said, "Oh, sorry. Okay. Okay. I'm sorry." Then she shook her little fists as if one more bead of electricity had to be shaken out.

"I need to hear about the interview now."

"Well, she asked me to come up with things real quickly. Like, if I was talking to someone. Say like Tanis. And I asked her a question, like, 'so this song was about birds,' and Tanis was like 'no, it was about kittens,' and I would have to recover quickly. What would I say?"

Rebecca frowned. "That's weird. It's not radio or television. Not sure why you would have to be quick on your feet like that."

Codi shrugged. Her hands were in her lap now and she was staring straight ahead – or, more likely, wasn't – through her large black sunglasses. "I guess it's journalism in general. Just basically asking like how I would adapt to a change in pace like that."

"Ah. I got ya. Well, I am just insanely proud for you. So happy for you," Rebecca said.

"Aww, thank you, Bec," Codi said, putting her hand on Rebecca's wrist and giving it a light squeeze.

"So what's your first assignment?"

Codi lifted her chin and held her hands in front of her porcelain face, as if she were guiding in a kisser on short final. "Four thousand words on the resurgence of the record, juxtaposed with the habitually lazy streamer."

"Good fuck. What is that?" Rebecca snorted.

"I think it's going to be fun, Bec. So many people stream their music now. Like they don't even buy digital music anymore and download it. Remember, we used to buy it and burn it on CDs? And now we mostly just stream it. There's no soul in that, is there?"

"There is a lot of soul in the record. I will give you that," Rebecca said, pointing sideways at the other woman.

"Yeah. These are things we talked about at length: how I consumed music and whatnot. Had I ever spun a record. How big is my CD collection. Shit like that. And so she wants me to write about it, because she said my passion for music was pretty obvious. And not just the music. But the way we hear it. The meta."

"Fucking wonderful. I get to be the first to read it though, okay?" said Rebecca, turning to look at the smiling face of Codi.

"Well, duh."

Walter sat across from her, chin resting on the fist of one hand while the other held the phone to his swollen cheek. His orange jumpsuit looked neat and clean, pressed. His hair was immaculate, as always, which was to say it was completely messy on his head, the same way he always wore it. There were cuts above his right eye and on his chin. The knuckles of both hands were bloody and raw. His right wrist was swollen. Left eye nearly black. Would be by tomorrow evening. Callie did not have to ask what had happened. And had not. When Walter had entered the room on the other side of the glass, she had flinched, probably visibly to him, and immediately swallowed hard, trying to hold back tears. She wanted to stay strong in his company, but boy, this was going to be hard. He had stared at her for a few long moments, expressionless, before he finally picked up the receiver. And Callie's only words, one hand still covering her quivering mouth, had been, "Oh, Walter!"

He furled his lips and licked his teeth but didn't say anything. He just stared her in the eyes. Maybe this was that 'lack of language', as Rebecca had called it, that she shared with Walter. Maybe they didn't need to talk. This look said everything. So Callie waited for words. After another long moment, wherein neither of them broke eye-contact, Callie started flicking her thumbnail across her upper teeth.

In all her years of knowing Walter, she had never seen him lose his composure. She had never seen him with a bruise on his face. Or a black eye. He had always been the man. Man of the hour. Man of the year. Man of her life. Whatever man she needed him to be at whatever moment of personal crisis she was going through, he was. But he had never been *her* man. She had maybe never needed him to be, just on the basis and strength of the fact that he was such *a* man. A good guy, through and through. A bruise on his face meant he had been on the other end of what he had served to Tim Blisk. But Walter, she reminded herself, looking at his fists, also had bloody knuckles. So someone hadn't just given it to him without taking some back. Callie finally broke the silence.

"How bad does the other guy look?"

Walter finally broke the stare-down, looking at the desk and reaching behind his head to scratch his neck. The vein on his biceps was strong and thick. In the few weeks he had been in, he had obviously gotten back to a strict workout routine. He shook his head and returned his eyes to hers. "You can't win in here. There's always another one. You take one down, the next one is there to take his place. Sometimes two or three at once. And it never ends."

Callie was shaking her head again. She hated seeing violence, but strongly supported it when it was necessary. Walter breaking Tim's face had been well-deserved. But seeing her friend in this state made her hurt in her heart. In her soul. She wanted to hug him. To lay her head against his chest and cry for him. Because she knew he wouldn't. She swallowed again, then changed the subject. "Been working out, I see," she said.

Walter leaned back in his chair. He nodded, widening his eyes. "Not much else to do in here. I've worked out like five or six hours a day for the last three weeks."

"You look good, Walt."

This finally got a smile out of him. "Yeah. Orange is the new black and all that."

"No," she said, shaking her head mockingly, "you." She said this last, bringing her hand down like she was presenting him an award. "You look good. Your muscles. You look fit."

"Thanks, Callie. So do you."

She beamed. "I'm sorry you're in here. Is there anything I can do?"

He shook his head. She couldn't stop thinking about how distant he looked. How *disconnected* he seemed. After a few long moments where she saw he wasn't going to say anything, she finally changed the subject again.

"I talked to Thad Cloys. Remember him?"

Walter shook his head, furrowing his brow.

"You might not have met him. Anyway, he was the forklift operator at Oliver Company."

"Yeah?" Walter said, not looking very interested. "What'd he have to say?"

"Lots. I'm on a mission again," said Callie.

"You're going *back* to Fiji?" he asked. And when he saw her smile and nod, he said, "Man, dude. Bro. You never learn, do you?"

"No, *bro*, I guess I never do. I don't give up that easy."

"What easy?" Walter said, finally showing some actual confusion. Some actual… emotion? Was this reaction? Like he actually cared?

"Like the bullshoot that I went through down there."

Walter sighed and furled his lips. "Homie, I don't know what happened down there. In case you haven't noticed, I've been a guest at the Fuck You Inn for the last few weeks."

Callie giggled, then stopped herself. Then she giggled again, putting her hand over her mouth. "I'm sorry," she said through a laugh. And now she couldn't stop. She was laughing with more than just her mouth. Her shoulders were shaking. She stopped for a moment, finally getting control, catching her breath. Then she was off again. This repeated several times, getting worse and worse, until she finally saw his face crack. And he started smirking. Then he shook his head, and then he was laughing too.

PART TWO

CHAPTER 17

Six months passed. Callie had all but forgotten her escapades to the lonely island south of the equator. All those fever-dream fantasies of going down and getting the bad guys had finally faded. Callie knew she had rushed into action without a plan. When asked what she had hoped Brian Bradley would say, or do, she couldn't really answer. Had she somehow thought he would suddenly be a good guy and admit he was wrong? Turn himself in? Offer to pay restitution? And if so, to whom? There was no one left.

When she had gotten home, she had gone to see Walter in jail, and he had asked her an even better question from behind the thick bulletproof glass: what do *you* plan to say if you run into him? And in her busy, I-can-fix-anything state-of-mind, there was no need to waste time answering nonsense questions. It just didn't matter. She had argued with him when he kept telling her she needed some kind of plan. "I'll make it up as I go along!" she had rallied. She told him she was going back, wasn't done with the mission, had new information, and all the other things that filled her blood with the fight. She was ready, by God! He had tried to make her slow down and count her eggs. Maybe move some into other baskets. Hatch a plan.

Nope.

Didn't work.

Her plan, still, was to go down there with as much force as possible and handle things. With new information, she would know what to do. Good guys always win! It would work itself out the way the universe tells it to. The way it's *supposed* to. Meanwhile, in her hot-blooded state, she had overlooked so many crystal balls in the process that she was nearly blind to reality. Those crystal balls that could tell her the future. They would tell her exactly how it would go down. Crystal balls like *they'll know what you're there for this time*. And *security will be tighter this time*. Among many others. Callie Simmons just completely failed to acknowledge anything but that her will would prevail over failure.

And what *was* there to do, come to that? What were her realistic options? She had no power – legal or physical – to administer a citizen's arrest. Without involving the local authorities, which required actual evidence and not just hearsay and memories of fake receipts, what were her options really? She had already tried going in and putting her finger down. Telling the only woman she trusted down there what had really happened. And she saw how far that had gotten her.

It was Jack who finally got her to recognize these things. They had spoken an hour after her visit to Walter, and he had said very simply, "Babe, you need to let this go." They had been sitting face-to-face. She had come breezing into his house and slung her purse into the corner of the couch. Then she plopped back against the cushions with her feet poking comically out in front of her. His couch was too deep for her knees to bend on the edge of the cushion and put her feet on the floor. So she had sat there leaning her head back, staring toward the ceiling, telling him all the things she had learned. Her ankles were crossed and she was playing with her hair. The portrait of someone who has it completely together. Jack had asked her if she wanted a glass of sweet tea. She had declined. Then he had brought her one anyway. He had handed her a tall glass of the stuff, ice cubes tinkling. Callie had thanked him and immediately set to imbibing. He held his own by the upper rim, dangling it between his knees as he sat on the ottoman facing her.

Callie's eyes had locked on Jack's, she had swallowed, and looked at him seriously. Thinking, seriously. Considering, seriously what he had said. Really taking in the meaning of the words. As if she had never considered that option as an option before. And for some reason, something had clicked.

"Jack, I…"

"Babe. You're a really smart girl! I've never met anyone with an IQ as high as yours. But you need to realize when you don't have enough. I don't want you getting locked up down there again, or hurt. Or even killed."

Callie sat in silence.

Jack had put his hand on her knee and shaken it back and forth slightly. "Trust me, hon. I'm on your side. I want what you want. But this just won't work. Until you get something more, something tangible, there's just nothing you can do."

And Callie had begun nodding slowly, focusing on something near Jack's shoulder as she really let it sink it. And then she had finally said, "Okay."

Then six months blew by like images on a screen. The warmest part of the year came and went. October brought in the cold winds and the children in their store-bought costumes representing the latest superhero crazes. The little girls were still princesses. The baby girls were still ladybugs. Callie still cooed and smiled that sad smile of jealousy when she put candy in their plastic pumpkins. And then it was November. That Halloween night had been the only real landmark date that knocked her back into a vision of how long her mission had stagnated. She had continually reminded herself that Jack had been right. There was nothing for her to do but keep living. Maybe more evidence would present itself. Maybe that mysterious sender of the Atlas-crash video would resurface. Show his face. Or at least send another email. But nothing happened.

They had spent many of those summer nights on the patio, grilling brats and burgers, blasting the music and standing around drinking beers. Rebecca, Codi, Sam and Thevi had been there for almost all of those nights. Fire pits and fantasies, long into the night, almost every Friday and Saturday night. Callie had really developed a closeness with Rebecca during this time. They had something to build on, having been down in that mess together in Fiji, and build they had.

On many of those summer nights, Callie and Rebecca would sit beside each other and talk in low voices, private from the rest of the group, covering everything they should know about each other, as if it were a duty. It felt perfectly natural to fill each other in. *Oh, I've been to the Grand Canyon too. I got a little freaked out on the helicopter. Oh I've been on a helicopter too.* And so on. Playing off each other's shared stories and holding nothing back. Rebecca had changed in Callie's eyes, from the stoic yet pleasant, not-quite-arrogant woman who held herself in a little higher regard than those around her. Callie finally understood that posture. It was real, but it had been misread. Rebecca was not arrogant. She was guarded. She was *careful*. But now that Callie had established herself as badge-worthy, Rebecca had let her into the employees-only sections.

Jack got on well enough with Sam, too. A lot of their initial conversations had revolved around Jack's curiosity: *What was it like to be blind from birth? What do you see in your mind's eye when I describe a color or a thing you've never seen?* They made good conversation, and Sam was a patient subject. But Callie could always tell that Jack missed having Walter around. And obviously, so did Thevi. Walter, who did not get to be part of this group of all-new friends. It was a very special time to Callie, who had realized early on that most of the group was comprised of new friendships. Most of them had only recently met each of the other people in the group. She was happy for having brought these people together, even though Walter was missing out on it all. That saddened Callie in a way that she could not well define for Jack. Or anyone, for that matter. But Jack, patient as he was, and full of the knowledge that Callie and Walter had a special kind of friendship, seemed to be sensitive about it regardless of what was said.

Callie had known since early on, when Walter and she had become so close as to be almost inseparable, that there would be no romance between them. They had both known it. Somehow, that just wasn't the direction their relationship had gone. And they had both known it without ever even discussing it. But in its progressing closeness, it had begun to look to outsiders like perhaps they were lovers in hiding. It seemed that no matter how many times Callie remarked that, no, they were not lovers and never had been – never would be, for that matter – some people always smirked at the answer. That knowing nod that says, *right. I got ya.* Those people simply would not be convinced that a man and a woman could be completely platonic – especially when the man and the woman were both attractive. There was just no way, in their minds. 'Men and women who are heterosexual,' one of her friends early on had said, 'begin to covet each other very quickly. And as an evolutionary absolute, they're going to end up in bed together.' Callie had rolled her eyes so hard at that statement that she had almost made herself dizzy. Needless to say, she was no longer friends with that person.

So it had come to be that Callie had decided to just not mention Walter to any potential love interest. If that love interest became serious enough to warrant moving to the next step, Walter would finally be introduced. But this was,

Callie reckoned, long enough into whatever relationship that the other should have formed a solid trust for her by then. And in seeing her with Walter, would therefore be at ease. *He's like a brother,* she would say with a dismissive wave. She would not make a big deal out of it. Don't hide it, but don't advertise it. And that mostly worked. Their unique brand of friendship, once people really got close enough to see a lot of them together, was actually something people came to be envious of. If it were truly possible for two hetero adults to be friendly but not sexually attracted to one another, then hell, they wanted that for themselves. Why wouldn't they? Why does friendship have to be constrained by a gender boundary? In Callie's mind, there was only ever a thought of anything sexual if there was something going on in her heart.

Well, that was all fine and good, she told herself, until she remembered *coveting* Walter a little bit down in Mexico. Having realized she had never seen him without a shirt in all the years she had known him, or at least not having paid attention if she had, she had begun to think of how good his chest would feel in her hands. And perhaps that had led to her wondering how good her own chest would feel in his hands. But the thoughts had not been allowed to prosper. Everyone was granted a fleeting thought occasionally, weren't they? She didn't act on it. She moved along with her day. Though it did resurface on occasion, she never voiced any of the attraction to anyone. Especially not Walter. Or his wife, Thevi. Heck no. *Oh, God, no, not Thevi!*

So this recent development with Jack had come on the heels of Walter's bringing the other man into the crew for the Monster Hunt operation. Callie had not been allowed to follow her protocol of not introducing Jack to Walter until she felt comfortable. Because it had gone the other direction, and Walter had already known the man, everything had just sort of *happened*. And it had happened quickly. Callie knew it wasn't a rebound. She had actively been trying to move forward in life, leaving thoughts and emotions of Chris and his death behind her. Callie's first true love, Chris, had drowned in the ocean on their SCUBA trip. And ironically, it had been Jack who had come along and helped Callie sell Chris's vehicle and get rid of some of his other personal things. Callie didn't want any of it around. She would have given the expensive watch away, but the only two men she knew who would wear it were the two men she was around most often. And she didn't want to see it. So she had Jack sell that as well.

But now, Jack, having known all along that Walter and she were only friends, was beginning to show signs of a little worry when it came to Callie's disposition on Walter's incarceration. It seemed well obvious to Callie that she would be grieving the horrific, life-changing circumstance of a best friend being behind bars for the first time. Well, why was Jack so upset about it? Maybe upset wasn't the right word. But he was concerned, for sure. Why was he so damned *sensitive* about her relationship with Walter all of a sudden?

It finally came to a head one night, now mid-November. The fire was blazing in the fire pit and the usual crowd was gathered, sitting in the Adirondack chairs. Codi's head was leaning back against the chair back, rocking slowly back and forth with the music. She was wearing her dark sunglasses. The fire played weird patterns in her brain if she looked at it too much. Sam sat close by, holding her hand. And since he could see nothing at all, his face was bare of any accouterments other than his usual slight smile. Rebecca and Natalie had been very inclusive of Thevi, trying not to let her feel like a third wheel since Walter couldn't be here.

One of Ryan Adams's slower songs was playing through the expensive speakers Jack had installed surrounding the fire pit. Callie and he were dancing slowly to the song. It was not a rare event for someone to feel the calling and stand up and dance. Especially when the drink was flowing. And it had been flowing that night. Jack was whispering in Callie's ear, asking her if she was sure she was okay with the Walter thing. His trial was next April, and if that went well he should be released. Callie was beginning to get annoyed with all the questions about Walter, having not been able to add anything new to the conversation. She had been to see him about twice a month for the last six months, spending an hour with him at the window, doing her duty as a friend.

She was about to tell Jack that she was getting tired of his always asking if she were okay about the whole thing. No, to be honest, she was not. But what could she do? She opened her mouth to speak and suddenly felt his finger against her lips. He had taken his left hand out of her own and put it on her chin. And then he said the thing that nearly tore them completely apart. He said, "Are you sure you're not in love with him?"

Callie had instantly backed up – or, rather, tried to. But when she pulled back, he had grabbed her wrist again, tightening his right arm around her waist. And then they were close enough to kiss. But not kissing. She was furious.

"Why would you…" she started.

But he was shaking his head, lifting his chin, holding her tighter. "Tssh tssh. Wait," he said.

Callie shut her mouth, and her lips became a thin white line of anger. But she stayed her distressed comeback.

"I only ask because I want to make sure. It's my final question on the matter. The last time I'll ever ask," Jack said.

Callie stared at him, still burning with the anger, but also still swaying mechanically back and forth – a mindless marionette unwittingly under his control. And after a long moment of heavy breathing, she finally said, "Why in the world, Jack? Why now? I thought we had something really special. I thought you *knew* that."

"We do. And I do," he said, nodding. "I just wanted to make absolutely sure."

She widened her eyes, shaking her head. *So?*

"Because if that's the truth, then that means I can have you."

"You already do have me, Jack! God!" Callie spat.

"Forever."

They stopped swaying.

Huh?

Huh?

He nodded very softly. Slowly. The smile still hadn't left his handsome face.

"Forever?" she asked, a little confused. Then his hands were sliding down her arms to her wrists. He had backed up a half-step and was now holding both of her hands in his. And then he dropped to his knee. Callie's gaze followed him down. She still had not realized what was happening, but their eyes had not yet left each other. And then Jack was reaching in his left jacket pocket and fishing out a small black velvet box. That's when Callie's mind opened up and let it in. And now her right hand was over her mouth. Tears were in her eyes.

"Forever, Callie," he said, opening the box. The fire danced crazily in the large diamond.

And now both hands were on her mouth. The underlying tones of the girls' talking on the other side of the fire had gone silent, but Callie only noticed peripherally. Her tears were now pouring freely down her cheeks. *Was this real?*

"Oh my God," she cried. And suddenly she was bawling. But Jack wasn't. Jack was smiling widely, presenting her with the most beautiful ring she had ever seen. It was white gold and blinding in its magnificence, a rock about the size of a house on top of it.

"Callie, I want to know that you can be all mine, forever. Will you marry me?" Jack said.

Callie, still in tears and breathing erratically, turned at the waist to look at the other five people across the fire. Rebecca was smiling broadly, glassy-eyed, holding Natalie's hand. Natalie's other hand was covering her own mouth and she was openly crying, expectantly waiting. It's all on you now, that look said. Thevi was jumping up and down making fists in front of her chest. Callie could tell Thevi couldn't wait to come over and hug her best friend.

Codi and Sam were looking in her direction thoughtfully, though Callie realized subconsciously that this didn't mean they could see her. But their attention was there.

Codi's hands were clasped in front of her excited toothy smile. And now Callie's hands were making tiny fists in front of her mouth and she was turning back to Jack. And magically – the music gods had seemingly smiled down upon them tonight – George Michael's *Faith* came on the stereo. And she was shouting, "Yes! Yes! YES, JACK!" and she was falling on top of him on the ground, embracing him with all her body, all her heart and all her might. And just over the bouncing rhythm of the song and the acoustic guitar, she could hear the shouts and applause of the others at the party. For this was now a party. The shouts were wonderful. And so was Jack's voice, once again in her ear, saying, "I love you, Callie Simmons. Callie Elaine Simmons. Soon to be Callie Carpenter."

Rebecca and Thevi, an unlikely pairing, were standing together in the lobby of the courtroom waiting for Jennifer Cambria, Walter's attorney, to come back through the courtroom doors with hopefully some good news. Or better news, at least. Thevi had called on Rebecca this morning when Thevi had gotten the call from Cambria. There was movement in the judge's chambers, apparently. There might be a chance of getting Walter released on his own recognizance, and Thevi was looking for support. Callie had not answered when she called, so Thevi had called Bec. They weren't very close, and never had been. They had just never spent a lot of time together. Rebecca had known Walter from her days at Royal with him, and had kept in touch with him for all these years, though their relationship was a mostly telephonic one. They almost never saw each other in person anymore. But since Callie had gotten them all together recently, and Codi had come into her life, Rebecca had been seeing more and more of more and more people. It was nice to expand her friend circle a little, and maybe to stop taking work so seriously. And having Natalie come back into town right at the same time was just crazy coincidence. But a nice one.

So here they stood. And while Rebecca stood looking at the pictures on the walls, the plaques, the civic mementos, her arms were crossed on her chest, and she swayed slowly back and forth on her heels. Meanwhile, Thevi was not so calm. She was sighing a lot, twisting around to look at the door every few seconds, and pacing in a small square she had deemed appropriate on the floor of the lobby.

After ten minutes or so, the heavy door opened in what seemed like slow-motion, and Cambria came out, not smiling. All business, this woman was. It was a shame, really. Because she could be so pretty if she smiled occasionally. Rebecca looked her up and down. *Dresses too much like a boy.*

Jennifer Cambria held a folio against her forearm and looked over her notes, then made the quick assessment of who she should be talking to here. On one hand, there was the man's wife. That made sense. Then there was this woman who was composed and business-like. The woman made eye contact with Rebecca and in the briefest instant, Rebecca read this thought and made a very subtle head-shake. Immediately, Cambria turned to the nervous wife, who was now scratching both elbows with the opposing hands. Fidgeting.

"Right. Okay, so here's where we stand. I'm moving to get Walt released on his own recognizance, and having this thing thrown out completely on the grounds that they can't with full certainty say this man died at Walter's hand."

Thevi was following along, but looked a little lost. She cleared her throat, but didn't speak.

"However, they probably can."

"Can what? I'm sorry," said Thevi.

"Prove he died of complications arising," Rebecca answered quickly, moving forward to get the woman's attention, touching her elbow. "There's no double-jeopardy at play here or something?" she asked.

"No. This is a whole new thing. New hearing. Not quite unprecedented, but not common either. Judges have some unchecked power we don't see too often." Cambria turned her attention back to Thevi and added, "And he doesn't like Walter. So we're fighting uphill here."

"Fantastic," Thevi whispered, shaking her head and breathing in deeply. She looked around as if for a way to escape. Rebecca put her hand on Thevi's back, a gesture of reassurance.

"Well, like I said, I'm working on it. I'll hear something back by tomorrow afternoon and I'll let you know, Theevy."

"It's Thevi," said Thevi. "Pronounced TEHvee."

"Sorry, Thevi," Cambria said, and touched her elbow, trying out the gesture Rebecca had used on her own elbow a few moments before. As if she were learning how to be a human slowly but surely. Rebecca smirked.

"Thank you, Jennifer," said Rebecca, reaching out and stroking the woman's elbow again. Showing her how it was done. The other smiled weakly, then looked like maybe she thought the smile didn't fit, and turned to go back into the courtroom.

The night Callie found her million-dollar check from Minus, she was sitting Indian-style on the floor of her bedroom with several boxes open around her, papers and memories spread out across the carpet like the remnants of a war. The stereo in her living room was blasting a never-ending Spotify playlist, keeping her company from down the hall. She was sorting through tax papers and license applications and merit awards, tossing the ones that were too old to matter, filing the ones she thought she still needed. There were loose

spiral notebook pages with the rat-chew still on the edge –
journal entries and poems. She found one Codi had written,
as well as her own. Codi had spoken the poem from memory
one night standing by the pit with a cane to keep her from
straying into the flames. Callie remembered the way she had
raised one hand and danced across the words with a
fingertip, emphasizing the proper parts and stunning the
small group with her poetic prowess. It was wonderful.
Callie had recorded it on her phone and transcribed it the
next day. When Codi had finished, there was wild applause
that sounded larger than the few people who were actually
there.

Callie read it again now and smiled. And when she
looked up, gazing at the wall, at nothing, just considering
what she had just read, there it was. The corner of a pink
rectangle hung out at an awkward angle from the bottom of
a mirror on the wall. Callie frowned wondering what the
heck it was, then flopped the sheaf of papers and notes from
her lap to the carpet beside her. She stood on creaking knees
and hopped across the piles like a child playing The Floor Is
Lava over to the mirror. As soon as she pulled the pink paper
out from between the wall and the mirror, the memory
flooded back into her mind. Along with a warm feeling of
excitement. And a cold feeling of dread in her blood when
she remembered how long ago she had put it there.

She had been so proud to have a check for a perfect
million dollars, that she had wanted to enjoy it for a while
before depositing it into her account. This was the second
such copy, having lost the first on the flight to Fiji. So she
was even prouder of it than the first one, even though the
sentimental value of the first should have been more
significant. But the night she had brought this second one
home, she had stood it atop the mirror, a paper balancing on
its edge on the top of a wooden frame and leaning against a
wall. And there it had stood for several minutes. Probably
just long enough for Callie to forget about it. And then it had
slipped behind the mirror into hiding, where its viability
would run out like the life blood from a dying man.

Callie looked at it now, seeing the *Void if not cashed within 180 days* at the top, and shook her head. *What an idiot,* she thought, and tossed the check in the trash.

Turning to face her piles of sorting, she stood with her hands on her hips and blew a lock of hair out of her face through the corner of her mouth. This was boring. Much needed work, but boring all the same. Callie hated paperwork. Sorting, filing, storing, trashing, recycling or whatever else you were supposed to do with dead trees, she hated every bit of it. But she had gotten it all out and spent the better part of two hours now trying to make a dent in it. She was mentally preparing for the fact that soon she would be leaving here. She would be moving in with her new fiancee as soon as they were married. This thought filled her with excitement. There may have been a little fear there as well, knowing her independence was about to be forfeit. But the overwhelming majority of emotion was happiness. Elation and excitement. Wonder and lust and tingles up her back thinking of his fingertips running up her bare belly. His mouth on her breasts. His hands on her hips, lips on her neck. These things came to her mind occasionally and made her feel like she needed a cool shower. Or to take a walk outside with no coat on. Frankly, she was so ready to be done with this *saving-herself* shit that she felt like she would spend at least the first month of marriage straddling her new love and giving no quarter. She planned, *frankly*, to fuck until she couldn't walk straight. She shook her head and quickly ran her hands through her hair, messing it up. Maybe a subconscious analog between being less physically attractive and thinking less about sex. Either way, it did clear her mind.

Callie looked at the bedroom window, where she had the blinds pulled open, and saw her porch light illuminating a peaceful snowfall. How nice. It would make driving to work the next day a stinky mess, but she loved it. She loved the muted sound outside when there was a carpet of snow on the ground. Back to the task at hand, she squatted and dropped back to a seat in the middle of the piles when something suddenly caught her eye. Again. *Surprises selling cheap tonight!*

It was a note the size of a generic Christmas card on creamy white stock. Callie picked up the note and read it again.

> *Callie... I look forward to hosting you on your visit, and hopefully getting to know you a little bit. I've heard so much about you – it's great to finally be meeting the legend. Enjoy the wine. Be well. ~ Cardna Darwyn*

How had she kept the note Cardna had written her on her visit to Fiji? She hadn't been able to go back into the room to collect anything. She had a vague memory of looking at it once more while she got ready that morning, and maybe slipping it in her back pocket, but found it strange that it would have ended up in this pile without her being aware of it again. But Callie also wondered *why* she would have kept it. Though she did keep a lot of things for sentimental reasons, this didn't seem like something worthy of the worry. Maybe it was Cardna's font-like script. Perfect penmanship really was attractive. Or maybe it was the part about Callie being a legend. She did like that bit. *It's great to* finally *be meeting the legend.* Finally. That word. Callie frowned and gazed at the window again. What did that word 'finally' mean? From this angle, she could not see the light from the porch, and therefore, nor the snow. But – BANG BANG BANG

"Great FUCK!" she shouted.

Callie slapped her hand to her heart and fell backward, rolling into the scattered papers. Walter stood at the window, smiling and waving like an idiot.

As he came in from the cold night, Walter stomped his feet on her rug, but Callie was instantly on him, wrapping her arms round his neck and pulling him close. "You scared the ever-living shit out of me, Walter!" she chastised, but she was rubbing her cheek against his beard stubble, as if in direct contradiction to her words. Her hands were trekking up and down the back of his felt pea coat, knocking off snowflakes and the drops of those that had melted. His hands were on her waist as he continued stomping, leaning over to allow her the full face-hug.

"GOD what are you doing here?! I missed you so much, Walt! GAAAAHHHHD!" she shouted and put her hands on his cheeks, kissing him hard on the lips, the nose, the cheeks. He was smiling and closing his eyes like the owner of a new puppy who was allowing it to lick his face.

"Haha!" he said, "Slow down, cowgirl! I'm here! I'm here!"

She had pulled him in for a full hug again, and then he stood up straight. With her arms around his neck, this picked her feet right up off the floor. Her body flattened against his. His hands were still on her waist, half on her pants and half on her skin. His thumbs were up under the hem of her shirt, stretched out from his fingers and almost reaching her belly button. Callie was laughing and scribbling nonsense into his ear at a thousand miles per minute while he stood there smiling and just letting her finish her welcome ceremony.

When she finally relaxed her hold around his neck, she slid down the front of him. Walter had not been prepared for it, happening as fast as it did, and thus failed to move his thumbs. His hands went up her sides all the way to her underarms, and his thumbs raked right across her braless breasts. Her shirt had gone up up over them, riding atop his wrists, as it were. And suddenly, there they stood, her hands behind his neck, his hands on her rib cage and thumbs on her nipples. Her eyes were locked on his gaze, mouth slightly open as she breathed him in. Her disbelief of his presence was palpable. Several long seconds passed in which neither of them said anything. But nor did either of them move. She was well aware that his hands were covering the sides of her breasts, and that her shirt was now bunched up, baring her chest to the cold air in the hallway.

She was also aware that there was still a warmth in her loins that she had not taken the time to extinguish earlier. Though it was a fire lit for another, it now burned hot for Walter, who stood staring at her through serious eyes.

He swallowed.

So did Callie.

His thumbs pivoted down. She reflexively flinched under his touch, and goose flesh suddenly covered her arms and shoulders. From the living room, Steven Wilson sang of how the summers were always slipping away. This flinch was uncontrollable. Instinctive. Unwanted. She could blame the intoxicating music.

Callie finally closed her mouth. Licked her lips.

His thumbs moved slowly back up. The response she felt against them was stronger this time. There was more to respond to. But she didn't question what he was doing. Or why. She knew it had been she who had inadvertently put his hands into this position. It had not been intentional, but it was also not unwelcome. Not as unwelcome as it should have been. Or as she should have wanted it to be.

She felt his thumbs move back down and stop on her nipples. And then her mouth was on his. Walter moved her back against the wall, one hand coming free from her breast to protect her head from a bump. His left hand though, was kneading and squeezing and caressing and doing all the things it should not be doing to her right breast. He breathed in deeply through his nose as he kissed her with a fervor she had never experienced. And she gave it back just as hard. Her hands were on his cheeks again, the tactile sensation of his whiskers against her palm every bit as intoxicating as his mouth on her own. She reached her tongue out, exploring his mouth. He met her halfway and the chills returned to her spine.

Walter's right hand finally moved down her back and grabbed a handful of her rear, squeezing and exploring. She allowed her leg to be lifted and wrapped it round his backside as his hand went lower, under her thigh, finding her soft spot. Callie cried out with a moan and intensified her kiss as his fingers began massaging that special place very few fingers had gone before. The soft cotton fabric of her pajama pants was quickly very moist between her skin and his fingertips, and then her right leg wrapped round him and she locked her ankles together. Both of his hands were now under her rear, fingers meeting in the middle working magic she had never experienced. Her back was against the wall and she suddenly felt hot and sweaty. With a deft move of her hands, she whipped her shirt up between their kiss and it disappeared into the living room, where the music played.

Callie straightened her back, which moved her chin up to rest on the top of his head, and put his face directly between her breasts. She squeezed her arms together, as if to try to make them bigger; to smother him with them. Walter turned and walked her to the edge of the living room, where he suddenly dropped her onto the couch. But as she fell backwards with a *whoop!* he took hold of the waistline of her pajamas. And faster than a flash, they were whipped from her legs and discarded. She now lay completely nude before him, looking up at him with a fire in her mind. His hands a flurry of activity, and his belt was separated. His jeans were suddenly below her level of vision, and before she knew it, he was inside her.

Callie's eyes rolled back and her breath hitched in her lungs. She arched her back up as far as she could in an effort to make as much contact with Walter's chest as she could. The sharp points of her breasts stuck up at him like they were reaching out on their own, nipples hard and covered with a sheen of his saliva mixed with her own sweat. Her hands, useless at this point, were down at her waist, just trying to touch anything. She felt the fronts of his thighs with her thumbs as he rocked into her. He pulled her knees up to her chest for full access to the woman below him. With the backs of her ankles on his shoulders, Walter moved quickly, and not without a little roughness that shook her head against the couch cushion behind her and caused her breasts to jiggle like plucked rubber bands. Her mouth was fully open and she was trying to cry out. Trying to put some voice to her ecstasy – her approval – but she could not cry out. There was no voice to be had. There was no breath to support it. Her entire body was locked in a state of such incredible pleasure that she could not even breathe. Under any other circumstance, she might have found a way to feel frightened. As it stood though, she was beginning to quiver and feel warm like parts of her were burning. She felt it first in her stomach, but it quickly spread like a gasoline fire to her loins and up into her thighs. Walter grabbed her ankles and spread them out as he fell on top of her, and he was sucking on her neck. His strokes became faster and harder and her panting more and more shallow. Her eyes opened wide and she tried to scream, but again, nothing came out. And then a bolt of lightning suddenly shot from her inner thighs all the way down to her feet and she was finally able to catch her breath. She screamed his name and lifted her arms above her head as he moved his own head down and licked her from her rib cage, over her breast and all the way up her neck to her open mouth. "Walter! Oh fuck, Walter! Oh God!" she cried as she was suddenly freed of a large part of him, and her stomach was being covered with his essence. Her body wracked with wave after wave of bliss. She closed her eyes again and her face contorted as if she were in a great amount of pain as she rode the waves that lit her arms and chest and face and neck and breasts on fire. She brought her hands forward and grabbed Walter's arms as he hovered above her. Her hands came to rest on his hard triceps and she was coming again. He kissed her lips and open mouth as she quietly repeated his name over and over. She could feel his tongue on the inside of her lips, quick little dashes as he tasted different parts of her mouth. The warmth slowly spread from her center like the ripple on a placid lake after a stone thrown in. And then it started to cool as the final jerks and trembles rippled through her tight thighs. A thin sheen of sweat now covered her entire body.

She was breathing heavily, holding tightly to his triceps and looking him in the eyes, watching his blue eyes stare back at her as he panted, completely unsmiling.

"Holy fuck, Walter. What have we done." It wasn't a question. It was a statement.

Between gasps of hot air, his pelvis still mashed right up against her own, he was licking his lips. She was slowly grinding against him, wanting more of that incredible sensation that had seemed to last forever only a few seconds ago.

"I don't know," he said seriously. "But maybe something we should have done twenty years ago."

CHAPTER 18

Callie sat on the edge of the couch, her knees together, face buried in her palms. Her messy hair spilled out between her fingers. She cradled a square couch cushion between her thighs and belly, but was otherwise completely devoid of any kind of covering. Walter lay a foot-and-a-half away on his chest, arms spread wide on the couch, and face turned away. He might have been snoring lightly in a post-coital daze.

"Why did we do that, Walter?"

It took him a moment to answer. He was still out of breath. "Well, it was bound to happen sooner or later. It just happened later."

"Bound to? Why was it bound to, Walt? What the hell?"

He turned his head and put his hand on her thigh. She reached down and pushed it away, feeling decidedly *yucky* at the moment. Yucky inside, yucky in her heart and yucky between her thighs. Quick glimpses of the event shot through her head, reminding her that it had not felt yucky – had felt anything *but* yucky, in fact – while they had been entangled.

"Why was it 'bound to' happen?" Callie said, making quotes with her fingers. "We've never crossed that line before. We've been best friends for twenty years now."

"I know, Callie," he said, rolling onto his side and propping his head up with the hand he'd used to touch her. "I just mean, it's a natural human thing. People have sex."

"Not us, Walter!" she shouted. "God! You're married! I'm engaged, for F sakes!" She was now shaking her head, fingers still splayed across her face. "What am I going to tell Jack? And what will you tell Thevi?"

Walter held a hand up, quickly changing his demeanor. "Whoa, Cal. Hold it. We can't tell them anything."

Callie looked angrily over at her friend, a frown consuming her visage. "How in the world…"

"Callie," he said, patting the air between them with his hand. He sat up and turned toward her, tried to take her hand. She pulled it quickly away. "Callie, we cannot tell them. I'm sorry if you think this shouldn't have happened, but-"

"If I *think*? Walter! Don't you effing think? What is wrong with you?" she snapped. She was feeling a coldness growing in her belly now. What if the others found out anyway? She knew she did not want to end up with Walter, so she would have to start over. All alone again. Though she could not say precisely why she didn't want to be with him, it just didn't feel right. None of this did.

"Yes. Cal, I don't think it's the *wrongest* thing in the world. It's better it was with you than some other woman. And don't you think in your thing with Jack that if it's going to happen with someone-"

"MY THING WITH JACK? My *thing?*" she said shoving him atop the head. A palm to the forehead. He deserved a lot worse.

"Callie, you're taking every word I say literally. Please stop. Just calm down. I just mean that if it were going to happen, isn't it good that it was between us two that it did?"

"No, Walter!" she shouted, standing up. Callie brought the pillow up with her, covering her private parts as she stood, but left her breasts completely exposed. She felt very vulnerable, but the anger was beginning to burn it up. "It wasn't *going to happen.* I would never ever have done this with anyone."

Walter made a face and crossed his arms, leaning back into a proper sitting position on the couch. She noticed he made no move to hide his secret places. The place that had been secret to her for the last twenty years. "Well then why with me?" he finally said, looking up at her.

Callie was breathing heavily, staring holes into him. Her anger was almost a physically tangible thing in the room. She noticed, with equal parts disappointment and appreciation, that Walter was concentrating hard on her eyes, and not letting his own drop to her chest, where she still stood out like fireworks against a dark sky. The cold air was making things ultra-visible.

As she stood here staring at him though, Callie began to remember who she was staring at. She was not staring at a one-night-stand. Not a stranger or a coworker. She was staring at one of the most important friends of her life. They had made a mistake together. And maybe he was right. Maybe it was good that it had happened with him. Though she could not imagine anyone else ever getting close enough to take something from her like this, she did have to admit that he was as safe as it could be, considering the circumstances. But she still felt horrible inside. She had just recently been engaged to Jack, and now she was heading the wrong way.

Callie finally breathed out and broke eye-contact, pulling her hair back behind her ear with one hand. "I guess Darwyn was right," she said levelly.

"About what? The dichotomy between monogamy and the evolutionary trait to reproduce?" Walter said, running a hand through his own hair.

"What the hell?" Callie said, screwing up her face. "No. Cardna Darwyn. She said I'm one of those people who only feels right when I'm facing north."

Walter spread his hands, a gesture that said *well why the fuck didn't you just say that, then?* He crossed his arms again, shaking his head. "Still. Charles Darwin was right. I mean," he said, leaning his head forward a little to emphasize the change of gears, "not about us coming from apes, but definitely about the sex thing."

"What the hell are you on about?" Callie said, shaking her head again. *Is this man crazy?*

Walter glanced at her again, but this time his eyes darted to her chest for just a split second before he returned his gaze to the floor in front of him. It had been an instinctive peek. "I mean, he said monogamy is not evolutionarily instinctive. We are literally *wired* to go out and have sex. And when women are no longer able to produce, they start becoming unattractive. What with menopause and all, they grow hair on their faces, they-"

She cut him off again. "Walter!"

"Hey," he said, holding a hand out to her, "You're still attractive!"

"You're not helping things!" Callie shouted. She was leaning forward pretty heavily, still trying to keep the pillow over her crotch. Though she didn't know why. He had seen – and had, now – all of her. "Why in the hell would I want to talk about evolution right now? About Charles Darwin?"

"Hey, you brought him up!"

"No, I didn't! I brought up Cardna!"

"I don't even know who that is, Callie," Walter said, trying to be patient. "I was just saying that monogamy isn't natural. It's a moral one has to practice. It's not easy. It takes an amazing amount of will-power and strength." He met eyes with her and she didn't say anything. She was allowing him to go on. "So we, as humans, don't always get it right.

Our evolutionary instinct is to fuck. It's only a moral code that keeps us from doing it."

Callie swallowed. Of course, she knew all this. But it did help to hear it. Every time her thoughts returned to Jack, though, she felt that sinking feeling in her chest again. A sudden emptiness that felt like a tractor had slammed into her chest, and that everything was going to end suddenly, and badly.

"Besides," he said, motioning toward her nether regions, "It's not like it's your first time."

"What makes you say that?" Callie said.

"You would have bled if I had taken your virginity," Walter said, matter-of-fact.

Callie nodded toward the carpet in front of the couch, where five minutes ago, her ass had been hanging over the edge as he slapped against her bodily. Crudely. In that disgusting act of fornication. Walter followed her gaze and leaned forward, peeking over the edge of the couch. When he saw the spots of blood on the carpet, his face went white. His eyes widened and he sat up straight, looking suddenly like he'd seen a ghost.

"Oh my God. I'm so sorry, Callie. I didn't know." He was shaking his head. Then after a moment, he stood up and embraced her. Held her head against his shoulder as she broke down and let it all out.

Callie stood in the bathroom drying her hair off while Walter showered behind her. While she had not yet completely restored her propriety – for she was standing here naked – she was quickly asserting her authority on the matter. He had asked, for instance, why not shower together. Save water. Callie had rolled her eyes and said 'forget it' while reaching in and turning the knobs. "This can never happen again, Walter."

Now as he stood under the hot water, not three feet away from her, he pleaded his case. "I understand what you mean. I mean, yeah, we can't make a habit of this."

"No. Not what I said, Walt. It can absolutely never happen again," Callie repeated. She got the feeling he had liked it a little too much, and was trying to shim his way into a semi-regular routine. Or at least a blue-moon tryst.

"Okay, okay. But you have to tell me that you understand – we can also *never* tell the others."

Callie breathed in through her nose, getting close to the mirror to examine the pores on her face. But she was reserving her answer. Maybe she needed to hear what he said. While she automatically agreed with what he was saying, she thought that maybe it should not be automatic. Maybe she should consider it. There was some merit to the argument. She felt pretty sure that Thevi would leave Walter if she found out. But what of Jack? And this played into Walter's argument, that he had been preaching for the last ten minutes. It had happened. *Now,* it had happened. There was nothing they could do about that, short whipping out the time machine. When he had said that bit, Callie had stared holes into him, for he had looked at her expectantly, as if maybe there was a chance she still had the quantum computer. She had had to remind him that it, like Amalie London's error, had disappeared like a dream in the sunlight.

But it *had* happened. Nothing could change that. So either move on, accepting that it was now part of their past, or dwell on it. Neither was easy. But one certainly had fewer repercussions. The problem was, Callie wasn't sure if she could live with the guilt. She could not remember if she had ever told Jack directly that she and Walter had never slept together. She had told him, of course, many times, that she had no romantic feelings for him, and that they had never been a couple. But had she directly ever come out and said, '*Look, Jack, we've never had sex!*'? Because if she had said that in their past at some point, then she could not – *would not* – contradict herself. She did not want to lie. But if she had not said it, then if the subject ever did arise, she could say they had coupled once in their past. And that was the truth. If he asked her when it had happened, however…

Could Callie live with the guilt though? Knowing? Hiding a secret from the one she loved? What about her part with Thevi? Thevi was her best friend. Could she hide that secret from her dearest, closest friend? *I've slept with your husband now.* What would cookouts be like? The fire pit Friday nights? Girls' shopping trips? Just sitting in the craft room while Thevi sewed her pillowcases and drapes and Callie kept her company, reading a book or just holding a cup of coffee and watching? Girls' time together, the men in the den watching *Western Wagons* reruns on a Sunday afternoon? Would it not be awkward now? Would that secret not be burning in Callie's mind the entire time she was with Thevi? And not only in her mind, but in the *front* of her mind… Ahead and on top of all the other thoughts.

Oh yeah, that looks good. I like the gold trim better than the bronze. I fucked your husband on my couch. That's my favorite so far. I like tassels you put on the corners. Your husband and I had sex while it snowed outside.

Callie shook her head, then turned and leaned against the counter, arms crossed over her chest. The water in the shower turned off. But Walter had not spoken again yet, until he said, "Callie, can you hand me a towel?" poking his head out the glass door. She bent over and fetched one out of the cabinet, aware that he was probably staring at her ass while she did it, and somehow not caring. What was the point? Now that he had been inside her, why hide herself from his view? She handed him the towel and considered that. Was this how it would be from now on? Any time they were alone together, she would shed the old prude posture? She would lose her modesty when he was around just because he had had her? Surely not. Surely this was a twenty-minute window that was about to close, and then her modesty – her tact – would return to normal.

Then Walter stepped out of the shower and stood directly in front of her. Callie could not help but glance down and see his ridiculous trunk hanging only inches from her own parts. That split where it had fit so perfectly a little while ago. He stood drying his face and hair, naked in front of naked, close enough for it to happen again. Her arms were still crossed, forming the only barrier that stood between them, but her breathing was already getting heavier.

"There would be absolutely no benefit in telling anyone about it, Cal," he said, as if he were oblivious to the situation in front of him.

"Yeah, I'm thinking about it, Walter. I'm not going to rush out and tell anyone. I have to sleep on this and see how I feel in the morning."

He stopped his toweling and looked at her wide-eyed. She reached out and put a hand on his chest. "I won't say anything ever though, unless you and I have talked first. Okay?"

He finally nodded. Why was she still standing here in front of him, naked as unpainted furniture? Why was she comfortable with it? Was this the new her? And comfortable was a funny word. It was more than just a lack of discomfort. She was feeling the tingling in her soft spot below again. Sideways, Callie worried that if she didn't move soon, she would need another shower.

Then he leaned in and kissed her softly on the mouth. She closed her eyes and allowed it. Just this once! It wasn't a cinematic kiss with a lot of movement and tongue, touching of the cheek, pinching the nipples. It was just an open-mouthed kiss. Every bit as erotic as any of the others, but very soft in its harsh reality. Very tame against the backdrop of their recent history. And it only lasted a few seconds. Then he closed his mouth and broke the kiss. Callie opened her eyes, again breathing heavily. Noting internally that her nipples were like daggers now. The chill up her spine was not a good sign. She was likely going to have to end her friendship with this man, or she would never be able so quash this desire. For, at the end of it all, beneath the blanket of all the feel-good thoughts and pep-talks that told her she planned on doing the right thing for the rest of her life, there was a coal-fire burning. At the bottom of all the forced emotion and prudence doctrine, she did have desire. She wanted this man again. And badly.

It was almost, Callie realized somewhere deep inside her head, as if the desire she had contemplated earlier in the evening regarding Jack had all been an illusion. The desire – the lust – had been real. But she had Photoshopped Jack's face over Walter's in her daydream. Now the facade was peeling back and she was seeing what was really there. As if she had wanted Walter all along. Maybe all of it. Maybe even the love. The in-love. Maybe it was all for him, all along, and she just had not realized it.

Because Callie knew one thing was certain. Had Walter put his hand on her waist, pulled himself closer to her as she leaned against the counter, putting his pelvis against hers, allowing the two to meet again, she would not have stopped him. She would have allowed him to lift her bodily up onto the counter, stepping between her thighs and taking her again right there. Her hands would have wrapped round behind his neck. His hands would have found her chest again. And she would stare into his eyes as he performed that magic trick down below her waist – making a rather obscenely large part of himself disappear inside her. And she would have watched that, too. With great fascination.

Yes, this was a bad sign, all right. She was feeling things that were only recognizable to those who had been had. Images like flash-cards deep in her mind were popping up, but what had been only shapes her whole life, now had labels on them. She now knew exactly what these trembling shivers meant. What the response on the tips of her breasts represented. What the tingle that ran that trail from her navel to just below the soft patch of blonde hair actually meant. Like her eyes had been opened to a whole new world. A veil had been pulled off, the curtain torn asunder – and now, she understood. She had missed a good twenty years of her life having something so wonderful, and so easily attained, that she wondered how she could possibly have ever thought it a good idea to abstain.

It would be so easy to fall into a pattern here. Here, and now, only a few minutes after her first sexual encounter and she was already wanting it again. God! Would it always be this hard? Callie tried to reassert her willpower. She had to be the strong one if there were any hope of salvaging anything now. She turned around, putting her bottom toward him. Which, in retrospect, was probably not much better. She had actually felt it brush against his excitement. He was obviously hoping her will would break down and let him in again. But then where would it stop? Would it ever end? Or would they be on a never-ending, unavoidable track full of frequent weekend rendezvouses? Hiding something that should never have been brought into the world?

"Walter, please step back," she finally said. And he did as he was told. Thank heaven and holy God above, he did as he was told. Because she would not have been angry at him if he hadn't.

They were dressed now. Callie was in fresh pajamas, wrapped in a robe to keep anything from poking through the thin fabric. Walter was back in his jeans and sweater. He leaned against the wall across the room, his legs straight out in front of him, crossed at the ankles. Callie was again sitting in the middle of her piles of paper.

"Who was this Darwin gal you mentioned earlier?" he said. The calm had finally begun to settle back over her spirit. The warmth – nay, the fire – had been raging inside her so hot that she had worried the only way to put it out would be to do the horrible deed again. But it had subsided. It had taken twenty minutes or so – and Callie had timed it. She was monitoring in a not-quite-subconscious way for a scientific purpose. She needed to know what she would be dealing with in the future if she felt those stirrings again. Oh, God, those stirrings. They were part of her life now. Dammit all to hell, Walter!

She breathed slowly, patiently working through the stacks and trying to keep her eyes off of him. This was a temporary resolution. She would obviously not spend the rest of her life – or her night, for that matter – trying to avoid his gaze. Just for now.

"Cardna. When I was flown into the complex, she had been the one who came to get me in the helicopter."

"She's a pilot?" Walter asked.

"No. She was on the helicopter with two men. They came and got me from where the taxi had dropped me off."

Callie could hear Walter's confusion without even looking up at him. So she explained to him how she had come to Fiji, and the zig-zagging maze of a trek she had taken to get to the plant. And then she answered the question that she knew he was bound to ask. "I don't know why they arranged it like that. Camrie had gotten me a badge and set up the travel arrangements to get me down there. The note she had texted me told me where to go in the taxi, when to expect the helicopter and all that."

Callie pulled her hair back on both sides of her head, with both hands, sighing. "And when Rebecca got there, she got a rental car and drove right into the parking garage."

Walter was silent. Callie finally met his eyes. He was chewing his lip.

"I really need to work through this, Walter."

He smiled, exasperation in his countenance. "I know, hon," he said, patting the air in front of him. "We'll get through it."

"No, you dumb dork, not the sex. The mystery. Why did they fly me into the place on a chopper in the dark?"

Walter frowned, putting his hand down and leaning his head back against the wall. "Oh. Well, I would think that was obvious. They didn't want you knowing how to get back there yourself."

Callie shook her head. "But Rebecca was able to find it, so why wouldn't I be able to?"

He stared blankly at her. "They didn't count on Rebecca coming to your aid."

She shook her head again, this time putting her hands on the sides of it. "No. I know that. But she was able to find it. So whether or not they expected her to come help me, she showed that the compound was findable," Callie said, waving at the made-up word.

He lifted his chin now, and looked the ceiling. "I got ya. Yeah, that makes sense." After a moment, he returned his gaze to Callie's. "But the point remains. Weak defense strategy, but doesn't mean it wasn't realistic. They were probably just doing what they could to keep you at bay. You know, like, to make sure you didn't have a car there?"

Callie raised her eyebrows. "So you're saying they had never planned to let me leave…"

He shrugged. "Maybe. But having a car there, or having a car rented in your name… That kind of leaves a paper trail. I don't know. Who knows what they were really thinking?"

Callie stared at Walter for a long time. "What are you doing here, Walter? I didn't get a chance to ask you earlier." She felt herself blush as the unspoken reason for the interruption flashed in her mind.

"I got out this evening. Thevi took me home. We ate, then I said I had to come talk to you."

Callie raised her eyebrows. Walter understood this to mean, talk to me?

"Yeah," he said, nodding. "I tried calling first, but you didn't answer. So I came over. We've got business to discuss. I've been locked up for six fuckin' months. There's shit we need to talk about."

"Well, I agree with you there. But why did you bang on my window?"

He shook his head quickly, waving in the general direction of the front door. "I banged on the front door, goof ball. You couldn't hear me 'cause of the music!" Duh!

"Oh, yeah," Callie said, suddenly looking around for her phone. She couldn't remember where she had last seen it. Probably on the kitchen counter or something. Or in a box of raisin bran. She had to roll her eyes at that. She giggled at the memory.

"What's so funny?" he said.

"Nothing," she said. But added anyway, "That night we met Minus at Brokeback Fountain?" she said, waiting for his nod before she continued. "When he called and told me to meet him there, I dropped my phone into the tub. I couldn't find a box of rice, so I dropped my phone into a box of raisin bran. I found it several months later and it scared the bejeezus out of me!"

Walter chuckled, lifting his chin. "So what's our plan, Calgirl?"

"I told you, Walter, we can't ever do it again. And I'd rather not keep rehashing it."

Walter sighed and rolled his eyes. "God damn, woman. You're the only one still thinking about the sex. I'm talking about your plan for Brian Bradley."

"Oh," she said, suddenly embarrassed. "Oh, yeah. Sorry." She swallowed. "Well, I have to go back," Callie started, but held up a hand in defense, a gesture meant to stop his interrupting her train of thought. But Walter didn't interrupt. He just stared at her. "Not like, right now or anything. Or anytime soon, for that matter. But I have to go back. There's just too many unanswered questions down there. And I have to find someone to go with me."

"Who the fuck else do you need to go with you?" Walter said, holding his hands out.

"Walter, I'm not going down there by myself."

"Callie, why the hell would you think I wouldn't be part of your team?"

"Oh," she said, then stopped. She swallowed. They would be alone in a different – exotic – part of the world. Together. Alone. Probably staying in adjoining hotel rooms, if there were hotel rooms to be had in the trip. Alone. Callie took a deep breath. *One minute at a time, sister.*

After a few covertly taken deep breaths, she concentrated on pulling her hair into a ponytail – though it would never stay in one because it was too short – and said, "I just guess I assumed you couldn't leave the country or something."

"Yeah, I don't worry too much about that shit."

Callie chewed her thumb for a moment. She had absently picked up an old photograph. It was not black-and-white, but it could have been. It was early-color photography. Back when they'd first started making color film – faded and washed looking. In it stood a woman in a red-checked dress leaning over with her arm around the tiny shoulders of a little blond girl. Bob cut, smiling against the sun. Callie's heart leapt in her chest momentarily. *Holy cow, it's my mom.*

"Do you want to see a picture of me with my mom, Walter?"

Walter leaned forward quickly, like he had been offended. Like someone about to attack. "You bet your fuckin' wallet I do."

Walter knew the story of Callie's childhood. Mom died when Callie was a teenager. Dad left before she took her first steps. He knew Callie had tried to reconnect with dad in her twenties. Likely, right about the time Walter and Callie were meeting. He also knew that it hadn't been anything to get excited over. Once a deserter, always a deserter. A father who would leave his perfect pudgy little darling baby girl in the first place was not man enough to suddenly be a good dad when she was older. Callie's mom, though short-lived, had at least loved the girl.

He took the picture from her and held it by a corner, staring long and hard at it. Callie watched him, sitting on the carpet with her hands on her ankles, which were pretzeled up under her. She was nervously running her thumbs over the ankle bones. Much the same way Walter had run his over her… She took a deep breath, shook the sparks out of her brain.

"Is this the only picture you have?" he finally said, looking up at her soberly.

Callie nodded. "Yeah. I think so. I didn't even remember having it. I haven't seen it in years and years."

"What was her name?"

"Elaine Madeline Carter. Née Simmons."

"You never took his name. But she did?" Walter asked, handing the photograph back to her.

Callie nodded.

Walter smirked, a mischievous little number that made Callie blush. "Gotta admit, Callie Carter would have sounded pretty bad ass."

She allowed herself to smile, and somewhere behind the thoughts, the name Callie Carpenter appeared. Would that still be her last name soon? Her heart had dropped into her stomach, a sick and twisting pit that seemed to be eating all her emotions and spitting out nervousness and fidgets.

"Yup. This is the only photograph I have of her anymore. Well, that I've ever had. I'm sure she had some, but I never ended up with any of them." She looked at the picture again, ran her thumb over her mother's long-gone smile, and tossed the picture in the To Keep pile.

"Why did you come here tonight, Walt?"

He had pulled his knees up and now sat with them caged in by his muscular arms, hand-over wrist. "Because, like I said, we have six months to catch up on. I didn't come here to... *take* anything from you, if that's what you're wondering."

She squinted and shook her head, displaying a weak smile. "Uh-uh. I just wondered what business you meant." After a long silence filled with them staring seriously into each other's eyes, she finally said, "Walter, have you ever been to Fiji?"

He shook his head.

"Cardna took me to this weird cabin-like place while I was there. Ostensibly to get away from far-hearing ears. Said it was for privacy. But it was the weirdest place. Only like ten minutes outside the gates, and down this dirt road in the forest. Like, you couldn't see it at all from the road. And I don't even know if there was electricity in it."

Walter was frowning. But he stayed quiet.

"Anyway, we talked there for like thirty minutes, maybe. Then we drove back. And that's when she locked me in a room with no door handle." Callie had spent quite a bit of time over the last few months filling Walter in on all the things she had experienced in Fiji. But she had not told him about the cabin until now. "What significance do you think that place might have played? I mean, don't you think we could have just stepped outside if she was really worried someone was listening?" Callie slapped her knees lightly with open palms, like she were taking up the timpani. "I mean, are there like microphones in the building, in every room? What the heck?"

Walter was furling his mouth, looking at the piles on the floor in front of him. Setting his analytical brain to work on the problem like a bloodhound set loose to look for missing children. He was running his fingertips over his beard stubble, repeating the motion over and over. A new, subconscious gesture he had picked up, apparently.

Callie looked up at the window, that not two hours ago had introduced Walter back into her life. The shock and the bang and the scare of seeing a ghostly figure just appear now sent chills up her spine as she remembered it. Again, she noticed how she could not even tell it was snowing out there. It was too dark. And too bright in here. The juxtaposition of the darkness against the light, with only a cold pane of glass in between made it a one-way view. She would either have to stand up and put the porch light into her line of sight, or put her hands right up to the glass to see through it. It was all about one's perspective. You just had to...

And Callie caught it at exactly the same moment as Walter. Their eyes locked and his mouth opened. But she spoke first. "Maybe the cabin was where they listened in."

Then he nodded, and said, "Yes. It's a place made to make people feel safe. Get them to talk. Maybe it looked primitive to lull you into complacence."

"Hidden mics in the walls. Cameras, even."

Walter was nodding. "Surely, that's got to be it. Why else would she take you there?"

"That freaking B-word!" Callie said, and Walter laughed out loud.

CHAPTER 19

Callie awoke with a start, grasping her pillow against her chest. The sun shone through the window. How long had it been since Callie slept until the sun was up? She glanced side-to-side on the bed, making sure she hadn't made any more mistakes last night. Making sure it had just... *been the one*. Her heart skipped a beat and her chest flooded with cold guilt. She was already shaking her head and grieving and her day had not yet begun.

Reaching her arms over her head, she grabbed the top of the headboard and pulled her chest into an arching, back-crackling stretch. She kicked the covers down to below her feet and sat up, then pulled her hair back. Having not put it away properly after her shower the night before, it was wild and exotic, and larger than life. Looking down at her chest, she realized she was in a state of attention once again. When would this end? Had he awakened some nerve or something that permanently put her on display? She grabbed handfuls of herself, not in a sexual way, trying to get them to stand down. But they were on edge and felt ready to be caressed. Like they were yearning for more attention. She quickly stopped and buried her face in her hands. This was bad. What had she done?

Callie felt like a machine had compressed her into a tiny ball of stress and anxiety. She had never had to worry about these feelings of guilt before, and thus did not know how long they would last. Or if they might be permanent residents now. The question was not *what had she done*, but rather, *what would she do*? It did not feel possible to move on with her life without putting this behind her. And the only way to do that was to tell the others what had happened. Suffer the risk of break-up with Jack, and possibly losing Thevi as a friend. But it seemed the more noble approach then moving on and acting like nothing had happened. Her heart was beating in a way she was not used to. This guilt felt like a heavy blanket. She picked her phone up to call Walter. Shaking her head, she said, "Hello, Robot."

The phone chimed.

"Call Walter Watson," she said. The feeling in her chest was rising to her throat. It was hot and restrictive. She shrugged the blankets off around her.

'Calling Walter Watson, mobile,' said the device in its semi-British accent.

He answered on the first ring.

"Walter, I can't do this. We have to tell the others."

She could hear Walter breathe in deeply on the other side of the line. A long, heavy-hearted sigh. "Yeah, I was thinking the same thing. Is it eating you alive?"

Callie nodded, then said, "Yeah. That's a good way to put it."

"So what are you thinking?"

She was flicking her thumbnail across her top teeth. "I think a group chat. Let's all get together. Someone's living room. Not a public place."

Walter sat silent for a while. "All four of us together, or should we start as couples?"

"I think we do it once. In the company of everyone. Give Thevi a chance to confront me. And Jack, you."

Walter was shaking his head. Callie could almost sense it. But he wasn't disagreeing. At least not vocally. After another sigh, he asked, "When?"

"The sooner the better."

Callie and Jack rode separately to Walter's house. And while she was trying not to make it seem like something big was about to go down, she could not think of an active way to downplay the ceremony. Instead, she passively coordinated the meeting, and they all made their way to the den. In Walter's house, the den was a formal sitting area, separate from the living room, where he had his television. The den was warm and cozy. He had his stereo in here. His turntable and his enormous record collection. The hundreds-of-dollars speakers on stands that stood comically several feet out from the walls. Thevi was sitting legs crossed under her in a high-back chair, lap covered with a blanket, while Walter had opted for pacing. Great. Talk about actively advertising.

Callie came in and leaned in to hug Thevi. She did not get much of a return hug. Maybe she already knew. A wife's instinct, Callie reckoned, was probably as strong as a mother's. And Callie was neither.

She found a seat in a large bean bag that probably cost over a thousand dollars. Its shroud was a thick suede, and had enough room on it for two adults. Jack, however, opted for the other high-back chair. Callie stared at Walter. Surprisingly, there was no music playing. Callie couldn't remember a time in her life that she had been over here and there had *not* been music playing at least somewhere in the house. Thevi's King Crimson, or Walter's Kings of Leon. Someone always had the background music. Not today. Today it was somber.

The den wasn't dark, but with the lighting style Walter had built into the crown moulding, it was indirect. And at the moment, it was tuned to a warm chocolate color reflecting off the cream-colored ceiling. This made for a near-dark atmosphere, casting a dim pall over the room. Callie already felt sick at her stomach. Riddled with guilt and already not good at confrontations, she was likely to self-combust.

Walter finally stopped pacing and put his hands on his hips. "Callie and I had planned to make an announcement today." Callie tried not to frown at this surprising news. If she were supposed to be playing along, Walter had forgotten to give her the script. She swallowed. "We plan to go to Fiji together. Her, again. Me, for the first time. To try to get done what she wasn't able to with the help of Bec last time. But that's become a secondary reason for the conference today."

And before he said it, Thevi bowed her head into an open hand, staring at her lap and letting out a loud *sssshhh* sound. Walter glanced at her quickly – they all did – but it was immediately obvious she was not shushing him. She was expelling anger.

Walter was nodding. Jack was staring at him, hands on his thighs and his left leg bouncing excitedly beside the ottoman. A nervous tic if there ever was one. Walter made eye-contact with the other man, then at Callie. Thevi was still not showing her face.

"Yeah. No easy way to say it," he said.

"We made a mistake last night," Callie blurted out, and Thevi's face shot up, red and full of anger.

"It's not a fucking mistake! It's fucking adultery!" she shouted.

Callie swallowed hard and saw peripherally that Jack was lost.

"Yes, honey, it *was* a mistake," Walter said. Callie saw Thevi's anger shift directly to him. Good. *Get that evil visage off of me,* Callie thought. She was breathing heavily, heart slamming in her chest.

Jack said quietly, as if to start a private conversation leaving out the other couple, "Babe? What's going on?"

Callie looked him square in the eye, and could feel her own rage. Anger at herself. Tears burned the corners of her eyes. But she couldn't answer. At least not before Thevi took the reigns for her.

"You don't know, Jack? They fucked last night! My husband over here," she shouted, her hand flinging out toward Walter, "put his dick alllll the way up inside your fiancee!"

"Come on," Walter said, making a sour face. "We don't need to be crude about it."

"You think I'm being crude, asshole?" Thevi said. "So it's okay for you to do it, but I can't call it by its proper name? You fuck?!" This last she said spitting with the harsh F, and twisting her ring off her finger. She threw the ring at Walter, hard. It hit him square in the chest and dropped to the floor at his feet. Thevi whipped the blanket off her lap and stormed out of the room. Momentarily, a door slammed in the back. Meanwhile, Jack was laying his head back against the headrest of the chair.

Walter paced some more, then squatted and lowered himself slowly onto the ottoman in front of the chair where Thevi had been sitting. His knees creaked. *Are we getting that old?* Callie thought.

"I'm sorry, man. Really, I am," Walter said, holding a hand out toward Jack as if to offer him a plate of ribs.

"What the hell happened?" Jack finally said plaintively. There was visible pain in his eyes, though no tears had shown up yet.

Callie, however, though she was trying to hold them back, had them running freely down her cheeks. She was trembling, fidgeting. Spinning the ring on her left hand with the fingers of her right. "Well," she said, taking a deep breath. "Walter came over last night because he couldn't get me on the phone. I was," she said, clearing her throat and glancing at Walter. He sat silently, staring at her with hopeless eyes. "I was sorting through some files," Callie started again and was interrupted.

"Look at me, please," Jack said, not forcefully.

She did. He deserved that much. She swallowed again. "Well, I was sitting in my room and had left my phone in the kitchen. Since I couldn't hear it, he came over." Callie adjusted in her seat, then returned her eyes to Jack's. "Well, I was happy to see him. When he came through the front door, I hugged him. I haven't seen him without glass between us in six months. So," she said, glancing at Walter again, then back to Jack. "So it just sort of happened from there."

Jack was chewing his bottom lip. "Sort of happened. So he goes away for half a year, and a hug undoes twenty years of 'nothing-but-friends' between you two?" he said, looking at Walter now.

Walter scoffed silently. An almost smile was on his lips.

"What's so funny, Watson?" Jack said.

"Nothing's funny, bro. But don't take that tone as if it weren't a real thing."

"Come again?" Jack said.

"Your cutesy little name for it. Twenty years. Yes. It was real. We had twenty years of absolute solid friendship. With nothing to hide."

Jack nodded. "My point. It comes undone that easily with, what? With a hug?" he said, offering that plate of ribs to Callie now. This imagery almost made her chuckle. She was able to push it down though. But the thought that she could have a chuckle at a moment like this made her wonder, in less than an instant of thought, why she wasn't a wreck over potentially losing this man. Did she care? The thoughts she had chased around her head last night had involved a lot of Walter. And a lot of him doing things to her in a lot of ways. And none of them had disgusted her. None of them had turned her off. And none of them had involved Jack.

"I guess so," she said finally.

Jack breathed in deeply. "You see, it's not the one time that necessarily worries me. It's the thought that now you've started something. Like it could happen again. And again."

Callie shrugged. Wherein coming into this duck hunt, she had pictured herself being a sobbing, gasping wreck of a woman, pleading on her knees for Jack not to leave her. To give her another chance. But now, sitting in front of him, she felt a little more aloof. A little less concerned of repercussion. Like, *oh well. Whatever may be may be.* This was rolling off her shoulders. Like she had made the high jump, and that was the hard part. Coming down was the easy part. And maybe now, she felt like she was coming down onto something safe. Something secure. Something that had maybe been there. For twenty years or so.

"It might or might not," Walter said. Callie's eyes shot toward him. "We can promise all day that it won't ever happen again. But we didn't see it coming this time. How can we say it won't again?"

Jack was shaking his head. "You guys really aren't making this easy to swallow," he said, leaning back again.

"Not trying to, Jack," Callie said. She glanced at Walter, who was nodding subtly. "Just trying to get it out there. It's the hardest thing I've ever done. And he's right," Callie said, again moving her eyes between the two men. "I never ever thought it would happen between the two of us. Not ever. But it did. So how can I even be sure myself," she said, putting a hand on her heart, "that it won't again."

"Unreal," Jack said.

"I'm not sure why you'd say that. See, it's not that I had to deny myself of Walter for half of my life. I didn't sit here and contemplate it. I just never thought of him in a sexual way. I didn't *try not to*, I just never thought of it at all. So when it suddenly happens, it made me aware that maybe it was waiting there all along. Who knows if I'll be strong enough to push it away in the future."

Jack breathed in deeply and stood up. "Well, thank you for your honesty. I do gotta admit, it takes a big person," he spun toward Walter, "a big man, to admit it." He shook his head. "Really. That's some serious courage." He stood there for a moment with his hands in his pockets, and then pulled up his jeans and approached Walter. "See you around, buddy." They shook hands. Walter had stood as he was approaching.

Then Jack turned to Callie. "May I have my ring back, please?"

Callie swallowed and removed it. She held it up in front of her, dangling it between her dainty fingertips. And without a word, Jack took it. After a few seconds, they heard the front door shut lightly, and Callie and Walter were alone.

Most of Callie's nervousness had passed by the time she trekked down the hall to where Thevi had shut herself in. The hard part was done. Facing the initial wrath had taken most of her courage. She had trembled and sweat that all out now, though. But she still felt duty-bound to face Thevi personally. To personally acknowledge the damage her actions had caused, and to apologize to her friend. With these things in mind, Callie reached up and knocked lightly on the door. So she was almost startled with surprise when Thevi actually opened it.

Callie breathed in slowly, then sucked her lips in, hiding them completely from sight. Maybe a subconscious analog to shriveling away herself, tail tucked between her legs. "Thevi, I want you to know this wasn't personal."

Thevi squinted. Her eyes were still red and full of tears. Her cheeks were red, wet and swollen. But she still looked gorgeous to Callie. Her pale complexion and fire-red hair was striking, no matter her mood. She was squinting hard at Callie. So Callie went on.

"This was not an action taken against you. Or Jack," she said, tossing her head back toward the direction whence she had come. "I've lost him, by the way." She waited for something. Maybe a little sympathy? Callie didn't know. She wasn't firing on all cylinders at the moment. She pressed on. "He took the ring back." Thevi was chewing hard on her bottom lip now. Only her face and a sliver of her body were visible through the crack in the door. She was leaning on the opening.

"My point is that we did not do this to hurt you or Jack. I did not want to lose him. And I don't want Walter to lose you. It was a selfish act, in the very strictest, most literal definition of the word. We were only thinking of ourselves."

"You mean each other," Thevi said in a hoarse whisper.

Callie swallowed and nodded, accepted it. "Yeah, I guess that's fair. But it more definitely paints my point. We didn't stop to think about who we were hurting. You and Jack were simply never in the equation. So please, while this is a destructive and terrible act, please at least know that we did not do it to hurt you."

"Jack left?" Thevi asked. Her eyebrows didn't raise.

Callie nodded. Then reached up and wiped a tear off Thevi's cheek. The other did not stop her. Then she said, "Yes. I have to start over again."

"Well, at least you have each other," Thevi said, and it took Callie a moment to realize what she was talking about. *Walter. At least Walter and I have each other. Does that mean...*

"Thevi, I'm really sorry. I truly am. I fucked up," Callie said. Adding the language would make the impact the rest of the words couldn't.

"No, Callie, people fuck up all the time. You fucked Walter." And then the door was closing. Callie stood staring at it for a few moments before she turned away. Down the long hardwood hallway, and to the right into the living room, then through the entry hall and out the front door, where Walter was waiting. As she looked up and saw him standing there, it surprised her. She had been hoping to sneak out. Leave with maybe a little dignity. But there he was, holding the door open. The glass storm door was closed, spilling light into the hallway.

They looked at each other, but didn't say anything. Callie had her hands up under her chin, and stood waiting for him to say something. Retribution. Punishment.

Scolding. Loving words. *Get the fuck out of my life, you homewrecker.* Anything. But he only nodded, ever so subtly. So she did the same. Then she was pushing open the glass door and leaving the Watson house behind her.

CHAPTER 20

Now what? That was the thought Callie had run through her head over and over that weekend. And then into the next week, as well. She would be standing at the sink washing a large pot in which she had just boiled six chicken breasts – lunches for the coming week – and it would just suddenly pop into her head. Or loading the dishwasher. Starting her car, or tossing another file she no longer needed into the dust bin. There was no escaping the thought. Though she had begun the morning of the Tell-All thinking she was drowning in guilt, she found this to be what clung. This new semi-emotion. This new question. *Now what?* It was what persisted now. The parachute pants or the Tickle-Me Elmo of Callie's week. The newest fad that raged so important in the hearts of those who let it in at all. But had she let it in? She felt like it was easier to tolerate, or at least to accept, than had been the guilty feeling. Then she wondered if that had been selfish. Guilt was an extremely personal and lonely enterprise in and of itself. No one on the planet knew what you had burning in your gut unless you told them. Was it selfish, therefore, to let it out and spill it to Jack and Thevi, so that Callie wouldn't have to burn with it anymore? Should she not have dealt with it on her own, in her own lonely, methodical way, saving the feelings of those not involved directly? There was no right answer. Every answer only led back to the question.

Now what?

Now what, indeed. There was no more Jack. What had started out to be such a wonderful prospect – a lustrous idea full of sexy, full of intrigue, full of new… She had gone through all that with him in just a short amount of time, but did not doubt it had been real. Callie knew she really loved him. So why, then, was she not feeling it now? Why was she not broken up inside about losing him? Why didn't she hurt like she had just lost her fiancee? Part of her thought it might be the empty hole in her soul that the guilt had ripped out when it came free of her. And whether or not she and Walter ever coupled again, or even spoke again, for that matter, she had lost something with him too. She had lost that purity. That friendship of twenty years, untainted by the destructive effects of sexual congress. When people spoke of not wanting to ruin a friendship with sex, Callie had never paid it much mind. How could it? It didn't matter to her, because just like she had told Thevi, she had simply never thought of it with Walter. And now, here she was facing it. They had done it, and – while it might not ruin their friendship – there was definitely something missing now. Maybe something they had never realized they had before. Or maybe they had realized it but had never given it name. That sweetness, that precious preservation of the one thing true friends should not share. They could have every bit of each other in complete innocent loving friendship. But not that. And now that had come between them. Like a wedge hammered into a log with a sledge, it was there. Burning like fire between them. Would they put it out, or let it separate them? Or had they called in a different department to deal with it, having told their secret to their respective lovers?

God, why was she so stupid? Why could she not have just waited a week or two and approached it with an intellectual mindset rather than emotional? Better yet, why could she not have just slapped Walter's hands away that night in the hallway? Well, Callie reckoned, that was a bell she could not unring now. And, as he had said so smartly, 'maybe it was something we should have done twenty years ago.' Maybe that was true. Maybe true male and female friendships just weren't meant to happen – always inevitably abounding in sex. Maybe it was destined to happen all along. *Maybe, maybe, maybe.* Boy was she tired of that word.

The boxes on her bedroom floor had been organized and culled down to one. The rest was all in thick black garbage bags that sat in her garage, ready for trash day. Two things she had kept from the Keep Pile though, she had now put on display. The picture of her mother and her was now tucked into the wooden trim on the edge of the mirror. The other, the note from Cardna, stood against the mirror on the dresser top. Callie stared at it now, hands on her hips, waiting nakedly for her bath to fill. Had she not seen something in the note the other night? The night Walter had come in and changed the course of her life?

She picked the note up and read it again. Studied it. That one line stood out to her.

...it's great to finally be meeting the legend.

What had caught her eye the other night? The word 'legend'? No, she thought not. Finally? *Finally! Yes! That was it! The word 'finally'.* That indicated that Cardna had known of Callie long before they had met. The word 'legend' held its own indications. That seemed to Callie to mean that they spoke her name in break rooms and hallways in the Fiji office. People knew of her. What did they say when they talked about her? Well, to reach legend status, it all had to be good, didn't it? Or… *legendary?* But what had she really done that was legendary?

She guessed, for one thing, that her name had been passed around pretty heavily when she had come up with the shield for the submersible on the Monster Hunt. She had made the company paper, even as a contractor. But why was she a legend? Most of her greatest work had been done for other companies. Other entities.

But that word 'finally' was what kept coming back to her. Was it complete facetiousness, a tacky hyperbole to boost confidence under false pretense? And for that matter, so might be the word 'legend'. Callie sighed and dropped the card back onto the dresser, then stepped into the bathroom where a slender glass full of dark red wine sat on a table beside a steaming tub full of bubbles. She turned off her phone, then lit a few candles that stood near the tub, then turned off the light. She clicked on the StreamBox and called up an Etta James playlist, then stepped into the heat.

Walter lay on the sofa, hands clasped behind his head as Thevi marched around shouting and cursing. Three days now, it had gone like this. Threatening to leave, telling him he didn't deserve her, and reminding him how much of an asshole he was to sleep with her best friend. He didn't have the heart to remind her that he had known Callie before Thevi had. And that were Callie to have to choose one best friend to save, it would be Walter she chose. None of that mattered, of course. Thevi was right, of course. He had truly not meant anything to happen that night. It was to be a night just like a thousand others he had spent in the presence of Callie Simmons. And to look at it that way, no one had ever questioned them before. And no one would have this time, either. It was by their own free will that they had come to admit anything had happened. And they had done so *so expediently*. They wasted no time in hiding it. He shook his head. Had that not been a little precocious? Ten years of marriage to Thevi and the darling had not once ever asked if he did anything with Callie. He could have easily kept it a secret and would likely never have had to answer for it. But that wasn't what Walter wanted. He didn't want to hide things from his wife. He also didn't think he *wanted* Callie. She seemed the obvious choice to fall back on after a failed marriage, but did he really want her? He didn't even know.

There had been plenty of women in Walter's pre-marriage days. Maybe a hundred of them. And he had never felt like he wanted them for anything more than the quick down-and-dirty. Callie was different, of course. She was a friend. A true friend. But did that equate desire on a more-than-physical level? Nominally, sure. Callie was worth it. He knew she would make a good wife. But he had simply never thought of her in that way. He had not really ever thought of her in a sexual way either. There had been a few times throughout the last two decades where he had seen her tits. She would be changing with a mirror placed favorably somewhere nearby. Or a few times when she would bend over to pick up a mug off a table, straighten a cushion or tie her shoe that he would see down her blouse. But that was the same for any woman. If she was showing something, Walter was looking. That didn't mean anything. Not really. But it had just *happened*. That was what was so damned weird about the whole thing. He had run over the events in his head hundreds of times now. Not without a little fervor, he found. But in trying to find *why* it had happened, he kept coming up blank. Of course there had been the touch. Incidental, inadvertent, accidental, but a touch worth remembering, for sure. But was that enough to make him want to do something inappropriate? To cheat on his wife, as it were?

Maybe there was something else there. Maybe a love for Callie – or rather, a lust for Callie – that he had just not recognized, realized or accepted before. Maybe, simply put, he really did desire her in that way. He had just never settled on the thought. She had given up her virginity to him, for shit's sake! He had not seen that coming. But now, as he lay here listening to Thevi shout and cry and curse and growl at him, he found he was leaning more toward the idea of exploring it. He loved Thevi dearly, no doubt. But this was getting old. He had come to her the morning after it happened, for fuck's sake. He had stood up like a man in the face of the obvious obstacle, and had been honest. Straight-up, straight-forward, no bullshit. Can't there be a little forgiveness?

Fotchie jumped up on Walter's chest and sniffed his chin. Walter put his hand on the dog's back and stroked him. "Fotch, you still love me, don't you. Yeah. You's a good boy. Still loves the mother fucker that feeds him."

Thevi's threats and stomps had not been hollow for the last three days. Nor, of course, had he lain on this couch that entire time. But it had been true that every time he came back through the door, she was still at it. Or at it again. But she had really meant what she was saying. She was methodically packing this one suitcase. *How the fuck long does it take to pack a suitcase?* He had almost gotten impatient enough to finally get up and go help her stuff her shit into it and toss it in her trunk for her. Just to stop the incessant shouting.

"Come on, TJ," he said, flatly. His arm was hanging off the couch now, the back of his hand an inch or two above the floor. "Why can't you move past this? Can you not forgive me? Give me a chance?" Of course, he had tried asking this same thing many times of the last few days. All to no end. This time, she came to a stop, standing right over him with one hand on her hip and the other flailing in front of her as she shouted.

"Because you stood there and admitted to me that you couldn't promise it wouldn't happen again! Even Callie said so much! The fuck does Callie know about fucking in the first place? Apparently everything she learned about it, she learned from you! Twenty years you've been friends and it never happens, but now it happens once and she can't *guarantee* she can keep away from you from now on?" And she was off stomping again. "Oh, no, she can't! Now she's had the D from you, she knows what it feels like. She's gotta have more of it!"

Walter heard a door slam, then reopen a second later. And Thevi came back into the room. "You realize that's what that means, right? When a woman says she can't guarantee blah, blah, blah – she's just saying she's going to do it again. It's just a nice way of saying, 'fuck you, it's happening again, but I'm just not man enough to tell it to your face!'"

Walter tried to touch Thevi's calf, which was a few inches beyond his reach. Just something to show her some feeling. Some humanity. He gave up when she didn't step forward to accommodate it. "Thev. Come on. You know it takes more than just her wanting it for it to happen again."

"What the fuck does that mean?" she said, an angry, mean frown on her normally pretty face. "You know you're going to give it to her again! You said so yourself!"

"I did not," he said, raising a finger in the air, "for the record, ever say that."

"You're right! You said it the polite way too."

Walter covered his eyes with the back of his arm, ready in his soul to just give up the fight. He knew Thevi was worth it, but she was off her rocker right now. Maybe a few weeks with her mom would calm her down, bring her back around. Fotchie dropped into the crease between Walter's left arm and his body and laid his head on Walter's chest.

"That's right, Fotchie. We men gotta stick together," he said, still hiding his eyes with his arm. "Even though you don't have balls anymore."

It had been two weeks since the destruction of everything Callie had built with Jack Carpenter. And what had in the beginning felt like a lack of emotion, finally came to present itself as pain. She really did miss him. Having had the bandage ripped off so quickly, she had been numb to the pain for a while. The guilt might have been part of the cocktail as well. But Callie had worried that maybe she had not really felt anything for the man at all because she didn't feel the pain immediately. It was therefore not a totally unpleasant thing to be able to welcome that pain. It meant she was human, after all. She had felt something after all. She had not been in an artificial relationship.

The weird thing though, at least in her mind, was that he had not reached out once. Not a *miss you* text, not a phone call… nothing. That hurt her in a completely different way. Maybe Jack was just hedging his bets. Maybe he was a one-and-done kind of guy. You got one chance with him. And when it came to sex, that seemed like a fair deal, but the irony was not lost on Callie that the one thing she could do to completely and immediately lose him was the one thing she had never done in her life. Until that one time. Every time she thought of it she cringed. How stupid must she look to him? To Thevi, who had not reached out to her, either?

Callie had texted Thevi. She had not been so bold or naive to call her. But she had texted her. On a couple of occasions. Just check-in texts. *Miss you, girl.* Or, *I'm so sorry.* But no response had come from her either. Callie had burned two bridges in one battle. Maybe *scorched earth* was a better metaphor. When I fuckup, I fuckup *all the way*.

Now she sat at the thick wooden coffee table in Rebecca's den, her back against the sofa and a cup of steaming coffee held atop her knees. Codi sat on the couch with a laptop, typing away at her next assignment, headphones over her ears and ridiculously large glasses over her eyes. She did not look at the screen very much. When it came time to read something, the computer would dictate it to her. But she had to move the cursor occasionally. To someone with good vision, it was almost as hard to read as a normal computer screen would have been to Codi. The cursor was a two-inch, high-contrast arrow that blinked and changed colors when she pressed the CTRL key. But she made do. It was nice to see her doing something productive. Not because anyone needed her to be, but because Codi herself needed to be. She wanted to do something to feel like she was contributing – to feel like she wasn't freeloading off the ever-generous Rebecca Judas. Callie's bare toes dug into the long fibers of the rug beneath the coffee table. She was listening to Rebecca tell her all about how they had run into the lead singer of One Last Orbit on the day they went for Codi's interview.

Rebecca was modestly proud of the encounter, but she was more excited telling the parts about how Codi had reacted. It was sweet to watch her speak of Codi in a matronly, doting tone, and Callie wondered how in love the woman was with her. She knew it wasn't a sexual kind of love, but that woman was most certainly *in love* with Codi. Much the same way a daddy is *in love* with his baby girl. It was a fascination – an enchantment – that Callie wanted to know someday for herself.

"Have you ever met anybody?" Rebecca asked when she had finished. She held her mug with both hands, sipping slowly as she looked over the high-top counter at Callie.

Callie sipped from her own mug, then leaned back against the couch again, hands out beside her on the carpet. "I ran into Matthew McConaughey once at the Pint and Barrel in Long Island."

"You're kidding!" Rebecca said with wide eyes. Callie didn't think it meant as much to Rebecca as meeting a woman would. But Callie also couldn't see how only hetero women would be attracted to Matthew. He was the definition of sex and manliness in her book.

"Nope. I was sitting at the bar finishing a cocktail. You know the little tiny straws they put in them? Well, I was leaning over to suck up the last bit of sugary lemon juice in the bottom of the glass, probably looking like a real dork with that tiny straw between my fingers. And he just walked up and leaned on the bar, signaling to the bartender, and looked at me. He smiled real big and said, 'Careful there, sweetheart, that looks dangerous!'"

Rebecca put her hand over her mouth, raised her eyebrows. "Oh my God!"

"Yeah, I think I must have smiled so big my face almost cracked. I was blushing like a schoolgirl, too," Callie said, reliving the moment in her head.

"Did you get a picture with him or anything?"

Callie shook her head, a disappointed smile touching her lips. "Nah. I was too shocked to even say anything. I think I managed to say 'Okay' or something. So embarrassing."

The timer dinged and Rebecca bent to pull a tray out of the oven. Then she shook the overstuffed glove off her hand and picked up her mug, coming to join Callie by the coffee table. As she sat with her back against the opposing sofa, Callie noticed the nonchalant way Rebecca reached behind her and squeezed Codi's foot through the blanket. Codi glanced in her direction, probably not seeing much behind those bug-eyed glasses, and smiled a routine little number. These were things she was used to, obviously. The subtle little gestures that Rebecca gave her, showing Codi that she was there. That one little gesture showed so much. *I'm back. I'm here if you need anything. Just let me know.* Callie felt warm inside being this close to that kind of love.

"How you holding up, girl?" Rebecca said, lifting the mug to her lips.

Callie sighed, chewing her lip. "Well?" she said, holding her hands up in a shrug. "I miss him!"

Rebecca nodded.

"I mean, I really do. I didn't think I did at first. I guess the shock and the guilt and everything else was just overshadowing that pain at first. But it's worn off, and I really do miss him."

"What's your plan with Walt?" Rebecca said, and Codi leaned forward, pulling a can off one ear and touching Rebecca's shoulder.

"Can I have a sip of your coffee?" she asked.

Rebecca, without answering, handed the mug back to the blind girl. Codi leaned back, replaced the earphone over her ear and put the mug to her lips. She sat with her eyes closed, listening to her computer telling her something. Codi showed no sign of giving the mug back any time soon. Rebecca also looked in no hurry to have it back. Callie giggled at this.

"I don't have a plan with Walt. I mean, I know what you mean. But as of now, I have to get my darn life in order first. I kind of need to stay away from him," Callie said, shaking her head.

Rebecca smiled at her. "I disagree with that, doll."

"Yeah? How so? Or, I guess, *why* so?"

"Maybe he's exactly what you need right now. Maybe you need to be as close to him as you can get," Rebecca said. She had one leg straightened out under the table, and the other knee up. Her hands rested, clasped, upon this raised knee. "See, the way I see it, you've *always* been that close to him. You two were like the hot dog and the bun. Oh, fuck sake," she said, rolling her eyes and looking at the ceiling. "That was the worst possible simile."

Callie burst out laughing though.

Rebecca finally smiled and giggled a little herself. "I mean you were like hot dog and mustard."

"You're not making this any better!" Callie shouted through her laughter, and now Rebecca was full belly-laughing as well.

"I know!" she said, twirling her hand in the air. "Why the fuck am I stuck on this hot dog analogy? I don't even fucking…" she said, but had to stop as she tried to catch her breath. She was leaned forward, hands on the coffee table and laughing so hard that no sound was coming out.

Callie was laughing into her palm, tears streaming out of her eyes.

After they had finally managed to restore their calm, the two women sat looking at each other. Each slightly out of breath, and a little giddy with the adrenaline rush. Rebecca,

Callie was sure, would have gladly explained this adrenaline rush as a dopamine injection straight into the brain. Maybe something like serotonin. Which would be a gateway to Bec's grand finale in letting Callie know that laughter was, quite literally, therefore, the best medicine.

Callie drained the last of her coffee. Codi, who had stolen that chance from Rebecca, was chewing the end of her finger and smiling at something. Rebecca saw Callie's reaction to this and peeked over her shoulder, then returned her gaze to Callie. "So I talked to my friend."

"Well, that's exciting," Callie said, giggling.

Rebecca raised one eyebrow. "Look at you. No. Seriously. Remember I said we might have a friend in the business?"

Callie was shaking her head. It wasn't coming to her. She had been through a traumatic few months, and could not remember anything of the sort. "I'm sorry, you're gonna have to refresh my memory."

"Well, why don't I do that while you refresh our coffee supply?"

"Deal!" Callie said, standing up. She touched Codi's shoulder on the way by, and Codi instinctively handed her the mug. As Callie stood making a new pot, she now saw the scene from Rebecca's earlier vantage point. All she could see was the top of Codi's head, where a messy bun had been formed quickly and without regard for fashion.

"Our friend at Royal is who I mean. Or Gray Horse. My college-friend's little sister. Remember me talking about her? She has an office there in Fiji."

"Yes!" Callie said, nodding emphatically, even though no one could see her. "I remember. You walked by an office and recognized the name."

"You got it," Rebecca said, and Callie saw her finger shoot up in the air as if to mark a score. "Her name is Cynda Lohm."

"Wow," Callie said, frowning. The coffee maker was beginning its chug and spew. "That is unique."

"Yeah. So anyway, I found her on OuterCircle. Not saying much, I know. You can find fucking *anybody* on the Circle. But with a name like hers it took less than a minute," Rebecca said. Callie leaned on the counter with both hands.

"Well, she is a friend indeed. She says she's not happy with the way certain things are going there, and the job isn't *quite* what she signed up for. At least not since the acquisition. So she's willing to talk, because I told her I could help her."

Callie came around the counter so she could make eye-contact with the other woman. This was getting deep, and Callie didn't do well without the facial language that came with the verbal. She needed to *see* Rebecca say this. "Whoa, whoa," she said, spreading her hands out before her as she rounded the end of the couch. Rebecca looked up at her, mouth closed and patient. "You told her you could *help* her? With what?"

Rebecca shrugged. "I didn't get that far. I just said I could help her. Didn't have time for details, but wanted to keep in touch. I just…" she trailed off, twirling her hands in the air, looking for the words. "I just *needed some information*." She looked back up at Callie with her eyebrows raised and a smirk on her mouth. "Whatever, it worked," she added, shrugging again. Her gaze returned to her toes, where she was picking at a nail. Callie watched this with a mild fascination as her brain tried to process what she was hearing. Then she started nodding.

"Okay. Well, that's good. So did you learn anything?" Callie said, heading back into the kitchen to fill the mugs.

"I sure did. There's some project that a few select people are working on. Called *Red Bell*. Says she knows all the major players but not the syllabus. And some of them are coming to town next month."

Callie was getting a curious feeling in her belly. Like a swarm of butterflies had awoken. *Red Bell?* What the heck was that? And who? *Who was coming to town?* "Oh, wait! He said that! I've heard of Red Bell!" She realized she was shaking her head and rubbing her belly at the same time.

"Who's coming to town, Bec?" She reentered the den with two mugs in her hands and stopped at the end of the couch. Rebecca's eyes were locked on hers again, but a mischievous look had now taken up residence there. Like she was about to share a secret.

"I think you know who," Rebecca said, and let the grin play across her lips. "All your favorite peeps."

As Callie drove, she pounded her steering wheel with excitement. She was, in fact, so excited that she almost forgot about the desert that now lay between Walter and her. Someone would have to cross it eventually. To make contact. Apparently that was her. And she was doing it without realizing its depth. She pushed the phone button on her steering wheel. The phone gave her its *ready* chime, then she said, "Call Walter Watson!"

'Calling Walter Watson, mobile.' With all this new info just boiling inside her, she had to tell her old friend. It was looking like they could finish all their business here in the states, and never have to go back to Fiji after all. Walter, if anyone, would surely see how exciting this was.

When he answered, he sounded nonplussed. Callie had apparently forgotten so much of the real world that she even asked him, "What's wrong?"

A long sigh from the car speakers, transmitting her phone call. "Really? Callie? Are you that much of a bird you don't know what the fuck's going on?"

Her face fell and she realized suddenly how much of a dope she had been. "You're right, Walt, I'm sorry. I just meant…" she said, but trailed off, not knowing how to finish the lie.

"I'm going through a fuckin' divorce, man. What do you want?"

Callie slapped her hand over her mouth. Suddenly the Royal take-down didn't seem so important. Her friend was in a bad spot and she hadn't even checked up on him. What the hell was wrong with her? Was this her normal tunnel vision, or was she trying to check out of reality for a while? Trying to put up a wall to keep the bad things from making themselves residents in her memory?

"Walter, I am so sorry. Oh my God, I didn't know…"

There was silence for a moment, then she heard the gasp and pinched exhalation that could only be duplicated by someone smoking a cigarette. "Yeah. She's leaving."

Callie's eyes filled with tears. She was stifling a cry with the one hand, steering the car with the other. Shaking her head. "Oh my God. Can I do anything?"

There was another pregnant pause. Then he sighed. "I don't know. I'm pretty fucked up."

Her chin was trembling and her eyes were now spilling heavily. Callie had to pull over. She turned into a parking lot and pulled into a space under a tree, put the car in park.

"Anyway, what's up with you?" he said. She could hear the pain in his voice. Ever the gentleman.

"Walter, do you need company? I'm sick about this."

"Yeah, me too. What are ya gonna do?"

She was shaking her head again. Her breathing hitched – a sob caught in her throat, and she expelled it in a throat-clearing cough. "I didn't think she was going to leave. I really didn't."

"I tried everything."

A woman walking by in front of Callie's car slowed to look through the windshield at her. Callie didn't bother to wipe the tears away, but waved at the woman and forced a smile when the woman held up a thumb, asking if she was okay. She swallowed and turned the radio down, then turned it back up, realizing it was the source of audio for her phone call.

"Well, I can come see you if you want me to, Walter."

She could hear him take another pull from his cigarette. The silence was long enough that Callie considered the possibility not only of his not answering her question, but even so much as hanging up on her. But he did finally respond. "Yeah. Sure. I guess that'd be cool," he said.

Ten minutes later, she pulled into his driveway and put it in park, then sat there, staring down at her lap. Was she about to make another mistake here? Were there any mistakes left to be made? If they were both single again, could they even make a mistake? Would it even be *considered* one?

Part of her was excited to be here for a whole other reason than just to see her friend. The parts of her that made Callie a woman were full of their own anticipation. It wasn't an overt excitement at all. It was just below the surface. But it was there, and it was recognizable. Even to she, who had such little experience with it. The other part of her was nervous and edgy about it. Was it that she was afraid that Thevi would return? Or was it that she thought, somewhere down in that mental dungeon, that she would be on top of Walter when Thevi returned?

She pushed the engine stop button on the dash and clasped her hand around the key fob. *Ugh! Why is this so hard?* She could not just leave now. Surely he had seen her sitting out front now. If not through the window, then surely on his security system. His phone would have told him by now, *'There is a vehicle in your driveway,'* in its cold British voice.

Callie rang the doorbell. Her purse was clutched against her chest. It would take her longer to get inside that way. It would keep a little extra distance between them. It would make her showing up look a little more innocent. She was aware that her eyes were red and glassy, and her cheeks were probably still puffy from the hard cry. When Walter opened the door, she had to keep from crying out. He had a full beard. Had it really been that long since she had seen him?

Callie raised her eyebrows and put her hand over her mouth. "Oh, Walter, you look great!"

He gave her a weak smile and stepped back, pulling the door open with him. He wore pajama pants and house shoes and a black t-shirt that said THANK YOU ELON in bold white letters. Callie peaked around nervously as she stepped into the entry hall, her purse clutched extra tight against her chest now. She looked like she was exploring a dark alley, nervous of being mugged.

"She's not here, don't worry," Walter said, shutting the door.

Callie stopped and stood up straight. Cleared her throat. "Walt, I didn't-" she started, but he cut her off with a kiss. Full of fire and passion, but it had no soul. He pulled away quickly, leaving her leaning forward and almost losing her balance. She opened her eyes to look at him and he was leaning against the wall behind him.

He stood with his arms crossed, looking serious. "I'm sorry," he said. "I know you didn't come here to make out. I just had this weird feeling," he said, moving his hand like he was bouncing a ball on it in front of his chest. Coaxing out the words. "Like, now that we're not bound to anyone else, maybe our little friendly welcome hugs could be like full mouth kisses now."

Callie smiled sideways at this and covered her mouth with the side of her finger, stifling a giggle. "That's cute, Walter," she said, stepping forward and running his hair back off his forehead for him with a fingertip. Then she nodded, biting her bottom lip. "I think I'm okay with that. But maybe…"

He held a hand up, stopping her speech. "I know. I'm thinking about that too. I think let's wait before we even discuss it."

Callie backed up a step. "Walter, I wasn't…" she started.

"It's okay. Whether you were or whether you weren't. Whether we ever…" he said and trailed off. He held his fist up and shook it in the air lightly. Rebecca's ridiculous hot dog analogy popped into her head and Callie smiled widely, again holding back a giggle. "What's so funny?" Walter said. He looked like he was about to smile.

"Nothing," she said, waving it away. "Just thought of something Rebecca said earlier."

Walter stared at her for a moment. "Well, I need to get this out. Whether we ever, you know," he said, shaking his fist again, "do it? Whether we ever *do it* again, or not, and either thing is fine, I just think we need to take some time. I need some time."

"Oh, of course, baby," Callie said, spreading her arms and stepping forward. He stepped into her embrace and she held him for a long time. "We're going to take as much time as you need."

They spent the rest of the evening sitting right beside each other on the couch, trying to pitch popcorn into a Solo cup that stood on the coffee table. This gesture reminded Callie of something in her past, but she couldn't put her finger on it. Walter's left arm was around Callie's shoulder, her head leaning against his chest while they played the popcorn basketball game. Callie, throwing with her left hand, was markedly worse than Walter, who was only making one of every third toss at best. Callie had only made three or four in the whole night. Popcorn covered the surface of the table, and lay all around it on the rug of the living room. *The Big Lebowski* played on Walter's large television across the room, but they weren't paying much attention to it. The sound was low enough for them to talk over. And that's what they did. They spoke of Thevi and her plans, how she had left; of Jack and how no, he had not reached out at all, and no, Walter had not heard from him either. They spoke of where Walter would go from here. Would he pack up and sell the house? Would he stay? Would Thevi keep the house? What would he do with his large train set in the back room? When Callie looked around the house, she saw a lot more rooms full of Walter here than Thevi. He had a presence in every room. The den, where his record collection took up most of the lower half of two whole walls, in here where he had movie posters on the walls, the lower den where his train set took up the entire room... Walter was everywhere. Thevi was almost nowhere. Confined to the small craft room where once she had sewn things, glued things together, created scrap books... Callie guessed this was just married life between two opposites. Walter was a wholly *materialistic* person. He needed *things* around him. Instead of streaming his music like everyone else did these days, he had to put on a record to listen to it. He had to stand up and flip the record when twenty-two minutes had passed. He liked the feel of things. To have and to own them. Very tactile, he was. Thevi, on the other hand, didn't need to own it. She just liked to see it in her magazines. She borrowed books from the library and took them back when she finished them. Walter would rather own his books – even the ones he had proclaimed he would only probably read once. *'When I die, people will judge me by my books,'* he had once said. Maybe it was true. But who cares what that judgment is when you're already dead? And if someone were to ask, *'Why do you have a copy of* The Stand *if you hate how it ends?'* you would not be able to answer. Because you'd be dead. Callie didn't fault him for it. He was a natural-born collector. He still had, in his train room, an eight-inch steel post that stood on a wooden coaster, filled with the iron rings he had once stolen from tavern puzzles in the mall as an adolescent. Why get rid of them now? Now they were a collection! He had a lot of money, but it wasn't just readily obvious, either. Not in the way that one would expect to see it on display, at least. He drove a nice car, sure. And had a nice house, at that. Not a mansion, mind you, but it wasn't small. And it was in a nice neighborhood. But he didn't wear showy ten-thousand-dollar watches and eat at the *Tin Fork Steakhouse* every night. Looking at his audio equipment, his record collection – you really had to be an audiophile to know what you were looking at in terms of value. Where most people would see a bookshelf full of records and see a couple hundred dollars, Callie knew what records actually cost. She had bought a few for him as gifts. Each one running somewhere in the twenty-to-forty-dollar range suddenly made those record shelves look a little richer to people. And one had to know his stuff to realize the turntable cost close to a grand. But these weren't flashy. He certainly didn't brag about their cost. And the television… who the heck *didn't* have a giant TV these days? As she looked around the place – on those mornings she had waited for him to finish getting ready over the years – she had just never seen materialism reflected in Walter's admittedly materialistic nature. She saw *collections*. She saw interesting things. And that was one of her greatest endearments of him. He treasured everything he had. Callie enjoyed the times when she felt like one of those treasures.

After the popcorn had run out – they hadn't eaten a single bite of it, for Walter had made it the night before and fallen asleep drunk before he even touched it – they also seemed to run out of the pleasantly flowing conversation. Then Callie finally pushed herself up off of where she had been leaning against him, feeling the sweat soaking her entire side, and he turned to look at her.

"Well, I guess I'd better hit the road, Jack," she said, snapping her fingers in front of her. She suddenly made a face like she'd stepped on an egg. "Uh… I was thinking Ray Charles. Not, um…" she said.

He smiled weakly, almost closing his eyes. "Thank you for the company tonight, Callie."

She nodded and slapped his knee. "You're welcome, big bro. I enjoyed hanging out with you."

As she stood up and straightened her blouse and pants, she turned back to him. "Oh. I almost forgot to ask you. Do you want to go to Manhattan with me next month?"

Walter frowned but didn't say anything.

"There's a Royal conference. A bunch of bigwigs from Fiji are going to be there," Callie said. Then she raised a finger along with her eyebrows, and added, "Some people I've been maybe wanting to see again, in fact!"

He tilted his head. "Callie, I lost my job. I can't get in anymore."

"I know. It's okay. I'll have Minus make you a badge" she said. "Besides, it's not that far away. Not that big of a deal."

Walter shook his head and put his hands on his cheeks. "Callie, I still have my badge and everything. But Minus is going to be there. I don't think I'll be allowed to stay very long."

"They won't recognize you with the beard," Callie said, reaching out and stroking it for him.

CHAPTER 21

It was mid-December before Walter joined the land of the living again. He had actually accepted an invitation to go hatchet-throwing with Rebecca, Callie and Natalie. Callie had approached Rebecca about making the call, fearing that Callie herself was likely the last person on the planet that Walter would want to see. She had sat nearby, trying to hear more than just the one side of the conversation as Bec asked him if he would like to join 'some of the girls'. Instantly, though, Walter had asked if Callie would be there. Rebecca's eyes had locked with Callie's and a slight smirk had found its way onto her mouth. The gig was either up, or she could play along. She had opted for the latter, and said, 'of course!' and Walter had almost instantly returned with an affirmative. So it was either *because of Callie's* being there, or in spite of it. Either way, she was happy about his joining.

The four were matched up as different combinations of teams until each had been paired with each other. Walter had ordered an old-fashioned at the bar before they got their lane, and had said it tasted so good that he just kept ordering them through the evening. He must have been on his fifth one by the time Callie finished her first vodka-tonic. But his axe was not suffering. He was still the best thrower of the four.

This didn't quite surprise Callie. What had actually surprised her was how poorly Rebecca had taken to it. Callie had imagined, based on this larger-than-life image she had of Bec from her performance down in Fiji, that she would just be a natural weapon master. It was, therefore, almost comical that she could hardly get the thing to stick in the wood. Callie was not much better, having had to have the host physically guide her wrists in the action until she finally got the hang of it. But now hers were sticking. They just weren't hitting the target.

It was Natalie who was shining though. Not in the light that Walter was, but everyone had expected him to be good at it. Natalie, though, was clearly second-best. While Walter was seemingly keeping his rhythm in spite of all the rye, the girls were all beginning to get even worse at it. Callie threw one that somehow flipped in the air and hit the boards with the butt of the axe, bouncing back and coming close to catching her in the foot. She had bounced backwards as if she were on a Pogo stick, trying to avoid the hatchet, screaming like a banshee, and everyone had had a good laugh at that. But otherwise, they were tiring pretty quickly from the physical exertion.

Callie leaned against the wooden plank that served as an armrest outside the cage, watching Rebecca try to stab a cherry in the bottom of her glass with the tiny plastic sword that had come with the drink. Callie was smiling and giggling as Rebecca got more and more frustrated, then finally reached in and picked it out with her fingernails and tossed it in her mouth. "God damn things," she said, rolling her eyes. "You should check on Codi," she said.

"Yeah. Good idea," Callie agreed, and picked up her phone, where it had been lying face-down on the bar. "Hello, Robot," she said quietly, mouth up to the microphone. When she felt the vibration in her hand, she said, "Call Codi Cohl."

'Calling Codi Cohl, mobile.'

Rebecca sloshed some ice from the glass and slung it into her mouth. "You call your phone 'Robot'?"

"Uh huh!" Callie said, putting the glass up to her ear. With her other hand she pulled her hair back. "That's what it is. He does everything for me, and fits in my pocket."

"Sister," Rebecca said, putting a hand on Callie's shoulder, "I have one of those too, but I can't make calls on it."

Callie laughed out loud and slapped a hand over her eyes, shaking her head. "God, I walked right into that one." The phone rang four times before voice mail picked up. Callie ended the call. "No answer."

"Yeah," Rebecca said. "She's probably got the music up. Or they're dancing."

"I can try Sam," Callie said. "What's his last name?"

Rebecca scoffed. "How many Sams you got in that fucking thing?"

"Probably just him, dork butt," Callie said, laughing. "I just don't remember if I put in his last name the other night."

"Well, it's Hakeen," Rebecca said, and set her glass down, wiping her mouth with a napkin and then clapping her hands together. It was her turn again, and she was trying to pep herself up. It was very loud in the place.

"Hey, Robot," Callie said again, waiting for the affordance of a vibration. "Call Sam Hakeen." She picked up her own glass from the bar and took a quick sip. "Hey Bec!" she shouted, "try to close out the twenties!" Though Callie knew there would be no closing anything out. Not from Bec. Not tonight, at least.

'Calling Shanna King, mobile.'

Callie looked down at her phone. "What the-" she said, staring at the screen. She frowned heavily. Who the hell is Shanna King? Did I not save his number? She looked back up to see Rebecca's throw bounce off the wall and drop to the padded floor below. Hakeen? Did I… The line was ringing. Callie shook her head. Her thumb hovered over the red circle that would end the call. "Hey Bec," she said, still looking at the phone, but then there was an answer.

Callie couldn't hear it because she had not touched the speaker icon. But the call showed connected, and the call timer was now counting up. *Oh shit, I just crank-called someone,* she thought. The thought of ending it anyway crossed her mind, then she decided to be polite. She put the phone up to her ear. "Hello?" she said.

"Yes? Who's this?" came a soft voice from the other end.

"I'm sorry, I mis-" Callie started, then frowned again. Shook her head. What the hell? "I'm sorry, but do I know you? I had your name and number programmed in my phone."

"Who is this?" the voice repeated.

"This is Callie Simmons. I uh.."

"Callie! Oh my God! What the fuck are you doing right now?"

Callie looked up, meeting Rebecca's eyes. She had come back around to Callie's side of the fence and was standing there staring at her. Callie's eyes were wide as moons. Rebecca's weren't. She looked bemused. She shook her shoulders in an obvious *what?* gesture. But Callie was speechless. Rebecca finally took the phone out of her hand and put it to her own ear.

"Boy, you better not be taking advantage of my little doll!" she said.

Callie's heart stopped and she grabbed Bec by her shoulders, mouthing, *It's not Sam!* But Rebecca learned soon enough for herself. Her smiled dropped and she frowned, then said, "Oh, I'm sorry. I apologize," and handed the phone back to Callie. "Who the fuck is that?"

"Who the fuck was *that*?" said the woman apparently named Shanna.

Callie had her fingers on her lips, looking like she was trying to figure out every possible color combination on a Rubik's Cube in less than a second. *Who is this? Why was she in my phone? How long has she been in here? Do I know her? If so, from where?*

She finally found her voice and said, "I'm sorry, Shanna, is it? I uh... I'm trying to figure out a bunch of things at once. I don't even know how you're in my phone."

"Callie! We used to work together!" Shanna said.

Callie felt a tickle of recognition somewhere in the middle of her brain. Right there where they say you store your memories of people's voices. But Callie did not recognize the voice at all. The name though...

"Oh yeah?" she finally managed. She was full-on biting the side of her thumb now. And hard. Rebecca slapped her hand away from her mouth and shook her head when Callie looked up at her.

"Yes! You don't remember me? We worked at the Oliver Company together. I managed the camera equipment for the Atlas mission! Good fuck, I was wondering when you'd finally call!"

They were in the parking lot, where the relative quiet was almost luxurious to her ears. Callie was pacing back and forth in the empty spot next to her car, while Rebecca leaned against it with her arms crossed, next to Walter. Natalie was still inside, using the restroom.

"She's alive, Walter. Can you effing believe this? She's a-freaking-*live!*"

Walter was shaking his head. He was sharing one of Rebecca's long cigarettes. That's at least what he would call it. Callie thought it more appropriate to say Rebecca was sharing with *him*. He never seemed to have his own anymore.

"Remind me who she is," he said.

"She was on the Atlas mission! She was a little girl, Walter!"

"A little girl? On the mission? To Mars?"

"YES, Walt!" Callie said, letting her hands slap against the sides of her thighs. "Not a little girl. Okay, not literally. A young woman. She was maybe twenty or so."

"Wow," he said, looking at Rebecca, who had remained silent. She had not even known Callie at the time she worked for the Olivers. "So who is she? I mean, not to sound rude, but what relevance is she to you?"

"Wait," Rebecca finally said. "I thought you said everyone died on that mission. How is she alive?"

"I don't know!" Callie said. "I didn't get to ask! She had to get off the phone. She's going to call me in the morning."

"Oh dear," Rebecca said, taking her cigarette back.

"What? What's that mean?"

"That means you aren't going to sleep tonight, honey," said Bec.

"What I want to know is how you've had her in your phone all these fuckin' years," Walter said, holding his hand out toward Callie, "and you've never come across her name."

"Walter, I've probably seen it a billion times! I have a billion contacts in my phone. When I get a new phone, I just sign into Google and it downloads them all."

"I know how it works, sweetie. I just don't know how someone doesn't know who's on her list," said Walter.

"It's not like I was looking for her! I had forgotten she even existed. Heck," Callie said, ceasing her pacing and putting her hands up on the sides of her head. "I don't even remember ever getting her number. I guess, surely I must have at some point." She was frowning now.

"One would think," Rebecca said, smirking. "So what's your move? What's this mean to you?"

"I don't know. She won't talk on the phone about anything, so I'll have to meet her. She's going to call in the morning so we can arrange something."

Callie was up most of the night, full of anticipation. What would she ask Shanna? What would Shanna *answer*?

Would they catch up like old friends? It had sure sounded like the other woman had been happy to hear from Callie. They had not been especially close during her tenure at the Oliver Company, but Callie had favored the girl. They had spent some fair amount of time together. She remembered Shanna being around a lot. Always following Donnie around like a puppy. But if she recalled correctly, Donnie liked it that way. If he ever had an idea, he wanted someone there to record it for him.

Callie also remembered Shanna being a math whiz. She had spoken it like a language. What would take most people several minutes to do on a napkin or scratch paper, Shanna would do in her head, as if staring at an invisible screen, touching numbers on it with her fingertip. It was fascinating to watch. And she could do it in seconds.

All in all, Callie was looking forward to catching up, and was, of course, full of nervous excitement about that call. Shanna did call the next morning, right when she said she would. And it became quickly evident that Shanna did not want to talk on the phone about anything meaningful. A little disappointed, Callie had given up trying to pry anything out of her. She respected the woman's wishes – *had to* respect them – lest she lose her chance at finding out anything.

The something they arranged involved Callie making another flight. This time, at least, she didn't have to spend all day on the plane. She got up early and ordered a plane ticket, then drove to the airport where she hopped a quick flight from Newark to Columbus. The flight was only two hours. But after the hour she spent in the car just getting to the airport, then parking, walking to the terminal and getting through the security line, the illusion of a 'quick flight' quickly lost its luster. By the time she got off the airplane and made it to the car rental shop she preferred, it was already after lunch time.

She rented the car with the prettiest color on the lot – a solid baby-blue that made her feel good inside – and slipped into the cloth seat. Callie didn't care how much a rental car cost. She didn't care what size it was, how many people it would hold, or what manufacturer's emblem she would find on the trunk. All she cared about was having something that matched her personality for the day, or week, or however long she called it hers. And this one was perfect.

The trip from the rental shop to where Shanna lived would take around forty-five minutes or so, Shanna had said. She lived in a little town called Amanda. A town so small it barely showed up on an *Amanda* town map, according to her. But Callie would have to stop somewhere and get lunch on the way. And probably take a pee break. Now the quick little flight to get her in front of the elusive woman with a royal surname was sitting at eight hours. At this rate, Callie reckoned, she could have just made the damn eight-hour drive in her own car. A bright orange SUV that *always* suited her mood.

She finally pulled into Amanda at close to four o'clock, exiting the highway and heading southeast on Main Street. The sudden change from highway to village was almost almost like a culture shock. The road that took her away from the highway lost its double-yellow line, and the pavement suddenly went from state-funded to cracked and rough. The small-town feel was instantly recognizable. It felt quaint, like a welcome mat at a favorite grandmother's house, and Callie almost already felt like this was home. A beautiful little town, she could tell, and she had not even made it a mile in yet. She then turned left on School Road, and as she approached Lutz, she heard what sounded like grinding coming from the back of the car. She turned at the intersection and tried to pull off the road as much as possible, though the roads out here were only about as wide as two cars. They didn't look like they got much traffic, either. Looking through her rear windows and trying to judge how much of her ass was still sticking out onto the road, she began to really take in the houses around her. The town almost whispered to her. It was the proverbial Spot on the Map. There were no cookie-cutter homes here. Some large, some small, some brick and some clapboard, trailers mixed in here and there. It looked like something out of a movie about Friday-night high school football games. Callie thought it was perfectly lovely.

She suddenly had the desire to trade in her wide concrete road with the perfectly spaced two-storey houses, all different shades of the same color, cut from the same cloth, for this… this utopia. The yards here had no fences on them, aside from the occasional chain-link. There was no pretentiousness about the place. Nothing to hide. No secrets. Probably no crime rate either. It was the kind of town where the only furniture shop was named after the town itself, and made visitors wonder how such a place could stay in business, when all your customers were from a town of eight hundred folks, and they already all had furniture. Presumably. Heck, maybe everyone did their part and bought new couches every couple of years to support each other.

Callie got out of the car and shut the door. The thump of the closing door was muted against the backdrop of the wind and the open air. There was hardly anything out here for sound to bounce off of. She pulled her belt loops up and walked to the back of the car. As she rounded the trunk she could instantly tell she had a flat. The right side of the trunk was visibly lower than the left, and she had not been able to pull far enough off the narrow pavement to make a difference like that. Nor was there a ditch anyway. Her tire wasn't the only flat thing. The entire landscape out here looked flat.

Shit!

She looked around but saw no one outside. The GPS on her phone – another of the special abilities attributed to the trillion-function robot she carried around in her pocket – told her she was two minutes from Shanna's house. That was driving, but it couldn't be much more walking. She had been driving about twenty miles per hour when she felt the flat. Sighing, she rounded the car and got her purse out of the passenger seat, then closed up and locked the doors with the fob. The car gave a reassuring beep as the locks all threw.

Callie smiled. "I'm gonna call you George," she said, patting the trunk. If asked where she came up with it, she would have been happy to explain the leap that took one from the color, baby blue, to the country singer, George Strait, to the song he sang, *Baby Blue*. She smiled again, and walked in the direction the car was facing. Without realizing it, she was now humming the song, an occasional word peeping out from her lips in a near-whisper – the words she knew.

Quickly, Callie came to an alley. Her phone, sensing she was now a pedestrian, had updated to show her a four-minute walk. "How 'bout that?" she said, and turned down the alley. She would take this alley all the way to Penn Avenue, then round the corner back onto the street, where Shanna lived, a few doors down. Callie would be back-tracking just a bit, but the air was nice. It was crisp and cool. She stuffed her hands in her pockets as she walked. So quiet out here.

A large white dog came tearing across a yard directly at Callie from the front and left, barking like the hounds of hell and sounding more like a bear. Callie's heart leapt up into her chest and she stopped short, yanking her purse up to her chest. The dog hit the end of its chain violently, flipping over backward, a loud unexpected yelp torn from its gullet. As it righted itself, it regained its angry disposition, staring at her and barking between growls that showed her its giant teeth.

"Good God," she said quietly, and began walking again. She was grabbing her purse strap across her body, unconsciously defending her center mass. Her heart was still slamming in her chest as she passed the dog and looked over at it. Her eyes darted around the backyard and up to the house, to make sure no one was out there, and said, "You're not a nice boy," with as much vinegar as she could manage. It was then that she noticed the man sitting in a folding chair up under the porch, smoking a cigar. This startled her, but she was able to conceal it in her gait along the rough pavement. The man was so large Callie couldn't believe she had been able to miss him. She returned her eyes to the road. *How about an 'easy boy' or a 'sorry 'bout that, ma'am – he doesn't bite'?* Nothing.

She began to slow when she looked up again, as there were two boys on bicycles sitting still, just off the side of the alley. One of the boys, a toe-head in a tank top, sat with both legs on one side of his bike, leaning back against the chain-link fence with his arms wrapped round the top bar. The other boy was standing straddled over his bike, leaning on his handlebars. They were both staring at her. Callie swallowed and made her mouth smaller, returning her attention to the road.

As she got closer, she could hear them whispering. She glanced up as she heard one of the boys say, "Scuse me, ma'am," but looked directly back at the road. The smirk he had been wearing on his face looked a little shady somehow. "I said 'scuse me!" the boy said again. She looked up, but did not stop walking.

"Yes?" Callie said, still not wanting to make eye-contact.

"You got some really pretty tits, miss. Can we see 'em?"

The boys howled with laughter, but Callie's heart was slamming harder than ever in her chest. She sped up slightly, hoping they wouldn't notice – hoping they wouldn't pursue her or antagonize her any further. Then she heard a woman's voice and looked up.

"Why don't you go look at your sister's tits, you fuckin' idiots," the woman said. She was leaning against the fence one more house down, on the opposite side of the alley.

"We'll look at yers if you'll show us, Shanna!" the boy who had not spoken said.

"Don't you wish," the woman replied.

Callie's eyebrows raised and she felt a skip in her heartbeat. Indeed, the woman looked like she remembered – the Drew Barrymore look of sexy mischief in her eyes, the blonde hair, the voluptuous chest... Her hair was a lot longer now, and she had put on about ten years, but it was her all right. Callie smiled and waved as she got closer. The woman smiled back at her and lifted two fingers off the fence rail. "You didn't have to walk, Callie," said Shanna.

The boys watched as Callie jogged the last few yards to the gate that Shanna was now holding open. As Callie stepped through it, Shanna flipped them the bird and made a sour face, then closed the gate and said to Callie, "Don't let them ruin your impression of Amanda."

"Well, I won't," Callie said, holding a finger up. "I actually do have really pretty tits, so I appreciate their compliment."

Shanna chuckled and leaned in to hug Callie as they approached the back porch, where two chairs sat beside a round wooden table. Callie got the cue quickly as Shanna settled into the chair on the right of the table, wrapping her hand around an old-fashioned glass full of ice and bourbon, judging by the bottle standing nearby. The table was faded bare wood, like an old fence in need of a sand and stain. It looked like it would give someone a serious splinter or two, were one not careful. Callie took the chair on the left and let her purse settle on the grass next to the chair.

"So how the hell are you, Miss Simmons?" Shanna said, leaning her head comically to the right, a wide smile on display.

Callie closed her eyes and shook her head, breathing in deeply. The air smelled sweet up here in Ohio. Fresh and clean. "You know, I've tried hard to rid myself of the Miss part. You would not believe the decade I've been through." She opened her eyes and ran her hair back, then looked back at Shanna. "But then, I wasn't lost in space on a doomed ship that never made Mars."

Shanna let a nice smile cross her mouth and nodded slowly. Almost a chuckle.

They stared at each other for a long moment. Callie didn't quite know what to say. This woman seemed like the legend. If there were a legend here, it was not Callie. Callie had never been in outer space, survived a doomed mission and made it back to Earth somehow. She had a billion questions she wanted to ask. It was going to be hard to be patient.

"Tell me about you, Callie. I guess you meant you were engaged?"

Callie smiled weakly and nodded. It was a forced smile and Shanna could see it. She pursed her lips and screwed up her face in response. An *ouch, that sucks* gesture. "Twice, in fact."

Shanna's eyebrows went up. Callie was immediately aware of how much the little girl had grown up in the last nine years. It was a shock to her senses, as the woman still essentially looked the same. There were the beginnings of some laugh lines around her mouth, maybe some pattern forming around her eyes. She just *looked* more mature. An older version of herself. One has a tendency to lock someone in at the age where the contact fell off. Shanna had existed in Callie's mind over the last near-decade as a twenty-one-year-old girl, a little immature, too eager to please, too obvious in her pursuit of her boss – who represented the only strong male figure in her life. She had also existed as a dead girl. Callie was in a state of shock sitting here looking at this woman who was suddenly back from the dead.

I was engaged to a wonderful man; his name was Chris," Callie said, wringing her hands in her lap. "I lost him on a dive trip in Mexico, off the coast. He drowned during a SCUBA accident."

Shanna shook her head slightly, but didn't make the usual wide-eyed face of horror and fake sympathy. She also didn't say any of the other bullshit lines people felt they had to declare in the face of someone else's loss – the *oh no,* or the *oh, I'm so sorry to hear that.* Callie was actually relieved by her abstract lack of tact.

"My second fiancee was a man named Jack Carpenter. I met him on the last project I was on. He was a former Navy man."

Shanna nodded this time. Very subtle. She took a sip of her bourbon and Callie watched the sweat roll down the glass and drip on her lap. Shanna saw her looking and suddenly reached out and touched Callie's knee. "My God, where the fuck are my manners?" Shanna said, rolling her eyes and shaking her head. "You want something to drink?"

Callie shrugged. "Sure, if it's no trouble."

"Ha!" Shanna said, staring straight at Callie. Then, turning her head back toward the house, she shouted, "JAY!"

Callie glanced back at the screen door, but could not see through it. After a moment, it popped open a few inches and a white face peaked out. The man saw Callie and nodded at her before saying, "Yes, dear?"

Callie looked back at Shanna, who stared right back at her, lifting her glass to shoulder-height. "Bring me another glass, babe."

The screen door shut. After a moment, it reopened and a man walked out, setting the glass down on the table. He looked at Callie and said, "You look familiar."

Callie looked up at the man but didn't recognize him. "Do I?"

"No, you don't," Shanna said, touching her knee again. "Go back inside, bubba."

The man turned and went back inside without saying a word. He looked downtrodden and lonely. Callie frowned and smiled at the same time, looking at Shanna. "Really?"

Shanna rolled her eyes. "You know him, Callie."

"I do?"

She nodded and took another sip of whiskey. "There's ice in the cooler here," she said and opened a miniature Igloo cooler that sat under the table.

"Oh, thank you," Callie said, and took a handful of the soft ice. It felt like it had been sitting out here for a few hours in the fifty-degree air. The cooler only partially helped. She dropped the melting ice into her glass and poured from the bottle that stood between them on the table.

"That's Jason Shepherd. He worked with us at Oliver."

Callie's mind reeled again. She tried to put the name with the face, but it wasn't working.

"He was a load master," Shanna said.

Callie shook her head and took a sip of the bourbon, licked her lips.

"Don't mind him. So what happened to Jack?" Shanna said.

Callie had to think back about what they had been talking about. She shook her head, trying to clear the sudden infestation of cobwebs. "Wait, darling. Are you married?"

Shanna smirked. Scoffed. "Shanna Shepherd? Boy that'd be a fuckin' mouthful." She took a sip of bourbon. "Nah. Not me, baby. I'm not the marrying type. I was in love once. But that didn't work out."

Callie was shaking her head dramatically now, leaning forward. "You really need to fill me in here. You're talking like we've been in touch for the last nine years!" She was still trying to get used to the fact that she was sitting across a tiny round table from a dead woman. In Callie's mind, for the last decade, this woman had literally been dead. And now, here she sat, living and breathing. And aged. Still as beautiful as ever. And Callie reckoned she had scars in all the right places. She had earned her age. Here was a woman who had a story to tell.

"I'm sorry, Shanna," Callie said, "I don't want to be rude, but I have to know…"

Shanna smiled widely at her. It was a genuine smile. Callie had to smile back. "You wanna know how I'm alive, right?"

Callie leaned back, holding her hands up and looking at the grass in front of her, eyebrows raised.

"I was crazy on a ship of fools, baby. Fucking incredible journey, that was. I'm sure you know how everything went down. But at the last minute," she said, holding her thumb and index finger a centimeter apart, "this close to Mars, I left the ship on an EVA. That was my resurrection."

Callie closed her eyes, letting the bourbon settle in her mind. She had not drunk it in a while, and was relishing its burn. Its warmth in her chest. The warmth that spread to all the nerves, all the blood cells. To the brain. She was trying to picture the words Shanna was saying, knowing she never could. Like describing a painting to a born-blind person. What good were words? Callie had never been weightless. She had never left a spaceship a thousand miles from another planet. She had never *been on* a spaceship. Or in space. How could she possibly relate to this woman? This woman, who still in Callie's mind existed as a little girl, had come back and claimed ascendancy over her. Over everyone, really. Holy hell.

"Anyway, you-know-who offered me a deal that saved my life. He offered me hush money to never mention his involvement or that he made it back. And I really didn't know what the hell was going on anyway. For fuck's sake, I was a goddamn kid, Callie!"

Callie nodded in agreement at this. She sipped her bourbon again. Breathed it in.

"I didn't know even what I was agreeing to. Alls I knew was that it didn't involve sex. I thought everyone dealt in sex back then. That was all anyone was trading. Well, he told me if I disappeared and never mentioned his name, he would let me live. He would… *save me*."

"How the heck," Callie said, turning suddenly in her chair, "did you keep the same phone number through all this?"

Shanna laughed out loud, staring at the sky and holding her glass up off the arm of the chair so as not to spill it with the ruckus. Her breasts bounced as she laughed and Callie suddenly felt a weird tendril of pride stretching out behind her. Like she had something to do with this woman. Like she had anything to do with her at all. To be associated with women like Shanna and Codi put Callie in a better place. Like she was on their level somehow. She imagined this was what a band manager must feel like. Someone who manages a Tanis Ransom or a Taylor Swift. Walks in front of the star and clears the way. Has her number in her phone. *You think she's cool? I manage her.* But somehow there was some pride to be had there. Callie had been the large-and-in-charge woman back then – just starting a career full of great big things – and Shanna just a little girl. Now, to see her having grown up and attained so much, having *been through* so much, Callie should have surely advanced in step with her, right? So if Shanna was now this, Callie had to be now, *that*. But then, just as quickly, reality set in, reminding Callie that she had not attained what she had wanted to. All her projects had ended in a failure of some sort. Shanna was definitely the winner here. Though her house didn't probably cost as much, her house had a back yard big enough to separate her from those little assholes who wanted to see nothing but tits. Callie's half-a-million-dollar home didn't have a yard like this. The weather here was relatively the same. But Shanna had lightning bugs. Callie had pointed at them while they were talking, but didn't say anything. Just a *hey, you have lightning bugs* gesture. Shanna also had a man inside. Apparently not marriage material, but she had gotten to make that choice, at the same time, somehow *keeping the man around!* Callie didn't. Callie had a house full of emptiness.

"That's the simplest question you'll ask all night," Shanna said. She reached over and spun the cap off the bottle of bourbon, one-handed, like someone who knew what she was doing. "I didn't have my phone. There was nothing to think about. When I got back, my phone was still in my apartment. That idiot Brian Bradley woulda probably broke it though, thinking it would end the number."

They both shared a laugh at this.

Shanna shook her head when the laughter died down. "Fuckin' idiot."

"Holy cow," Callie said, covering her mouth with her fingers. "Well I'm happy you do still have it."

Shanna finally turned sideways in her chair and looked at Callie through the tops of her eyes. "Do you want to see something crazy?"

And in the middle of Callie's brain – that part the scientists will tell you they associate with things like recognizing people's faces – birth-dates, movie titles, actors' names – she felt a sparkle. "You sent me that video didn't you," she said. She didn't ask.

And Shanna just smiled. "Of course I fuckin' did."

Shanna's desk was covered with magazines and papers, bills and junk mail. It looked as though this was her dumping ground for anything that came into her possession that had no immediate other place to be put. Her junk drawer, out in the open. She had to restack several piles to make room for her keyboard to slide forward enough to reach. Callie stood behind Shanna as she logged onto the computer and navigated through a directory structure. A post mounted to the desk supported two wide-screen monitors.

Callie stood with her arms crossed not sure what she was supposed to be looking forward to here. She turned her head and saw Jason sitting in the living room watching a fight on the television. He had a beer bottle in his hand, resting on his leg. She took in the décor, the furniture. The complete lack of a cat, which actually surprised her. They had a nice fireplace, but it looked like they might never have used it. More piles of junk sat in front of it – magazines and empty Amazon boxes. It was a cute little house, but apparently Shanna and Jason appreciated the function over the form. There was a large picture on the wall – something one might find at a garage sale for ten bucks – a terrible painting of a bull running toward the fourth wall, directly at the painter. A bullfighter stood in the background with the cliché red cape draped out beside him. The perspective was off somehow. Though the man was only a few steps behind the bull, he was rendered too small. Even smaller than some of the people in the crowd. The overall effect was that of a second-grader's effort – cute, but ridiculous. Callie smirked. The kitchen was messy, but there were no piles of pots and pans in the sink like she would have expected to see. Here in the den where Shanna had her computer desk, there was a tall dresser on the wall to her right. Several Day of the Dead dolls stood atop the dresser. They were covered in a thick layer of dust. Behind the desk was a window blocked out by cheap plastic blinds, yellowed and cracked. A dusty black curtain was held back with a frayed rope. Callie raised her eyebrows and returned her attention to the desk.

"I like your house, Shanna. It's cute and cozy!" Callie said, trying to make herself feel better.

"Oh, ha. Yeah, it's Jason's. He inherited it from his mom when she died a few years ago." Shanna looked around the room, waiting for something to load. "Could use some interior decorating, if you ask me."

Callie almost agreed but caught herself just in time. She was beginning to get the idea that Shanna was using Jason Shepherd for something. Maybe the house. Maybe companionship, but Callie didn't think that was it. Sex? Callie made a face at that and shook her head. "What is it you're showing me?"

Shanna looked up over her shoulder at Callie and said, "Look here. See this?" She was jiggling the mouse around, making the mouse arrow dance around the address bar in a window on the right screen.

Callie leaned in to look more closely. "Yeah, I think so…" she said, unsure.

"This is a Samba connection to a secure server. Look at this directory structure," Shanna said, moving the mouse down into the bottom part of the window.

Callie focused on some of the file names and felt her heart rate begin to increase. *Mars Mission Day 23. Mars Mission Day 51-56. Mars Mission: science experiments and Andy.* They all had something to do with the Mars mission, as far as Callie could tell. "Holy fuck!" she whispered, then immediately clapped her hand over her mouth. "Sorry."

Shanna grinned at her. "No need for that. Crazy shit, right? Watch this," she said, and double-clicked on a folder. Inside there were twenty or so files. She double-clicked on one of them and immediately Callie felt unsafe. Like they were doing something extremely illegal. There, in the middle of the screen, was a video player opening the file. It took a few minutes to buffer, as it was a video file coming from a network Samba share, from God knew where. When it finally finished loading, she was staring at the inside of a space ship. Callie had never been on a space ship. But it didn't take an astronaut to be able to tell what they were looking at.

"Oh my God," she said, leaning over the back of Shanna's chair, unconsciously trying to get as close as she could. There on the screen, Andy Duryea was performing some experiment or another, talking to the camera. Documenting the event. With the realization that Callie was watching video of a woman who was no longer alive, she suddenly got tears in her eyes and her skin went cold. Goose flesh covered her spine. "I can't believe this, Shanna. Where did you get this?"

Shanna looked at her again, the smile just a shadow on her face now. "This is on the Royal server."

"You're not afraid you're going to get caught? Get in trouble, I mean?" Callie said, covering her heart with her hand. She was not even aware she was doing so. Her eyes were wide and her chin was trembling.

Shanna closed the video and backed up a level, then entered another directory and played another. This one, when it finally filled the screen, took Callie's breath away. She literally yelped and slapped a hand back over her mouth. There, in fantastic color on the screen in front of her, was a camera view of the cockpit of the ship. Donnie Oliver and Mike Thurman were engaged in piloting the craft. The tears came a little harder this time for Callie. Shanna looked up and saw the emotion in her eyes. Callie tried to hide it quickly, tried to fake a smile. But Shanna had seen it. Slowly, Shanna backed her chair out, careful not to back over Callie's feet, and stood up. She embraced Callie and put her hand on the back of her head. "I know. I went through the same thing, Callie. Many times. I've cried over and over about this. I sometimes watch this stuff just to bring them back to life. Just for a minute."

Callie was openly weeping now, and had to sit down. Shanna guided her to a chair nearby. She dropped into it and cupped her face in her hands. Shanna retrieved a box of tissues and offered them to Callie. She stood at Callie's knees, putting her hand on Callie's back, pulling her in close.

To see them alive again in perfect clarity, it was too much. Callie had never expected this. She didn't know what she had expected when Shanna had said she wanted to show her something. But she knew it wasn't this. *My God. It's all on video.* When Callie was finally able to catch her breath, she looked up and saw that Jason had joined them. He was standing next to Shanna looking down at Callie. There was no scorn or mockery on his face. Just reverence. He had known these people too. It was obvious by the seriousness of his face that he had done his fair share of mourning over them too.

"How much is there?" Callie said through a gasp. The tears were freely falling down her cheeks.

"The whole mission," Shanna said. The ascendancy Callie had witnessed earlier – that easy-going arrogance that wasn't quite arrogance, but something more than confidence – it was all absent right now. Here was a human watching another human grieve the loss of these people she had known to have died so many years before. But the wound was so fresh. Callie would never have imagined that this stuff was even extant. Much less that she would ever get a chance to see it. "Up to the crash," Shanna said quietly. "Every camera, every angle, every minute."

"Oh my God," Callie said, shaking her head.

Jason Shepherd put his hand on her shoulder. "I've gone through this too. I want to kill that mother fucker myself."

Shanna looked at Jason through seductive eyes. Eyes that looked like they wanted either great amounts of sex, or vengeance. Callie guessed in this case, it was the latter. Then she looked back at Callie. "I am so glad you're here, Callie. We want to help you bring him down."

Callie's heart skipped a beat. She had not yet considered that as a viable option. What a perfect setup though! Two prior Oliver employees – did it not make perfect sense? And especially considering that one of the two was actually *on the ship!* Maybe she was even meant to die on it. And surely would have, if not for the last-ditch magnanimity Brian Bradley had found in his shitty black heart. She felt a new pulse in her veins. Maybe she actually had a chance. And these were indeed the perfect people to help her. Maybe she could even get Thad to join in on it – though she doubted his kind-hearted nature would allow him anything resembling an act of revenge.

Callie looked up at the two of them standing over her, offering her comfort, wondering what to say. She gulped and used the tissue to clear away her tears, trying to get some control of herself. "I'm sorry. I just wasn't expecting that."

"I know, hon. I didn't want to introduce it to you. I wanted it to shock you."

Callie was shaking her head. "How is it… How does it… How did you get it?" she said, holding a hand up.

"I managed the cameras for Discovery Channel on the mission."

"Yeah, I remember that," Callie said, pointing a tissue wad at Shanna.

Shanna nodded. "I had to get credentials to the server on the shuttle for the camera to connect to it. All the video I took recorded directly onto the shipboard servers. Well, there was also a constant trickle-feed of data being sent back to Royal's servers. Bradley had installed all that shit without anyone knowing. So the whole time we were gone, all the video feeds were being transmitted back to Earth."

"But how did…" Callie started, looking down, trying to figure it out on her own. Then she got it. "He used the same fucking credentials, didn't he?"

Shanna's mischievous smile returned full-force. She nodded. "That stupid fucker uses the same password for everything."

Callie was shaking her head slowly, just trying to take this all in. "Oh my God." She stared at Jason and Shanna for a minute. Jason had his arm around Shanna's waist, while she stood crossing her arms. In his left hand, he held a beer bottle. He took a swig of it, then Shanna took the bottle from him and took her own swallow. She offered the bottle to Callie. *Why the hell not?*

"So what's the plan?" Callie asked.

Shanna looked confused. Shook her head quickly, frowning. "You're in charge here, sister. You tell us what to do. We're in."

Jason nodded slowly and shook his fist in the air. *Damn right* that gesture said.

Callie had her team.

Chapter 22

Y ou wouldn't believe it, Rebecca," Callie said, putting her hands on the sides of her head. "I mean, I know you have no point of reference. But I'm telling you, she was a little girl when I knew her. Like early twenties. And smart as a whip, but not very mature. It's so insane to see her grown up. She's smart! She's… she's just this…" Callie fumbled for the words. "I don't know. She's just a woman now. It's unreal. When the last part of someone you knew was someone so young, to see them all grown up is just surreal."

Rebecca was nodding. "I know what you mean. I have a cousin like that. He and his family moved to Vietnam when we were like ten. So I didn't see him for many years, until I was in my mid-twenties. And in my mind he had just stayed in place as a kid. It was so fucking weird to see this grown-ass man who sounded just like the boy I remembered.

Looked like him too. His face was just a little more rugged. Crazy shit."

Callie sipped her wine. "So I think I finally have my team," she said, licking her lips.

"Oh yeah?" Rebecca said, leaning back on a hand, taking a sip of wine with the other. They were sitting on her living room floor, which seemed to be their headquarters of late. Callie felt like their friendship had really grown over the last few months. The experience down in Fiji had obviously put them in pretty close proximity, but what it had also done was to break down some final wall, and Rebecca had finally let Callie in. Now she felt she could really call Rebecca a true friend. And hanging out at her place just felt warm. Natural. It had just organically happened. No one had made a conscious decision to base most of their get-togethers over here. But when broken down, it did make sense. Codi was here. Codi was *comfortable* here. Natalie was here, too. And Rebecca did have the better sound system.

She had a computer hooked up to her receiver. On most nights, Rebecca would have Spotify open on that computer, just playing stations based on songs she liked. Anyone could walk up to the keyboard and add whatever song they wanted to the queue. So there was always an endless stream of music. This made the place warm to Callie. Cozy. Safe. *Home.*

Callie leaned back on her own hands, fingers digging into the thick carpet behind her, and stretched her legs out in front of her. She sat on one of the large pillows Rebecca kept on the floor for nights like this. "Yep. So I think we'll all pile in the minivan and spend the day in Manhattan next month."

Rebecca giggled at the minivan comment, but held her hand up, closing her eyes momentarily – trying to break through the light-heartedness and get to a little seriousness, at least for a minute.

"Callie, you know you're going to have to be very careful there. They have major fuckin' security at these events."

"Yeah," Natalie chimed in from the couch. "You know what your best bet is gonna be, Callie?"

Callie looked over at Natalie, who lay back against the arm of the sofa, smoking a joint and shaking her foot to the music. "Uh-uh. What's that?" asked Callie.

"They're having the meeting at Astor on the Park. They will undoubtedly spend many hours out on the grass. The festival part of this thing is your best bet. That's where they let loose and stand around drinking, socializing and listening to the live bands and shit."

"They have live bands?" Callie said, raising her eyebrows. "Holy shit!" The language, she found was coming easier and easier these days. She attributed this in large part to the new friends she had been spending so much time with lately.

Natalie nodded. "Yeah. Well, one, at least. But yeah, it's a big to-do. So like, the major players will be attending the private conference," she said, twisting her hand in the air as she spoke, "but there will be hundreds of others from all over the world doing these little workshops and side-meetings and shit. So they always spend the week in meetings and conferences, then have a big hoo-rah on Friday night. "

Callie nodded, looking up at the ceiling, trying to imagine the chaos of the day.

"What *is* your plan, doll face?" Rebecca asked, tilting her head and pouting her lips. She looked genuinely interested.

Callie looked her in the eyes, dropping the smile. "I need to iron a couple things out still. But we have a lot more tools in our bag now."

Walter hung up the phone and tossed it on the couch beside him. He had just gotten off the phone with his probation officer. Before that, he had spoken with Jennifer Cambria, his attorney. Things were looking up on that front, at least. She had gotten the judge to reduce his sentence to time-served and two years of probation. In his mind, probation was just their way of keeping a leash around his ankle. They would know everywhere he went, everything he did. He would have to submit to random drug tests, sometimes as often as twice a week. That was not a problem for him. Cannabis was legal. Everything else was of no concern to him. Walter had never been one to dabble in that stuff. Cambria had rolled her eyes when the DA had mentioned the frequent drug-testing. She knew Walter was good for it. And after the first few, they started grasping, finally, that they wouldn't be catching him on anything. This guy was white-collar all the way.

He leaned his head back against the couch cushion. His left hand warmed a short glass of bourbon, sitting on a coaster atop an ottoman tray. That was one thing he did dabble in. And it had become a lot more frequent of late, and had begun starting earlier and earlier in the day. He rolled his wrist to look at his watch. Almost eleven in the morning. And this wasn't his first glass.

In the courts, he was getting closer to that light at the end of the tunnel. At home, however, there was no light. No tunnel, either, for that matter. Thevi had come several times and taken out large swaths of her belongings in a large suitcase that she would presumably dump on the floor wherever she was now, and come back for more. Each time she came, Walter tried to talk her into sitting and having a conversation. Anything. But she only said there was nothing to discuss. He wondered how over ten years together could just vanish so quickly. How it could be turned into something so meaningless – not even worth fighting for – because of one mistake. The way Walter saw it, was that she – of all people – should have seen it coming, even though he couldn't. But the part she didn't get was that he *hadn't* seen it coming. Thevi believed that surely, he must have seen it. He must have known it would happen someday. Not that she had always believed that. But once it *did* happen, her thoughts retroactively corrected themselves to accommodate the new belief. Like some sort of quantum eraser for his relationship, his sin had gone back in time and dropped hints along the way for her to pick up. Hints that would never have shown up had he not put his dick in his best friend.

Walter slapped his forehead, closing his eyes, and ran his hand back through his hair. Shook his head. He still couldn't believe how royally he had fucked this up. The walls were bare. The parts of Thevi he had taken for granted seeing around the house – they were all gone. The parts of the house that were Walter didn't have the same life about them. The Uma Thurman *Pulp Fiction* poster, the John Goodman *Big Lebowski* poster, the Leo DiCaprio *Inception* poster, where he stood in the middle of a street... All three of them featured handguns in them. And not a smile to be seen anywhere. There was very little life in the faces he had hung around the living room. Thevi's photographs – friends laughing and holding cocktails up for the camera, the two of them as a couple, family from both sides – they had all had soul to them. Life. And now they were all gone. How had she been able to make such a sudden and decisive cut?

He leaned forward and put his hands on his knees, ready to stand up, when his phone vibrated. He picked it up, swiped the answer emblem. It was Callie.

"Hey, big bro. How you holding up?" she asked. He could hear her smile and it gave him a little comfort.

"I'm using a whiskey bottle as a cane. But other than that, I'm doing great," he said.

"Oh, no, Walt. You're drinking alone? This early in the day?" she said.

There goes the comfort. Now I'm being judged? "Well, yeah. Sorry," said Walter.

"No. No need for that. Get another glass ready. I'm on my way."

Just like the old days. Walter sat on the left end of the sofa in the den. Callie sat right next to him, wrapped in by his arm, her feet curled up beside her on the couch. Callie, being the lightest, was tasked with getting up to flip the records when the tone arm reached the dead wax. Elvis Costello and the Attractions' "Punch the Clock" was the current spin. They were vaguely paying attention to the music. Callie was indiscriminate in her selection. When it was time for the next record, she would pick one at random. Not having near the appreciation for music that Walter did, she liked just about everything she heard, and thus didn't care what came next. In Walter's mind, "Goodbye Cruel World" would come next. But that was the least likely candidate with Callie being in charge, since it sat right next to the place-marker board she slipped in when the current selection had come out.

"Walter, I would like to have our Christmas dinner at my house this year," Callie said, taking a sip of the bourbon. She could feel his shoulder move around her, and knew he had shrugged. "Good," she said, patting his knee. "I think it will be less likely to remind us of the bad shit in the air." She now felt him nod.

"Whatever's clever, bub," he said. "Who's all coming?"

"Well, I've already invited Rebecca and her gang. That's Natalie and Codi and Sam, of course."

"That's cool. Is that it?"

Callie shrugged this time. "I don't know. Who else you have in mind?"

"I guess you're not inviting Minus this year?" Walter said.

Callie sighed. "No. Let's stick to couples only. Besides, seven is a weird number."

"So, I guess you're saying we're a couple then."

Callie looked back at him. Their faces were only a few inches apart, but in the odd, twisted-around position she was in, she was not able to get any closer. Her desire had been to give him a quick kiss on the lips. A friendly reminder that she was here for him. But she couldn't reach, so she just said, "Yeah. I guess so," and patted his knee again. But he didn't move. So neither did she. They just looked each other in the eyes for a long moment. She saw Walter's throat move as he swallowed. She felt a tingle in her tummy. "Walter, kiss me."

So he did. He leaned in to meet her mouth with his own, putting his hand on the back of her head. After several long seconds, she finally twisted in her seat, bringing her legs around, then whipped her right leg over his and sat atop him, putting both of her hands on his cheeks. His hands were on her hips. Why did this feel so right? As their tongues danced together, lips wet with the newfound passion, light kissing sounds audible over the music, she considered this – how damn *right* it felt. And the underlying thought there was: how did it feel so right, yet they had only just discovered it? Twenty years it had taken! And now, after her first time actually experiencing sex, she wondered why the hell she had taken so long to let him in. To let anyone in, actually, as he had never actually tried to get in. But boy, had she been missing out or what? Had she known what it actually felt like, she would have given up that ghost long ago, she reckoned.

The kiss itself lasted well into the next song. When Callie finally broke it, her entire body was on fire. She could feel sweat under her arms and on the small of her back. She kept her hands on his cheeks and sat up straight, staring into Walter's eyes. She could feel him beneath her, a *something* right in the place where it felt best, that had not been that same *something* a minute or two before. Breathing deeply, she swung back off of him and fixed her hair with a finger from each hand. Then she stood up and went to the turntable to move the stylus off the dead wax.

Walter sighed loudly. "Are you fucking kidding me?"

"Calm, calm, little sailor!" she said, turning back to him with her shirttails in her hands. "I just can't listen to that for another thirty minutes." She pulled her shirt off over her head and retook her position on his lap. There was simply no way she could stop this train. Not now.

Three weeks passed. Christmas was here. Callie's house smelled like cooking from the moment someone entered the front door. She and Rebecca had been in the kitchen all morning. Rebecca had shown up at 6:45, knocking quietly, an arm full of paper sacks. Callie had let her in with a hug, and they had gotten right to work. Callie was excited about having Rebecca be part of the Christmas dinner. This was her second year to be part of it, but this year she was acutely involved. It felt like she had come in and taken part ownership of it, which was exactly how Callie wanted it. And it wasn't so much a dinner, as an all-day celebration of friendship, gift exchanges and eating. The cooking part of it was actually for all three meals of the day.

Walter was still asleep, in Callie's room. He had stayed over last night. And a few nights here and there before that. It was not a rare thing now. What had been once non-existent was now a frequent event. They had decided to announce their official status today. But it really didn't need announcing. Their whole crew had already gotten used to seeing them together in a different way than it used to be. Now they held hands a lot. Now they sat snuggled together on the couch when people were around. They kissed and smiled together, hung on each other. Callie would stand with him when they were standing around, arms wrapped round his, head on his shoulder. Touching his stomach. Touching his cheek or nose. Standing behind him with her head against his back, arms locked round his waist. Like two people in love, in other words. Everyone had seen the slow transformation. The patient transition that all had been sure would happen eventually anyway, was therefore not much of a surprise when it did. They all expected it, and thus let it happen organically, without feeling the need to comment on it. Furthermore, everyone was completely accepting of it, and, in Rebecca's case, had even wondered why they hadn't just gotten together ten years ago. Or fifteen. Or hell, twenty. Callie had told her at one point that she had not been ready for Walter at any time in her life like she was now. She wasn't sure if it had been the death of her first fiancee, the loss of her second or the sex that had caused that loss. But something had clicked, instantly changing everything. And maybe it was the blissful enterprise itself, opening her eyes to a reality previously unimagined that finally allowed him to look like a contender.

Natalie showed up around nine with Codi and Sam in tow. She showed them to the den and helped them find a place on the couch before joining the other two women in the kitchen. Hugs all around, then she washed her hands and dug in to the meal preparation. After she had been there for an hour or so, Walter finally appeared in the doorway, fresh from the shower. His longish hair was combed neatly and his beard was soft and squared. He wore a long-sleeve shirt that was form-fitting and expensive looking. It showed off his physique, and Callie found she couldn't keep her eyes off of him. He still looked like his normal rough and rugged self, but like someone trying to hide his masculinity – his alpha – behind a comb and a dress shirt. He wouldn't fool anybody, Callie thought. There was no hiding that chest and those thick arms. He oozed sexiness and manliness. Her hands found those muscles for brief brushes and touches throughout the day.

Callie had to admit to herself, when the thought made its way into her brain – as it was doing with a greater frequency these days – that she had probably been holding out for Walter all along. It felt so natural to be with him now that she felt like maybe her most recent two love interests were only preludes to the real love. This felt completely different. Natural was a good word for it. But it wasn't the only word. Right was another. She even considered words such as 'duh', 'of course' and 'what the hell were you waiting for, you idiot?'

When they sat down to dinner that evening, Callie looked around the table and smiled, mostly to herself, feeling very proud for the way things had turned out. This looked so much like her future that she almost didn't want it to end. They had eaten, listened to loud music, danced, played games and eaten again. Sam and Walter had gone out back after lunch and smoked a cigar together, clinking glasses of whiskey together. This had made Callie smile too. It was nice for Walter to have another man here to share his own tradition with. Rain or shine, snow, blizzard or hellfire, Walter smoked a cigar and drank whiskey on Christmas. A few of them had taken light naps on the couch while others sat in whispered conversations nearby. They had exchanged gifts and laughed and joked and told stories and loved and drank and enjoyed each other's company in great loads. And then, in keeping with the final dictum of the day's ritual, they gathered on the couches to watch a Christmas movie. This year's pick, which Walter had brought on BluRay disc, was *Home for the Holidays*. Codi and Sam were excused for this part of the evening, and they retired to the spare bedroom to spend some private time together.

Natalie dozed off halfway through the movie, wrapped in Rebecca's embrace like a child with her mother. Rebecca lay lengthwise on the couch, facing the television, with Natalie facing her, head buried in Rebecca's chest under the covers, snoring softly. Several half-full glasses of eggnog stood on the coffee table; wrapping paper and bows still littered the carpet near the tree; the lights around the fireplace blinked and changed colors festively, reflecting in the shiny bezel of the TV. The night was winding down on another successful Christmas get-together, and Callie was wrapped in her own set of arms, lying across Walter's lap, both of her hands holding both of his, drifting in and out of a doze while Anne Bancroft and Robert Downey Jr. danced in broken eggs on the kitchen floor. Before she fell asleep completely, lost to the rest of the movie, Callie had one more thought of the near future. In about two weeks, they would embark upon the next step in her journey toward closing the biggest chapter of her life: bringing down the dark horse. She had started her investigative poking around in what seemed like a different lifetime. She had learned little bits over the last decade, putting her puzzle together one tiny piece at a time, never bothering to try to speed through the thing. Never picking up the pace, never worrying about the fact that at her current pace, she might die before she ever got her hands around Bradley's neck. But now, here it was. Right in her sight. So close she could almost reach out and touch it. And funny, the last feeling she had before her eyes closed against the movie screen, was not one of dread. Rather, it was one of pride. Excitement and wonder. She had a great team around her now, who all had the same goal – even if not all of them shared the closeness of the initial tragedy's effect. The closeness of her new group of friends was so apparent, so unique and wonderful, that she knew everything would be all right. There was no dread to be had here. Nay. There was success in their near future. And that same group of friends would stand around in someone's kitchen, or in a bar wearing formal clothing, holding up tall, skinny glasses of bubbling champagne while Callie made a speech about victory and good-over-evil, and how persistence prevails in the face of the enemy – another one they could finally put to rest. And then they would clink and drink and she could finally let it go. She could move on with her life, satisfied that the right thing had been done. And with the right people. A faint smile moved her lips and she adjusted her head on the lap that held her. Squeezed the protective hands. And then Callie closed her eyes. And slept.

CHAPTER 23

The new year came and went like a swift breeze. After Christmas, Callie had spent the entire week at Walter's house with him. It was almost like she had just forgotten to go home. There was always a nagging nervousness in the back of her mind, in her stomach, where she feared Thevi would come back. Walter had assured her that this wasn't going to happen. That Thevi wanted no part of him, or Callie, or being back in this 'damned house' as she had called it. He said it with a reserved acceptance, and Callie could tell part of him was still mourning the loss of his marriage. All that remained was the paperwork. And Thevi had already filed to end that as well. All her stuff was gone, and Walter had changed the locks anyway. So if she were to show up, he had said, she would have to knock like the rest of 'em.

Callie's leave of absence from work had dragged on, to the point where she finally had wondered if she needed to reapply before going back. Would she go back? She had no pending projects under the scope at the moment, and nothing pressing. They would find work for her if she returned, that was sure. She was useful in everything she touched. But at the moment, she was taking Mr. Lancey at his word, taking her sweet time, and taking a breather from the chaotic maze her life had dropped into over the last couple of years. There were entire days where she would stay in bed naked with Walter, stretching her boundaries. Stretching her rules for sleeping in. Stretching her laziness as far as it would go. When late one night they heard fireworks coming from somewhere down the street, they had stopped what they were doing, Callie looking up at the window as if to be able to see through it, hands on the bed beside Walter's head, her eyes wide in the dark, wondering what the hell was going on. They'd had to remind themselves it was New Year's Eve before they finally caught on. It was then that Callie had realized how quickly the week had gone.

She spent many mornings sitting at the drafting table in his bedroom journaling, writing out plans for the big event. He would sneak out of bed and surprise her with his hands, reminding her she was naked, and carrying her back to bed. In this light she was seeing a completely new side of her longest-running friend. A side they had necessarily denied themselves for half of their lives, and were now allowing it to prosper. So the newness of him felt authentically wonderful.

The Sunday before the event started, Callie got up early and got on the computer, looking for an agenda of events. All she had found so far was a bulletin that mentioned the event, welcoming the personnel of Royal Research, and mentioning the band that was playing in Central Park next Friday night. The band, Rising Atlantis, was one Callie had heard before, and she got a little sidetracked with the excitement of seeing them live, even if her focus was to be elsewhere.

She sent Shanna a text to see if she could get into anything with her white-hat skills. Sadly, Shanna replied, no. Shanna said she was planning to join them the day of the concert though, for whatever mischief and malarkey they might get up to. She was always up to ruffle a few feathers.

Callie leaned back in her chair, staring at the ceiling fan, a tall mug of coffee steaming on the desk, her fingers loosely looped through its large handle. She thought about all the things Shanna had told her that evening in the yard behind Shanna's – or rather, Jason's – house.

Shanna had admitted she was ready to be done with the anonymity she had sworn herself to in regards to Atlas and Brian Bradley. She had taken a pretty good sum of money – in the couple of hundred thousand dollars range, Callie guessed – to keep quiet about his involvement, and, she had understood, to sort of disappear. But in retrospect, Shanna couldn't really define what that had meant. There had been no paper contract, of course. Nothing to which she could refer back. "That fuckin' idiot," Shanna had said, "didn't really tell me what the hell I was supposed to do. Just lay low, I guess." And so Shanna, being the naive, young girl she was at the time, had mostly complied. Mostly. She had done some talking to her circle of friends. That never went anywhere. No one from any news stations or papers ever contacted her. And, she doubted they would have believed her had she told them she went. *Uh huh. Sure, sweetie. You got so close to Mars you could see it in your windshield. Right.*

She had known that Brian Bradley would stay the hell away from the Oliver Company when he got back. So Shanna had sneaked around a little. She didn't quite let them know she was back. But she did contact a few of the ground crew to ask if they knew anything. None of them had known her well enough to recognize her voice on the phone. Except Jason. Jason Shepherd had been a little smitten with Shanna, and had 'about flipped his shit' when she called him. After she had finally calmed him down, she had told him to please keep quiet about her being back. He had agreed, but had wanted to see her. Which worked out nicely, because she had been in need of a place to stay.

After the company broke up, he moved into his mom's house. Shanna followed as a matter of convenience. And the sex wasn't bad. So when his mom died a few years later, Shanna and Jason had the place to themselves. She sort of just took over a spot in it. Shanna never denied the man whatever sex he wanted, but she thought he knew she wasn't really into him. And like that, he had also fallen into that convenience factor. It was too inconvenient to break up, to kick her out. And they were at least pretty good friends.

But in recent years, Shanna had begun to feel like she was missing out on a lot of living. Not so much because of her 'vow of silence', but because of who it had made her become. She had stopped being the outgoing, fun-loving person she had once been. She seemed to blow through her entire twenties as a reserved, self-conscious dud who never did anything fun for fear of being 'discovered'. She never went to clubs or concerts during the best decade of a person's life to do such things. She had, therefore, decided to stop playing by the rules of some asshole who was no more looking after her than the man in the moon.

It was almost exactly two years before Callie had come back into her life, that Shanna had started trying to connect people in Royal who were still alive. She thought if she could get them in touch with each other, they would naturally get curious and start talking. And if the right people talked, maybe someone would open an investigation. Sending the video to Callie had been one of her bolder steps. But seeing that it didn't bounce back had given Shanna hope. After a year of not hearing anything made of it though, she began to wonder if she had screwed up. That old psychology came back easily, she found. She doubted herself again. But the calls to Thad Cloys had gone out around the same time. They were texts and emails, specifically, in which she tried to get him to reach out to any of the others she had contacted. Cloys was apparently not big on checking emails though, and did little with the texts except probably to suspect they were spam. The one about Callie did get through though. He had looked her up on OuterCircle and sent her a message. Not knowing Callie only got onto her Circle account about once a year, it had sat unread. So he had finally looked up the company number for Bohr Enterprises, which she had listed on her profile as being her employer. And that was that.

Of course, Shanna King had no idea it had worked. She had no clue Callie and Cloys had met up. But the project had served its purpose. Callie was asking. And with the video Shanna had sent her, Callie had known there was something worth looking into. Callie's accidental call to Shanna had just been a bonus. Shanna had never expected to actually get back in touch with her. It was nice though, Shanna had admitted, to be back in touch with a real friend from back in the day. And Callie's heart had warmed at the mention of the F word. She had never known Shanna had thought of her as a friend. It was sweet, but also a little worrisome, as Callie had to think back, wondering whether she had been unkind at all. Of course, she hadn't. Callie wasn't unkind to anyone.

When Callie got the text from Shanna saying she planned to join them at the outdoor festival, Callie yelped with excitement and instantly touched the call button. *Calling…*

"What's up, girlfriend?" Shanna said.

Callie yelped, "You're coming? Are you serious?"

"Yeah, hell yes I am! I figured I would fly up Thursday night and crash your couch, if you're cool with it, then we could roll in there together and stir up a little shit."

"I am so excited, Shanna. You have NO idea." Callie took a sip of her steaming coffee.

"Oh, I do. It'll be fun. I'm all for a little mischief," Shanna said and giggled.

Callie laughed and almost blew coffee through her nose. "You're effing crazy, Shanna King!"

"I'm really good on a full moon," she replied.

"Well, hell yes, you can crash at my place. I can get a couple of my other friends who are going to come over that night too. We can have some drinks and get our ducks in a row."

"I look forward with great enthusiasm, Callie Simmons. I want you to know me," Shanna said and Callie instantly got glassy-eyed.

"Wow, Shanna. I'm…"

"I'll see you Thursday night, okay? Text me your address!" she said, and hung up.

Callie set the phone on the desk and wiped her eyes.

Monday.

In the morning, Callie called reception at Astor on the Park, figuring it would be hectic with a lot of people checking in and showing up for the many conferences. She was right. She could hear the noise of a crowd in the lobby over the phone. "Yes ma'am, I just need to know which ballroom the meeting is in this morning."

"I'm sorry?" the woman said.

"Which room is the conference in this morning, for Royal?"

"Oh, no ma'am, we don't have any conference rooms. I think the ones you're thinking of are at the Saint Regis."

Callie frowned. "I'm sorry, I thought the Astor was hosting the Royal party."

"Uh…" the woman said, "I'm not sure how that could be. There are some of your co-workers who are staying here, but we don't have any ballrooms. Oh! You know what? Maybe you're thinking of Mister Astor. He founded the St. Regis… Is that where you might have heard the name?"

"Ah!" Callie said, playing along, "You know what, you're absolutely right. I'm so sorry to bother you." She hung up. No way she could have made that mix-up. She had no idea who had opened any of the hotels, and didn't think she would ever find the time to care. But at least she knew where the conferences were now.

Tuesday.

Callie and Natalie took Callie's car into Manhattan to go scope out the scene. They found the St. Regis on the complete opposite end of Central Park from where the Astor was located, and Callie found it hard to believe anyone would stay at one and commute to the other every day. It was a twenty-minute drive from one to the other, without traffic. That would be nonsense. But, she remembered, the receptionist had said some of the employees were staying at the Astor.

Natalie had the idea that they should go in and just ask how many of the employees were staying there. So that's what they had done. Callie had let Natalie do all the talking, as she had no idea what the plan was. But it turned out to be as simple as Natalie had advertised it.

"Excuse me, can you please tell me how many Royal Research folk are staying here? We're from accounting. We're trying to consolidate and maybe do some shifting around, since some rooms have become available nearer the events."

The woman she was speaking to was shaking her head before Natalie had even finished though. "I'm sorry, ma'am, but I don't know what events you mean. I don't know if any Royal employees are staying here. Certainly no one checked in with a company card from that company."

"Oh, maybe they've already moved then. That's good," Natalie said, patting the counter. "Thank you for your help."

As they exited the building and went down the steps, Natalie looked over her shoulder at Callie and said, "Okay, that's a bust."

"Well at least we ruled it out. Let's go have a look at the other hotel," Callie offered.

"Do you just want to walk into one of the conference rooms and see if they're in there?" Natalie asked.

"No, I was thinking more along the lines of sitting in the lobby and seeing what moves and shakes," Callie said, pulling her hair into a ponytail. It was muggy this morning and her neck had started sweating under her hair.

As they made the drive back to the Regis, Callie passed four hot dog vendors, and wondered to herself how those damn things were so popular as to warrant that many vendors on the streets. It's a hot dog, people! When she mentioned this to Natalie, Natalie had turned to look at Callie and said, "Have you ever tried one?"

Callie's smile dropped away.

"Guess that's a no," Natalie said, and turned to look out the window again. And that was the last on that subject.

The lobby of the St. Regis made a ridiculous statement in beauty, Callie thought, all marble and gold. It looked like what she pictured the entrance to heaven looking like. With that thought, she had almost giggled, picturing Saint Peter standing by the stairs checking a list for names as one approached.

They found chairs, and they were comfortable. But very quickly, Callie could tell this would be a bust too. There were far too many people wandering in and out, hustling and bustling about like they were on a mission. And not one of them wore a shirt that read ROYAL EMPLOYEE across its back. What had she been thinking? Well, she couldn't answer that, not even to herself. But she had imagined it would be a little easier, at least. Maybe spotting a group of them talking about it, and following them into a room or something.

Natalie suggested it would be very easy, dressed nicely as the two women were, to blend in anyway, and just ask one of the concierges which rooms the conferences were in. Callie nodded at that, but held her back with a hand on the wrist.

"I'm still not sure I want to go into one though. What if we get caught?"

"Look," Natalie said, holding Callie by the shoulders. "There are probably only a few people there in that whole fuckin' company who know you. The odds of one of them being in-"

"Callie? Is that you?" a voice interrupted. Callie and Natalie both turned to see a woman approaching with a mischievous smile on her face. *Holy cow, it's Cardna,* Callie thought. She shot a hard look at Natalie that said *Don't ever talk to me about odds again!*

"Well hello there, Miss Darwyn," Callie said, faking her best smile.

Natalie stared at the approaching woman with little surprise on her face. She, of course, didn't have the advantage Callie had. Cardna came to stop between Callie and Natalie, forming a small triangle with them, still smiling.

"Hello, I'm Cardna Darwyn," she said, jutting her hand out toward Natalie.

"Natalie Reese," she said, shaking the proffered hand.

Cardna turned her attention to Callie at that point. "What brings you to town, Callie?"

Callie felt suddenly sick to her stomach. What were the odds, indeed? This woman's saccharine bullshit should be so easy to see through. Only, it wasn't. She looked truly, genuinely happy to see Callie standing here in the hotel lobby. What a great actor she was.

"Well, you know, Cardna," Callie said, overcoming her fear quickly and touching Cardna's shoulder, "I actually live here." She was rewarded with the raised eyebrows. The delicious flinch that spoke of surprise.

"Here?" Cardna said, pulling her chin back and holding her hands out like she was about to play a piano.

Callie offered a sour little smile and said, "How's the conference, Cardna?"

"Oh, it's just going swimmingly well," she said, smiling so wide Callie thought the woman's face was going to crack in half. Cardna was looking at Natalie as if she were showing off her friendship with Callie. "I'm surprised to see you here, Callie," she added, turning back to Callie.

"You mean," Callie said, mimicking the move Cardna had made a moment before, like she were playing a piano, "here? Or do you mean *anywhere*, since I escaped your unlawful restraint?"

Cardna raised her eyebrows and blinked quickly. *Ouch.* She cleared her throat. "Let me know if I can do anything for you," she said, grasping Callie lovingly by the upper arm. Then she looked at Natalie and smiled.

Natalie raised her chin and gave back a natural, gorgeous smile of her own and said, "I think you can go fuck yourself," without a note of irony in her voice.

Cardna swallowed, dropping the smile, and made a quick exit. Callie and Natalie looked at each other. Then Natalie said, "Well. That was fun."

Callie nodded slowly. "Yeah. But you know what? We're outnumbered here. Why is she acting defeated?"

Natalie looked around and shrugged. "I dunno. Public place? Humility? Maybe she found Jesus."

Callie grabbed Natalie by the arm. "Yeah. Right. Let's get the hell out of here."

Wednesday.

"It's no longer a surprise. That's all I know," Callie said.

"Yeah, sure. But if she doesn't see you for the rest of the week, I mean, until Friday, she may just think of it as a coincidence," Walter said, holding a hand out, palm down. The veins on the back of his hand stood out like pipelines. Then he shrugged. "If you weren't wearing a Royal badge or anything, there's no reason for her to think you'll be back."

Rebecca was nodding, pursing her lips, squinting in that peculiar way she had that told you she was really thinking about something. "Yeah, but I think there's another angle to this," she said.

They were all sitting on her sofas, drinking homemade martinis and trying to regroup. Any time Rebecca made a drink at home now days, she called it a homemade drink. Callie guessed she thought it made it sound more organic somehow, though Rebecca was not particularly interested in being 'organic'. Callie had actually found it a little surprising when she had first gotten to know Rebecca. She had stricken Callie as a vegan. Feminist. Hates men. Won't eat steak or carry a purse that ever touched leather. So when they went to Owen's Steakhouse one night and Rebecca had gotten the rib-eye, Callie had put her glass down, tilted her head and widened her eyes at Rebecca. She had smiled back at Callie and winked. She knew the image she portrayed.

"What angle would that be?" Callie said, frowning.

"Maybe you're there with Royal. You were down in Fiji with Royal under a temp badge, right?" Rebecca said, holding out her martini as if to offer it to Callie. One of the fingers on the stem was pointing at her. "Wouldn't it be possible for you to still be under that contractor badge or whatever?"

"Holy shit!" Callie said, slapping the sides of her face with both hands, holding them in place for a minute, so much like a young Macaulay Culkin that Natalie burst out laughing. "I do have a badge!"

Walter squeezed her thigh. He was looking sideways at her. She turned to face him, putting her mouth only a few inches from his. "Seriously!" she almost shouted. "Minus said he would get me another badge. I have a company badge."

"Well there you go," Rebecca said. "So you can just walk into whatever conference you want."

Callie was shaking her head. Walter giggled and took a swig of his martini.

"Where is Minus in all this?" asked Rebecca after a moment.

"What do you mean?" Walter asked, hiking his chin at her.

"I mean, where is he? Literally. Is he at the conference?" said Rebecca.

"Oh, surely," Callie said. She adjusted on the sofa, putting her feet up beneath her, sloshing her martini a little and spilling some on her lap.

"Fuck sake, woman," Walter said, trying to wipe it off her jeans with his bare hand.

"Are you sure you can love a girl like me? Chasing down this dark company and doing my own thing so much?" Callie said, out of the blue.

Walter smirked at her and shook his head. "No. Not at all. But I'm giving it a shot. And for now, we're good."

"You two are too cute to fuckin' resist," Natalie said.

Rebecca turned suddenly, pointing at her with her martini, sloshing some of it in the process. "Holy fuck, you just used all three toos in one sentence!"

Thursday.

Callie drove up to the Royal building, knowing Minus would come in to his office before going to whatever conferences he had that day – if he attended those at all. If he would not be called on to participate, or if no one would notice his absence, Matt Minus wouldn't even show up. Such things were a waste of his time. So Callie was counting on his dedication to his current project, which would most definitely have him in the office at 6 a.m. If one thing could be said about the man, it was that he always got to work on time. He hadn't missed a day of work in so many years it was ridiculous. And he was never late.

Callie, without a badge, had little trouble getting into the building. The security guards were used to seeing her. She had been here so many times she could have walked the path from the front door to Minus's office in her sleep. As she got to the end of the hall, she was rewarded with the light spilling in from his office.

She knocked on his doorjamb and he turned in his chair, eyebrows raised. "Well, well. It's you again," he said, clearing a stack of papers off his desk.

"Well, I was just in the area. Thought I'd drop by," she said, smiling weakly.

"Right. In Manhattan at 6 a.m. on a Thursday. That's reasonable," he said, leaning back.

"Am I disturbing something?" Callie said, pursing her lips.

He blinked at her and shook his head. "I'm sure you are. We all are. Entropy and all that. But your disturbances elsewhere usually make shit better here, so who cares, right?"

Callie made a sour face. "What the heck are you even talking about?"

He sighed and waved his hands. "Who knows. Just a little hungover, probably."

"I totally get it," Callie said, smiling. She shrugged and looked around the room.

"Anyway, I was wondering if you still had that badge," Callie said.

"What badge?" he said, spreading his hands on his desk.

"The badge I lost in Fiji. You said you'd get me another one?" she said.

"Ah, yes. I think it's right here, in fact, Minus said, opening his top drawer. He pulled out a badge on a lanyard. As he handed it to Callie, she realized her picture and name were already on it.

"Perfect! Thank you, Minus!"

He was looking at her wide-eyed, shaking his head. "You know, I had that made months ago. You forgot to come get it." He sat staring at her. Then he added, "How are you so spritely in the mornings?"

"Spritely all day, baby!" she said, slapping the armrests and standing up. "Thanks, friend," she said, turning for the door.

Minus waved her away. Callie knew people could only take so much of her energy this early in the morning.

For the rest of the day, Callie felt like Ray Liotta at the end of Goodfellas, running back and forth, here and there, trying to take care of a bunch of errands and last-minute preparation details before she had to head to the airport to pick up Shanna. She had to go to the grocery store to get steaks – Walter had insisted they should cook steaks on the grill for the whole gang this evening – then to the liquor store to restock the cabinet. She also needed to stop by the mechanic, because her Check Engine light had started coming on. Secretly, she had been hoping Walter would help her with that part, because she was intimidated by mechanics – having heard how they were prone to taking advantage of women. Walter, however, begged out, saying he had something very important he had to take care of. He had told her not to worry about it and that it would hold for a day or two. But Callie was nervous about it. What if her engine blew up?

When Callie finished her chores, she was sweating and hungry. She really wanted to go home and shower before she went to the airport, but was running too short on time. Shanna's plane touched down at 6:10. Callie watched the updates on a phone app, and felt excitement in her spine when it said she had landed. She sat in the cell phone lot waiting for the call from Shanna saying she had her suitcase and was ready for pickup. The call came nearly forty minutes later, and Callie remembered that arrival times did not mean instant pickup. She could have showered after all. Heck, she could have bathed.

When Shanna came waltzing out the sliding glass doors, Callie squealed and hopped out of the car to give the woman a hug. They met in front of the car and embraced, kissing each other on the cheek. Shanna was wearing a very out-of-place sunhat and large sunglasses that took up most of her face. She looked like a tourist in Rome on a summer morning. Not someone dressed for January weather in New Jersey. In the evening. But she looked good and Callie was happy to see her. She popped the trunk, helped her load the small suitcase and they headed for the highway.

The sun had long since set when they pulled into the driveway at Walter's house. It was after eight and everyone was pretty hungry. Fortunately, the steaks were almost done. Walter had his chef's apron, a comical red thing that read in large black letters, 'FUCK YOUR SALAD, WE EAT MEAT'. Shanna instantly loved him. She squealed with delight as she approached him at the backyard kitchen. Sam leaned against the counter top nearby, drinking a beer while Walter held a short glass of something amber. Callie made the introductions.

Rebecca and Codi sat by the fire pit with Natalie. Rebecca hopped up and shook Shanna's hand, then took her by the arm to the fire and introduced her to the other two. Natalie instantly loved Shanna. She hopped up to hug Shanna and took her by the shoulders when she noticed they were almost exactly the same height. "Oh, nice, I'm not the shorty anymore!" Natalie said.

And Codi piped up from her chair across the fire. "Shut it, woman."

"Oh. Yeah. Sorry, forgot about you, dear," she said, looking over her shoulder with an exaggerated frown. "Hey! You want a drink?" she said, taking Shanna by the hand.

"Not just yes," Shanna said making a face that advertised her readiness.

Natalie giggled and led her by the hand to the counter top, where there stood a large array of liquors and a bamboo tray full of assorted glasses. Callie watched all this with a smile on her face, holding onto Walter's arm but facing the opposite direction from him while he manned the steaks.

"How do you take your steak, sweetheart?" he asked as Shanna stepped up beside him with a glass of whiskey in her hand. He looked over and saw her glass and added, "Hey, cheers. You do eat meat, right? You're not one of them fuckin' weirdos, right?"

"Walter!" Callie said, slapping his butt for him. "What if she were a vegetarian? You just insulted her!"

But Walter was looking at Shanna, who was shaking her head and smiling. "Nah, babe. She wouldn't be standing this close to the searing cow meat if she didn't love it."

Shanna held up her glass and they clinked them together. "Run it through a warm room, I like to say."

"That's my kinda girl," Walter said, and began shoveling them off the grill and onto a waiting platter covered in parchment.

"What's the paper for?" Shanna asked, pointing.

"Keeps the steaks warm until they are ready to be consumed."

Shanna frowned. Then she saw the trick. When he put the last one on the tray, he pulled the remaining edge of the paper over the tops of them, then laid the spatula on top of the heap. "Steaks hold the paper down," he said with a wink.

"Yeah, I got it," she said, putting her hand on his shoulder.

Rebecca had cut her steak up so that she could sit by the fire and pick up the tender morsels with her fingertips. She had done the same for Codi. Shanna sat next to Callie on a bar stool at the bar overlooking the counter top and the grill while Walter and Sam stood by the grill. Walter had asked Sam how he ate his steak and Sam had looked in his direction and said, "Like a fuckin' man, bro," and Walter had laughed so hard he almost spilled his drink. The others had laughed too, but Walter was visibly impressed when he saw Sam using the steak knife, guided by the backs of his knuckles, slicing off perfect bite-sized chunks that he then speared perfectly with his fork and delivered to his mouth. He had obviously been doing this a long time. Walter wasn't sure he was even that good at cutting steak himself.

After everyone had gotten through about half of their meal, Walter remembered something and looked at Callie as if for approval. But she had no idea what the look meant. She tilted her head and frowned at him, a mouth full of baked potato. He only smiled at her then said, "Hey, cheers everybody. This is to Callie for – well, for dragging this dream along for ten years. Hopefully tomorrow, she'll get to see how it ends!"

There were shouts and hollers at that. "Cheers! Woohoo!" Callie said. Some of them clinked their glasses. And everyone drank.

"So you up for a little malarkey tomorrow, Shan?" Rebecca said. Callie noted the lack of the last syllable and again thought of how close everyone had become so quickly.

"Malarkey and then some," Shanna replied, holding a finger off her glass to illustrate. "I'm all about shenanigans."

"Yay," Rebecca said, smiling widely. "Glad to know you don't limit yourself." Then she rolled her finger in the air and added, "So... if we happen into a little chicanery, tomfoolery or sneak-thievery, you're okay with that, I suppose?"

Without missing a beat, Shanna said, "Oh, I'm more than okay with them. And I submit that there may be a little ballyhoo, or even some skulduggery..." After a brief paused accented by the pursing of her lips, she added, "if the moon is right."

Everyone laughed out loud at this exchange, including Walter, who had to lean forward, coughing hard, as he had sucked down some of his cigar smoke at the exact wrong moment.

Rebecca was even laughing. She leaned forward, holding her wine glass out to Shanna, who met her over the empty space and touched her whiskey glass to the stem. They drank and smiled at each other. Rebecca turned to Natalie, who sat very close to her with her knees bent, feet up in the chair. She put her hand on Natalie's knee and said, "Don't you just love her, Dommie?"

Natalie, staring into the fire, nodded and smiled widely.

"Hey, where'd you get the nickname 'Dommie'?" Callie asked. "Sort of always wondered."

"Natalie Dominique Reese," Natalie said, speaking through held breath.

Callie raised her chin, putting to bed one more mystery in her life. Rebecca smiled a 'there-ain't-that-better?' smile at her and looked back at Shanna. "So what do you do, hon?"

Shanna held her glass up high and looked through the bottom of it at the invisible stars. "I drink."

They all laughed again.

"Yeah, not much of anything. I worked as a graphics designer for a home builder out in Columbus for a while."

"Oh really? That's interesting." Rebecca said.

"Nah, not really," Shanna said, putting her feet up on the seat and twirling her hair with her fingers. "What *is* interesting is the name of the home builder I worked for."

"Do tell," Rebecca said.

"I worked for Sherlock Homes."

Rebecca twisted her mouth up and nodded slowly. Natalie laughed, coughing out a chest full of smoke. Callie leaned her head back, rolling her eyes.

Walter said, "Seriously? It was named that?"

Shanna nodded, a tight-lipped smile just barely showing itself. "Yeah. The owner's name was Dan Sherlock."

"That's fuckin' great," Walter said, pointing his cigar at her. "That is fucking great, man."

"Oh, yes, it was, my dear Watson," Shanna said. This brought everyone to laughter.

"Well played!" said Rebecca, leaning forward to give a high-five. Credit where it was due.

"So who's house is this?" Shanna finally said, looking around the backyard with clear approval.

"This is Walter's house," Callie said, pointing her fork at him.

"Oh, okay. I thought we were staying at your house is all." Shanna said, taking a sip of her whiskey.

"Well, we can if you like. I just figured everyone would gather over here for the evening since he has the better backyard," Callie said.

"Yeah, this is hard to beat," Shanna said, nodding. "Is anyone here grass friendly?"

"Boop!" Natalie said, raising her hand over her head and pointing straight back down at herself. "Over here, sister. Whenever you're ready."

Rebecca, sitting with her legs crossed, her hand holding a glass of wine that stood on her knee, waved and raised her eyebrows. "We're all friendly here, by the way. She's just the purveyor of the goods."

After everyone finished their plates, they stacked them in the sink by the grill and refilled their drinks, then found seats around the fire pit, where they stayed until late in the night, smoking grass, sharing stories and laughing a whole lot more than Callie would have ever believed possible. This was the perfect antithesis to what she had imagined the night to be like. She had imagined stress and fretting, anxiety, worry and a bad stomach.

CHAPTER 24

Friday.

Callie and Shanna had sat up by the fire until everyone else had given up the ghost, talking and catching up about things they had no idea they needed to catch up on. When they stopped adding logs to the fire and it finally went to embers, it was well after two o'clock. Callie had shown Shanna the spare bath and handed her a fresh towel, then crept into the master to wash the smoke off herself. It was almost three when her head finally hit the pillow next to the softly snoring man of the house. She slipped in next to him, shivering and naked, and snuggled up against him, her hands made into tight fists that she sandwiched between her chest and his back. She kissed his shoulder and the alarm was going off.

Callie sat up and swiped the alarm dismissal on her phone screen. It was suddenly seven o'clock. *Good wow. I just laid down.* She ran a hand back through the mess on her head and stretched, then stepped out of bed. The towel was still wet from the shower she had taken a few hours before, but she took another just to warm up and wake up.

When she got to the kitchen, thick robe and her fuzzy slippers, she put on a pot of coffee. She slid onto a stool at the island and pulled the newspaper over in front of her. It was a week out of date. She didn't remember ever seeing Walter read a newspaper, but for some reason he always had one in the kitchen. Callie rested her face in her hands, elbows on the counter, yawning. She wished she had three more hours of sleep, but did not regret the time she had spent with Shanna. She also wished she would have gotten in touch with her many years before. It seemed they had a great friendship ahead of them.

A hand touched her shoulder and she turned to see Shanna sliding onto the stool beside her, all smiles.

"Good mornin' love bug," said Shanna.

"Hey, girl. How'd you sleep?" Callie asked.

"I have no idea. I slept through most of it," she said. "Coffee smells good!"

Callie turned to look at her, shaking her head. "Is that a general declaration on the state of coffee, or were you referring to my pot specifically?"

"Oh, both. But I do await, with great excitement, the steaming mug I shall see in front of me shortly," Shanna said, holding a finger up.

"Why are you up so early?" Callie said, smiling.

"The curse of the Kings," she said. It took Callie a moment to realize she had referred to her surname. "I've always been an early riser. Even those days I really wanna sleep in, my eyes pop open around six forty-five." She rolled her eyes.

The coffee maker started gasping for breath and Shanna stood up. "Allow me…"

"Of course," Callie said.

"To have the first cup."

Callie and Shanna drove up to the doughnut shop and bought a big box of kolaches for everyone. Several of them had disappeared by the time they came back through the front door. And the rest of them were cold by the time everyone else finally woke up. Callie felt a nervous excitement in her stomach, but it wasn't the bad kind. It was more excitement than nervous. About that, she was happy.

"So what's the plan, guys?" Rebecca said when they had all found seats around the den. The sofas and chairs formed a rough square facing inward. Codi and Sam were on the love seat, but were not planning on taking part in the malarkey, as Rebecca had called it the night before.

Walter spoke up first, raising his hand as he did so, "Has anyone verified that Bradley is actually here?"

Callie nodded. "Yeah. Our girl on the inside said all the key players are here," she said, looking at Rebecca.

Rebecca nodded and added, "Yeah, she said all the offices down there have been dark all week."

Walter nodded, pursing his lips.

"I think our best bet is to wait until everyone has had a chance to get a few drinks in them," Natalie said. She had pulled out a notebook and began flipping through the pages until she found the page she wanted. "Last meeting gets out at one pm. I expect they'll be in the park by two."

There was no *minivan* for them to cram into, so they ended up taking two cars: Callie's Kia and Walter's Bentley. When they had gone into the garage to decide who rode with whom, Shanna had stopped and turned to look at Callie. She had not laughed at Callie's Seltos when she'd been picked up at the airport, but now, Shanna looked like she was about to laugh. "Wait. You drive a Kia?" she said, but was pointing at Walter's Mulliner. Callie frowned, not knowing what the joke was.

"Don't bother trying to figure that shit out," Walter said, putting his hand on Shanna's shoulder as he came up behind her. He pulled her in for a tight one-arm side hug. "She only buys cars for the color."

Rebecca, on the other hand, came into the garage from the house and walked right past the little group. One hand was in the air over her shoulder as she said, "They all move faster than feet," and then added, as she passed under the still-rising overhead door, "I call shotgun." She pulled the handle and swung gracefully into Callie's orange conveyance.

Natalie came hot on her heels and climbed into the backseat without saying anything. "Sorry, Callie, darling, but I've never been in a Bentley. And may never again," said Shanna.

Callie grinned and rolled her eyes. "It's fine. Hope you like his music though."

Parking was more terrifying than usual for a Friday afternoon in Manhattan. They ended up having to park on the street near Carnegie Hall, so they had a few blocks to walk to get to where they wanted to be. The party they intended to crash was on the Great Lawn, but the bands wouldn't be starting until around seven. There was already a crowd several thousand strong near the stage, staking out their little spots of grass in anticipatory excitement. Callie wondered how spread out the Royal crew would be, or if they would be easy to spot. If they walked directly to the Park from the St. Regis, Callie reckoned it would be much like watching a fire drill. Several hundred people in nice attire streaming out the double doors and heading toward the music. But her better mind knew that wouldn't happen. They would probably walk straight across, indeed, but it wouldn't be until they had changed clothes, and probably freshened up.

There were several large awnings erected on the east side of the park where there could clearly be seen Royal branding. There were some tables that looked like the type to hold the shiny silver implements of the catering trade. The buffet would surely attract employees, even if they went back to their rooms before the rest of the party took place. Walter wandered over and spoke to a couple of young ladies who worked in the company party business. They were standing there in their nice, ironed khaki pants and tucked-in black Royal polos, smiling, hands behind their backs – just waiting for the party to come to them. They were ready to work.

Callie turned to Rebecca and Shanna, who stood looking around the Park, taking in the sights – tourists with parasols, locals walking their dogs, eager young teens hoping to get close enough to the stage to catch a pick from the guitarist, maybe get a good Insta shot with their iPhones. "You know what, girls?" she said. They both turned to look at her. Shanna in her ridiculously large yet chic sunglasses and sun hat, Rebecca in her breezy cotton pants and a sweater, they looked like models for Opposites Day. "I'm hungry as an ox."

Rebecca pursed her lips and nodded. "Yeah, I could eat my weight in soba right now."

Shanna burst out laughing at that. "Soba? Fucking soba? Out of all the perfectly good dishes to be found in Manhattan, you want soba?"

Rebecca tilted her head and shook it – a look that said, 'you just don't get it, do ya?' "Sweetie, I didn't say I wanted it. I said I could eat my weight in it. But now that you mention it, I am actually fucking craving it."

Shanna stifled her giggles with a curled up hand, then wiped her eyes.

"Well, I'm going to have one of them street dogs," Callie said, pointing in the general direction of nowhere, behind her.

Shanna followed the direction of her outstretched arm and spotted a dog-walker. "Callie. It's not that desperate yet," she said, putting her hand on Callie's shoulder.

"Ha, ha," Callie said.

Natalie walked up at that moment, using the tips of her fingernails to arrange the onion pieces perfectly on a street dog covered in mustard and ketchup.

"SEE!?" Callie shouted, turning and pointing both index fingers at the hot dog. "Where the heck did you get that?"

Natalie looked around. "Seriously? They're fuckin' everywhere. You said so yourself, 'member?"

Callie put her hands on her hips and tried to act matronly. "Well, you could have asked if we wanted one."

"Ew," Rebecca said. "No thanks. I'll stick to real meat."

"Sorry, I thought you weren't interested in them," Natalie said.

"I wasn't. Then you talked me into trying one."

"I did?" she asked, looking genuinely lost.

Callie stomped off in search of a vendor. It didn't take her long to find one. She paid her eight bucks and had him dress it like she liked – relish and sauerkraut and onions with mustard – and began walking back to where the rest of the girls waited. But having taken her first bite, she stopped dead in her tracks, looking up toward the park and holding her free hand up near her mouth. Someone watching her might have thought she was about to ask to speak to a manager. Then she said to herself, *What the actual fuck.*

Licking her thumb, she turned around and meandered very slowly back toward the vendor. Callie timed it so that when she got to the cart she was already working on her last bite. "Yeah, I'm gonna need another one of those, please," she said.

As the hour of action grew nearer, the crowd thickened and the clouds seemed to clear a little. It wasn't cold; it was in the mid-fifties. But it was still chilly enough to make Callie happy she had worn a windbreaker. They had staked out their own spot, about a hundred yards from the stage and on the eastern side of the crowd, within view of the Hotel St. Regis. They were close enough to the stage to see people milling about, running mic cables and making other excuses to walk across a five-foot elevation to be seen by thousands of eager spectators.

Walter stood beside her, hands in his jacket pockets, calmly taking in his surroundings. He had no care in the world for seeing Rising Atlantis. *Too much arena, not enough rock*, he had said. He had also called them Kings of

Leon wannabes. Callie had rolled her eyes heavily at that. She never judged someone for the music they chose – that was what made the world go round – but that had been a ridiculous statement, and he deserved to be judged. Harshly and swiftly.

A man walked by wearing a t-shirt that caught Callie's eye. It simply read *Bill Stickers is Innocent!* Callie frowned and pointed at the man, grabbing Walter's arm. "Babe!" she whisper-shouted, "That's the second time I've seen that shirt today! Who the heck is Bill Stickers?"

Walter looked down at her, dumbfounded and awestruck. "Ah, uh… I -" he stammered. "You, uh… wait. Really?" he said, leaning in closer to her. "Are you serious?"

Callie suddenly felt stupid. "How the heck am I supposed to know who he is?"

Walter breathed in slowly, shaking his head. Then said, "You need to keep up with current events, babe. Bill Stickers will be prosecuted. Bet your fuckin' wallet on it," he said, pointing his first two fingers at her.

Rebecca, hearing the exchange, shook her head, looking up at the clouds. She stood with her arms crossed, slowly rocking back and forth between left foot and right. "Walter, you really are an ass, you know that?"

Natalie and Shanna, meanwhile, were laughing so hard they couldn't breathe – only, they were doing it in perfect silence, and behind Callie, out of her line of sight.

Callie threw her hands up. "Guess I need to read more of the flippin' newspaper."

The stage lights went out. The crowd got loud. The sun was setting behind the buildings on the far side of the Park. The air was redolent with the scent of human beings. Sweat and laughter and beer and happiness. People were shouting and raising fists to the sky as someone walked out onto the middle of the stage and asked if everyone was ready to have their asses rocked off.

Rebecca, ever the picture of perfect posture, stood straight like a rod, clapping with her hands in front of her chest, smiling like she knew something secret. Callie had to smile at that. The woman did know something secret. The whole of the tiny group did. And they would finally get to share that secret with the world.

Walter pinched Callie's waist and whispered in her ear that he was on a beer run. Then he disappeared.

Within the minute, a band took the stage and started into a hard-hitting bass line with a metallic edge to it. The crowd suddenly came to a roar, making it impossible to have conversation. Three gigantic screens came to life. One on either side of the stage, and an even bigger one that took up the entire back wall behind the band. A drone-shot landscape soared by on the three screens, adding an element of flight to the music. Shanna turned to Callie and said, "Holy fuck, it's Ninet Tayeb!" then turned around to shout and clap her own welcome. Natalie turned around and held Rebecca by the upper arms and stood on her tiptoes, kissing the taller woman on the lips. "I'm going in. Love you."

Rebecca patted Natalie on the hips and winked at her, then returned her arms to their previous position, crossing her chest. Shanna looked at Rebecca and smiled a crazy, excited number showing lots of teeth, then held both her thumbs up and hopped up and down. She then turned and put her arms around Callie, moving her with the song. Callie had not heard the band before. Apparently, everyone else had. Though she knew it was not the music about which these women were excited. Their plan was finally in the last stages. Shanna held onto Callie and she held back, resting her chin on top of Shanna's head, swaying with the attractive beat. How happy she was, being back in touch with a woman she never knew she was missing.

After a time, Walter returned holding four giant cans of craft beer. They were twenty-four-ouncers, and had probably cost a hundred dollars for the set. Callie rolled her eyes as she took two of the Pirate Flags and handed one to Shanna. Walter handed the third to Rebecca. At least in the double-can size, their trips to the beer stand would be halved. Callie reckoned their trips to the portable toilets, however, would likely be doubled.

After an hour and a half, the first act said their thank-yous and left the stage. It was now fully dark outside, save for the Central Park lighting and the purple spots from the stage. The crowd was so thick now that one couldn't move to the edges of the Park without twisting and turning like a snake, holding beer against the chest and trying to suck in the gut, as if that extra half-inch would get you through the next squeeze.

Walter reached into his jacket pocket and slipped out a steel flask with his initials on it. The triple-W caught the lights from the edge of the park as he twisted the cap off and offered it to Callie. She took it in his hand and twisted the whole conglomerate up to her mouth, sipping long from it. He then offered it to the other two women, who gratefully accepted their own draws. Shanna licked her lips and closed her eyes. "That's Evan Williams!" she said, holding a hand over her heart.

"Callie, is it okay if I fall in love with this woman?" Walter said suddenly. Shanna grinned at them, proud to have gotten it so right.

"Well, I already beat you to it," Callie said, running her hand down the shorter woman's arm all the way to the wrist, where she took hold and squeezed. Shanna leaned in and put her arm around Callie's waist, her head against Callie's shoulder.

"I'm so glad you found me, bayba!" Shanna said.

Rebecca leaned in and put her hands on Shanna's cheeks and said, "We're so happy you're here. You're a perfect fit for this little entourage."

Shanna pursed her lips and nodded her head dramatically. Callie was smiling too. But as the word settled on her, the smile faded. "Wait," she finally said, "Entourage?"

Rebecca smiled lightly and put her hand on Callie's upper arm. "Baby, stars take the lead. All the planets fall in line."

Shanna was still nodding. *What the hell?* Walter was looking down at her too. There wasn't so much a smile on his face as there was the shadow of one. Something proud. Something *paternal*. The corner of his mouth twitched up. Then he said, "Honey, don't act like you don't know the power you have. You command a lot more than just this little group of ours. You could run the fuckin' world."

There was a haze in the sky. The lights didn't quite reflect off of it, but they didn't penetrate it without a bit of a fight. A progressive rock band was on the stage now, beating some heavy percussion into the cool air, riding people's drunkenness like a surfer finding the perfect wave. Callie was almost in a state of euphoria. Walter had pulled out a pipe a few minutes ago and they had all taken a puff or two. She was on her second Big Beer. In congress with all the Tiny Sips she had taken, she was now beginning to feel some altitude.

It was almost time.

Finally.

Rebecca had squeezed her hand a few minutes before, then turned to Walter, standing up on her tiptoes to whisper something in his ear. He had bent slightly to listen, then stood back and nodded. Then Rebecca had given Callie a thumbs-up and disappeared into the crowd. Some of the people around them were dancing. Callie guessed the percentage of the crowd that was actually dancing was somewhere near the holy shit mark. This crowd was a happy one.

Callie could feel the slight vibrations in the ground itself as people stomped and jumped and danced and stamped and clapped and shouted. The very air was alive with the night. The music was loud and rich. The best part of it all, she reflected, was that the Plan didn't call for her to actually do anything but wait. Everyone else had been appointed their own tasks. They would report back to her, or the results of their personal endeavors would necessarily show themselves to her accordingly. Maybe she was a good delegator, after all. She took a moment to be proud of what she had put together. She had assembled a team to go out and get the very bad guys she had spent the last decade chasing while she stood here, arms crossed, listening to the band, getting high and standing next to the man she now called a true love.

The smell of cotton candy reached her nose. She lifted it a little higher and closed her eyes. Enjoying the moment. For it would all be over soon. The music. The high. The drink. The companionship. The standing in the greatest fucking park in the world and being part of history in the making – bringing down the mother fuckers who had killed all her friends. It was only a small history, maybe, but it was a real history. It wasn't the future. Not anymore.

The band on the stage was called Luxury Trailer. Callie had never heard of them either, but was finding that with each passing song they played, she grew closer to being a fan. Walter was doing a lot of swaying back and forth, eyes closed against the sky while he took it in. He, too, knew what was coming.

When the band hit their last note, thanked the crowd and exited the stage, Walter grabbed Callie by the shoulders, kissed her on the lips and looked her in the eyes. "If I don't come out of this alive, Callie," he said through tight lips, "avenge my death." She looked at him with love in her eyes. Loving him was getting to be so much fun.

Callie laughed out loud and squeezed his hand. Then Shanna took her turn hugging Callie, and kissed her on the cheek. Walter and Shanna disappeared into the crowd, and Callie stood alone. The next time she saw everyone, Royal would be a different company.

CHAPTER 25

Walter ducked his head under the edge of the awning and smiled at the two ladies, girls, really, who stood there. "Hey girls!" he said, making a small show of slipping his badge out from inside his jacket. "Y'all can take off, I'm gonna get all this packed up."

"Oh," said one of them, looking more excited than surprised, "that's great. Thank you!" Walter guessed she was a fan of Atlantis and would be as close to the stage as she could get within the next few minutes. The other girl, not quite as sure, grabbed a backpack off the grass and smiled weakly at Walter as she exited the tent. Then Walter took a seat in a collapsible chair and checked his watch.

Shanna stood close to the middle-left side of the crowd, looking intently for anything that looked like a group of Royalites. She pulled her phone out of her pocket, checked the time, then sent a quick text letting the others know she was in place. Within the minute, a woman walked out on stage and came right to the center. She adjusted the microphone and smiled at the waiting crowd. There was light applause, as no one knew what to expect. Shanna giggled and rolled her shoulders.

"Good evening everyone! I hope we're all enjoying the show so far!" The applause was a lot greater this time. "Let's give a great big thank-you to Ninet Tayeb and Luxury Trailer!" she said, and stood back clapping, a wide smile on her face. She was too good at this shit, Shanna thought. Rebecca waited for the cheers to die down, then said, "The main act will be up here shortly. Are we all ready for Rising Atlantis?" This time the sky almost came down. The eruption was sudden and fierce. It sounded like a hundred thousand people shouting in unison at the top of their lungs. Shanna wondered how far off that number was from reality. This time, Rebecca didn't clap. She just smiled and looked across the sea of bodies as she waited for the roar to return to normal levels. When it finally did, she pulled a piece of paper out of her pocket and unfolded it, then said, "We'd like to give a big thank you to our friends from Royal Research Corporation, one of the parties joining us here today. Hey, Royal! Can you show me where you are? Let's see those hands!"

Fucking brilliant, Shanna thought, shaking her head. About three hundred hands went up, and – thank God – they were in about the same general area. They were off the stage-right side, about a hundred meters back from the apron. Shanna began making her way toward the group.

"That's great! Hey guys," Rebecca said, waving at them from the stage, all smiles. "Okay, so we had a drawing and would like to congratulate Mr. Brian Bard – um, excuse me, Brian *Bradley* on winning the prize!" The sound of weak applause scattered around the place. "Brian, if you'll meet the team under the Royal awnings, we'll get you hooked up."

She assessed the crowd for another second, then said, "Okay, that's it for me. Enjoy the show, everyone!" Then she walked off the stage, waving at the crowd, again to light applause. There were some wolf-whistles and cat-calls as she disappeared into the curtains on the stage-left side.

Shanna sidled up to Cardna, who looked exactly like the picture Callie had shown her from the company intranet page. She was surprised the woman didn't have red hair. *If I were named Cardna, I would have red fuckin' hair.* Cardna noticed her and looked down at her briefly. When Shanna saw this peripherally, she half-glanced up at the woman and gave her a wan smile. Cardna returned the half-smile – obviously only trying to be polite – and returned her attention to the screens that were showing the crowd, much like a Kiss Cam at a baseball game.

She glanced down at her phone again, then texted Natalie saying she was ready.

Brian Bradley came ducking under the awning with a look of dumb wonder on his face, and Walter stood up to greet him. "Hey, Mr. Bradley, how's it going?" he said enthusiastically. "So happy for you, man!"

"Yeah, I guess I am too, but I don't remember entering a raffle," Brian said, losing a little of his smile.

"Ah, no," Walter said, waving the comment away. "No one had to enter. Just a company thing. The execs did a drawing from the week's attendees and you're the lucky guy!"

"Well, hell, what did I win?" Brian Bradley said, leaning back a little and spreading his hands wide. Walter thought he looked a little like a used car salesman. Walter felt a little like one himself. *Takes one to know one, I suppose.*

"Well, if you'll follow me, I'll show you," Walter said, and guided Bradley out the back of the awning and off the Park toward the street. As they stepped to the edge of the sidewalk, a beautiful wine-colored Bentley Mulliner pulled to a stop, just in front of them. Bradley's eyebrows went up. No fear there. Not yet. Not with a Bentley. Walter opened the front door for him and swept his hand inside.

Bradley ducked to look at the driver, then stood up and looked back at Walter. "You want me to get in? Who is that?"

"Ah, she's Jennifer Cambria. She's just here to take you back to the shop."

Bradley looked fully concerned now, shaking his head, his mouth open like he wanted to say something, but couldn't.

"Mr. Bradley!" Jennifer said, leaning out as far as she could across the passenger seat. "Hey, how's it going? I'm Jennifer from the Detroit office!"

He looked back at Walter once again, and Walter smiled at him again. Then he shrugged and dropped into the red leather seat. Walter closed the door for him, then got in the backseat.

Suddenly, the gigantic concert screens went black. Interpreting this as the start of the next band's show, the crowd erupted. Cardna bounced up and down on her toes, clapping and trying to get the best view of the stage. Shanna smiled and clapped, keeping an eye on the woman peripherally. Then the footage came on. It was a scene from the inside of a space ship. The crowd didn't know how to take this. There was general applause and some laughter, but nothing real committed. The three large screens showed what looked to be footage from a helmet-mounted camera looking through a window into the cargo bay of a shuttle-type ship. As the helmet lowered, an astronaut came sailing across the void and slammed into the window. "Jesus Christ," said a voice in quiet tone. Then the camera moved to show gloved hands opening a pressure chamber door and letting the other man in. The spacesuit the other wore clearly read THURMAN on the left breast. Shanna swallowed hard, trying not to let her eyes fill with tears. She had seen all this footage many times, of course, but now, here, on these gargantuan screens… This was surreal.

The view changed again to see across a void of space where apparently another ship stood waiting. Then suddenly, there was flame blasting out behind it, and the other ship slowly moved out of frame. The crowd was growing more and more silent, having no idea what was going on, or what to expect. Shanna looked at Cardna, who had stopped jumping up and down as soon as the footage came on, and was now standing and staring, awestruck, with her hands clasped in front of her chest. Clearly, she did not yet know what she was looking at either.

Suddenly, Cardna turned and started to walk away, toward the awning that bore Royal's company emblem and name. Shanna reached out and grabbed her by the wrist. As the woman jerked around at her, Shanna said, calmly, "You're going to want to see this."

The woman stared down at her with anger in her eyes, then glanced up at the screens and then back down into Shanna's eyes. "Who the hell are you?"

"Right now? I'm a friend."

As Cardna turned to fully face her, she crossed her arms, staring down at Shanna, the anger still pulsing. Cardna's lips trembled like she was about to say something with all that anger, but Shanna smiled confidently at her and nodded toward the screens. The other woman finally turned, conceding, toward the screen in front of them, where it now showed a woman's hands moving lab equipment around, snapping things into place and turning dials and knobs whose meaning Shanna could only imagine. The camera turned in place and put the woman's face up on the screens. "Andy Duryea. Tenth of March. Mission day twenty-nine. We're going to fill these vessels up and see what changes in them over the next few months," said the woman. The crowd was beginning to rumble a little, wondering what the hell was going on. The scene switched to a chase of some kind, down through the hallways of the ship. It ended with one man slamming another man up against a wall and pinning him in place. The pinned man was very clearly Brian Bradley. Shanna watched as Cardna's chest rose and fell, taking in what she was seeing. Her face had dropped its anger, and was now full of something more like fear. She glanced around at her peers, who were now talking quietly into ears and looking around nervously. Everyone from the Royal group was starting to take part in this general fidgetry.

Cardna turned quickly toward Shanna. "Who the fuck are you? What do you want?"

Shanna smiled again and tilted her hand. "I was on that ship, you know?"

Cardna shook her head, incredulous and full of interrogation. "What fucking ship?"

Shanna pointed at the screen, looking up at it like a doe might regard its mother. "That fucking ship." And as if she had summoned it purely by mentioning it, there she was on the three huge screens. Shanna was almost startled herself by her own appearance in such a fashion. "Oh. There we are!" she said, pointing. She was holding a camera facing herself as she floated through the corridor of what was clearly a ship in zero-gravity. *'We're getting close now! Let's go see what Mars looks like without a telescope!'* said the woman on screen.

There was no missing that Cardna made the connection. Her eyes widened and she glanced back at Shanna, seeing there was no way to fake this. She was talking to the woman on that screen. Her mouth opened as if to speak, then she shifted uncomfortably and closed it again.

Then came the crash. The video Shanna had sent to Callie that showed a cockpit view of the ship hauling its last few hundred miles toward a barren red landscape that was unmistakably Martian. The crowd did react to this. There was a roar of approval and applause. Obviously they were catching on. That, or they thought this was the next action movie sequence.

Cardna was still shaking her head, but she was watching. The ship was getting close now. The crowd was getting louder. One could not look at the video and not see that it was going to crash. It was a destined disaster, like a train heading for the end of the tracks. It was well obvious what was about to happen. And they were riding it like passengers, the collective *ahhh* of the audience growing in volume and intensity with each passing second.

Right at the last second, just before the nose slammed into the red dirt and rocks, Cardna turned and walked away. The crowd was at full swell, extremely loud. And then the videos stopped, as did the audio. But the crowd carried it from there, hollering and clapping, jumping up and down and roaring like this was just part of the show. The crowd, that was, excluding the Royal employees, who were now looking like they were about to head for the exits. Shanna followed Cardna until they got to the other side of the trees, just south of the Met museum before they reached the road. Cardna had her phone up to her ear. Shanna stepped in front of her and said, "You can come with me and we'll settle this, or you're going to go down with the rest of them, Ms. Darwyn."

Cardna was looking at her with eyes that were almost glassy now. There was definitely a new level of respect in there somewhere. And perhaps a little more fear. She certainly wasn't interested in aggression, as Shanna had expected. Darwyn shook her head quickly, looking at the face of the phone, and Shanna could tell what had happened by the look in her eyes. The woman had called Bradley and reached his voice mail.

"What do you want?" Cardna said, crossing her arms and making her mouth into a tight mess of nervous anxiety.

"I want you to come with me. We're just having a little pow-wow with your buddy Brian."

Cardna stared at her for a moment, then swallowed. Tears formed in her eyes. She looked away, trying to hide them. She also tried a fake smile. "Is it too late for me to change sides?"

Shanna shrugged, slipping her hands into her pockets and looking up the road. The lights of the city ended abruptly at the edge of the Park. It looked like a glitch in the Matrix. "Hon, it was probably too late already by the time you took the job."

Callie witnessed the stage presence by Rebecca and the ensuing video montage with equal parts horror and elation. Her plan was working like a well oiled machine. It was perfect. Literally, absolutely perfect. No one had approached Rebecca on the stage, asking why the hell she was talking in the mic, addressing sixty thousand people. No one stopped the video feed before it reached its end. No one shut the power off to the whole thing, or announced, "Ladies and gentlemen, we seem to be..." Callie could only assume – only *hope* – that Shanna and Walter had caught their respective charges. The horror came from seeing the videos again, some of the bits for the first time. Seeing Rebecca walk out onto that stage so confidently... There was no *way* Callie could have done that. Her palms had started sweating as soon as she'd seen the woman appear out of the curtain. No effing way. Everything sure seemed to be working, though. And she had more confidence in Walter's part than in Shanna's, as far as their respective successes. Not necessarily just because she had more confidence in Walter, but because Brian Bradley was his charge. He was not near as trig as the young and spunky Cardna Darwyn. In fact, Callie considered, he was actually kind of a fucking dunce, when you got down to it. How he had landed a job at one of the top companies in the world was anyone's guess. Of course, if his gateway had been selling out his friends at Oliver, that could make sense. He deserved every bit of what he was about to get, either way.

Callie's plan did allow for Cardna turning coat though. She had felt a genuine connection with the woman, and did not take that lightly. Callie was naive a plenty. But she usually read people right, and couldn't imagine getting Cardna completely wrong from start to finish. That just didn't scan. It felt more realistic to Callie to accept that Cardna had made a decision somewhere, halfway through whatever operation she was running – a decision that turned her against Callie and her quest. There was just no way that *some of that* emotion wasn't true. Callie had never been *that* wrong. Unless Cardna Darwyn was just that good of an actor. Roll eyes. Shake head. No way. Not even Helen Mirren could have pulled that off.

The logical progression, in Callie's mind, was that Cardna was divided. Half of her wanting to be the girly gal – the feminine woman Callie saw taking her hair out of a ponytail as they stepped off the helicopter on the roof of the Royal complex – and the other half having to play the corporate whore that Royal was known for breeding. She had been secretly in battle with herself, half wishing to side with Callie and be her friend – Callie truly believed that – and half wanting to follow policy. Girls connected. Women. They connected in ways that men would never understand. That mythical intuition always spoken of was real. Had she not experienced it with her new friends already? They just *knew* shit. They read each other's thoughts sometimes. It just happened. Cardna was not a fake. She was just faking it.

Callie looked at her watch and took a deep breath, mentally patting herself on the back. It was time to go. Time for the next phase of the plan. If she pushed open the door to the meeting place and found it empty, she would know all was lost. But if it was not empty…

Walter had offered the man coffee, but Bradley had refused. He kept asking, over and over, 'What the hell is this about?' while Walter paced in the small room, rubbing his chin. Bradley had obviously, finally, caught on to the fact that he had not won anything. He would not be driving away in the beautiful Bentley he had been brought here by. That had most likely been his hope. Who the fuck wins a Bentley from a raffle they didn't enter though? *Come on, dude.*

They were sitting in Jennifer Cambria's office. And Walter was only pacing because she wasn't in the room. He had no problem with the notion that he could keep this man in the room. He could get violent and make sure it happened, but that was not in the plan, and he didn't want it to be. He knew Cambria had a tongue as smooth as silk and would get this son of a bitch talking in no time, if he were going to talk at all.

When Jennifer finally entered the room, it was with a confidence Brian Bradley had probably not been prepared to see. She no longer looked like the friendly executive offering him a ride. She now looked like a high-powered attorney who was about to bring the book down on him. Walter noticed the man's hands trembling slightly as he fidgeted with them under the table.

"Okay," Cambria said, sliding her chair up to the table across from Bradley. "Where do we begin?" She had a thick manila folder in front of her. Walter wondered what the hell was in that folder. Could she really have *that much* data on the guy? Either way, it looked plenty intimidating.

"I'm not even sure why I'm here," Bradley said, looking between Walter and Cambria as if looking for a little sympathy.

Cambria looked at Walter and said, "I guess he missed the video montage?"

Walter nodded.

"What montage?" Bradley asked, twisting his head to look back and forth between the two others. "What video?"

"They just showed a nice little medley of your Mars videos," said Walter.

Bradley frowned, squinting his eyes almost closed, making a sour face. "What fucking Mars videos?"

"You know the ones, ass-hat. From the ship full of Olivers you let die."

Bradley's face went white. After a long pause, a pause allowed by both of the others, he finally said, "Who showed it? What…"

"On the big concert screens," Cambria said. Her fingers were poised over the edge of the folder as if she were about to open it, but she stared him dead in the eyes. "Now you know why you're here?"

Bradley gulped. "I want my attorney."

Cambria chuckled amiably. "I'm not the police. But you don't have to say anything. I can do all the talking."

Walter leaned against the wall with his arms crossed, suddenly feeling like he was playing the good cop.

"I didn't do anything. Seriously," Bradley said, spreading his hands wide. He looked like he truly believed it. "Nothing I did was criminal."

Jennifer Cambria flipped the folder opened and lifted the first sheet out. "Oh, let's see… Corporate espionage, embezzlement in excess of a hundred thousand dollars, conspiracy to entrap or endanger…" she trailed off and looked up at him again. "Shall I go on? Negligent homicide?"

Walter was now afraid the man would pass out. Bradley's breathing had gotten very heavy, but now he was just about hyperventilating. He looked even whiter than he had a few minutes before.

"Look, Mr. Bradley, this is all well documented. We have tons of evidence. Receipts from where you bought cheap parts in lieu of space-hardened parts, videos of you installing them… We have videos from every camera in the ship. Everything you did on that ship." She was shaking her head. Walter smirked. If the other man didn't feel the doom and gloom in the room before, he was swimming in it now. This woman was laying it on heavy.

"Okay," Bradley said. "Okay. What do you want from me?"

Cambria leaned back in her chair and looked over at Walter with her eyebrows raised.

Walter stepped forward and put his fists on the desk, leaning over it. "I want you to escort Ms. Simmons and me into the vault."

Brian Bradley's eyes suddenly filled with confusion. It was a look he couldn't have faked. Walter's heart skipped a beat, worried suddenly that the scene had been misread. Maybe there was no vault.

"What vault? I don't know of any vault," Bradley said.

"Yes you do," Walter said, doubling down. "The vault in the basement in the Fiji compound. The double doors with the big red signs on them."

Brian Bradley's eyes got wide. "Why do you want to go in there?" he said, suddenly looking confused.

Bingo. Confirmed, Callie. There is *a vault.* Walter stood up, feeling a lot better all of a sudden. "We want to know what you're working on in there."

"You mean Red Bell? What's that got to do with…" he trailed off. Then he was shaking his head. After a long, thoughtful pause in which Bradley stared at the table, considering his options, he finally looked up at Cambria and asked, "And then what? What happens to me after that?"

Jennifer calmly and coolly slipped the paper back into the folder, closed it, then patted the top lightly with a ring-bearing hand. The diamond on her finger was large enough to put reflective sparkles on the ceiling. "We make this disappear."

"That seems simple," Bradley said.

"Yeah, it would sure seem that way. But I want you to keep in mind," Walter said, leaning on the desk again, getting very close to Bradley, "if you fail to comply with any of the commands given during this little trip, I will personally take you outside and find the nearest curb, then stomp your fuckin' teeth into it." He stood up and crossed his arms again. Bradley stared up at him, wide-eyed. "And then we will proceed with prosecution."

Bradley was shaking his head, incredulous. He looked to Cambria, held a hand above the desk and said, "You can't do this! You're just going to let him stand here and threaten me?"

"Oh, I'm sorry," Cambria said, pursing her lips and widening her eyes. "I didn't hear what he said. I guess I was off in my own little world." She returned her gaze to the man and put her elbows up on the table, began twisting the ring on her finger as she smiled pleasantly at him.

The man stared back at her, but looked a lot like a child scolded. His face was full of fear and uncertainty. He swallowed and breathed in deeply. "Okay. I'll do it. You'll let me go?"

"There's a lot better chance of that if you cooperate, sure," Walter said.

"Okay," Bradley said, looking back at the desk again and shaking his head. His face bore a sardonic look as if he was trying to find some sense about the deal. "This is stupid. You realize that, right?"

Walter raised his eyebrows as the man looked at him.

"If this is so important for you guys to… to… to make right," he said, waving his hand in the air as he searched for the words, "the uh… the deaths of all those people, then why would you just walk away so easily?"

Jennifer Cambria backed up from the desk and stood up, keeping her hands flat on the shiny surface. "Because, you have no future with the company any longer. Everyone already knows your involvement. You're going to go away. You're going to walk away from everything you have and just disappear."

Bradley was still frowning. Shaking his head.

"Like a mafioso turning witness protection," Walter said.

Cardna's posture was written on her like big red letters on a white wall. She was scared to death. Shanna stood looking at her nonchalantly. She pulled her phone out to text the others, but held off on sliding it unlocked just yet. Something was happening with the woman's demeanor.

"I guess you're with Callie Simmons?" Cardna said, looking around as if Callie herself might be hiding in the trees.

"What makes you say that?" Shanna said, not changing her face.

"She showed up at my hotel the other day with another woman. Short gal like you," she said, holding her hand out at chin height, "mousy brown hair. I thought it was odd that she happened to be there. Now, here you are. She was after all that Oliver Company business."

Shanna raised her chin. "So I guess you're catching on how serious it all is."

Cardna sighed. Nodded. "I know it's serious. Seeing those videos was haunting. But you should know, I had nothing to do with any of that," she affirmed.

"Oh, we don't think you do. But it's the accessory part of it that concerns us," Shanna said.

"I was serious. I can help you."

"You mean about changing sides? You want to be one of the good guys, now that you know we're winning?"

Cardna smirked, then shrugged her shoulders. "Well, yeah. I guess, when you put it like that. I mean, I have a lot to say. You might want to hear it."

"That's why I came and found you, Cardna."

"Right. Okay, so where do we go from here?"

Shanna smiled and opened her phone, then sent the text. Behind her, she could hear the crowd suddenly burst into a roar. The next band must be taking the stage. Shame she would have to miss that. She looked up at Cardna and saw the nervous anticipation thicken on her face. Then after a moment, peripherally, she saw why. Rebecca was approaching from the northeast – from the other side of the museum. Shanna glanced at her and smiled, then back at Cardna, who was now visibly shaken. Tiny beads of sweat stood out on her forehead. What the hell was going on with her? Rebecca must have some great power over her or something.

"Piper?" Cardna said, staring at her, mouth agape, as she approached.

Rebecca smiled a sour little number, holding her purse strap at the shoulder with both hands.

"I saw you on stage," Cardna said, pointing weakly at her as she closed the last few feet and stopped, forming a triangle with the others. "I couldn't place the face, but I knew I recognized you."

Rebecca tilted her head, but still said nothing, just stared at Cardna, sending in that intimidation. Shanna watched her, trying to read what was happening, but was coming up empty. Nothing was happening. That was the sickly funny part about this, nothing was happening at all, but Cardna was freaking the *fuck* out! And what was this 'Piper' business? This was all too great.

"I see you two have met," Shanna said, just trying to fill the void.

"So are you going to tell me who you really are?" Cardna asked, ignoring Shanna's comment. Shanna could see the gears turning in Cardna's head though. She had just seen this tall, attractive woman waltz onto a stage in front of sixty thousand souls, just like she owned the place. Surely, Cardna was wondering how the hell she had managed to pull that off, unless she was every bit as important as she appeared to be.

"Who do you think I am, Cardna?" Rebecca said.

"Ahuh," Cardna scoffed. "Well, shit, I know you as Piper Beck. I'm guessing that's a pseudonym."

"Everything you think you know about me is pseudonym, darling. So did you come to play ball, or did you want to ride the hansom down with Brian Bradley?" The crowd noise was now overshadowed by the bass line of the band's first song. It was getting too loud to hear one's self think. The only relief was the great big Metropolitan Museum of Art standing directly between them and the stage, and it was only *just* helping.

Cardna swallowed, shifted, looked at Shanna, then back at Rebecca and said, "Right. Well, I told your associate here I would be willing to talk."

"Actually, she asked if it was too late for her to switch sides," Shanna said.

Rebecca smiled at this, again with that matronly *ain't that darlin'* smile that wasn't really a smile at all. "Don't it always go that way?" She stared at Cardna for an uncomfortably long time before finally nodding and saying, "Yup. Okay, let's just call the boss." She pulled her phone out and turned around, walking a few meters away.

Walter answered on the first ring. "Looks like our girl wants to turn state's."

"Okay. What does she know?" he asked.

"We haven't asked anything yet. Still standing outside the Met."

"Yeah, I can hear the music. Well, find out one thing she knows that would prove her loyalty. Tell her if she doesn't give you something then you'll have to let her go," said Walter.

Rebecca held the phone away from her face and frowned at it, shaking her head. "Why the hell would I do that?"

"Because, trust me, Bec. She wants to be in our custody right now. I'm guessing she's very afraid. We have her buddy. She knows that if he goes down, he'll bring her with him."

Rebecca nodded, slowly. She had turned back around to face the other two women, who were staring expectantly back at her.

"Listen. If you set her free, and she *does* walk away? Then we're completely wrong about her culpability. But this is not about Atlas anymore. This has become more about *Red Bell*," Walter said.

Rebecca shook her head, to clear it. That damned code name again. "Red Bell?" she asked.

"Yeah. Doesn't matter, but all that shit about Atlas, it's too old. Not enough evidence. Red Bell is the new thing. That's how we bring him down! We start talking about stuff involving that project and he gets really tight."

"Got it," Rebecca said, and found herself nodding.

"You're in front of the Met?" Walter said.

"Yep."

"Okay, hang tight. Cambria's gonna pick y'all up. Look out for my Bent."

"Got it," said Rebecca, and slipped the phone back into her purse.

"Will you ladies accompany me to the street please?" Rebecca said as she returned to the small group. Shanna guided Cardna with a light touch on the elbow, careful not to put herself in range of an assault. It didn't seem like that was on the horizon, but Rebecca was proud that she was being smart about it. *Anything is possible.* Cardna seemed pretty demure right now.

The three women walked over to the wide sidewalk directly in front of the Met to wait for Cambria. As they walked, Rebecca fell in beside Cardna on her other side. They could have been three friends out for a Friday-evening stroll. As they approached the gigantic staircase that led up to the building, she slowed and they came to a stop. She turned to face Cardna and said, "Give me one thing."

Cardna raised her eyebrows. But before she could verbalize her question, Rebecca spoke again. "Tell me one thing I don't already know. One thing that speaks to your loyalty."

Cardna looked at the ground, smiling nervously. "Okay. I know where Brian Bradley's safe is. And I know the combination to get in."

Rebecca shook her head, a flat smile returning to her lips. "Nope. That won't be good enough."

"I know, I know. You can't resolve it yet. Look. I knew he was involved in some shit, but I had no idea to what extent. I didn't even know he was on the space mission with the Oliver Company."

Rebecca raised her eyebrows, a look that said *go on, I'm listening.*

"I mean, I do now," Cardna said, putting a hand over her heart. A subconscious gesture that showed someone she truly believed what she was saying. Could have been rehearsed, Shanna thought, but it was good. "But I just learned a lot of this on the way up here. We sat together on the plane and he told me that we would need to be watching out for Callie and her crew while we were in the states."

"What was his reason for saying that?"

"He was scared shitless of coming to this event. He thought he'd be safe because, well, safety in numbers and all that. But he knew she was still out to get him. I don't know why. But down in Fiji, he told me to stop her and find out what she knows. What all she 'had' on him."

"Uh huh," Rebecca said. She adjusted her stance and looked out at the road. She looked like she was losing patience with this woman. Shanna was just enjoying watching this show.

"Anyway, I had to run interference. That put me in a really bad place. Like I had to be this bad fucking guy. I'm totally not that person in real life. I've been sick about it ever since. But I did do one thing to protect her. Only thing is, I never got to hand her that bit of information. Shit went south so fast when we got back to the office, that I lost control of it."

"I'm sorry, Cardna," Rebecca said, looking very suspicious, "I'm not following your back and forths here. *Back* to the office? Whence had you come?"

"I took her to this safe house out in the woods. Brian Bradley doesn't know about it. But I left a bunch of stuff there for her. A get-out-of-jail-free card, if you will. I hid it in a vault under the floor and was going to tell her where to find it, and help her get out of there, but she wasn't reading my signs. I couldn't come out and say it all directly. We just… I guess we just didn't connect like I had thought we had." She stared off down the one-way street for a moment, letting the wind from the north catch her full in the face.

"So let me get this straight," said Rebecca, holding a finger up. "You were trying to hide stuff for Callie, from Brian Bradley, where he wouldn't know about it. Is that what you're saying?"

"Yes," Cardna said with a friendly smile. "It's still there in the cabin. My goal was to get her out of the building and back to that cabin. I was going to tell her where to find the vault."

"What was in it?" asked Rebecca. She was slipping her phone out of her purse again. A wine-colored Bentley pulled up, getting Cardna's attention with a quickness. Rebecca thoughtlessly aimed her hand at the car, but did not yet move toward it. She waved at the driver, holding a finger up to buy a moment.

"There was some Fijian currency in there. Some phone numbers of people who could help her. And her phone.

That's the big thing. I had gotten Callie's phone from her room and put it in there."

"Why didn't you just give her the phone?" Rebecca said, now turning toward the car and holding her hand out again, indicating the other two should get in. "Shanna, let our friend ride in front."

Shanna winked at Bec and walked to the curb, opening the front door for Cardna. Cardna said, "Because Bradley would have just confiscated it from her. This kept it safe for her."

And as Rebecca turned as if to head to the back door, Cardna reached up and touched her arm. "There's something that's been eating at me. I want someone to know about it."

Rebecca looked up. She tilted her head thoughtfully, looking at Cardna with an expectant visage. Cardna said, "I've heard for years and years about some ties to Mars. Like stuff that goes on down in the basement. I think there's some equipment down there that they brought back from Mars. Or were going to take there. Something. I don't know exactly what. But ever since Callie walked into my life, it's started making me more and more nervous. I'm afraid it's bad."

Rebecca nodded thoughtfully. All of this was pretty vague, she knew, but she was also good at reading people, and right now, she was reading Cardna as nothing but genuine. The woman didn't know what was going on in the basement, but she did know there was something *to know*. Something *to be* worried about. And breaking the confidence of Bradley's trust to at least let Rebecca know that much seemed to be a step in the right direction. She was trying to switch sides.

Rebecca nodded and turned for the car, sweeping her hand toward the front door, which still hung open. Then she began swiping through her contacts. As she closed the door for Cardna, she looked over the top of the car and met eyes with Shanna, who was standing beside her own open door with a bit of mystery in her eyes. She raised an eyebrow and

Rebecca winked at her. Then she got in and they both closed their doors.

"Hey, Jenn," Shanna said, reaching forward and squeezing the woman's shoulder. They had not yet officially met, but Cardna didn't need to know that. Jennifer Cambria turned and winked at her, then looked back at Cardna.

"Hello, Cardna. I'm Jennifer Cambria. I hear you would like to speak to us."

Cardna gulped comically. She nodded like a child. Cambria smiled and returned her eyes to the windshield. Rebecca was plugging her open ear with a finger and talking into the phone intently. After a few minutes, she got in the car too. As she closed the door she said, "Okay, we're good. So we're going to know in about thirty minutes if what you say is true, Cardna."

"How…" she said, wide-eyed.

"We have a friend who's going to swing by the cabin 'no one knows about' to check it out for us." She leaned forward and patted Cardna on the shoulder then said, to Cambria, "All right, let's go."

Five women sat in a room. Natalie, Rebecca, Shanna and Cardna sat around the coffee table on the floor. Jennifer sat on one couch with her legs crossed, bouncing one foot as she ran her thumb up her phone screen over and over. OuterCircle. It sucked away lives. It ended marriages. Social media in general, but the Circle specifically, ate away close to a trillion-and-a-half hours per year, the studies had shown. It even affected lawyers, apparently.

There was some timidity in the room. Initially, the stranger had been brought here with reservations. She had been offered the amenities – scotch, vodka, coffee – and had been treated like a friend. But there was some unsure in the air. Especially from Rebecca, who was cool to the touch until she had the confidence of signed contracts guaranteeing insurance against such things as betrayal and espionage. She was very weary of newcomers. But this was not her game. Not her call, not her house. And it wasn't like she was completely against the idea. She was just cautious. Wanted to be sure. She had seen this woman down in Fiji, at her worst. Thinking back, she had not had the same interactions and experiences as Callie – and certainly had not spent any time bonding with her – but she could not remember any serious hitches that required attention.

So for now, they were sitting in Callie's living room between the couches, drinking and passing a bong around, and including Cardna Darwyn – treating her like she was an old friend. They had been given specific instruction not to exclude her from anything or make her feel like an outsider. She was to feel as welcome as any of the rest of them. At least until such time as it was deemed they had made a misstep. And at that time, she would be dealt with swiftly and forcefully.

Natalie had turned on the streaming music player and thus had a classic rock playlist running as background noise. They all waited expectantly and tried to act – with this strange woman sitting with them – like everything was completely normal. And for all intents and purposes, it kind of felt like it. There was some laughing – some ribbing, for certain, but all in good spirit – and joking, some story-telling, and the ever-important inquisition that felt completely necessary. A new hen had entered the coop. They had to peck at her a little. They had to find out from where she had come.

No one had apologized. That was not the way of it. No one had asked for apology. No one had begged forgiveness, or expected it. It was a completely neutralized – or as Natalie would later call it, neutered – conversation. Almost sterile. Sure, there was humor and friendly banter in abundance. But it felt like there were certain topics they were not allowed to broach. No one was unhappy though.

And no one felt endangered by the presence of the newcomer.

All the women, short Cardna, of course, had known the plan: Rebecca had made the call to Cynda, down in Fiji, to go check the safe house and report back to Callie. Once Callie heard back, they would decide what to do with Cardna. Rebecca felt pretty sure she was being honest though, because sitting here around the rug in Callie's living room, Cardna looked completely relaxed. Not like someone on the edge of sanity knowing she was about to be caught in a lie. Walter had taken to his next phase of the plan, which was to escort Brian Bradley down to Fiji, where he would find out everything he could get his hands on about Red Bell, gathering evidence if necessary. His thought was that it wouldn't be necessary. Bradley would just give himself up somehow when he was truly faced with being exposed.

When the front door opened, nearly an hour after they had all settled in, everyone got suddenly quiet. Callie Simmons came into the living room, slinging her purse off her shoulder and up onto the hook by the entryway. She had a look of seriousness in her eyes that was hard to read – even to Rebecca, who fancied herself a professional Callie analyst by now.

She walked to the edge of the group and took her coat off, tossing it over the back of the couch just to the right of Cambria. Jennifer cranked her neck to look at Callie, who stood with her hands on her hips, taking inventory of the women on her floor. She took a deep breath. Jennifer shifted on the couch, ready to pounce if needed.

Callie locked eyes with Cardna Darwyn and stood there staring, just breathing. Cardna stared back, solemn. Patient. Ready. Peaceful.

Finally, Callie stepped forward, her feet at the edge of the rug the women sat on. Cardna stood up, almost like a private getting ready to take a verbal licking from the sergeant. She swallowed. "Callie," she said, quietly. Her palms faced Callie, down at her sides.

Callie stepped forward and embraced her.

Instantly, there was laughter and applause from the rest of the group. They were on their feet. Even Jennifer Cambria sat up straight, smiling, and clapped, a big grin showing lots of teeth. This meant a lot of things to Rebecca. Of course it meant Cardna had been honest about the stashed care package. It also meant they could let her in; they had *another* friend in the office, in fact. Cardna was surrounded by all the women, hugged and patted like she'd just scored the winning goal in a soccer match. She closed her Egyptian-looking eyes, her exotic, pleasant smile a pale painting across her pretty face. She looked like a woman sitting in the sun at a picnic, taking in nature. She looked at peace. Callie kissed her on the lips.

"I knew I was right about you," she said, and Cardna nodded, her eyes still closed.

After a moment of the bliss, Jennifer Cambria broke in with some reality. "Girls, I hate to ruin the moment. I know you're all high, and maybe this doesn't need to be said, but Cardna, don't make me regret trusting you."

Cardna opened her eyes slowly and tilted her head to look at her. "Jennifer, listen. I've never had any reason not to like this woman." She looked now at Callie, her movements in slow-motion due to the alcohol and grass. She put her hand on Callie's cheek. "Seriously. I've loved her since the moment I met her. I'm very thankful I wasn't part of all that mess that happened on your Mars mission. And I'm glad I met you all." Then she sealed it with a kiss on each of their cheeks. "Thank you for giving me a chance."

Jennifer leaned into the group, slipping her arm between Natalie and Callie, and grasped Cardna by the hand, squeezed. Smiled at her. "Nice meeting you. You're standing among some of the most amazing women I've ever met in my life." Then she grabbed her purse off the couch and showed herself out the front door.

CHAPTER 26

Walter had his tablet open on his lap playing poker, legs stretched as far forward as they could reach within the limitations of airline seating. There had been no first-class seating available. Not two seats together, at least. So they sat in coach with the rest of the steerage passengers, trying to be comfortable. He had Brian Bradley's phone in his pocket, lest the man try to make some duress call, or have someone waiting. He was excited to be going to Fiji, but that excitement didn't quite reach the level he had for getting to put this business to rest. To finally see Callie be able to let go all her stress – all the darkness she had been carrying around for the last near-decade – it would be wonderful to have her back.

Brian Bradley sat silently staring out the window. He had not tried to engage Walter much on the trip so far, which was just fine with Walter. Every time Bradley opened his mouth, Walter wanted to punch him out. The girls had told him about Rebecca laying him out flat, and every time Walter thought about that it made him giggle and get warm inside.

Walter had initially thought this was a tenuous leash at best – this hold they had over Bradley. Making him promise to show something, get rid of something, give them something – whatever he could come up with on the fly – all in return for dumping the Atlas evidence they had on him. Very likely, the statute of limitations had run out on most of that stuff anyway. But to get to see Red Bell and what it was about… *That* had begun to show a whole new face of promise. Walter had to keep reminding himself they weren't dealing with a genius here. Bradley was a dullard at best. A total fucking idiot, in fact. The sheaf of papers Cambria had stuffed in the manila envelope had been blank printer paper. Walter, upon seeing it, had almost gone white, worried that Bradley would notice. He had not. Tenuous or not, it was a leash on which Bradley had not yet tugged too hard. How smart was the man, who, when presented with some evidence of a long-ago project starts spilling hints that there's an even more sinister one in play right now?

Most of the other Fiji execs who had attended the week-long conference in New York were not returning until Monday. There was some festival of lights or some other bullshit that had been scheduled for Sunday, and all had been invited and encouraged to attend that as well. So the offices should be pretty much a ghost town, according to Bradley. There would be a skeleton crew answering emails and phones for those execs who were out, but that was about it. Not that anyone in Fiji got too many calls. It was a mostly private office, and therefore quiet. Not to mention the sixteen-hour difference in time between there and the closest office in the United States.

Walter's mind had wandered a little at the possibility of using the time zone differences as some sort of time-travel device. If in New Jersey it was Friday at noon, then in Fiji, it was Saturday at four pm. The next day. The future. But then he reckoned all the great minds had already covered all that shit, so he let it go. It wouldn't be *true* time travel, of course, but it had been fun to think about for the few minutes or so that it had lasted. Of course, time being a human invention kind of bunked the deal anyway.

He had grilled Matt Minus pretty hard about the Mars Mission Callie was on and on about. It wasn't that Walter wasn't interested in helping her – obviously he wasn't being forced to fly to another country – but it just wasn't, at least in his mind, *his* battle. It wasn't *his* passion. It was truly, and wholly Callie's. He respected her for the tenacity and persistence she had put into it for all these years, and would support her until it had run its course. But if she had said yesterday, "You know, fuck it. Let's drop the whole thing," he would have shrugged, pursed his lips and said, "Okay, what's next then?"

So his 'grilling' of Minus was understood between the two men to be grilling from Callie, by Walter proxy. It was unspoken, but the spirit was obvious to Minus, who had known Callie and Walter for many years. Walter simply just didn't get that passionate about stuff like this. Callie did. And Minus had seen her passion for it for the last several years. It had, in fact, interrupted and thrown several wrenches into his Scylla Scout deep sea dive. But he had to be patient with her, because she always got results.

The 'grilling' had, therefore, been pretty relaxed. But Walter had been told to make sure Minus was not lying when he answered. They both knew Minus wasn't a liar, but under corporate shush contracts, no one knew what could happen. The basic gist of the thing was this: everyone knew that the Fiji Department of Royal Research worked on the top-tier, top-secret projects that no one else in the company was cleared for. If you got put on one of those projects, you moved to Fiji. You had a stack of Non-Disclosure Agreements to sign if this happened, and they were pretty much *by threat of death*, if not officially, then at least official enough to seem official. People obeyed them. And part of being in Fiji, on the other side of the world, was the seclusion. It would be easy to make someone disappear down there. So with everyone knowing there was some next-level shit going on down there, or at least if there was some next-level shit going on, it *would be* down there, it was understood that if you *weren't* down there, you probably didn't know the current next-level shit that was going on. Maybe you had worked on a project that required absolute secrecy in your past, and you had relocated to wherever you were now. Fine. But what Walter had been tasked with getting from their closest associate was assurance that this was true. That he *truly* didn't know what Brian Bradley was working on there. That no one did. Walter had worked for Royal himself, and he sure as hell hadn't known. But Minus was higher in the food chain than he, and he just needed to verify that it wasn't an executive-level knowledge of some sort. Simple enough.

If they could trust that, if they could *know* – as much as one could know something they didn't know – that it wasn't common company knowledge – then they could use that against Brian Bradley effectively. Even in the court of law. And this had seemed to be the case with a certainty, at least so far. Because Bradley was playing the hand they had dealt him. He had been acting like it was true. And he was no Leo DiCaprio. Walter couldn't be talked into believing Bradley was faking anything. They would see right through it. The colors of his cheeks too easily told whatever he was holding back. No one could fake that. Well, maybe Leo could.

So Walter and he would land in Fiji and take Brian's car back to the compound. Walter would be driving this car. He would be the one to go through the security gate – to use the special hand gesture that told the guard he was not under duress. Bradley would be under duress himself. If he fucked up the entry, he would be the one who would suffer. Walter had watched Cynda do the hand signal several times on a video meeting. It hadn't taken long to learn it. She had also told him that literally *any* sign other than the right one meant duress, but that people screwed it up all the time. Security, it seemed, was not quite as serious as some made it sound. The main reason was because of that Fijian seclusion. It took a special will just to get down to the island. So bad guys attempting to get onto the base were a rare thing. And thus, the hand signals were more of a routine pantomime show they all complied with because of policy. Not because of any real fear of intrusion.

Walter looked over Bradley's seat out the window. As far as the eye could see, there were nothing but stars in the sky. He sighed and slipped his tablet into the seat pocket in front of him, then clasped his hands on his stomach and closed his eyes. They were only a quarter of the way into the flight. Traveling to the future was slow and boring, he decided. This aircraft, flying at almost the speed of sound, was the slowest goddamn time machine he could imagine.

Callie's comfort with Cardna was not based on hunch alone. Her hunch had almost never failed her in life. Whatever hitches and hangups she had experienced with it were insignificant at worst. Almost not worth mentioning. Her gut instinct, simply put, was usually right. And very right, at that. So while it had been comforting to confirm she had indeed gotten it right about Cardna Darwyn, it was the phone call to Cynda who had really solidified the comfort level. This woman Callie had never met. This Cynda Lohm had really turned into a truly wonderful boon for their mission. In fact, Callie didn't see how it would have been possible to have carried on without her aid. When Rebecca had made the call to her last night and given her the location of the suspected Help Box Cardna had supposedly planted, it had been about one o'clock in the afternoon in Fiji, on Saturday. So Cynda had been able to hop in her car and run out to the cabin, where she had actually spent time herself. When she arrived and pulled up the floorboard, revealing a vault beneath, she had called Callie to review the contents of the secret box.

Callie's phone had indeed been in there. There had been some money, a map with certain key elements circled and notated in thick marker right over unimportant parts of the map. There was a key to a company loaner car that wouldn't help her very much, as the car was left parked at the airport. But she could chalk that one up to *thought that counts* territory. There was a stun gun, a flash light and a few other things that might or might not help in a getaway. And there was a note folded up on top of it all. That note, which Cynda had read to Callie in full, had read:

> *Hello Callie. If you're reading this, then things have gone the way I hoped. I hope you can hear me out. And I hope you can believe that I arranged this as a backup plan to what I really wanted to happen – and that was your success in what you're calling your mission. Shit went south pretty quick as soon as you arrived. I tried to calm him down. I tried to turn it around, to make him see you weren't here to do anything stupid. If you're reading this, then I wasn't able to turn the tide. But you were able to get away, rather than succumbing to whatever fucked-up plan he had to exact his version of justice on you. I brought you here hoping you would remember how to get here. To give you a safe place to come. I regret deeply ever having to play the bad cop, to take his side on any of this – to act like I was protecting his interests. But it's the only way I can stay in the game and help you at all. Someday I hope we can talk, and I can tell you everything I know, and what*

The fact that Cardna had put Callie's phone in the box had made the biggest impact. If she were able to make it back to the safe house, she would have gotten her phone back. Unfortunately, it didn't work without the international plan, but hey – *thought that counts*. Cardna hadn't known that.

Now they sat in the circle on the floor, sharing a bottle of vodka and a pipe. The others were still here too. Cardna had indicated pretty quickly that she didn't think there was any need for privacy at this point. She was trusting Callie as much as Callie trusted her. And there was no point in thinking whatever she told Callie in confidence wouldn't be shared with her closest friends. So might as well skip the Telephone Game and just say it all in front of everyone. That way they would all get to see for themselves how up-front she was being.

"I've been trying to find a way to let shit slip for years. Something that would make it look like someone else, without getting anyone else in trouble. Unless that someone was Bradley himself," Cardna said.

"See, I started learning things a few years ago when he asked me for help on the project he was working on. I'm cleared for top secret on my own engagement. So it was nothing to bring me over there. To even be stationed in Fiji, you have to have so much reliability with corporate Black Boxes. That's what they call them. *Black boxes*. Red Bell is a Black Box. I've been there for five years. There's never been an issue with trust. But that doesn't mean I *needed to know* about his project. And the weird thing is that he's the only fuckin' one working on it!" She took a deep breath and stretched a little. "Others have worked with him over the years, but slowly and surely, they've all sort of phased out. It's ended up where he's the only one left on the project. So he's down there a lot more these days."

Callie shook her head, looking at the others as they all listened. No one was willing to cut off the woman. They all just listened.

"I mean, he's asked for help from a few people over the years, but he has this gargantuan budget, and a whole fuckin' floor for testing and experimenting, or whatever the hell he does," she said, waving her hand like that wasn't the important part. "And he's got half the damn basement. As you saw, Callie," she said, now holding that hand out to Callie, "half the basement is storage for old projects, or components just not currently being used."

"Have you ever been in the other half?" Rebecca asked, remembering for herself what they had experienced in the gigantic basement.

Cardna shook her head. Furled her lips. "Nope. No one has, to my knowledge. I mean, he's obviously working with some seriously big bio-hazard shit or something. He has these Level Four contagion suits down there."

"Suits?" Rebecca asked. "Like, more than one?"

"Yeah," Cardna said, pointing at her. "But no one else gets to use them. I asked if I could go in there one time. Nope. They're backups. Spares. Whatever. That guy has spare backups, and backups for his spares."

A few of the girls giggled at this.

"Anyway, I started getting worried when he started taking people in there, and they didn't come back out."

Natalie's eyes got very wide. She sat up straight. Rebecca shook her head. Shanna mouthed *what the fuck?*

"Yeah. Like people who were low in the command chain. Cube farmers. You know, the assistants and shit. So he would take one of them down there, *put them in a suit*," she said, pointing at Bec again, "and take them through the bio-hazard doors with him."

"Holy fuck," said Natalie.

Cardna looked at her, all seriousness in her eyes. She nodded. "Yeah."

"How did you find out about this?" Callie asked.

"I staked out down there and watched. Now it wasn't like it happened all the time or anything. But I had seen him take this guy, Billy Adams, down there one time. I was standing at someone's cube and saw him come out the elevator and look around. Then he walked up to Billy's desk and asked if he could get a hand for a moment."

Callie stared through wide eyes now, her chin resting on her hand, fingers covering her mouth to keep from speaking her discomfort. The other girls in the circle looked much the same. Rebecca looked down at the floor. Refilled her glass and took a big swig of the clear alcohol.

"I was just sort of watching out the corner of my eye while I talked to a friend of mine, you know? And Billy hops up and follows him into the elevator. We never saw Billy again."

"Holy shit!" Rebecca said. "And no one caught on to that?"

"No. No one knew anything. It was such an innocent little thing. I think I was the only one who saw Brian come get him. No big deal, right? And it wasn't even until like a few days later that it finally registered with me that that was the last time I had seen him. I mean, I still wasn't sure. I didn't think much of it. Just a weird coincidence."

"Sure," Shanna said, picking up the pipe and taking the lighter when Natalie held it out to her. "Why would anyone think anything of someone coming to ask for help? No one probably connected it to his disappearance. Shit, no one probably knew he was missing for a day or two anyway, right?"

"Right," Cardna said, nodding. "Then it happened again like a year later. I was walking down the corridor, scrolling through something on my phone, and glanced up because I sensed that someone was coming toward me. You know how you can just sort of do that?" she said, looking around the group. They all nodded. "Yeah. Well, I looked up right in time to see Brian coming toward me. Looking a little lost. He asked me, 'Hey can you come give me a hand down in the lab real quick?' And I said, no, that I was on my way to Kendall Mitchell's office. I said I could help him a few minutes later, but that Kendall had called me up there and I had to go see her first. He said, 'Never mind. No biggie', or something like that."

Cardna took a sip from the glass that she'd been twisting on the carpet with a finger. "So I walk on, not thinking anything of it. Again. Of course. Why would I? You know? Then I hear him ask someone behind me. Same thing. Can you come give me a hand. Only be a minute. You know?"

"Oh my God," Shanna said. "Don't tell me."

Cardna looked at her and nodded. "Yes. Brandy Clarke. She had just started working there like a week before or something. *Fwip.* Gone."

"Christ on his throne," Rebecca said. The others mumbled similar interjections. Callie was actively covering her mouth now. Speaking *oh my God* into her hand over and over.

"Again, I just happened to be the only one who noticed, and why would anyone think anything of it?"

"No one thought to check the cameras on that floor?" Natalie asked.

"No cameras on that floor. Not for the cube farm, anyway. And think about this. If you get into the elevator with someone you don't know very well, and he goes and leans against the back wall, where do you stand? When he asks you to push the B button."

"Right by the door," Rebecca said.

"Right by the door," Cardna repeated. That's a blind spot for the elevator camera."

Rebecca closed her eyes, faced the floor. Shook her head. "My God," she whispered.

"Yeah. So Brandy was gone. Never came back. When we found out she was missing a few days later, I remembered the encounter, and the hair on the back of my neck stood up."

They exchanged words, all expressing similar feelings of sickness. Natalie said, "And no one ever investigated these disappearances?"

"Well, I'm sure they did. But not within the building. No one can *disappear* inside a building. You know? At least not for long. Everyone kind of assumed they didn't like the job, or the lifestyle, and they just ghosted. You know? Like decided to go back stateside or something. Hopped a flight to Miami Beach. *New York State of Mind* style."

Rebecca smiled at this. It didn't bring much levity though.

Cardna refilled her glass and took a long sip of vodka, sighing and shaking her head, obviously uncomfortable from reliving all this again. Rebecca reached out and stroked her shoulder for her. That made Callie happy – to see the other woman who had been screwed over down in Fiji – to see she wasn't the only one accepting this woman's return.

Cardna breathed in deeply again, then continued. "I started watching him closely after that. I was scared shitless. So I set up another monitor on my desk that always showed the camera view of the elevator. 'Cause Brian almost never shows his face on the floor or in his office on the days or weeks he's working down in the basement. He'll go long stretches of like months in one place or the other. But not back and forth in the same day, you know? Or week, for that matter. Anyway, any time he would get on the elevator, I would run out and sit on someone's desk in a cube nearby where he went."

"How long did that go on for?" Callie asked, shaking her head. *What dedication!*

"Oh, too long. I became obsessed with that fuckin' elevator screen. I watched it like a hawk for months. Hours go by with no movement. But anytime there *was* movement, it would catch my eye and I'd look over real fast, just to see if it was him getting on. And when it would be him, my heart would start beating real fast. And I couldn't breathe well. Like I got seriously anxious, you know?"

Callie could tell she was getting anxious now, just reliving it. She reached out and took the woman's hand. Rebecca nodded, staring at Cardna, and reached her own hand out to put it on Cardna's knee. *Smart.* That left Cardna's right hand free to pick up the drink.

"Well, I finally started easing off of it a little. Like I started to think maybe I had been wrong all along, and it *had* been a huge coincidence. So I stopped watching the screen so intently. Kind of forgot about it a little. Then one day, I hear his voice, *right outside my office*. And here's the fucked-up thing. This was a new-hire. A woman I was *literally* sitting in my office filling out paperwork for. I mean, not new to the company. But new to Fiji," she said, waving her hand quickly in the air. "Whatever. I was filling out her paperwork, and I hear Brian come up and ask her for a hand. My spine went cold. I got up and walked as quickly as I could to the stairs at the end of the corridor. I ran down all five flights of stairs and hauled ass across the basement to where the pallets of cargo are. I hid there, and watched. When the elevator dinged, there they were. He helped her put one of the suits on, and they were all laughing and talking. Like nothing big was going on. Then they went through the double doors."

Callie was getting tears in her eyes. She was shaking her head. God, how she had misread this woman. She couldn't imagine the terror, knowing what you suspected was probably the truth, and you were about to witness it. Her spine tingled with that thought. She took a sip of her drink and licked her teeth. Tried to stop thinking about her own experience of being down there in that very basement, only a few meters from where this maniac had been doing all these bad things to people.

"Well, I sat down there for two hours before he came out."

"And I'm guessing he was alone?" Shanna asked.

Cardna nodded. There were tears in her eyes as well. Her nod was even a stutter. "He was carrying the empty suit."

<h1 style="text-align:center">CHAPTER 27</h1>

Walter was actually able to get some good sleep. Not being one who was really ever able to sleep on planes, he found this surprising. Twenty minutes before landing, he made his way to the lav to freshen up, swish some mouthwash and look in the mirror. When he got back to his seat, Brian Bradley had his head against the headrest with a force, his knuckles white, wrapped round the ends of the armrests. He looked like he was on the big climb on a roller coaster. Not an airliner.

"Relax, dude," Walter said, slapping the man's knee. "You're more likely to die in a crash on the way to the airport than on the actual airplane."

"I know that!" Bradley snapped. "Doesn't make it any less nerve-wracking for me."

Walter lifted his chin, pursed his lips. "Ah, I guess you probably have some PTSD from that little flight out to another planet," he said.

Bradley tried to stare holes through him. Walter could see he was being stared at peripherally. He turned to face the other, the hints of a smirk still on his face. "Need something?"

"Why don't you just shut up?"

Walter nodded, leaned his head back. "You got it, bub."

When they disembarked, Bradley asked Walter for his phone. "Who do you need to call?" Walter said, strolling casually toward the luggage carousel, hands in his pockets.

"Don't you want me to arrange a ride?" the other man said, looking like it should have been well obvious.

"Nah. Where is your car parked?"

"It's in long-term parking, which is a hell of a walk!"

Walter turned to the man and took him by the shoulders. "That's why they make shuttles!" he said, shaking Bradley a little bit. They had just landed and gotten off the plane and Brian Bradley was already trying to scramble something up. Walter reckoned he shouldn't be surprised that he was already trying to slip something under the rug. This was a desperate man, about to divulge secrets he had held fast to for almost a decade. And it had all been so easy. Well, would be so easy. Hopefully. He hoped there wasn't a hitch when it came to show time.

The shuttle dropped them in the middle of the parking lot, only a few feet away from Bradley's car, a black late-model Lexus that was in bad need of a wash. Remarkably, Brian had handed over the keys before they got off the airplane. Walter had told him the plan, as far as he'd seen it anyway, from start to finish. And Bradley had remained silent, accepting his position as the puppet while Walter held the control. The left rear tire needed some air. Walter pointed this out, somewhat magnanimously, in his estimation, with a smile. As he got in the driver's seat he was greeted with a foul smell. He kicked his door back open as Bradley was settling into the passenger seat. "What in fuck's name is that? Does it always smell like this?"

Bradley shook his head, then turned to look in the backseat. "Oh. Yeah. I forgot to finish my breakfast on the trip to the airport." He reached back and brought forth a foam box, then held it over the console as if to offer it to Walter.

"What the fuck you want me to do with that?" Walter said. "Put that thing out, dipshit!"

Brian Bradley got out of the car and walked over to a large trash barrel with it. Here was a guy who would assist in the demise of an entire team of astronauts, but wouldn't drop a bad sandwich on the asphalt. *Unreal*, Walter thought. Perhaps the man was just scared straight in his presence. Maybe that was a good sign. As he got back in the car, Walter shook his head and rolled his eyes, then rolled down the windows. "Looks like it's gonna be a windy ride."

Approaching the gate house, Walter could see the guard on duty knew the vehicle. Walter took Bradley's left hand and pulled the thumb back toward the man's wrist. Bradley flinched but did not try to pull his hand back. The gesture wasn't painful, but it was quite obvious that it could bring instantaneous pain with very little effort, if Walter pulled any harder. Slowing to the posted entry speed, he hiked his knee to steer and smiled at the guard like an old friend. Held his left hand up above the steering wheel and made the gesture. It was Sunday morning, and the guard was about as excited to be working as one could imagine. He waved at the oncoming vehicle and turned back into the gate house. And that was that.

Walter looked over at Bradley, let go of his hand and said, "That's some security you got here." Bradley apparently didn't feel the need to respond. "Tell me where to go," Walter said, but it looked pretty obvious. There was a long, curvy drive that only went to one place. The 'compound' as they had been referring to it, was a series of structures that were all grouped together. Not a campus-like layout like a college, with large, sprawling greens and nice little concrete sidewalks for the attendants to make their way leisurely between the different buildings. This was all business. The color of the stucco looked like it might well blend in with the surroundings when viewed from above, though Walter could see a helicopter on the roof of the nearest building.

As they rounded a final curve, the road dived down under the ground level of the building and into darkness. He slowed and let his eyes adjust as they entered the parking garage. Brian Bradley finally spoke. "I have a reserved spot, just over there. D44."

Walter found the spot and pulled in, killed the car, pocketed the keys. He patted the bulge they made in his pocket with the other man's cell phone, and smiled at Bradley. "You ready to do this?"

"No, honestly. This is my life's work you're about to ruin."

Walter shook his head. "Damn shame it wasn't something a little more noble, then, huh?" he said, grasping Bradley by the shoulder and squeezing hard enough to make the man cringe in his seat. "Let's go."

As they came out the elevator on the fourth floor, Bradley peeled to the right and headed down the corridor, saying he needed to get his badge from his office. Walter followed behind, leisurely, peeking into the cubes and offices as he walked by them. Suddenly he saw the name placard on a door to his right that read Cynda Lohm. He almost stopped, as the door was open, but remembered in the last instant that it might be better to keep her in his pocket. It wouldn't hurt for him to have a few secrets of his own. Still, he was able to slow enough to peer into the office as he walked by. There she was, sitting behind the desk and staring at him through the doorway. She had obviously seen Bradley walk by and known Walter would be close behind.

Cynda held up a long-fingered hand, smiled very subtly at him, but kept quiet.

Walter winked at her and kept walking. Cynda had bright red hair. The orange kind that kids made fun of in schoolyards. The kind it takes an adult to fully appreciate, to realize how exceptionally gorgeous it really is. She wore it shoulder-length all around, but the bangs were longer, hanging down past her chin. Her face was covered with hard freckles that at first glance might be taken for a rash. Walter felt his heart speed up. *Where the hell has that woman been all my life?* He shook his head as he walked, blowing out through pursed lips. Cynda was, in Walter's estimation, one of those women who was so ridiculously beautiful that no one ever asked her out. Men were afraid and aware that they'd never have a chance with her, so it was easier to just give up the dream, when in reality, she was probably just dying for someone to pay her attention. To say hi.

As he approached the door to Bradley's office, Walter looked back over his shoulder, then turned and leaned on the jamb before realizing what was happening. Bradley was sitting behind his desk, hands on the blotter wrapped round a handgun. The muzzle was pointed directly at Walter's midsection.

Walter scoffed and looked up at the ceiling, rolling his eyes. "Seriously?" he said.

"I'm in charge here, asshole," Brian said.

Walter shrugged. "Yeah, okay. Whatever. The plan stays the same though."

"Oh, I'm going to show you what you want to see. But then it's over."

Walter didn't have much trouble believing that Brian would show him what he wanted to see. He also leaned toward believing the man would actually shoot him. The trick would be to find out exactly what point the innocence was over. That pivotal second where the game switched and it was time to pull the trigger – Walter had to keep his eye open for that very instant. He certainly could not turn his back on the other man. He wasn't necessarily afraid of being shot. He felt like he could avoid that when it came down to it. Bradley was probably not a great shot, for all that. Walter could tell by the way he was holding the gun that it was a foreign element in the man's hands. He looked girlish and limp-wristed with it. There was a very real possibility, in fact, that he would miss Walter altogether, and end up shooting someone else entirely. Fortunately there weren't a lot of bodies in the office. In fact, Cynda had been the only one Walter had seen on his walk to Bradley's office.

On the way back to the elevator, Walter noticed that Cynda was no longer in her office. Maybe she was in the break room getting coffee. Maybe she had left. Or maybe she was perched over a doorway ready to drop down on the man holding Walter at gunpoint.

When the doors opened on the basement, Walter was immediately astonished by the size of the place. The basement sprawled away to the right into darkness that had no end. Down that direction were crates or some other monstrosities covered with tarps, spaced wide enough to allow forklift maneuvering, and they followed that darkness as far as he could see. To their left, about twenty meters away, there was a concrete wall. Since the elevator was almost exactly in the middle of the floors above, Walter knew the wall wasn't the end of the basement. The double doors on the close end gave that away too. But he didn't see any bio-hazard suits hanging outside these doors, so they must not be the double doors Cardna had spoken of.

Walter looked back at all the looming blocks of hidden technology that sprawled away in the darkness, full of wonder. How many years'-worth of research was this? What could be under all those tarps? The badge reader beeped and the door unlocked. Bradley pushed the door open and tried to shove Walter inside. It was like turning a log on the water though. Walter looked back at him and said, "Tell me where to go. But put your fucking hands on me again and I'll break that thing off in your ass."

The man with the gun swallowed. Then nodded curtly. Walter walked into the room beyond. He wasn't sure what he had been expecting, but this wasn't it. It was simply a square room, largish, with counter tops running almost the entire perimeter. On the back wall was another door, wide and tall, that looked strong. The hinges were gigantic, like a bank vault. Next to the door hung several white suits. The bio-hazards. In the middle of the floor was an array of tables and other equipment, but none of it was that interesting. On entering the room, Bradley had tried to coax Walter to walk to the other door, but Walter was taking his time. Running a finger over the backbones of steel equipment skeletons, peeking under dust covers and generally just slowing the man's pace. When he finally made it to the inner door, he turned and looked at Bradley. "Well? What now?"

"Put on the suit," Bradley commanded. Now here was the trick, Walter thought. The suit itself had built-in gloves. In fact, every part of it was closed except the front zipper. Even the feet. What this told him was that at some point during the donning of the suit, Brian Bradley would have to put the gun down, slip his hand into the gloved portion, then pick the gun back up. Walter registered this with a silent quickness, then turned and looked back at the door.

DANGER! Absolutely no admittance without prior approval from administrator!

Walter sighed and grabbed a suit off the hook by the door, tossing it at Bradley. Bradley caught it with his free hand then motioned for Walter to turn around, using the barrel of the pistol. "Go ahead. You first," Bradley said.

"What the hell's in there? Am I going to get radiation sickness?"

"Just put the damned suit on!"

"All right," Walter said, raising his hands. He took the other suit off the hook and started stepping into it. His shoes fit easily into the closed feet. As he pulled the suit up over his waist and stuck his hands in the armholes, he took in its texture. It was very thick fabric, but fabric wasn't really the right word. It felt like something metallic mixed with a very strong fibrous plastic. Its texture was beyond description, but it did feel nice to his fingertips. He finished pulling on the suit, pushing his head into the face-covering area, then grasped the zipper below the crotch and pulled it up. The quality of the steel zipper treads was undeniable. It felt very expensive – very *fine*.

"Now sit over there while I put mine on," said Brian Bradley.

Walter shook his head and dragged over to a steel stool. He watched as Bradley struggled with each part of the suit still holding the pistol. When it came to the arms, he switched hands. He never set the gun down, but it was a clumsy hold. Walter could have easily charged him, knocked him over and taken control of the situation. But what then?

"You know where we're going?" Bradley asked as he zipped his suit up.

Walter nodded toward the vault-looking door. "I'm guessing into the bio lab."

"Have you seen any signs that say Bio-hazard on them? Or 'radiation' for that matter?" Bradley asked, a little too cocky. Walter was going to have fun with this one when he wrested control back from his weak hands. Bradley turned and punched an eight-digit code into a keypad above a toolbox, then slid a drawer open. He pulled out a belt that looked much like the one Chewbacca wore in *Star Wars*. Black nylon or leather with steel blocks spaced evenly around it. They had a dull sheen to them. Bradley slung it over a shoulder – again, like everyone's favorite Wookie. Walter smiled at this, amused.

"Let's go."

Walter stood up and joined Bradley in front of the door. "Do I get to play Star Wars too?"

"What the fuck you talking about?" Bradley said.

Walter reached out and fingered one of the steel blocks. "You look-"

Bradley knocked his hand away, shouting, "Keep your hands back!"

Walter held his hands up. "Whoa, okay, sorry. Sheesh!"

Brian Bradley turned and grabbed the large steel handle of the vault door, and pushed it down. Walter was surprised not to see some sort of iris scanner or keypad, a badge-reader of some sort. It was just... the honor system?

As he slid the door open, Walter was aware of a slight change in the atmosphere. It felt heavy all of a sudden. Like when one wakes up from a nap in an airplane, before the ears pop, there's a dulled sense to all the sound. Everything sounds loud inside the head. It felt like that. He suddenly felt a little queasy. But he recognized the sensation. *Magnets. Must be some magnetic device going in there.*

Say all you want about not being able to feel magnetic force, Walter knew better. He had lain on the gurney under an MRI. When those magnets were spinning, he felt it in his bones. Maybe we have enough iron in our blood, in our bones, our bodies, to react to magnetism. This was a powerful sensation. At one hand, Walter was excited by getting to see what ridiculous, top-secret project this man was working on, to see this giant magnetic contraption. But on the other side of that hand, he was not excited about feeling this way while he saw it. If this shit didn't subside soon, he might have to bow out.

"You get used to it eventually," said Bradley, reading the green on Walter's face. "Go," he said, waving the gun into the darkness beyond the vault door. *Why is it dark in there?* The light from the lab was all the light there was. It was enough to see that it was not another room, but in fact, a tunnel of some sort. It actually looked like a very low-tech brick passageway one might see in the catacombs under Paris. Concrete floor, red brick walls. Weird.

Bradley came through the door and pulled it closed, turned the handle. They were in absolute darkness now. Walter began to feel very uneasy. Was this where it would happen? Where Bradley would shoot him? He felt Bradley's hand on his shoulder, then a light switched on. It was a very bright flashlight. "Here," he said, handing it to Walter. "Lead the way." He could feel that the man now had the gun in

Walter's back. The worst place to put a gun if you were leading someone. Walter could so easily have twisted round, his arm hanging down by his side, and knocked the gun out of the way with no real force needed. Spinning round like that would move the gun off his back and put him in a position to head-butt or otherwise incapacitate the other man before he would have a chance to do anything else with the gun. Walter rolled his eyes and moved down the tunnel. He could not see the end of it from where they were. It was getting colder though, the farther they moved away from the vault door. Why not install some lighting in the passageway? What's the point of keeping it dark? The ceiling was plenty high to avoid hitting the bulbs.

After a few minutes of walking, the air getting heavier and heavier, Walter finally saw a steel band around the tunnel. It looked like a black channel of steel that formed a rectangle, perfectly encompassing the inner perimeter. It looked solid and strong, but was only about two inches thick all the way around. As they got even closer, he could make out circles on the inner perimeter of the band. These circles were like little glass eyes flush with the black steel, spaced about a foot apart from each other.

"What is that?" Walter asked, a little nervous. The heaviness in the air around him was now causing his shoulders to drag.

"It's the security gate," Bradley said, as if talking to an old friend. You don't get through it without this belt," he added, thumbing the Chewbacca belt he wore cross-body like a satchel. Bradley got real close to Walter, grabbing him with both arms, from the side, like he was a drunk man needing some assistance walking. They stepped through the steel band and Brian let go, returning to his previous state of following.

The two men moved a few more meters down the hall before coming to what looked like a dead-end. There was a step up in the concrete, and another steel band forming a sort of ring that hung above the step. It was mounted to the ceiling and walls with long carriage bolts that kept it spaced about six inches away from the brick and concrete all the way around. They would have to step through this ring to go any farther. And through the ring was about two meters of more hallway, then a brick wall. Attached to this ring, evenly spaced, were eight large black capsules. They had a dull luster to them, and looked to be constantly freezing over and thawing in parts: a scrim of misty ice that danced slowly about the surfaces. On each side of the step, at floor level, one of these capsules was attached. Then one on each side exactly halfway between floor and ceiling, and then two more directly above the two on the floor. Something about them was just… creepy. Just eerie. Not *right*.

Walter stopped and stared. "What is this, Brian?" he said. He was beginning to feel real, legitimate fear now. Brian Bradley stepped up beside him and took the flashlight from him. By the light reflected off the wall behind him, Walter could see the man had a friendly smile on his face.

"This, Mr. Watson, is where it all happens," he said proudly, spreading his arm out to offer the greatness that lay before them. "See, if I told you, you wouldn't believe me." He stood staring at Walter for a moment, amused. Then said, "Go ahead. Step through."

"It's not going to zap me to death or anything, is it?"

"Well, I guess you'll just have to find out, won't you?" he said, jamming the pistol in Walter's side.

With a scoff and a shrug, Walter stepped through the ring. During the transit he felt a terrible heat, like he was walking through a foil-thin wall of fire. It seemed to scan through him like a laser, taking him apart atom by atom. He stumbled when he reached the other side, reaching out for that brick wall to steady himself. But there was no brick wall. He was in a sort of greenhouse, with glass ceilings and semi-translucent walls. It was very bright all of a sudden, and he sensed movement in the walls. Wind. It was windy. This shed-like structure was outside, somehow, and there was a strong wind pressing the walls. *What the hell is going on here?*

He turned to look back at the ring he had come through, but it looked different – *was* different from this side. He saw Bradley literally materialize from it, as if he had emerged from black cloth. "What the fuck?" Walter shouted, staggering back a few steps.

The ring on this side was the same steel oval, the same – or at least he assumed it was the same – eight black capsules bolted to the outside of it. But through the ring here, he could see the wall of the shed he was in. A plastic-looking wall that looked as viable as a painter's drop cloth. Bradley was still smiling that smug, arrogant smirk of his as he came through. Then he spread his hands as if to say, *what do you think of the place?*

Walter was shaking his head. He took another step back, but gravity just felt wrong somehow. Everything seemed wrong. "What the hell is this place?"

"Congratulations, Walter," Bradley said, putting a hand on his shoulder, "you've made it to Mars."

Callie sat in her dining room with her chin on her arms, folded on the table, staring out the back windows at the rain. Two birds were flying around, landing on the fence, flirting, pecking each other, flying off and repeating the whole cycle. Over and over. It had a peculiar resonance to some part of her life, but she couldn't put her finger on it. The coffee cup by her left elbow sat half-empty, the steam having long since departed. Everyone had left the night prior. Gone. Returned to their lives, their jobs. Their own homes. Callie had grown to really love and appreciate Rebecca over the last couple of years. She was the closest thing to a sister Callie had ever had. And Codi, well, they shared a special kind of bond as well. They were not as close as Callie and Bec, but there was a very real connection there. They had danced together, being the center of the universe on that dance floor. They had cried and laughed and eaten ice cream together, sat up late by a fire talking about their childhoods together. There was a true love there as well. But with the closeness she had attained in these two friendships, Callie was feeling a weird emptiness right now, and that was for the strange and perplexing Cardna Darwyn.

Why did she feel this sudden emptiness with her? The roller-coaster woman; the woman who had at once felt like a friend, then betrayed her, then become a friend again... True, it had been a corporate betrayal – a business thing. Callie got it. It had still felt real at the time. Either way, they had barely had time to bond at all. To get to know each other, to share stories, find a common passion for anything. It was so new, there was hardly time for her to have developed enough like for the woman to call her a friend. So why did she miss her so much? Was this like a platonic puppy-love thing? Callie had no illusions about sexuality. Even the gorgeous Codi Cohl, at whose body Callie had found herself gazing many times with more than tinges of jealousy didn't turn Callie's dials enough to warrant experimentation. It was just fascinating to look at something so perfect, male or female be damned. You could take gender completely out of it. This was art. Callie loved to look at gorgeous bodies. Of course when she looked at Walter's chiseled chest and veiny arms, sex came flooding into her, but it wasn't like that with other men.

Cardna was mysterious and enigmatic on the surface, but once you broke through the ice, she was pretty normal beneath. Very human. Very humane. Sweet and caring, compassionate and generous. But complex in a simple way. She was sharp and witty, funny and interesting. Callie had kind of fallen quickly for her, in that weird friendly, and completely non-sexual way. But wow, this fast? Already enough to miss the woman? When Cardna had squeezed her hands last night and said, "Callie, I *really* have to go home," Callie had felt a sadness sweep over her, like she was next in line at the carnival ride, but they had to shut it down. It felt very girlish. Young. Immature. And Callie's face had obviously betrayed every bit of it. Cardna had put her hands on Callie's cheeks and made sad eyes, cooing and speaking soothing words like a mother to a toddler. How embarrassing!

She was right, of course. Cardna still had a job she presumably wanted to keep. She had a plane ticket back to Fiji. She had a life. And Callie had known it. It wasn't like she had thought the woman would say, 'fuck yeah, Callie!' and stick her middle fingers up, eschewing all responsibility in favor of Callie's mission against that asshole, Brian Bradley.

So was everything going according to her plan? Callie was no longer sure. Necessarily, in this phase, she was counting on everything to go smoothly down in the bottom half of the planet. If all those pieces slid smoothly along their tracks, then Walter would be coming home to her in a relatively short while. All would be well. But she had no way to tell. No way to check on him. Callie had been reticent to enact the last bit of the plan, which would involve Walter leaving for Fiji without her. But he had comforted her, as he always did, a hand on the cheek, a kiss on the lips, a promise that all would be fine. There was no way that spineless idiot would get the better of him. Walter stood a good five inches over the man anyway, and that was before you started measuring front to back. Callie was confident in his words. She knew what Walter was capable of.

But… But, but, but. There was always a but. *What if?* There was always that lingering what-if that resided in the back of her brain. What if something stupid happened – something completely out of Walter's control? Something that allowed Brian Bradley to take control of the situation? Callie had to force herself to change the subject in her mind. To think of other things. Almost every thought she ever had these days revolved around Walter, so that would be especially difficult. Which was one of the reasons she had hoped Cardna would stay a little longer. Rebecca and Natalie and Codi and Sam – they all had their things. That was fine. Callie knew them as working people. It was routine for them to go back to work. Could she just have this one friend spend the night?

She chewed her lip and sighed, then sat up, grabbing her coffee mug and throwing back a large swig before realizing it was cold. *Bleh!* She spit it back in the mug and stood up, stretching her arms above her head and arching her back. She had been sitting in the wooden dining room chair for over an hour in nothing but her panties and a night shirt. Her butt was sweating. She needed a shower. Her legs and underarms needed a shave. It was time to clean up and get dressed. It was time for her to be one of those routine followers. She reckoned she had been away from the job long enough. It was time to go back to work.

On the drive into the Bohr office, she thought back about how long she had actually been gone now. She was fortunate to have such a lenient manager. And the involvement she actually had in the jobs she oversaw was such that she could get away with such leaves. But it might be good to actually show up occasionally. To get involved a little. To do some real work.

The rain beat against the windshield so hard, she could barely see the end of her hood. The trek to work took almost forty-five minutes. By the time she pulled into the parking garage, Callie was in a bad mood all over again. She wanted to back out of the space reserved for her and just go back home. Get back in her pajamas and crawl back under the covers. She could take one more day. Maybe another week. Just to be sure she was truly ready to come back.

She stepped off the elevator and dragged herself across the marble floor of the reception area with a force of will. Said hi to the receptionist. Some new gal Callie had not seen before. That shouldn't have surprised her. When you're gone from work for months at a time, stuff has a tendency to change. She wondered how foreign – how *alien* her office would look now. Would there be stacks of mail and paperwork on her desk? Books? Boxes? Other people's stuff? Would they have turned it into temporary storage? *Hey, that Callie Simmons is never here, just set that shit on her desk.*

But it wasn't like that. It was still perfectly neat, the way she had left it. She set her purse on the file cabinet and pulled out her chair. There was a stack of mail on the middle of her blotter, about an inch thick. Not bad. Not as bad as she expected. The amount of mail she had received at home – albeit junk mail – in the time she had been gone from work, would have filled a dumpster by now. She flipped through the envelopes, tossing each of them in the trash as she identified them as irrelevant. Until she got to the fourth or fifth letter. It was a folded paper with a beautiful bouquet of flowers on the front. Frowning, she opened the card and scanned the inside – her eyes in an almost robotic automation – knowing exactly where to look. For this was a familiar type of card. One that didn't require reading in its entirety. No, the only part that required reading was the Who. And maybe the When.

She suddenly covered her mouth with her hand, sucking in a breath. "Oh my God!" she said, tears immediately flooding her eyes. The who was Charles Lancey. Her boss for time out of mind. "Oh my God, no!" she said, dropping the mail on her desk and bolting out of her office. As if to try to disprove the card as a prank. Some prank that would be. But her boss's office, right next door to her own, was empty. Callie had planned on popping in and taking the chair across the desk from Mr. Lancey, as soon as she had gone through her mail – her return ritual. But there was no Mr. Lancey in here. Not anymore. Not ever again.

They had cleaned everything out. The blotter was empty. The shelves and the cabinets, even the walls – they were all bare. She stood there, heartbroken, staring at the empty chair where the best-dressed man she had ever met once sat. *God, what a dolt I've been!* She shook her head. How come no one had told her he had died? Shouldn't someone have at least let her know? She would have liked to attend the ceremony. It had happened over a month ago.

Callie dropped into the seat across the desk from his own. Slumped back, staring at the empty throne where the man would never sit again, putting his elbows on the desk and tapping his fingers together, smiling at her wise ideas. She wasn't downright crying, but there were tears. She had nothing but fond memories of the man. And they were rolling through her head like an old reel-to-reel film.

"Hey, Callie," a voice called from the doorway behind her. She turned to see Debra, the executive assistant to the man who used to call this his office, standing with her arms crossed, leaning against the jamb.

Callie wiped her eyes and stood up. "Hey, Deb. I'm so sorry." She stepped forward and hugged the other woman. When she stepped back, she could see tears in Debra's eyes as well. "I had no idea," she said.

"Well, he wasn't big on advertising anything. He went quietly."

"What happened?" Callie said, taking the same posture as the other woman, crossing her arms.

"Stroke. Died in his home."

Callie shook her head. Breathed out. "I wish I would have known."

Debra shook her head as well. "Well, you didn't miss anything. His family, his children, had a private thing for him. Apparently he didn't want a funeral at all."

Callie just stared at the woman, not knowing what to say. Debra stared back at her. After a long moment, Debra finally said, "Listen. I have something to give you. Mr. Lancey said when he was gone, he wanted you to have it."

"So he did know it was coming?" Callie asked, suddenly confused.

"No," she said, waving her hand, shaking her head, "no, gone was meant like, as in retirement, when he originally said it." She bit her lip for a moment. "I never thought of it as his dying. But he wanted you to have it."

"What is it?" Callie said, raising her eyebrows.

Debra flicked her head over her shoulder and turned to walk out of the office. Callie followed Debra to her office, one more down the corridor. Debra rounded her desk and opened the top drawer, removing a small, square box that was wrapped in brown paper and taped immaculately. There was a thin crossing of cord that formed a bow at the top. She handed it to Callie, who was frowning again.

"What is it?" she asked again, holding the box near her ear and shaking it.

Debra shrugged.

Callie stared at her for a moment, wondering whether to open it right here or if she should take it back to her own office. "Hmmph," Callie said, shaking her head. "I have no idea what he would want to leave me."

Debra smiled and raised her eyebrows, putting her hands on her hips. She didn't have any answers for Callie.

"Okay, well, thank you, Deb," she said, turning to leave the office.

"Oh, Callie?" said Debra, stopping her in her turn. "Ms. Simmons?" Callie frowned at the sudden shift. "One more thing."

"Yeah?" Callie said, tilting her head. She left her mouth open, chewing her tongue. *More mystery?*

"I work for you now."

Brian Bradley had assumed the role of a benevolent dictator, offering the charity of a *quick tour of the place* under his good graces. Walter was still reeling in shock from what the man had said. He was not yet on board with the belief that he was standing on another planet, though the sun did seem more distant. The general atmosphere around the place seemed more red. It wasn't something one could perceive directly with any specific detail. It was like the green that came before a hail storm. No one thing looked any greener than normal. But it was just there. As it was here. It was red.

Something felt different, for sure. Gravity. Atmospheric pressure. Everything? Walter couldn't quite tell. But if something didn't show itself pretty quickly – something that would break the facade and reveal the trickery – he reckoned he would have to consider the thought that there had indeed been a transit.

"You see those black capsules there," Bradley said, pointing lazily at the ring through which they had emerged, "those are Entangled Transposition Buoys." The smugness on his face was almost enough to send Walter into a rage, were he not so overwhelmed with fear and confusion already. He needed a moment to sit and sort this out. To think about what was going on. He had seen science work in ways only a very small fraction of a percentage of the population ever had. Walter had ridden back a hundred years under the direction of a quantum computer. That had seemed completely natural at the time. There had been no shock. No need for time to sit and consider the possibility of what he was witnessing. Horse-drawn carriages in the road, gas lanterns lighting the buildings – it had all just felt *contemporary*. There had been no temporal shock to it. But this – this traveling through great distance…

"They form what the lay would call a teleportation portal. A perfectly reasonable moniker for it, I suppose. But it's so much deeper than that," Bradley said, shaking his head. "See, if I slip my hand inside the ring," he said, doing just that, "my hand is coming out the other ring instantaneously, back on Earth. That means my arm is over sixty million kilometers long!" he said, and actually laughed.

Walter was shaking his head. Indeed, the man's arm was disappearing as it broke the barrier of the air betwixt the capsules. He felt the blood drain from his face and staggered. He had to sit down. There were plastic chairs in this greenhouse-looking place, so he sat in one of these and put his hands on his head, feeling the thick non-fabric between them.

"You know about quantum entanglement, don't you, Walter?" Bradley said. He completely ignored Walter's reaction to the science he was living.

Walter looked up at him, feeling faint and dizzy, excited and overwhelmed. He couldn't speak. His wide eyes answered for him though.

"Yeah," Bradley said, smiling. "You know. Each one of these canisters has an analog back on earth. A perfect duplicate in every way. So special in its quantum state that none of them can be discerned as independent from the rest of the group. So it's more like stepping through a doorway than actually teleporting." He then went over to a door cut into the wall of the structure they were in. He pushed it open and held his hand out, offering Walter the red-brown dirt of another world.

Walter was still dumbfounded, though he was able to find his feet. He went to the door and peered out, a little dizzy. The view was instantly rewarding. He was very obviously not standing outside the building he had entered less than an hour ago. This was not Fiji. Red mountainous and rocky landscape surrounded him in every direction. He took a few steps, staring down at the dust on his boots and let the door slam behind him. How long would he last in this suit? Surely he would run out of oxygen soon.

"Beautiful, isn't it?" Brian Bradley said from behind him. "You know, you should feel lucky. Only a handful of humans have ever been granted this vision."

"How the fuck did you do this?" Walter said, turning to look at the man. Part filled with amazement, part a complete lack of understanding of how he should be feeling. Everything was coming at him so quickly, he hadn't even had time to stop and appreciate the fact that he had transited over sixty million kilometers, assuming Bradley's calculation of distance was correct.

"Oh, it wasn't just me. Red Bell is my baby, for sure," Bradley said, putting a hand over his heart. "But I couldn't have done it on my own."

"You mean without standing on the backs of those on the Atlas crew?"

Bradley made a sour face behind the clear part of his suit, the part that formed a mask. "You still don't get it, do you? One thing has nothing to do with the other!" Bradley said, waving the pistol around like an idiot. Only someone who never handled firearms would handle a firearm that way. Walter stared at him. Biding his time.

"That Atlas bullshit was just a small part of the bigger picture. I mean, that's how we got this set of the buoys here, I'll grant that. But Red Bell was about connecting them!" He was talking like a motivational speaker, about to warm to his climax. "And testing them, of course. Sacrifices have to made in any world-changing advance, right?" he said, standing up straight and frowning. Like he wasn't proud of that part. "You have to slaughter some pigs to get the bacon. No one misses them anyway. They were fuckin' peons."

"Huh?" Walter said, and now he was frowning too. "Who the hell are you talking about?" He stood up and turned to square off at the man, getting ready to make his move. He had seen enough. Maybe he didn't have enough to satisfy Callie's curiosities, or to bring down the company. But he had enough reason to put this man's face through the back of his skull. And that would have to be enough. He took a deep breath and flexed his hands, but Brian seemed to sense something was off. He turned and looked at Walter, and raised the gun again.

"Well, I think we've talked enough. I have to head back now. Feel free to make yourself at home," Bradley said, then backed through the door, letting it shut slowly as he looked at Walter through the translucent plastic barrier. All Walter could do was stare in disbelief. He finally caught on that Bradley was about to abandon him here.

"What the hell am I supposed to do here, asshole? You can't leave me here!"

"Oh, yes I can. It wouldn't be the first time, anyway." Bradley slipped one foot through the ring and stared back at Walter for a moment. And then he was gone.

The pistol was the last thing to go through. As soon as it was gone, Walter charged the ring. He dived through thinking he would slam bodily into the man who had vanished through it less than five seconds before. But he only came into an empty hallway, stumbling and almost falling onto the stones. There was no sound in here. Bradley was long gone. *What the hell?*

A tinge of fear began to settle in on Walter. His head tingled and burned. He was back, for he could feel that much. He was back on Earth. The gravity – the atmosphere, it was all *right* again. All the way he had gotten used to feeling it be over the last forty or so years of his life.

Walter made his way as quickly as the darkness would allow, back up the hallway. Soon, it was over though. He slammed into a wall. He couldn't remember a wall being here before. The tunnel had been straight as a board. He began feeling around the edges, trying to find an opening. He felt a steel rectangular channel, and as he slid his hands up, felt small holes in the inner perimeter of it. Then he remembered. "Fuck!" he shouted. It was the band that kept people from wandering onto another planet by mistake. *The belt! The Chewbacca belt!* Walter stepped back, putting his hands on his head, finally feeling the sweat in his hair as the helmet portion of the getup came into contact with his head.

Holy fuck, I am actually trapped on another fucking planet. This can't be real. This can't be real. This can't be…

Then the real fear began to settle in.

Callie sat at her desk, chin resting on a hand, staring at the box in her other hand, tumbling it over and over. Fingering the thin cord. Picking at the perfect tape with a fingernail. Feeling its assumed importance through its heft. Fidgeting. Serena McAlister was on her way down. Callie had gotten the phone call about ten minutes before. When the woman had heard Callie was back in the office, she had called and told her to hang tight. Serena was Charles Lancey's boss. The natural assumption was that Callie was now her direct report. But who knew? Debra's telling Callie that she worked for Callie now had been a shock. Callie had only met Serena a few times. Once in the office, a couple of times at corporate events, like dinner parties.

Serena worked on the top floor of the building. Up there with all the 'Big Ballers', as Rebecca called them. Charles Lancey had an office up there, in fact. He just chose to office down close to his subordinates. He was one of them. The fact that Callie had only seen Serena one time in the office revealed the stark contrast between the two management types.

Shortly, Callie heard the elevator ding from down the hall. She straightened up, pulled her blouse down, checked her hair with practiced fingertips. Serena stepped around the corner. She stopped and spread her hands out. Smiled.

"Well, Ms. Simmons, nice to have you back!"

Callie nodded and stood up. "It feels nice to be back, thank you, ma'am."

"May I sit?" the older woman said, raising her eyebrows and holding a hand out at the visitor's chair.

"Of course," Callie said. She waited until Serena sat, then took her own seat again.

"Well, I guess you know why I'm here."

Callie didn't speak. She nodded once, slowly.

"Mr. Lancey always spoke so favorably about you. You were the natural selection."

Callie almost smirked at the phrasing. She shook her head. "I'm sorry, ma'am, I'm not sure I…"

The woman waved Callie's words away. "Don't be prig." She leaned back in her chair, grasping the handholds. She looked around the room.

"Pardon, but I don't think I was being prig. I've never been fanciful about my diction."

The woman raised her chin, smiling a smug number. "Well, then forgive my misdirection. I came to ask if you wanted the job. You were the natural *choice*," she corrected, even though Callie thought she had cleared that up.

"Do you mean Mr. Lancey's job?"

Serena's smile faded. "Well, of course, dear. What else would I mean? We've owed you this for a long time."

Callie was unsure how to take this. Being offered an executive position was not entirely attractive to her. She had always preferred to have her hands on the science. Taking a position such as Serena was offering would mean long hours. It would mean more meetings. More responsibilities. Higher pay, sure, but Callie felt like she made too much money already. In the short list that sprinted through her mind, the first bullet she actually did find attractive was a parking space closer to the elevator.

Callie realized she had been staring at the box in her hand. She looked up and saw that Serena was looking at it too. Probably wondering what the hell was in it. She still had that smile on her face.

"We're prepared to offer you a forty-percent salary increase. You would be in charge of the Research Department."

Callie met her eyes. "Can I take some time to think on it?"

The woman's smile left her face again. All this back and forth was going to ruin her makeup, Callie thought. "More time off?" she asked, raising her eyebrows.

Callie shrugged. "Well, I didn't know I was coming back to an orphaned position here. No one told me that Mr. Lancey had passed away."

The other woman tilted her head a little, looking like she thought Callie might be something of a dolt. Then she shook her head quickly and leaned forward, still grasping the handles of the chair. Her old knuckles were white and looked fragile. "Ms. Simmons, the position has not been orphaned. We just feel that you might have… *outgrown* it."

"How would that be?" Callie asked, frowning heavily, pulling her head back. "I love the science! Research is… it's my- my life!" She was getting angry all of a sudden, and she couldn't quite pinpoint why that was.

The older woman sighed, looked around the office. Clearly, this was not how she had envisioned this meeting going. "Sure. Take your time. How much time do you need? Another month? Three?"

"That's not fair," Callie said, finally putting the box down on the desk. She set it so neatly and gently down, so precisely in the center of the blotter that it caused Serena McAlister to frown at it. Now her curiosity was almost palpable. She was dying to know what was in that little wrapped package, no bigger than a bracelet box.

"Look," Serena said, holding a hand out with the palm up, "I know Charles always granted you whatever time you wanted to go gallivanting around working for other companies. And that's fine. But it's over now. We're offering you a very fair upgrade to your existing position." She stood up and straightened her trousers, then tapped a finger on the edge of the wooden desk. Callie looked up at her. "If you don't accept it, then yes, your position would be," she said, and held her fingers in the air to make quotes, "orphaned."

Then she turned and walked out of the office. Callie leaned back in her chair and began twisting the ring on one hand with the fingertips of the other. She had just been given a strong ultimatum. Serena McAlister obviously didn't know Callie very well. Working under pressure, or a deadline, was sort of a specialty of Callie's. Working under duress of an ultimatum was not. She looked around her office, shaking her head. "I don't need this crap," she said, then stood up and walked out the door, flipping the light off as she left.

CHAPTER 28

Walter had sat on the floor, knees up and arms wrapped round them, burying his head in his arms for the better part of two hours. He tried everything he could think of to stay calm. After the first hour or so he had begun to feel lightheaded, and realized he was running low on oxygen in the suit. Sitting in the dark outside the admittance band, he wondered how the oxygen level was in the hallway. Realizing he had no other real options, he unzipped the front of the suit to test the air. The relief on his sweaty skin and the cool rush of air into his face was both instant and magnificent. He had never felt such a vivid and powerful transformation from one extreme to another. In the instant that the cool air blasted his face, his head started tingling – the sweat in his hair almost feeling like sleet – and he began gasping long, deep breaths. The asphyxiation had been creeping up on him.

He didn't know how the contraption worked, and thus, didn't know if it blocked oxygen from passing through in one direction or the other, but guessed it probably didn't. He had not been able to inspect it on the trip coming in, but didn't remember it looking air-tight. The ring with the entanglement buoys on it, however, well, that surely had to be doing something about keeping the pressure regulated.

Walter finally gave up on waiting beside the band and stood up in the dark, then took a few deep breaths and zipped the suit back up. It was good to know that he could always come back into this short run of terrestrial tunnel to refill his oxygen supply. What he would do about water and food was another story. His thought was that there might be something outside – perhaps another entrance back into the lab area, even. Anything was better than sitting in the dark and waiting for something to happen.

He maneuvered his way down the tunnel in the dark, hands on the walls, until he finally got back to the teleportation ring. It had not been as drastic an event coming back the other way, but he had also dived through it. Unsure if that mattered or not, but dreadful of the transition sickness, he stepped through a little more gingerly. Again, the flash of intense heat as each part of his body came through, but also again, the nausea and fogginess seemed even less than the last time. The sun was definitely in a different place in the sky now, as the tent had a different angle of shadows crossing its floor. The sky was cloudy as well. He stared in amazement for some time, just relishing the reality of this magic. He shook his head. No, it wasn't magic. It was science. He had not been moved here by séance or spell, but by science. Fitting. That's the way Walter lived his life. He even refused to read Fantasy books because of that one thing. Magic. If there were dragons or spells or any other nonsense like that, he'd drop the book and never look back. *Science over séance.*

He knew he had at least a couple of hours to do some exploring before he would need to go back and refill his breathing supply in the suit. But he also knew there was not much to explore here. The word 'desolate' didn't quite capture it all. This place was so forlorn, so lonesome and far away from everything he knew that there probably were *not* words that would capture it. He had seen a small building behind the tent when he had gone out that door earlier. He could at least go check that out. So that's where he headed.

And it wouldn't be bad to watch a sunset on the red planet, would it? If he were destined to die out here anyway, he might as well try to find something redeeming in the experience. As he pushed open the almost comical storm door, he turned this time to the left and made his way around the back of the tent. He could see now that it was more than just a tent. The rods and spars that made up its structure were steel and solid. The plastic walls were semi-malleable. But it looked like it would stand up in a pretty good wind. Maybe there weren't destructive winds out here. He realized there was so little he actually knew about Mars, and wished suddenly he had done some research on it back when he had the chance.

The building behind the tent was a dome, and not very large at all, maybe only ten meters across at its base. In the side, there was a somewhat simple notch that allowed for a door. The door had an even simpler handle on it. There didn't even appear to be any locks. He reached out and tentatively put pressure on the handle. It indeed turned with little resistance. Apparently if someone wanted to break into this place, all they had to do was fly to Mars and turn the door handle. Walter smirked at this thought, then pulled the door open.

Light flickered to life inside the door, and he was greeted by an unexpected site. A steel staircase leading down was directly in the middle of the floor. There were rails around the other three sides of it. There was not much else in this dome, either. A couple of boxes sat in the back behind the stairs, but that was it. He stepped on the top stair, carefully, and suddenly feeling a little foolish. Here he was sneaking down a staircase in a strange building on *another fucking planet,* and acting like he might be about to wake a giant. He could almost certainly say he was the only human being – and for that matter, the only living thing – on the entire planet. Probably not much need to be sneaking and whispering. But the goose flesh that accompanied that thought was reassuringly poignant. There was definitely reason to be cautious. No telling what he might find down there. Machinery? Booby traps? Who could say. Brian Bradley had obviously not tried to keep Walter from coming in here.

Then a thought occurred to Walter, and he stopped. Brian Bradley had mentioned bringing the eggs or buoys or whatever-the-fuck they were called out here on the Atlas trip. So that meant they *had* made it to Mars. Or at least the Royal ship had. Could it be that there *were* people down here in this cellar? Others who were still working on the project? Another chill ran up his spine at the thought. It wouldn't be impossible, especially considering it only took a few minutes to get from the parking garage to the transposition buoys. It would be a lot like coming in to work. Never mind the step that takes you across the solar system in the blink of an eye.

He moved downward in the dark for the fifteen or so stairs. But when he got to the bottom, there was a door, and a light switch. There was enough light from up above to see that the door was a little more sophisticated than the entry to the dome had been. This one looked substantial. Maybe airtight. He grasped the handle and though it did turn, it took a little more effort to make it happen. He heard the sound of a seal breaking as he pushed it open. A light flickered on inside the new space, and it was immediately obvious what the room was. *Airlock.*

Walter had seen enough sci-fi movies to know an airlock when he saw one. He closed the door behind him and looked up, wondering if it would happen on its own. Then he glanced around the small room and saw a panel to his left with two buttons on it. One had an arrow pointing back the way he had come, and the other had a mirrored image of the arrow. He pushed the one that pointed forward and was immediately rewarded with hissing and the sound of a bolt throwing in the door behind him.

After thirty seconds or so, the same bolt-throw sounded from the door in front of him. He pushed down on the lever and pulled the door toward him. This chamber was a locker room. Lockers and benches lined one wall, enough for about a dozen people. A couple of the lockers hung open and he could see suits like his own stuffed into one of them. Extras?

Walter took a deep breath and unzipped his own suit, relishing the refreshing sensation of new air coming in to replace the stale, used air. It smelled a little metallic, but not bad. It was obviously recycled here, so one had to expect it wouldn't be perfect. The room beyond the locker room was visible through the doorway, which had no door. He ducked through and looked into the next room. He was greeted with warm lighting and a very cold decorative schema. It looked very utilitarian. Hospital-like. All business. A couple of couches and a table, some steel boxes and a wall full of cabinets. He shook his head as he took this all in. Across the room was another doorway, again with no door. Walter stepped carefully to the doorway and peeked through. Hundreds of jars sat on metal shelves, large and filled with unclear liquid. Most of them had unidentifiable things floating or resting in them. In the corner where the corners of two shelves would come together was yet another doorway. It was dark back there and he couldn't see into it.

As he stepped into the room, his eyes fell across one jar in particular, and his heart almost leapt out of his chest. It looked like a mix between a lobster and a spider, floating in the viscous green liquid. Its ten legs looked as thick as pencils and it had a gigantic – at least by what Walter would consider *Earth standards* - bulbous abdomen. If this was a spider, it was definitely not one he was familiar with. This one would give a camel spider a run for its money. And as he stood looking at it, a woman appeared in the doorway in the corner. The movement startled Walter so bad he fell backward, crying out as he stumbled into a shelf, bringing down several of the large jars, where they popped and exploded on the floor.

Walter stared dumbfounded into the curious countenance of a young woman.

Callie Simmons sat in her car, head leaned back against the headrest and hands tight on the steering wheel, eyes closed and locked in thought. She didn't need to work. Not yet. She could sustain for quite a long time on her savings before she would need to worry about working. But her lifestyle dictated that finding a new job would be the smarter decision. Steak and lobster dinners several times a month, drinks out with friends landing in the several-hundred dollars a night range and buying every pair of shoes and every purse or cute top she saw without regard for whether or not she would ever even wear it… These were things she understood she was not willing to give up. So she either got a job to fund all the fun, or she paid for it with savings. And then she wouldn't have the savings.

The hurt in her heart came from what felt like a betrayal. Charles Lancey had always treated her so well, like family. This woman to whom she would now report was cold and callous. Very un-family-like. Being given an ultimatum was the farthest thing from what she had expected coming into work this morning. Well, second-farthest. Her boss's death being first place in that short list.

And it wasn't as if Callie had a bad work ethic. There were two sides to consider. Number one, she did put in the hours when it was necessary to do so. If she were deeply involved in a project, she had many times in her life, and for many companies, found herself working until two or three in the morning, sometimes even crashing on a company sofa, then going at it again a few hours later. She had definitely given herself to the jobs, when those jobs called on her to. When they were worthy. But when there was nothing really going on, Callie had a hard time agreeing with what Corporate America deemed appropriate. Forty hours was a standard work week. Well, who the hell came up with that policy? If there wasn't forty hours'-worth of work to be done in that week, why the heck should she sit behind the desk and surf the internet, just killing time? She did not believe in busy work. Needless, mindless bullshit tasks meant to justify the pimping of her time. And it wasn't just at her job, either. At any of the jobs she had worked. She didn't believe in it anywhere. If you worked a fast-food counter and wanted full-time work, then of course, forty hours was appropriate. But if you worked in an envelope-stuffing mill and the company ran out of envelopes, why stick around? Or if your work was based on fulfilling a quota, why should the higher-ups care how you managed your time, as long as your quota was filled? If she could stuff two hundred percent more envelopes than everyone else around her, and only had to stuff five hundred per week, should she not be allowed to stuff them all in one shift, then take the rest of the week off? *Shrug. Why not?*

Callie had a bitter taste in her mouth about being made to accept a promotion she didn't want – all in the name of assigning her to more hours in the office. It didn't just *not appeal* to her, it made her feel downright *icky.* She pulled her hair back behind her ear and looked out the window. The sign was right there, a giant, black marble block two meters wide, glistening and beautiful with raindrops running down its face. It read Royal Research Corporation. She knew she could walk into that building and have an employee badge again within thirty minutes. Minus would hire her sight unseen. But was that what she wanted? Had she not given Royal enough of her life? Had she not taken enough of their money over the years? Money… *Hey, wait!*

She was out of the car and dashing for the smoked glass doors of the building entrance before she even realized she had not shut off her car. F it. It could wait. Her heels clicked as she made her way across the lobby, replete with its own austere beauty. The fountain by the elevators provided a nice backdrop of trickling water as it spilled over the black marble steps down into the basin. The security guard didn't even look up at her as she walked past. Callie knew that looking like she belonged was the biggest key to getting into places she wanted to go.

The elevator took her to the sixth floor. Dinged. The doors slid silently open. Then she was marching down the carpeted corridor, offices on her right, cubicles on her left. Phones and printers, fax machines and coffee makers. She popped into Minus's office without even the courtesy of a knock. There was another woman standing at his desk with her hands clasped together in front of her, listening to him talk quietly. When Minus saw Callie enter, he stopped talking and looked up at her.

"Did you blow through that ch-"

"Minus, you used that joke last time I was here. And for your information, I forgot about the damn check and it expired. Can I please get another one?"

Matt Minus shook his head as if trying to clear out a colony of bees from within. "Are you serious? This would be, what? The third one now?" He looked up at the girl standing by his desk, who was in turn staring at Callie. Callie did not recognize her. And that's what she was. Just a girl. Couldn't be more than twenty years old. More cute than pretty. "You have to be the only person in the history of the planet who cares so little about money that you forget to cash a million-dollar check."

The girl's eyebrows went way up, and she looked down at Minus, then back at Callie.

Callie furled her lips and tilted her head to the side, dramatically showing how irritated she was with the direction this conversation was going. "Look, Minus. Can I please have another check? Or direct-deposit it? Something?"

Minus stared at her for a long moment. Callie looked at the girl, who was still staring at her. She actually caught the girl looking her up and down. She looked amazed. In awe. Here she was, a regular gal standing in a regular man's office on a regular Monday morning. And only two meters away stood a woman who had let a million-dollar check die.

"Well, yeah, I can get finance to cut another check. If you need money that bad though, I can-"

Callie cut him off. "No, Minus. I still have plenty in savings, thank you. I just quit my job, and I don't really want to go back to work yet. So I figured, if I had that extra money, I could stretch that time out a little longer and not have to worry about rushing."

"Kkhah," Minus seemed to say. It was an expulsion of breath and voice, a perfect representation of his complete and utter befuddlement. The other girl was still staring. Not in a weird way. She truly looked like she felt as if she were in the presence of a superstar. That made Callie feel a little better. So she smiled at the girl.

"Hi. I'm Callie," she said, holding up a hand in a wave that looked more like she was swearing in at a court.

The girl's face lit up in a bright smile. "Hi, Callie, I'm Laynie," she said. She tried to hold back a huge smile, allowing instead a very slight one to make its way through. She waved back.

"You do realize you could completely retire and live off the interest from a check that big, right?" Minus said. His elbows were both on the desk while his fingers twiddled with a small gadget of some sort. Maybe a fidget spinner. Did they still make those?

"After taxes?" Callie said. "Pssh. I'll maybe net six hundred."

Minus held up his hands, tossing the gadget in the process, rolling his eyes and leaning back. "Christ, Callie."

She looked back at Laynie. Callie realized on closer inspection, especially with the now permanent smile on the girl's face, that she had been wrong before. She was not just cute. She *was* pretty. Darling, in fact. She had pretty white teeth and a contagious smile. Callie decided she liked her. *I think we are going to be friends.*

After a moment, Minus said, "What is it you plan on doing with all this time, Callie? You still chasing the ghost of Christmas past?"

Callie frowned. "What does that mean? No, Minus. I just want to be free of the work world for a while. Maybe do some traveling. You know, see the world."

"Let me guess. Hmm. Like, maybe… Fiji?"

Callie sighed. Put her fists on her hips. Tilted her head again. Did she look exasperated enough? She went to work chewing on her bottom lip.

"Why the hell are you standing here giving me those angry eyes? Are you wanting something?"

"Just the check, Minus," Callie said.

"Okay!" he said, throwing his hands up again. This time the gadget went flying. Landed somewhere off behind his desk. He turned and looked for it briefly, but gave up without moving too far. He grunted. "I told you I would have finance cut a new one for you."

"Can we get that going?"

"Fuck sake," he said, picking up his phone. While he dialed and spoke, Callie looked back at the girl.

"So who are you, Laynie?"

"I just started today. I'm going to be an apprentice for a few months while I decide what I want to do in college."

Callie looked back at Minus, wide-eyed. "Apprenticeships now, Minus? What the F? Pay this poor girl some money!"

He waved her away, shaking his head. He looked defeated. Meanwhile, Laynie was trying hard to hold back a gigantic grin. She was barely succeeding. Callie could tell the girl liked her.

"You're going to Fiji?" asked Laynie. Her blond hair was only slightly longer than Callie's but about the same color. It swung forward as she moved her head.

"I might. Already went once."

Laynie raised her chin. "Ah."

Minus hung up the phone. "Will there be anything else, Queen Callie?" he asked, holding a palm above his blotter.

"Nope. That'll do it. Thanks, Minus." Callie said, smiling. "It was nice to meet you, Laynie. Good luck working for this guy."

Laynie looked embarrassed. She looked down at Minus, then back at Callie, not sure what to say. Minus, meanwhile, was making a face that registered disappointment.

"Just kidding. He's a wonderful boss," Callie said. The tension broke. The girl laughed out loud. And as Callie turned for the door, she shouted over her shoulder, "I'm serious, Minus, pay that girl some money!"

The girl stood staring back at Walter with wide, fear-filled eyes. She had jerked her hands up into fists in front of her chest as the jars fell and burst on the concrete floor. Now she stood trembling, too terrified to speak. Walter, breathing heavily, looked back up from the wet mess he'd made and held a hand up toward the girl, almost like a wave.

"Who are you?" she asked. Her voice was hoarse and rough, but not unpleasant.

Walter expelled breath through tightened lips and put his hand on his chest, willing his heart to slow. "I'm Walter," he finally said. "I'm not going to hurt you."

The girl nodded somberly, slowly. She swallowed. "Well, it's nice to see somebody else for a change. Are you my Prince Charming, here to rescue me?" she asked, and although her mouth had twisted in a smirk as she said it, Walter thought she sounded sincere in her hope.

Walter squinted at her, tilting his head slightly. His heart was still slamming in his chest. He stood up straight, finally coming out of the stance one takes when jars pop around his feet. He wiped his hands together. "If you're serious, then yes," he said, nodding slightly. "You bet I am."

Her eyes widened. "Really?"

"What are you doing here?" Walter asked her, ignoring her question.

She sighed. "I'm slave labor, I guess. He won't let me come home. That's why I was hoping you were here to save me. I haven't seen anyone else in ages."

"Oh my God," Walter said quietly. He wiped his hands on his pants and then rubbed his cheeks, trying to find calm in his raging head. That sick fuck had been keeping this girl down here? For how long?

The girl stared at him. She had dark circles beneath her eyes and hollows in her cheeks, but looked like she might be pretty with a little attention. Her long black hair was pulled messily back into a ponytail and she wore a white t-shirt and cargo pants. She was barefooted and her feet looked dirty. She probably hadn't worn shoes since she'd left home. "So? Are you here to save me?" she asked.

Walter shook his head, clearing his mind. "Well, that's not why I'm here, but yeah. I mean, I'll make it my mission to get you out of her, assuming I survive," he said, finally finding his voice. The girl stared at him with no emotion in her deep-set eyes. She looked like she was trying to have hope, but maybe she was used to having that bubble popped for her.

"Do you mean you're trapped here too?" she said.

"Well, it appears so," Walter said, looking around the room. "But two heads, all that."

"Huh?"

He breathed in deeply and put his hands on his hips. "I just mean two heads are better than one," he said. "What's your name, darlin?"

"I'm Kenna."

Walter stepped forward reaching his hand out tentatively, trying to avoid intimidating her. The girl didn't appear to be afraid. She shook his hand then returned it to her side. Her other was resting on the door jamb. She looked to be in her early twenties, but with the sunken eyes and lithe muscle on her bare arms, he reckoned she could be unfairly aged by this abuse. She might be only eighteen or nineteen. *Christ.*

"How did you end up here, Kenna?" he asked, stepping back a little to give her space. But she stepped forward quickly and embraced him, pushing her cheek up against his chest. Walter was too shocked to react. In the split second before she wrapped her arms around him, he had thought she was about to attack him. His thinking mind would have recognized the thought as ridiculous instantly. As the reality settled in on him, he relaxed a little and let his arms fall. He reached them around her gently and wrapped her in, pulling her tight against him. Now his fear was that he would break her in half if he hugged too hard.

"It's all right, hon," he said, and slid his hand up to hold the back of her head. He could hear her breathing deeply, but she wasn't crying. This, he reckoned, was just a long awaited and much needed touch of humanity. "It's okay. We'll figure this shit out together," he said.

When she pulled away from him finally, she backed up and looked up at him. She was short. Like no more than five feet or so. She looked as if she were ready to ask him, *'What now?'*

"Do you have somewhere we can sit?" Walter asked.

She reached her hand out and waited for him to take it, then turned and lead him through the doorway. The place opened up, and Walter had to stop and think about the insane amount of engineering that had gone into this. How do you ever make anything big enough? Tractors would have to be brought. Earth-movers. Well, Mars-movers. This was a serious feat of construction. She showed him into the kitchen, which was really just a corner of the larger living area. There was a stove and a refrigerator – all the things that would make it a normal kitchen – but there were no walls delineating it from the other rooms around it. Very utilitarian.

The kitchen table was a small stainless steel square that jutted out from the wall. Two steel-framed chairs stood beneath it. As he came to the table Walter glanced into the kitchen area and took note of how neat and tidy it was. Not a thing was out of place. No dishes in the sink, no food left sitting out. Kenna obviously understood the importance good housekeeping had on the psyche.

When they had both pulled up chairs, Walter said, "How long have you been here, Kenna?" but immediately regretted it, realizing she might not have any idea how long it had been. Days and years had different definitions on different planets. That thought startled him. Each time his mind took him back to the realization that he was actually on a *different planet* he felt a wave of shock and fear. He had to maintain his cool though. If Kenna had been here for 'ages' then she had suffered a lot worse than his couple-of-hours adventure.

"I guess you might not know that," he said, reaching out and patting the table, trying to perhaps distract her from the oddity his previous question had brought about. "What do you do here?"

"I don't know," Kenna said, sighing. "If I had to guess I'd say I've been here for two years or so. Maybe not quite that long. My watch died a long time ago. But before it did I had counted four months on the little date number thing." She swallowed and looked away from him, her eyes getting suddenly glassy. Then she smiled. It looked like a good effort. "Anyway, I work. I run experiments and whatnot. It's all bullshit, really, but ostensibly they were to have a lab crew out here."

Walter turned his hand over on the table, inviting her to take it. She did, and gave it a squeeze, then politely withdrew. He sat up and glanced around the room trying to gather a little information, but there was nothing to gather. It was just a big wide-open room with all the normal things one would expect to see in a living space.

"Two fuckin' years," he said to himself, shaking his head.

Of course she heard him and then responded. "Yeah. I think."

"You think all the experiments you do are bullshit?" Walter asked.

"I know they are," she said, scoffing. "I'm not a scientist. What help can I be? I just keep doing the same stupid shit over and over, just to stay busy."

"Wait," Walter said, leaning forward again. "Why were you brought here then?"

"Dipshit sent me through that portal thing to test it and see if it worked. Then he wouldn't let me come back."

Walter was shaking his head. "So you didn't sign up to be out here."

"No. Of course not!" she said. "I was a lab rat. At least I made it," said Kenna.

"What do you mean by that?" he asked.

"There were others, apparently, who weren't so lucky."

Walters eyes went wide. "Where are they?"

"Oh, they're long gone, Walter. Buried out back. Left in the wind. I don't know. I never saw them. Just heard hints about them over the first few days I was here. Hints like about how it had finally worked and he was so excited. Great! Can I fuckin' come back then?" she said, mock-smiling.

"How long had you worked there when you came over?" Walter asked.

"I think it was my first day. When this man came and told me he needed a hand with something. I remember that. But I don't remember much else."

"Good God," he said.

Kenna only nodded, looking at him with that distant hope in her eyes.

Walter stared at her for a long time. Then he nodded. How could he guarantee this woman anything? What if he promised her something and couldn't fulfill it? How much worse would that make things for her? "Listen, Kenna, I'm going to do anything I can to get you out of here. But," he said, holding out his hand again. He was trying to show her a calm, but she surprised him by reaching out and taking his fingers. His heart swelled and his eyes got glassy. She had her whole life ahead of her. She didn't deserve to end it here in this dank, dark room buried beneath the red sands of an alien planet. She had yet to find love. Happiness. A career. A family. He couldn't imagine the desperation she was feeling. He squeezed back with his thumb. "That man has a gun. If he uses it on me, then I won't be able to fulfill my promise to you," Walter said. "But if things go the way I plan when I see him again, I will get you out of here. Back to your family."

Kenna's resolve finally broke and the tears poured down her face. She came forward in her chair and reached for him, then fell onto his lap, wrapping her arms around him as she cried. Walter held her close and let her.

Callie drove home like her tail was on fire. Both fists formed white knuckles on the steering wheel as she held her arms straight like a Formula One driver. She had a new determination in her blood. The rain had let up a little, but the streets were still draining of it. By the time she got home, she had her plan in order. She went inside to pack a small suitcase. She grabbed enough clothing for a week or so, a journal from beside her bed and her laptop. She smashed the suitcase closed and zipped it, then wrote a note and left it on the dresser, in case anyone came looking for her.

On the way to the airport, she spoke to her phone. "Hello, Robot," she said and waited for the hum. "Find me a plane ticket to Fiji."

'*From which airport would you like to depart, Callie?*'

"Newark."

'*To which destination: Nadi International, or Nausori International?*'

"Nadi."

She stopped at a red light and looked over at the passenger seat. The small brown paper-wrapped box Charles Lancey had left her caught her attention. She reached over and picked it up. She tucked it in her jacket pocket. Looked left and right at the cross street. There was no traffic coming. She blew the red light.

'I've found you a flight, Callie. It leaves at eighteen forty-five this evening.' Her friendly robot rattled off the price of the ticket. *'Would you like to purchase this ticket?'*

"Is there a first-class ticket available?" Callie asked.

'Checking.'

There was no point in wasting time or comfort. If she was going to do this, spur-of-the-moment as it were, then she was going to do it right. All the way. Was leaving with no real planning *doing it right?* Was leaving without notifying any of her closest friends the right way? She had to shrug at that. The phone told her the price of a first-class ticket and asked if she would like to purchase it. She said yes. What *was* the right way? She could plan until the cows came home and it still wouldn't be right. The only thing she knew now that she had not known before, was everything. And nothing. Everything could have changed. She knew the layout of the building now. And she knew the hand signal to get in the gate. She also knew that Cardna was on her way there now as well. So Callie had two friends in the building.

'Your plane ticket has been purchased.' Excellent. What more plan did she need? Callie had found that if she took too much time trying to plan stuff, it would bite her in the ass. It was better to fly by the seat of her pants. Go completely spontaneous. That gave her room to improvise. It was impossible to get things wrong when you had no expected outcome.

She merged onto the highway and turned on the stereo. Touched the Spotify icon on the screen. Selected a playlist. Her music came to life on the car's speakers. Callie felt nervous. But it was a good nervousness this time. Nervousness was healthy, and would keep her head straight. When there was very little planning at all, it was best to stay on one's toes. Be ready to dance. A good dose of fear was good for keeping those toes limber.

When she pulled into the long-term parking at the airport, the sun was dropping behind the buildings on the horizon. Maybe she could sleep some on the flight. She was not tired yet, and too full of excitement. But once she reached altitude, she knew the quiet dark of the cabin would lull her to a sleepy state. The vodka tonic she planned to drink would help with that as well.

She locked her car with the fob and dropped her keys into a zipper pocket inside her purse, where they would be sure not to get lost, and made her way to the shuttle waiting area. The rain fell through the narrow opening high above the tracks upon which the shuttle ran. It made a comforting sound splattering against the rocks. Callie stood with her purse clutched to her chest, her suitcase standing on its wheels at her leg, the handle near her hip. She stared blankly at the sky through the narrow opening above. Mist from the rainy evening made its way onto her face. It cooled her skin. She was beginning to sweat under her coat, but didn't want to remove it until she was on the plane. One more thing to carry.

The shuttle came whistling out of the tunnel a mile down the track, its single headlight growing in size and intensity quickly as it approached. She felt a smile fighting its way to the surface, and Callie realized something about herself: she was not nervous. She was excited! This was exciting! She had always known she would come back to Fiji. Or at least it sounded good to say that in her mind. She knew she had business to finish down there. So of course, she should be going back. Walter might need her help. But what if he didn't? What if he was finished by the time she got there? Well, then that would be just fine, wouldn't it? They would be in Fiji together. And that could only be a good thing. The way it was supposed to have been the first time.

With a groan of metal against metal, the shuttle car came quickly to a stop in front of her, a completely autonomous feat of engineering. When the doors slid open and she stepped inside, welcoming the smell common to every train car and shuttle interior in the world, she felt a sense of peace wash into her stomach. Yes. This was going to be good. This was the right thing to do. Plan or no plan, this was what she was supposed to be doing. Surprised she had not thought of it before – joining Walter for the final phase down in Fiji – Callie actually felt relieved about her decision. It was as if she had been searching for the last piece to a jigsaw puzzle, and she had finally found it. Holding it up to the light, admiring its smooth cut edges, and relishing the final seconds of holding it before it was put in place, where it would dissolve into the bigger picture; where it would become just like every other piece. Right now it was special. She had found this piece – the only one that could fit in the final hole the puzzle had presented her – a thousand different possible outcomes of where the hole would be finally resolving into one. This one. This piece. Before slipping it into its final position, she would enjoy its importance for one last moment. One glorious hour of staring at the future through the blurred vision of concentration, and then it would be over. The past ten years of her life came down to this one tiny slice of cardboard cut into a funny shape. Callie was finally going to bring it to a close, then step back and look at the wonderful masterpiece she had assembled. She grasped the vertical post, leaning in and resting her cheek against its cold metal surface and smiled. Tonight would mark the beginning of the end.

Chapter 29

Walter paced as he talked to the disheveled woman who sat on the steel chair with her knees up under her chin, wrapping her arms around her legs like a little girl in the presence of a bear. Walter had learned that Bradley brought food ration boxes in once a month or so, and it was always more than enough for the period provided. So she had surplus in the cabinets and on the shelves in the pantry. She drank water from the tap and took showers every day. It was recycled water, somehow, but Kenna couldn't answer when Walter tried to learn the details of the system. Was there a reservoir here? A water tower of sorts? She simply didn't know.

Another thing she didn't seem to know was what the plan was for her, long-term. She had naturally come to assume this would be a permanent installment as the days had turned to weeks and nothing ever changed. The same routine. Brian Bradley would come check on her and bring her used magazines filched from dentists' offices or rags from the newsstand, puzzles with missing pieces – whatever he felt his good grace was worth that day. He truly thought he was being generous. Benevolent.

One thing he didn't do though, was to sexually abuse the woman. And a woman she was, but just. Kenna had turned nineteen when she started working at Royal. She was probably somewhere around twenty-one now, they agreed. Walter had been happy to hear the man had at least kept his hands off her.

And all this equipment – the appliances and furniture, the structural components that comprised the superstructure of the building – it had all been brought on all those missions by ship and shuttle. All those trips from Earth the long way, like a slow boat across the ocean of space. Callie had told him once upon a time that Royal had been coming out here for decades. This was the product of those trips, apparently. But now it had all died off and Bradley was apparently the only one left who had any involvement with it. Certainly, no one else ever came out and checked on her. She hadn't seen a single soul besides Bradley the entire time she'd been here.

And now here he was, pacing the floor while he delicately questioned Kenna. And that's when she said something that stopped him in his tracks. "So how'd you get in here? Did he push you down the stairs, or did he give you the app?"

Walter frowned and looked at her. "App? No, I just walked in the door," he said, throwing a thumb over his shoulder toward the general direction of the entrance. "What do you mean, app?"

"He used to brag about it. Saying he was the only one who could open the door and no one would be able to save me or anything," Kenna said. "I think there was an app, or a chip or something on his phone that only he had."

Walter's heart stopped in his chest. He suddenly slapped his right thigh and felt the uncomfortable clunky rectangle in his pocket. Brian's phone. He still had it in his pocket, along with his car keys. "Holy shit," Walter said, staring at the floor. Could that be right? Was it the phone? If so, that meant – at least presumably – that Brian Bradley could not get back in here. Unless he had another phone or another backup badge of some sort. But Walter somehow didn't think that likely. He wanted to protect his secret with an absolute. Having a backup meant that someone could inadvertently discover what he was hiding out here. The Chewbacca belt was one measure. It prevented transiting through the first band. Likely that would prevent other things – maybe even including Martian air – from coming back through the tunnel. Then there was the teleporter, which had no security whatever. But this door on the dome… A final step in security that ensured only *he* would ever know what was inside.

Walter stood up. "Kenna, this is good news!" he said, returning to his former posture, scratching the back of his head.

"It is?" she said. But she didn't look surprised or interested. She was probably so numb to emotion by now that it took a concentrated will to feel anything. Her breakdown earlier might have been on the edge of happening for months.

"Yes!" he said, coming to a squat right in front of her. He took her by the shoulders. "This gives us time to come up with a plan! Because he can't come back through that entrance door without his phone!"

She was shaking her head. "But…"

"But!" Walter said, and slipped the phone out of his pocket. He held it up between his thumb and index finger for her to see. "I have his phone."

A remarkable flood of relief washed over Kenna's entire body. Her face, her posture, everything looked more at ease. She leaned forward and embraced him for a second time, full of elation and crying happy tears.

"I'm so happy you showed up, Walter," she said. "I've been praying for a miracle and here you finally are."

The first vodka went down smoothly. The second, even smoother. Callie had still not learned her lesson: alcohol at altitude did her no favors when she landed. But how could one object when it felt so right? There was no proof that she would feel bad when she landed, previous experience notwithstanding. What if those were exceptions to the rule? She felt just fine now, and that was all she was worried about. Even still, two might be plenty. And it was a long enough flight for her to get drunk, sleep it off a full eight hours, then do it all again. Trapped in an aluminum mail-tube at five-and-a-half miles above the sea could get a little claustrophobic if she spent too long thinking about it. Callie was a physicist. She knew there were no 'water landings' from this altitude, at this speed, if something went wrong. Oh, they would land all right. But there would be nothing to walk away from. That pilot who had landed on the Hudson after a double bird strike had set expectations for a new reality in people's minds. But people didn't realize – or at least didn't consider – he had not even reached five thousand feet yet. Had barely made any air. An aluminum cylinder hitting the ocean at two hundred knots would come apart like a handful of BBs.

Callie took a deep breath and closed her eyes. She leaned her head back against the headrest and concentrated on the sounds around her. The sounds of engines and wind doing exactly what they were supposed to be doing. She had never had a real fear of flying. It was only on these treks over a dark ocean that she started thinking about all the things that had to work together to make a successful flight. The five million tiny servos and wires and sensors and motors and everything else that created the miracle of flight. But… But there were twenty thousand flights a day that took off and landed without a single issue. She just had to remind herself that the odds of a plane crash were so ridiculously low that she would probably not even ever *see* one. Much less be involved in one. She popped her left eye open to look at her watch. Only eighteen hours to go.

After her first sleep session, she awoke with a start, clutching her purse as if someone were about to try and take it from her. No one else was near. No one was even awake, seemingly. All was quiet. Her ears needed to pop, but she let them stay. She liked the soft cushion of auditory cotton that grew on the eardrums during a nap at altitude. Callie unbuckled and made her way to the lav to relieve herself and splash some water on her face. As she stared at herself in the mirror, leaning on the basin, she had that feeling of dread wash over her again, knowing she still had more than half the flight to go. Then she would be doing this all over again on her flight back home. Hopefully on that flight she would at least have company.

As she walked back to her seat, she thought about all the friends she had made in the last couple of years, as well as all the experiences she had lived through. It seemed like she had been through so many life-changing trips and projects in such a short time. She lost two loves, one of those having died. Her boss's death didn't hit her quite as hard, but it did resonate. She had seen the end of her best friends' marriage. Callie considered Thevi and Walter both best friends. She couldn't help but feel guilty for that one. But whether or not Thevi ever talked to her again, Callie had a net gain of friends. Rebecca and Codi and Shanna and Sam and Natalie, and now Cardna – they all felt so close. She was so happy to have expanded her friendship circle by several hundred percent in such short order, that she could afford the loss of one. Losing Thevi hurt pretty bad, but what could she do? All the apologies in the world wouldn't bring her back. Thevi had said, 'People fuck up all the time. You fucked Walter.' That had stung. But she had been right.

Callie thought about the prospect of having Shanna come with her to Fiji. It almost made sense to have her along. Let the girl who had been directly affected – the girl who had been *on the trip* – hand out some of the punishment. Shanna had flown back to Ohio yesterday. Callie hated to see her go. Watching her walk through the sliding doors and disappearing into the airport had hit Callie maybe a little harder than she had expected. On the heels of Cardna's departure, she wasn't ready for another so quickly. Everyone had just vacated all at once, it seemed. Her house had been left empty, where quite recently it had been the central hub for all action and entertainment. The sudden emptiness had sparked a memory of her coming home after the trip to Cozumel with Walter, Chris and Thevi. The four of them had gone down there together, but only three returned. Opening her front door and coming into a house where Chris still existed, but would never again *live...* That's what it had felt like. Or at least reminded her of.

But at least she was in touch with these women now. And though they lived in different parts of the world, she would definitely be keeping in touch. Callie had promised Shanna to buy her a plane ticket to come out to New Jersey any time Shanna wanted. And Shanna had not taken it as insult at all. She knew Callie made more money, and that Callie was genuinely more interested in the friendship than the cost of a plane ticket. She had smiled and nodded, then hugged her wordlessly.

Callie looked out the window at all the stars, reminded of the last trip she had made down this way. It seemed like so long ago now. A different era. And once again, she had no real plan. But with two friends on the force, she would fair a little better this time, she believed. She also looked forward to meeting Cynda, who had been such a big help with the logistics of proving Cardna's loyalty. When Callie had spoken to her, she had not told Cynda what she expected to be in the hide box. So when Cynda had said there was a smart phone in a sparkly gold case, Callie had felt instant levity.

She leaned forward and reached under the seat in front of her, retrieving her purse, and pulled out her journal and a nice pen. She pulled off the cap and began to write.

"Kenna," Walter said. He hated to disturb her celebratory cry but he needed to let her down quickly, before she got too excited. "Kenna, there's something you need to know. I have his phone, and that will get us out of the dome." Kenna pulled back from him, sensing a 'but' on the way. She had a look of concern in her eyes.

Walter nodded, knowing she was about to say so. "But we can't get back to the lab in Fiji without that belt he wears."

She was frowning now, and looked like she was trying to sort through a hard math problem in her head.

"You know the one I'm talking about?" Walter asked, making shapes with his hands at intervals across his chest and torso.

"You mean the one with the blocks on it?" she asked. And when Walter nodded, she stood up abruptly, putting her hands in her hair. "Oh my God, that's what that's for?" Walter shrugged. "Holy balls, dude," she said, turning toward the kitchen area, still holding her head, elbows sticking out to the sides like weather vanes. "I remember walking through some doorway when he brought me in here! And then like the next day, I tried to go back several times, but he had closed the door. I couldn't find a handle or anything!" She turned back around and looked at Walter. She must have realized how silly she looked with her hands in her hair, so she dropped them to her sides. "So, what? He carries keys on it? I thought I had it."

"No. It *is* the key. There's no door, Kenna. It's a special kind of barrier. You can't get through it without the belt."

She was staring at him again. "So it's like one of those doggy doors that only works if they're wearing a special collar."

Walter shrugged again. "Yeah, I guess that's a good analogy. I would imagine it wasn't intended to keep people from getting back to Earth so much as it was to keep people from accidentally discovering he had a secret passage to Mars."

"Oh, totally," she agreed. "But he sure is using it for that." After pacing back and forth on a small track for a few moments, Kenna finally returned to the seat, sitting on one of her legs and resting her elbow on the table. "So, what's our plan then?"

"Well, we need to get him back over here so we can hijack that belt. But if you're right about the phone thing, he can't get back in, either. It's like a Mexican stand-off," Walter said. He leaned back in his chair and looked around the place again. He could already feel the weight of solitude. He could not imagine spending two years here, only occasionally seeing one other human. And that wasn't even getting into who that human was.

"No secret entrances or anything?" he asked after a minute.

Kenna shook her head. "No. I don't think so. I felt every corner of this place when I first got here, just looking for something like a latch or a secret panel or something." She pulled her hair back, making a fresh ponytail. With her thin arms up in the air, she looked like a lady doing normal lady things. It reminded him of Thevi. That made his heart drop momentarily. He had been putting her out of his head a lot, hoping that by the time he thought of her, he would be over the guilt, sadness and grieving. But there were still times she broke through his consciousness.

Kenna caught the look. It might have translated into something lustful in her mind. She was pretty, but he only had eyes for Callie now. Walter quickly looked down at his hands. She put her arms down.

"What's her name?" she asked.

CHAPTER 30

allie's plane had touched down uneventfully, reminding her that she was just another statistic. One of the billions of people who made up the larger number of the fraction people quoted when they spoke of airline disasters. She had rented a car from the Avis and realized pretty quickly that it was the same exact car Rebecca had rented. That had given her a good vibe. She talked herself into believing in fate for a few minutes, that the stars had aligned to tell her something good was going to happen down here.

She drove along the dark road toward Suva feeling completely exhausted. Something just felt wrong about the time zone exchange – like she'd had a terrible accident involving a time machine. They had left Newark at 6:45 in the evening. And it was now almost ten o'clock. But she had lost an entire day. She shook her head getting lost in confusion. Time zones, jet lag, International Date Lines, day corrections – it all gave her tired-head. If she wanted to figure it out, she would have to put pencil to paper and draw it out. As it stood, she had to accept that it was now Wednesday. Poof. A whole day. Gone.

She pulled into Suva a couple of hours later and checked into a place called Crusoe's Retreat, on the south end of the island. For a three-star affair, it was peaceful and serene in ways Callie couldn't imagine any other place on Earth could be. She tossed her suitcase on the baggage hammock and opened the window, letting the cool air fill the room. Then she plopped onto the bed, still in her shoes and promptly fell asleep.

At just after five o'clock the next morning, Callie's eyes popped open. She was lying on her back with a pillow on her chest, on top of the comforter and sweating like she'd slept in a sauna. Her heart was slamming in her chest. Had she just been having a bad dream? She couldn't remember anything of the sort. She just knew that one second she was asleep, and the next she was awake. Callie didn't feel the usual drag of waking that required lying there for a few minutes before getting up. She didn't feel sleepy at all, in fact. Sitting up and swinging her feet off the edge of the bed, Callie realized she had not woken up a single time to go pee during the night. She had actually slept all the way through the night. *Imagine that. I bet I could count on one hand the number of times I've done that.*

She scooted her feet into her slippers and into the bathroom where she sat on the warm toilet seat. *God, why is it so hot in here?* She looked around trying to locate the thermostat, but could not see it from her current position. It felt like maybe the air conditioner had failed during the night – though she honestly couldn't remember if it had felt good last night when she had come in. She should have checked it then. She washed up and put a toothbrush in her mouth, then made her way into the room again. The thermostat, which she found by the front door, was set to 'off' and the interior temperature was a nice, stale 78 degrees. *F sake!*

Callie slid the switch to the 'on' position and heard the air kick on a few seconds later. Oh well. She needed a shower anyway. She just wouldn't make it as hot as she normally liked it. She made her way back to the bathroom and started the water, then spit in the sink, looked in the mirror. She even *looked* refreshed. Callie couldn't remember the last time she had felt this good when she woke up. Maybe it was the heat that had made her sleep so well. She stood in the shower for a very long time.

When she got out, she noticed she had a missed call from Cynda Lohm – the woman on the inside at Royal Fiji. Callie frowned at the screen. *This early? Wow.* Callie went back out and sat on the bed, still wrapped in her towel and pressed the call button. Cynda picked up on the first ring, talking quietly and quickly.

"Hey, Cynda. What's up?" Callie said. She felt in her chest the concern that her words weren't betraying. She wanted to sound casual. Calm. She was anything but.

"Hi, Callie. I am about to go in to work. I just wanted you to know that Walter came in the other day with Brian Bradley. They went down to the basement. Well, Brian came back out a little while later, but I haven't seen Walter come back out," she said.

Callie was chewing on the side of her finger, staring at the carpet, trying to imagine what could have happened. "Did they go into that lab downstairs?"

"I can only assume so. But Brian came back upstairs to his office a little while after they went down. My office is between the elevator and his office. Walter never came back by." Cynda waited a moment for Callie to talk. Callie stayed quiet. "Now that might not mean anything. Right? I mean, Walter could have just gone out through the lobby and I wouldn't have seen him. But I thought…"

Callie now waited for her. After a few longs seconds, Callie realized Cynda was leaving her dangling. "You thought what?"

Cynda made the verbal equivalent of a shrug. "I thought the plan *didn't* involve Bradley being the one to come out alone. I don't know."

Callie's heart was beating so hard now that she was seeing purple streaks in her vision. She needed to calm down. "Okay. Well I'm here."

"You're where?"

"I'm here. I'm in Suva," Callie said.

"Oh my God! Really?" Cynda said, sounding genuinely excited. "Do you have a car?"

"Yes. I rented a bright yellow Camry."

"So are you coming into the office?" Cynda asked.

"Well, yes. I was hoping to get an escort. I mean, I have a badge, but not a Fijian badge."

"Absolutely. I can come by and get you. Where you at?"

Callie gave her the address then hung up and got ready. This all seemed like a bad deja vu trip somehow, being escorted into the company's secret base by a local. This time she checked everything carefully, making sure she had everything she needed. Phone, purse, badge – for what that was worth – and her coat. She decided to leave the rental car keys on the dresser. Just in case. They wouldn't do her any good anyway, if she didn't have the car. But it felt like she was taking a precaution, which made her feel more prepared.

Twenty minutes later, Callie was standing on the front sidewalk – what passed as a porch at a motel – waiting expectantly. She, of course, had no idea what Cynda Lohm looked like. Would she be fun and pretty like Cardna? Or would she be a dud? All Callie knew was that this woman was the little sister of someone Rebecca had gone to college with. One of the many small-world connections that seemed to happen throughout life. A few minutes later, a black BMW two-seater pulled into the parking lot. Callie could hear loud music pumping through the windows. Cynda turned it down as she pulled into the spot, a few feet from Callie's knees. She immediately hopped out and came round the front of the car to meet Callie.

"Hey, Callie! So glad to finally meet you!" she said, coming toward Callie with arms already extended for a hug.

Callie stepped down off the short curb to meet her in front of the car. The hug lasted longer than Callie thought was necessary, but she wasn't put off by it. Just a little weird. It was as if they were long-lost friends. Not new acquaintances. When they separated, Cynda held onto her upper arms, staring her in the eyes and said, "I've wanted to meet you for so long, Callie!"

Callie tried to smile. She knew it didn't come out right though. But Cynda didn't seem to mind. She probably knew how awkward she was making this. Cynda stood about five-foot-four and had sharp copper-colored hair that hung long beneath her chin, but was shoulder length around the sides and back. A style Callie thought was unique out of all the styles she'd ever seen. It didn't look odd at all. Just different. She had thick patches of freckles on both cheeks, though the rest of her face was covered with a light spattering of them. The cheek patches gave her face – at a glance, or from a distance, Callie imagined – the look of having dark red discolorations. Though seeing them up close, Callie thought they were striking. Beautiful, even. Her eyebrows were thick and red over dark brown eyes that held just enough back to make one believe she might know some secrets about the future. She wore a dark sweater that disguised her figure completely, running long over some dark blue linen pants that were so loose and baggy they might have been a dress. Callie couldn't even see her feet. Her hands were covered in freckles as well, and she wore silver rings on several of her fingers.

Cynda smiled at Callie, a pinched number that almost replicated the one Callie had tried to make, showing that she did indeed know the state of awkwardness they stood in. "Sorry. I know that must sound weird. But you're sort of a legend around here, you know?"

Callie's heart might have skipped a beat. There was that damned word again. *Legend.* Cardna had written it on the card she had left in Callie's room. How in the world was Callie even known around these parts – much less, as a legend? "I'm sorry, Cynda, can I ask you a question?"

"Sure!" she said brightly. Her fists were down at her sides and she was bouncing slightly, like she just couldn't wait to get going.

"I don't want to sound arrogant or anything, but you're the second person who has said I'm like a legend around here. Where does that come from?" Callie asked, squinting and trying to evade the blush that must surely be falling into her cheeks.

"Ha!" Cynda said, eyes widening. "Well, you've been written about in our corporate rag many times. Mostly by Matt Minus. You're like this superhero who always comes in and saves the day. It's cool to finally meet you."

Callie was shaking her head, mouth agape and speechless. She felt the incredible weight of honor that statement put on her shoulders, but wasn't sure she was very deserving of it. She blinked away the beginnings of some tears, resolving to try and track down some of those articles and read about herself someday.

"Do you have everything?" Cynda asked, turning and almost skipping to the driver's door, which still hung open on its first detent.

Callie said that she did, and stepped over to the passenger side. As she slipped into the seat and dropped her purse in the floorboard, reached for the seat belt, Callie noticed that Cynda was sitting there staring at her with a grin on her face. "Do you like Orbit?" she asked, fingers reaching for the volume knob on the stereo.

Callie thought about this for a moment, then noticed the screen was displaying the name of the artist currently playing – One Last Orbit. She nodded and looked back at Cynda. "I do, indeed." *Is this woman always so enthusiastic? Excited?* Callie thought that might be the right word. Cynda seemed eager to get to the next second. Like each second bored her, but the prospect of a brighter future awaited just the next second over. And she was *excited* to get to it. Callie put her age at about twenty-eight. *Old enough to know better, too young to care.* Callie missed being that age. This girl had spunk and energy that couldn't be captured. It was nice to see someone so happy to be alive.

"How's this for legend though, Cynda," Callie said, putting her hand on Cynda's on the shift knob. "Your sister's friend, Rebecca, actually knows Tanis."

Cynda looked over at her, wide-eyed and said, "Get the FUCK out! Seriously?"

Callie couldn't help catch the excitement, and grinned widely. "Yeah!"

"Wait," Cynda said, the giant smile turning to something that looked like fear. "Was that the Rebecca she posted on her Insta a few weeks back?"

Callie nodded, then said, "That's the one!"

"Holy cow, I'm almost famous."

The trip into the office was not boring. Cynda kept the radio turned up loud, exercising the full capabilities of her vehicle's sound system. But she also talked the whole time. Callie found it odd that one wouldn't turn down the music so they could have comfortable discourse, but didn't say anything because she was getting a kick out of Cynda's general sprightly energy. And the greatest part about it was that the smile never left the woman's face. She talked with her left hand on the wheel, while her right hand made the motions she used to illustrate the words she was beckoning. Callie reckoned if she were to hook up electrical leads to this woman's earlobes, she could power a small city with all the energy coming off her.

When they pulled into the lane leading up to the security shack, Cynda never even looked at the guard. Her right hand just naturally took the wheel so her left hand could make the duress gesture, which she did with such casual finesse it made Callie think hard about who this woman really was. A gesture well practiced still took concentration to generate.

She likened it to a concert pianist: the right hand was free to roam the higher notes, but the left had to maintain the rhythm and the bass. Sometimes the bass clef was every bit as complex as the treble. But it had to be there, and it had to be mindless. This woman was displaying those signs. She was presenting the picture of someone so intellectually advanced that she could make complex gestures without so much as a thought. Callie knew these duress gestures changed every couple of months at the least. Something was at work here. Something was going on. It might be minutes, weeks, months before she latched onto it, but she would be thinking about its significance. This Cynda Lohm woman was more important than what she presented. *Something is going on.*

Callie was finally able to get a word in edge-wise when she held up a hand and looked at Cynda. She pursed her lips like she was about to talk, and Cynda just stopped. Mid-sentence, she was ready to listen. They were pulling into the parking garage. Somehow, she was able to drive and pay attention to Callie at the same time. She would look back at the road ahead every few seconds, but it seemed like most of her attention was on Callie.

"Hey, Cynda, what is your IQ?" Callie asked. She knew Cynda knew. There was no way this woman didn't know her own IQ. Most people might go through life not knowing where they rank, but someone, somewhere in Cynda's past had asked her to take a test. *She knows.*

Cynda only frowned for about a fifth of a second, then said, "I think it was 185 when I took the test." She rolled her eyes and waved her hand dismissively. She pulled into a spot and pushed the Engine Stop button. "You know, Einstein had a low IQ."

Callie did know this.

"Yeah. He tested poorly. He was a slow-thinker, which made him test badly. So his IQ was low. But no one would call him dumb, right?"

Callie scoffed. Cynda giggled. Her chuckle was a fast, high-pitched staccato, and reminded Callie of a chipmunk. *Adorable.*

"Yeah. So I don't put much stock in it. Why do you ask? What's yours?" Cynda asked.

Callie looked forward at the wall in front of the car. She reached down and picked up her purse from the floor, then popped the door open and got out of the car. Looking over the roof at Cynda, she said, "I don't even remember."

Their plan wasn't a great one, but they did have limited resources. Kenna had gathered up a couple of flashlights, which was a welcome addition. She was trembling as she put on the suit. Walter was still having trouble grasping how she could have spent two years here, alone, and not gone crazy. He had seen *The Shining,* and it hadn't taken Jack two years to go mad. When the airlock finished its cycle, a blue light went out and was replaced with a red one. Walter looked back at Kenna – her face blurred by the mask – and gave her an OK sign. She nodded and gave the sign back to him. Then he pulled open the door. He stepped through it and stood with his back against it as Kenna tentatively stepped through herself, ducking as if she might hit her head on the seven-foot frame.

Walter held his hand out, telling her to go up the stairs first. He was right behind her. When they got to the top, she turned around and looked at him. She was saying something but he could not hear her. Walter pointed at his ear and shook his head. She got real close to him, put her hands on his arms and leaned in, touching her mask to his. He was then able to hear her muffled voice.

"Why can't you hear me?"

"Very little atmosphere in here. Go ahead," he said, nodding toward the door that would lead out of the dome. She stared at him for a moment, then turned and put her hand on the handle, then pushed it open. It was dark outside. Walter clicked on his torch and aimed it at the dirt outside the door. He put his boot against the door, holding it open, and Kenna went past him turning on her own torch. Kenna turned quickly back to him and Walter could see fear through her mask for the brief instant he was able to see through it at all. Kenna was ripped away from him and thrown to the ground, and another man in a white space-suit was coming at him. Walter put one foot back and squared his shoulders, taking the man's momentum and transferring it forward. Brian Bradley went sprawling in the dirt past Walter, and the gun in his hand tumbled soundlessly across the rocks into the darkness.

Walter rushed forward and stepped on Bradley's hand just as he was about to grab the pistol, then twisted his boot heel. He should have stepped on the gun though. Bradley's other hand seized it and then he was rolling over, firing up at Walter.

Walter leaned back instinctively as soon as Bradley had started his roll, and thus the bullet missed his face by inches. But it didn't miss his suit. A quick puff of mist escaped anticlimactically and he suddenly had no air to breathe. He was reaching up and pinching the hole closed, quickly forgetting about Bradley, the gun and the girl. But it was no use, and it took his brain a few precious seconds to register the fact that he did not have any fresh oxygen pumping into the suit. Even sealing it closed right now was a useless endeavor. He was out of air.

He turned quickly, just in time to see Brian Bradley chasing the girl through the open door and throwing it closed behind him. "Fuck!" Walter shouted, running for the door. He flung it open and saw Bradley at the bottom of the stairs already, forcing Kenna in front of him as he dashed toward the airlock. Walter had Bradley's phone in his pocket, but that wasn't the problem anymore. Now the problem was that the airlock was re-pressurizing, which would take too long to recycle – phone or no phone. He would run out of air before it could empty again.

Walter turned quickly and began running back to the hallway where he knew he could at least get some air, and the seeds of true panic spilled into his blood. He had very little time to figure something out. As he banged through the door of the plastic shed, he realized they had effectively traded spaces. He had been holding the door open, so Bradley was able to go through it. And now that man was trapped inside the compound with Kenna. And he had a gun. Walter had never felt so hopeless in his life.

By the time he got to the iron ring with the black canisters on it, he was about to faint. How long had he been holding his breath? It couldn't have been more than thirty or forty seconds. But he had not gotten a good, full breath before his suit had been punctured, either. He stepped awkwardly through the ring and fell into the darkness on the concrete floor on his home planet, gasping and spitting.

For a long time, Walter stayed on his hands and knees just pulling in fresh air, thankful that at least he had that option, even though he couldn't get through the next section. The true weight of his problem now settled in on him. If the phone was what gave him access to the dome, and the Chewbacca belt was what let him back out of this hallway into the lab area, then there would have to be a trade-off somewhere down the line. And unless Walter just got super lucky with his timing, and caught the other man right as he was depressurizing the chamber, there would be no trade-off. His plan had been tossed in the air like a bowl full of popcorn. It had come down in a mess, all over the ground of two entirely different planets.

He finally rolled onto his butt and leaned back against the wall, looking up into the darkness at nothing as he tried to work out a plan. He could not get a new suit. He had nothing to patch this suit. He was stuck in this hallway. Shaking his head and closing his eyes, he began to consider the danger Kenna was in now, as well. Bradley had the gun, and he had been in a shooting mood. Walter felt like kicking himself for losing control of the situation like that. He shouted as loudly as he could, cursing himself and pulling on his hair at the sides of his head.

Can't go back to the airlock without a fresh suit. Can't get a fresh suit without going through the airlock. Can't go through the airlock without it being depressurized. Claustrophobia began to settle in as Walter realized he had absolutely no plays left. He was now at the unforgiving mercy of the universe.

Callie was standing in Cynda's office, waiting for her to get off the phone. Her phone had been ringing as they approached the office door, and she had been stuck on it now for several minutes. Cynda was rolling her eyes and making the universal blah-blah-blah hand motion at Callie.

Callie finally opted for sitting down, and pulled out a chair from in the opposite side of Cynda's desk. She sat down and crossed her legs and set her purse on the floor. When Cynda finally said goodbye and dropped the phone into its cradle, Callie looked up at her.

"Do you know why I'm here, Cynda?"

Cynda smiled and leaned on the desk for a moment, then decided to sit down, herself. She pulled her chair up and stretched her arms out across the desk, toying with a pen. "No, I guess I don't. I mean, I know what you and your group are up to, if that's what you're asking."

"No. Funny that, I don't know what I'm even asking. I was asking you hoping you would know why I'm here. Because I don't know what I'm supposed to do." Callie swallowed. "I guess I need to go into the lab after Walter. Assuming he's in there."

"Well, I'm sorry, Callie, I can't give you access to that. That's like the one thing I can't do," Cynda said, looking regretful.

"It's okay, she's with me," proclaimed a voice from behind her.

Callie turned and looked over her shoulder at the same time Cynda said, "Hey Card."

Cardna was walking in with her arms stuck straight out in front of her like a robot. Callie stood up and stepped into her embrace. They hugged for a long moment, rocking back and forth before they finally separated. "So good to see you," Cardna said.

Callie nodded. "Yes. Feels like it's been forever."

Cardna smiled at her. "You coming, Cyn?"

Cynda stood up excitedly. "You mean, I finally get to see inside the fabled lab? Of course I'm coming."

They took the elevator down together, armed with nothing but their collective intellect, a few smart phones and a will to find out what the hell had happened to Walter. Callie's stomach was in knots, worried about what they would find. Cardna had confirmed that Bradley had come into his office that morning, and then gone right back down the elevator. Presumably to the lab. So he had to be in there still.

As they approached the double-doors, Cardna pulled her badge out and ran it against the badge-reader. It beeped, but the indicator light stayed red. *Damn.* "Try yours," she said, looking at Cynda. Cynda did as she was told. Same result.

"Want me to try mine?" Callie said. Cardna looked back at her.

"Might as well," said Cardna. *Beep.* No entry though.

Cardna put her hands on her hips, then said, "Bang on that fucker, Cynda."

Cynda proceeded to pound on the door with both fists. After a few seconds, Cardna stepped up to it and yelled with her mouth close to the metal, "I know you're in there, Brian. Can you come out, please? I need to talk to you about something urgent." Then she pounded on the doors herself.

She finally stepped back, shaking her head. Then she sighed and looked around the warehourse-like area behind them. "Hang tight, gals," she said, and walked off, quickly disappearing into the rows of tarp-covered mysteria. Callie and Cynda stood watching the lights turn on over Cardna, following her progress.

Callie looked back at Cynda. "So none of you have ever gone in there?"

Cynda shook her head, making a bored smirk with her mouth. "I don't think anyone has any access but dipshit. I didn't mean I *wouldn't* help you earlier. I hope you know that."

Callie nodded, closing her eyes. "I got you."

"Yeah. I just know this shit is above my pay grade."

They both turned as they heard the motor coming toward them. Cardna sat in the high seat of a forklift, and it was bearing down on them with a quickness. Callie and Cynda stepped back, splitting up, each on one side of the double-doors. The motor grew loud as it got closer, and Cardna raised the forks to hip-level. Without so much as a hint of hesitation, she rammed straight into the doors, but instead of slamming them open, which Callie had expected, the forks stuck straight through them, one on each of the doors, puncturing the steel like a knife through butter.

Callie's heart sank for an instant, but before she could fully register the dreaded feeling of disappointment, Cardna was raising the forks. A sickening squeal of metal on metal forced the two women to slap their hands over their ears. Callie instinctively stepped back, as well. The bottoms of the doors lifted off the ground as the tops folded in on themselves. Then she tilted the forks back and backed up with the lift. The squall intensified as the crumbled mess that had been the doors came backward and ripped out of the final hinges. She backed up until the forklift was ten feet away, then shut off the machine. Callie felt a rush of adrenaline pumping through her veins. *Holy shit!* A strand of thin steel hung from the doorjamb, bouncing. She saw

Cynda look up at it, then peek around the edge of the door frame.

Then she looked back at Cardna, who had dismounted the vehicle and was coming toward the doorway. "He's not in there," said Cynda.

"There's another door," Cardna said, pointing as she walked right in like she owned the place. Callie followed Cynda in, who in turn followed Cardna. They marched right up to the inner door. It looked like the door on a bank vault. It stood open a few inches. Cardna looked at Callie as she gripped the edge of the massive door and began pulling. "Lucky that. I have no idea what his PIN code would be."

"Probably his birthday," Callie said, rolling her eyes.

"Or one-two-three-four-five," said Cynda. They laughed out loud.

"Help me!" said Cardna, laughing her strength away. The three of them pulled hard on the door and it came open wide enough to see a hallway that ran into darkness.

"Is there a light switch?" Cynda said, backing up and looking around.

"Find a flashlight," said Cardna. "There's no lights in the hallway."

Callie peered around the door and into the hallway, a chill suddenly making its way up her spine. The air was cool in the hallway, and it was coming into the lab area. She turned to look at the other women, who were both searching the room for a torch. Opening steel drawers and rifling through them, slamming some, leaving some others open.

Finally, Cynda held up a flashlight. She clicked the button but it didn't come on. She began shaking it.

"Fuck it. We all have flashlights on our phones, girls," said Cardna.

The other two laughed again. "Duh! How long have we been carrying these things, and we still forget they do everything!" said Cynda. Callie shook her head and pulled her phone out. They all turned on the flashlights and crept into the hallway. Some meters ahead there was a steel black band attached to the concrete walls, ceiling and floor.

Callie's light played across something in the darkness beyond the channel and she flinched and yelped. Everyone stopped. Callie's heart was slamming in her chest as all three lights came to rest on a person sitting a few meters beyond the metal channel, squinting back at them and raising a hand to try and shield his eyes from the light.

"Holy fuck!" Cynda shouted. "Scared the hell out of me!"

Cardna was standing still, wide-eyed, staring at the person beyond the channel. "Walter?" she said, leaning in and squinting. Callie's heart suddenly filled with elation as she realized Cardna was right. It was him!

"Oh my God! Walter!" she said, bounding forward and slamming face-first into nothing. Walter was standing and coming toward them. Everyone lowered their lights.

"What the fuck?" said Cardna. "What happened?"

Callie, meanwhile, was staggering back, holding her nose. It felt like she had broken it.

Cynda reached out with a tentative hand, feeling for the glass that must be there. Her hand stopped on the close edge of the black channel, but there didn't appear to be any glass there.

"Don't bother," said Walter, approaching and putting his hands on the channel itself, as if leaning against a doorway. "You have to have a Chewbacca belt to get through it," he said. He looked rough. In need of a shave. Covered in sweat. Callie was staring at him, tears streaming down her face from the pain of the hit on her nose. But she was smiling inside, thanking God Walter was alive.

"Are you okay?" Cardna said, putting her hands on Callie's shoulders, looking her in the eyes. Her phone hung between her hand and Callie's left shoulder, shining bright light onto the wall behind her.

Cynda was standing at the gate, putting her hands all around the invisible wall, looking so much like the mime pretending to be caught in a glass box that Callie had to laugh out loud in spite of the pain. Cardna turned to look at what was so funny.

"What is a Chewbacca belt?" Cynda said. She was giggling too. Walter was just standing there staring at them all.

"Bradley was wearing one. It looks like that belt that Chewbacca wears in the Star Wars movies."

"Never saw 'em," Cynda said, now standing with her hands hanging down at her sides.

"Go back into the lab area and look around. See if you can find a belt that has gray, steel blocks on it," Walter said, trying to illustrate with his hands.

Cardna nodded over her shoulder toward the lab, looking at Cynda. The latter turned and quickly jogged back into the lab behind them.

Callie stepped up to the invisible divider that was keeping her from hugging her man. Blood was now running down her hand.

"Sorry, babe. I tried to warn you but couldn't get it out fast enough," said Walter. They each put a hand up on the invisible barrier. It looked like their hands were touching, but Callie couldn't feel the warmth of his skin. Just – nothing. Just resistance.

"Are you okay, Walt? You look like you've been beat up."

He nodded. "Yeah, I'm fine. How'd you get here so fast?" he asked.

"What do you mean? It took twenty flippin' hours."

Walter was shaking his head, frowning at her. "Huh? I've only been here a few hours. When did you leave?"

"The day after you did. How did you get over there, Walter? What's going on? Where is Bradley?" Callie said. She was growing concerned again, and couldn't think of all the questions she wanted to ask fast enough to ask them.

"Look. You're not going to believe this, Callie," Walter said.

"Got it!" said Cynda, running back down the hallway to meet them. She held the belt in both hands, approaching the gate. "Is this what you meant, Walter?"

Walter's eyes got real big and he nodded, pointing at it. "Yes! That's it! But hang on!" he said, waving his hands at her. Cardna was meanwhile inspecting the belt. "One of you needs to wear it to come through and get me. Then we can come back through together."

"I'm going," Callie said, turning to look at the other two women.

"Of course you are," said Cynda, immediately handing her the belt.

Callie slipped the heavy belt over her shoulder and looked back at Walter. "What's over there, Dubs?"

He held his hands up. "I'm not sure you're ready for this, babe. Come on through. Then we'll go back in there and talk about this."

Callie was too excited about being reunited with him to let that statement sink in – the fact that there was something that needed talking about…

Callie held her hands up in front of her and gingerly stepped through the gateway. She fell into Walter's arms on the other side. He stepped back, embracing her and swinging her side to side, holding on tight. He had his hand against the back of her head, and was lifting her slightly off the ground.

"God, baby, I thought I was never going to see you again," she said, kissing his neck and head repeatedly. She didn't even care that he stunk to high-heaven. She loved his scent. He smelled like a man. That brought on another whole slew of feelings, some of which were tingling in her nether regions.

He pulled back and kissed her hard on the lips, then said, "Let's go back. We all need to have a pow-wow."

Oddly, there were enough rolling stools and chairs in the lab for everyone to sit. Walter did not sit, though. He stood, leaning back against a steel table with his arms crossed. After their shared hugs and a proper introduction between Cynda and him, Walter had asked the group collectively, if anyone in here knew what was out there at the end of that tunnel.

The three women exchanged glances, and a consensus was reached. No, no one knew anything. No one had ever even been inside this lab. Cardna had commented that she was surprised to see this many stools and chairs, seeing as how he never allowed anyone else in.

He closed his eyes momentarily, shaking his head. Then sighed. "Okay. Where the fuck do I even begin. This shit is so fucked."

Callie could see that Cardna's patience was being tested when she cleared her throat and crossed her legs. All of them were ready to hear what the hell the big mystery was all about.

Walter looked up at the ceiling, then pursed his lips. Cleared his own throat. "Right. So there's no easy way to say this." He uncrossed his arms, held his hands out in front of him, then clasped them together in front of him. "Beyond that tunnel," he said, "is Mars."

They all stared at him. Speechless. What in the world was he talking about?

"Callie, you just walked through the gateway that was designed to keep people out. And things from coming back in. If you go down that hallway, there's an iron ring with these black capsules all around it. Somehow, they are entangled with counterparts that exist on Mars. You walk through that ring, and you instantly walk out onto the surface of Mars."

Cardna was pursing her lips now. "You know how crazy that sounds?"

Walter smiled wanly and nodded. He had recrossed his arms. He sighed again, then continued. "I'm not bullshitting. It's Mars. I took off my suit back there in the tunnel. Bradley shot a hole in it and I almost fucking asphyxiated."

Callie was staring at him, tears forming in her eyes, her hand over her mouth and chewing her lip. Cynda was staring at him through the tops of her eyes, head tilted forward, but remaining silent.

"I know it's hard to believe. You can go witness it yourself if you want. But you need to know some things." After a moment, he began pacing and put his hands in his jeans pockets. "There's a little tent thing that you come out into. A ridiculous plastic fucking tent. And outside of that, is Mars."

Walter looked at each of them in turn, waiting for one of them to interrupt, or to say how fucking crazy he was. No one did. They all just waited. So he continued. "There's a little dome outside of the tent. That dome has a door on it that can only be opened by whomever is in possession of this phone," he said, pulling the phone out of his pocket. "This is Bradley's phone. So right now, he's trapped in there."

"Good!" Callie said, leaning forward as she said it. It felt good to spit that word out. "Leave him!"

Cardna looked at her, shocked. Cynda looked at her too, but she was almost smirking. Walter turned toward her. "We can't, babe. There's a woman in there with him."

Cardna bolted up out of her chair. She had her hands on the sides of her head, grabbing handfuls of dark brown hair. "Oh my God. Are you fucking kidding me right now?"

Walter shot her a look. Obviously, the question had been rhetorical. But what was her real question? Callie stood up, too. It seemed like the thing to do.

"What is her name, Walter?"

"Her name's Kenna. She's been there for as much as two years. Maybe longer."

"Kenna Sharling?" Cardna said, stopping in her tracks. "She's still alive?"

Walter nodded. "Yeah. In pretty good health, too. A little gaunt, but…" he trailed off and shrugged, a *what do you expect* look on his face. "She's in surprisingly good spirits, too."

Cardna was covering her mouth with both hands, tears streaming down her cheeks now. "Oh my God, I'm so happy she's alive!" Cynda stood up and went to her, putting her arm around her shoulders, but staring back at Walter.

"What about the others?" Cardna managed through her tears. This breakdown was reassuring to Callie in ways that spoken words would just never do. This was humanity the woman was showing.

Walter shook his head, looking lost. "Others?"

Chapter 31

There were only enough suits for two of them to go in. Walter did not feel safe or comfortable trusting the suit he had been wearing, even though Cynda had managed to seal up the hole with duct tape on both sides of the fabric-like material. Though the suit wasn't pressurized when in use, there were just too many reasons to worry about it. If it failed and they didn't realize it, someone could literally have less than a minute to live. He knew that most women couldn't hold their breath for a minute. And even he could only hold his for a minute, when he knew he was about to have to, and took a big lungful to prepare. So he ruled it out.

Walter himself was the obvious first candidate. Having been the only one to have actually made the trek, and who knew the inside of the dome building was the first reason. The other was simply that he was a man. There was a man over there with a handgun. It would take a man to seize control of the situation. It was a coin-flip already. They were taking a big chance. He had not recognized the make of the handgun, but had told the women that they had to assume the magazine held twelve or thirteen rounds, and that it was only down one. Which meant there could still be twelve or thirteen rounds in it. They absolutely must proceed with the assumption that it had been full to start, with one in the chamber for good measure.

He did not think the man would have used the gun on the girl over there. But there was no telling, either. Now that Bradley knew Walter had made it *into* the dome, all bets were off. His secret revealed, he could have become desperate and tried to tie everything off. Hell, there was even a possibility – remote as it might be – that he had killed the woman and then taken himself out. They had searched the drawers and cabinets in the small lab area to no avail, and Cardna had sent Cynda upstairs to Bradley's office to search there as well. Other employees were starting to show up now, so they had to be as inconspicuous as possible.

When Cynda returned shrugging and holding her hands out, they had all felt a subtle punch to the gut. It had been a long shot, but Walter had been hoping the man had stashed at least one more handgun in the office. He had told Cynda to look for magnetic mounts up under the desk itself, and not to ignore any instinct. It looked like there had only been the one, though.

Cynda had also told them that stuff was starting to happen upstairs – a general buzz about the place. She had thought she heard someone talking about a bunch of big-wigs flying down to handle the PR mess – nightmare might have been a better word – that had ensued during last week's concert. Whoever was responsible for the video evidence of the Oliver Company's failed Mars mission, and its leaking to someone who had shown it to sixty thousand people, well, heads were going to roll. Executives were showing up and asking questions already. Cardna, standing with her hands on her hips, had turned to face the wreck where there had once been a double-door, shaking her head. She had shrugged and said they had no other choice. Callie was inclined to agree with her. Desperate times, and all. No one knew how long it would take for them to start storming the castle, as it were, pouring out the elevators to come interrogate Mr. Bradley. Surely, some native upstairs would tell them that he split his time between the empty office and somewhere down in the basement.

Cynda had looked about the place and said, "You know, we could send them in and pretend we were working here in the lab, if only there were some shit to work with."

Callie had scoffed. But Cynda was right. There were no beakers or Bunsen burners, scales and testing equipment. It was so *not* like a lab that there would be no way to fake anything. If the execs were to come out the elevator, they could look straight into the 'lab' and see two women standing around dumbly, doing nothing, with a destroyed double-door between them. Hard to be nonchalant in those circumstances.

"Okay, so we need to roll," Cardna finally said. "Walter, you and Callie go see what you can do out there. Cynda and I will run damage control up here. We'll go back upstairs and try to intercept them."

Just then, a man came wandering into the lab wearing jeans and a sweatshirt. He looked quizzically at the destroyed double-door, but didn't mention it. He came in and stood just inside the threshold and looked at Cardna. "Excuse me. But are you done with the forklift?"

After about three seconds of silence, everyone in the room – except the newcomer – burst out laughing. It was nice to let go a little of the tension. The man stood there, smiling wanly like he had missed the joke – he had – but not asking any questions. This was obviously well above his pay grade. *Smart man*, Callie thought.

"Yes," Cardna said, turning to him. "Thank you for letting me use it. Obviously I had an accident. I need to take a refresher course." As she approached him, he did not back away. He did lower his head a little, as if he were intimidated by her. The man wasn't stupid. He knew it had been no accident. But he was smart enough to be politic about the situation.

"Um, well, if you say so, ma'am," he said, rolling his shoulders.

"What's your name?" Cardna asked, stopping directly in front of him.

"Stephen Widup," said the man.

Cardna nodded, then said, "I'll come see you later to discuss how we'll finance your silence on this matter."

"Uh, well, no financing necessary, ma'am. I don't know anything, and that's the way I like to keep it."

"You're a smart guy. You'll go far here, Stephen."

He nodded, then looked at each of them in turn, a slight nod in Walter's direction, then turned to leave.

"Oh, and Stephen?" Cardna said. He stopped and turned. "Thank you for letting me use the lift."

"Okay," she said, turning back to the group and clapping quickly several times. "Let's go! Get those suits on!"

Cynda instantly ran to the hook and grabbed one of them, heading for Callie. She held it out and assisted as Callie stepped into it. Cardna stood by the threshold keeping an eye out for any other visitors while Walter stepped into the other suit. Callie was a little nervous as they had no time to plan, but it had seemed to work favorably for her up to now. No reason why things shouldn't keep going the right way now. She was trembling as Cynda helped her run the zipper. These 'space suits' were so unlike anything Callie had ever seen or imagined that she wondered how they could even work. Why did they not need to be pressurized? She would obviously only be working with whatever oxygen was trapped in the suit. And Walter had assured her it was enough to make it to the outpost. As soon as they heard the clunk of the inner door unlocking in the airlock, she would be safe to unzip it and start breathing 'fresh' air again. He had made quotes when he said that word, having no idea how long that air had been recycling itself over there. How many times had that air been breathed and re-breathed? It was crazy to think about.

When she was all zipped up, Cynda gave her a thumbs-up. Callie instinctively flashed on OK sign with her right hand, instead of the thumbs-up. The diver in her reawakened. She was filled with nervous excitement now. Walter had warned her of the 'transition sickness' she might experience on her first transit. And Callie thought it was at that moment that all this BS became a reality. All jokes aside, all pranks, any thought of pulling one over on her – this had to be real. He wouldn't let her get this far, zipping up into a space-proof suit just to say, "Ha, I got you!" It was not that she believed he would do such a thing. And even moreso not in the case of something so staggeringly epic as teleporting to another planet. It was not in his nature to joke about things of massive importance. But still, somewhere in the depths of her mind, the possibility had reared its head that maybe he had been fooling around. Or at the very least, embellishing just a tad. Just enough to cover a historically non-existent technology that allowed a human to instantly pass from one place to another, some sixty million kilometers away. What if he was mistaken, in other words? What if this supposed ring just led out back where there was a rocky and dirt-filled landscape? Callie had to roll her eyes at that. Standing on the roof of the building the first night she had come to Fiji, she had seen the landscape around them. Rocks and dirt just weren't in it.

There was just something in her humanity that tried to prevent her from believing it could be true. Callie had seen some weird science herself. But still, a new proposal such as this just struck her as impossible. And now, standing here face-to-face with Walter, his hands on her shoulders and asking her if she was okay, and was she sure she was ready to do this, she was trembling. She believed. The look in his eyes. The seriousness and the depth of his concern was on his face like red spray paint on a white wall. Callie could hear him well. Apparently the suits had transmitters in the helmet portion that allowed them to speak to each other. His voice sounded confined. Alone. Calm.

Callie swallowed and nodded, then said, "Yes, I'm ready. I'm ready. I love you, Walter."

Walter smiled at her, squinting his eyes. "I wanted the first time to be in a better place," he said, putting his hands on the sides of her head covering. "But I love you, too."

Then they were off. Cynda and Cardna had waved and given thumbs-ups to them, then turned and headed for the elevator, disappearing. That left Callie and Walter on their own. And now they were heading down the dark tunnel. Walter wore the blocky belt he had called a 'Chewbacca belt' slung over his shoulder. He held her close as if to hug her as they stepped through the steel black channel that ran the perimeter of the tunnel like a doorway. That which had almost broken her nose less than an hour ago now admitted them like a ticket-taker at a theater. Welcome. Enjoy the show.

All the memories of her discussions with Donnie Oliver and Mike Thurman and Thaddeus Cloys all came flooding back to the surface as soon as she saw the black canisters attached to the iron ring that sat on a step in the tunnel. She could see through it. Just a blank brick wall on the other side. No proof that it did what Walter said it did. She wondered in the back of her mind why light wouldn't come through, thus providing a vision of the other side. She would have to revisit that thought another time. Either way, here they stood, and she remembered everything she had ever heard about the black canisters. She remembered talk of them being added to the manifest unauthorized. About how they went missing. There had almost been a trip to the Space Station to take them up or something. And then the empty crate where they had once been, in the back of the Atlas. It had been shown on the video in front of the concert crowd. With the mystique and unknown purpose about their origin, they had an eerie rumor about them. A mythology created completely from unknown facts about them. And now here they were, covered with a misting of frost that seemed to dance around like fast-moving clouds. They looked downright creepy to Callie. And she was about to step through them.

Walter looked at her again and said, "Are you ready? You might feel a little sick, but it passes quickly." Callie nodded once. Then again. She was pumping herself up for it. Her heart was racing. Her mind was filled with a billion scenarios – not one of them attractive – and she was beginning to feel sweat on the small of her back and under her arms. Now was the time. It was finally here. The culmination of a decade's running around after shadows. *Here we go.*

Everything happened so fast that Callie couldn't remember what had happened in what order, sometimes confusing things upon recollection of the events. And some of those seemed distinctly like dreams, or maybe the other way around. Even years down the road, she would still have spotty visions and nightmares involving the instantaneous trip to Mars and its aftermath. What she did remember, she tried to journal. Sometimes unsuccessfully. Sometimes that would end with tears dropping onto the paper, blurring the ink and forcing her to clap the book shut, burying her face in her hands to have another cry. The cries seemed endless. For months and months after the event, the cries would revisit, unannounced, sometimes several times a day.

Having stepped through the teleportation ring, she immediately stumbled and became incredibly disoriented. It had not passed quickly, as Walter had promised. It clung to her like a haunt in a hotel. The rest of the experience on the other side, was therefore a hazy, blurry, dream-like series of events that were accented by screams, panic and fear. Walter's theory that they airlock would have a way to recycle from the outside had been accurate. They had stood there, Callie bending over at the waist, crying out in discomfort and panic as they waited for the air to be evacuated from within. Then something about Walter dragging her into the chamber. Re-pressurizing. She remembered very little of this. Leaning back against him, closing her eyes against the nausea and dizziness, Callie had never felt so bad in her life. This was worse than any sickness she had ever had. She felt completely useless, and regretted coming along. She would be absolutely no help.

As it turned out, that was exactly wrong. Had she not been there to take the shot, Kenna would have died.

Brian Bradley had come round the corner with a woman locked in by his arm around her neck. Callie thought the woman was screaming. She was definitely crying. She wore a white t-shirt that had blood all over its front, and khaki cargo pants. She was reaching up and prying at the arm that wrapped her in. Her face a mess of pain and fear. Callie's heart had gone out to her, but the confusion and disorientation was too strong. She crumbled to her knees grasping at her stomach, feeling like she was going to throw up. Walter had shouted something and let go of her at this point, charging forward and tackling the man who held the woman. Callie knew the gun Bradley had been pointing at the woman's head had gone off. She also knew it had not hit the woman in the head. But the nausea in her belly had turned to burning pain, and suddenly, Callie's gloved hands were covered in blood. Confusion washed over her. Sweat was pouring down into her eyes – sweat that she could not wipe away with the back of a hand. Had she unzipped the suit, she might have been able to clear her vision. As it lay though, she had fallen against the wall of the airlock, lying on her side in a near-fetal position, gasping for breath and wondering if she would ever see Earth again. The next time she was aware of anything, Callie would be in a hospital millions of miles from where she now lay bleeding out.

Walter knew instantly he was the reason Callie had been shot. But he also knew that bullet had been destined for

Kenna's head. He had the awful, sickening thought that he had just traded his girlfriend's life for a stranger's, and hoped this woman would be worth it. Not to him, of course, but in her life. All these thoughts flashed through his head in the instant it had taken him to watch Bradley's hand go down and fire. The deep red spot on her space suit didn't look that bad. But he also realized peripherally that the blood wouldn't be soaking through that. It would be ruining her blouse, hidden by the suit.

But he was already in motion, tackling the man who had fired the shot. As Walter's momentum hit Bradley, they all fell back into the hallway and Bradley's left hand went up, knocking Kenna in the face. But Walter landed on the man. And now, sitting on Bradley's chest, he began punching him in the face through the plastic hood, over and over. The anger and rage he had felt ever since finding Kenna locked in the room here was all boiling over. Walter wanted to make sure every drop went where it belonged. He didn't want to spill any on the floor.

"Kenna!" he shouted, looking over at the girl, who was just starting to sit up. "Can you get Callie out of here? She's gonna need medical help, and fast!"

Kenna, suddenly looking like she'd seen a ghost, hopped to her feet. "That's Callie? Oh my God, Walter!" she screamed, and then she was busy picking Callie up by her armpits.

Walter adjusted his grip and did the same with Bradley, getting behind him and turning the man around, pulling him toward the airlock. He was at once surprised and relieved by the display of strength Kenna was showing in her ability to move the dead weight of his girlfriend ahead of him. His heart was beating double-time and with a new fear in it. If Kenna didn't get Callie across fast enough, or if they couldn't get an ambulance to the complex fast enough, or if the ambulance couldn't make the hospital fast enough...

There was no good to be had thinking down these pathways though. He could only do what he could do. The two conscious humans stood in the airlock looking at each other, breath fogging up the plastic windows that would normally be helmets on a proper space suit. They both had their hands under the arms of their respective charges. The two unconscious humans hung limply at their knees. Walter nodded at Kenna. "Thank you, Kenna. I'm proud of you," he said.

She smiled at him, head moving forward and back with her own heavy breathing. She looked proud to receive the compliment. Beaming. She nodded. "I'm gonna save her, Walter," she said.

Walter nodded back. "I know. I know."

The airlock cycled and the light went on. Then Kenna was on the run, dragging Callie across the smooth concrete floor to the bottom of the stairs. "Fuck!" Walter shouted. He had forgotten they had to go upstairs. "Drop her!" he said, dropping Bradley at the same time. "Come stand with your foot on this fucker's neck!"

Kenna nodded and did as she was bid. Walter took her place and hoisted Callie up on his shoulder, fireman's style. "Up we go, baby," he said, and heaved, carrying her up the long flight of stairs. When he got to the top, he realized the futility of trying to carry Bradley up. Callie had been heavier than her normal mass. The gravity was different here. There was no way he would be able to lift the man. He changed his plans on the fly and shouted back down at Kenna. "Kenna, come on!" The girl looked up and then ran, bounding up the stairs to meet him as he turned around and banged through the door. He carried Callie across the dirt to the tent, where Kenna ran ahead of him and opened the door. Then to the ring. He stepped inside the ring and his foot came down onto something hard, scraping it across the concrete.

Walter, almost stumbling, stopped and turned, waiting for Kenna. She popped through the ring a moment later. "Hey!" he shouted, putting a hand out. She ran into his hand. He remembered she hadn't been able to hear him before, where there was no atmosphere. But in here, they were back on Earth. Callie felt lighter as well. "There's a flashlight beneath my foot!" He could sense Kenna bending down to fetch it and then shortly, the hallway was filled with light. She looked up at him expectantly with wide eyes. "I'm gonna have to set her down to give you the block belt."

Kenna nodded and began reaching out for Callie. She helped Walter set her down gently against the wall then held her hands out like a baby asking for a toy. Walter pulled the block belt off his shoulder and slung it over her arm for her. "Okay, Kenna. You'll have to get really close to her to get through the gateway together." Kenna nodded again. Walter took her by the shoulders. "Save my girl, Kenna."

"You got it, Walter." Then she leaned in and they embraced. Walter hugged her hard before letting her go and turning back to the buoys. "Walter!" Kenna cried as he reached it. He stopped and looked back at her. She was shining the flashlight onto the ground between them. "Thank you. Thank you for saving me."

He gave her a thumbs-up and smiled, then dived through the buoys. As Walter came out into the shed, he noticed it was a little lighter outside. Something pinged in his mind. Maybe it only felt like an instant trip. But somehow, time was passing differently in both places. Or at least the transit screwed things up somehow. Callie had somehow made the flight from home to Fiji in the short span where he'd only been in the bunker for what felt like a few hours. He didn't have time to think about that now, though.

And when he got back into the dome, he had other problems to deal with. Brian Bradley was back up and conscious. He stood outside the airlock, knees bent, peering at the recycle button like he was having trouble seeing. Likely that was because of the five or six hard punches he had taken from Walter's fists. Walter's plan had been a simple one: he would come in and slip the block belt off the unconscious man's shoulder and dash back up the stairs, leaving the son of a bitch to die a slow and lonely death. The same way Bradley had basically done to Kenna. But now that he was awake, that changed things. Walter, coming down the stairs, had to act fast on the plan change.

Fortunately, the gun was still in the pressurized part of the bunker, on the other side of the chamber they now stood outside of. As Walter came off the last stair, he was thankful for the lack of atmosphere, as the other man did not hear him approaching. A blue light came on and Bradley stood up, but Walter was there. He slammed the other man bodily against the pressure door and actually heard him grunt as their hoods came briefly into contact with each other.

Walter stepped back, pulling Bradley by the belt he meant to take from the man. He swung him around like a rag doll and slammed him into the concrete wall by the stairs. Then it was up the stairs. "Let's go, asshole," Walter said, understanding that he was probably only speaking to himself. He set to pushing Brian Bradley up the stairs, thankful the man was conscious enough to take that bit of the burden from him.

When they got to the top, Walter slammed him into the door. As Bradley rebounded, Walter used the momentum to lift the block belt off his shoulder. He spun his hand smoothly in the air, reorienting the contraption to fall over his own arm where it slid down onto his shoulder. He grabbed Bradley by the shoulders and spun him round and slammed him against the wall beside the door. He finally got a look at the man's face, bruised and broken, through the splattered and smudged face shield. There was blood everywhere in that suit.

Walter grabbed two handfuls of the front of Bradley's suit and looked at him, breathing heavily. "You're the worst excuse for a human being I've ever run into. Your life ends today," he said, and nodded. Bradley was shaking his head inside the hood. Then he dragged him out the door and walked him away from the dome. They were not heading for the tent, either. As Bradley finally realized what was happening – what this walk meant – he started trying to resist. And when Bradley spoke, Walter could hear it. It dawned on him that some of the suits had communications devices in them. Maybe they all did, but some needed new batteries. He almost smirked at the thought. "What are you doing?"

Walter had his suit in two fistfuls by the back. And Bradley wasn't strong enough to get away from him. Walter marched him out away from the compound. A hundred yards. Two hundred. When they finally got to a place Walter felt like was far enough, he turned Bradley around and shoved him to the ground. "Can you hear me?"

Brian Bradley nodded and replied, "Yes, yes, I can hear you. Please don't do this."

"I want you to tell me what happened to the others."

"What others?" Bradley said, his face a mess behind black eyes and bloody lips.

"The others who didn't make it through," said Walter. "There were others before Kenna Sharling."

Recognition dawned on Bradley's face. "Nothing! I didn't do anything!"

Walter rared back to kick him, but Bradley held up a hand and shouted, "Walter, let me finish!" Walter stayed his punishment momentarily, righting himself and squatting, getting close to Bradley. After a moment, Bradley lowered his hand and caught his breath. "I didn't do anything because I didn't have to. They didn't make it. When they came through the transposition ring, it just didn't work. They just never came back."

"You never found a body or anything?"

"No!" Bradley said, almost shouting. "I had to fine-tune them. Adjust them on the ring. The position of them is what's important. They have to be perfectly evenly spaced."

Walter stood up straight. "How the hell did you adjust the ones out here if you couldn't go through?"

Bradley was shaking his head, holding his hand up again. "I didn't! I just had to match the position. I was working with a diagram and a picture. I had set this side up many years ago. The Atlas mission brought them out here. All I had to do back on Earth was match the exact position here to form the link."

"And you got it right in two tries?"

Bradley looked confused. "Well, yeah. They didn't have to be moved much," he said. He held that hand out to Walter as if asking for reprieve. "Walter, you have to believe me. I regret losing those two people. I'm sorry."

"Tell that to their families. They don't even have bodies to bury, you fuck."

"I know! I know, but there's nothing I could do. But it works now! Don't you see how this can make things better?"

Walter looked around the barren landscape. Took a deep breath. It felt light in his lungs. He was beginning to run low on residual oxygen in the suit. He was probably within a few minutes of passing out, and needed to start heading back now. He turned back to Bradley, who still sat with his hand up, pleading.

"A lot of people died for you to get your science experiment working," he said. "You have to pay for that, Bradley."

"Okay," the man said. "Okay. I will. I promise. I will turn myself in. I will hand over all the information I have on it. I'll hand it all to the authorities."

Walter shook his head. "You already did. Sorry, Brian. I am the authority." He stepped forward and pushed Bradley onto the ground and knelt on top of his chest. He reached over and grabbed a sharp triangular rock and flattened out part of the hood with his left hand.

"What are you doing?" Bradley cried. "No! Walter, no! Please!"

With his other hand, he began stabbing down into the plastic that served as a window for the hood. It was tough. Tenacious plastic. Not easily torn.

"NO!" Bradley screamed. He was beating his hands against Walter's legs and sides, wriggling his body and trying to get free.

It was the fifth or sixth stab that did it. The rock punctured the plastic and a white puff of air like a tiny ghost blew out and disappeared instantly. Bradley's eyes went wide and he immediately started grasping for the hole, trying to pinch it closed, the same way Walter had done not so long ago. Walter stood up and dropped the rock on Bradley's chest as a slight tinge of sympathetic claustrophobia began to creep in. He had felt the fear this man was feeling now. Only, this man had no chance at redemption. No chance of recovery. And surely now, Brian Bradley was staring headlong into the very short future that lay ahead of him. Knowing this was his final resting place.

Then Walter nodded reverently. "Sorry, man. But this is how it has to be." And then he turned and walked back to the tent. He could hear the struggles of the dying man behind him, but steeled himself against turning around. While Walter believed in the work his hands had performed, but did not want to watch the results. That was a level of sinister he hoped never to attain.

It was done. He had done the hard part. The gravity of the situation began to settle on him. Walter reckoned he could come to a peace with it, especially knowing the stakes. Knowing the evil the other man had committed in the past, and some of that a *very recent* past. But for now, he was despondent. Revenge was a dish best served cold, they said. Well, he certainly felt plenty of that in his soul. The worry for Callie's outcome, the worry for the rest of them – the woman, Kenna, whom he had only just recently met… There was plenty of coldness in his heart. He just hoped that stepping back through that portal to another world would help cleanse his spirit of it. And maybe give him back a little warmth.

There were times when the lights were too bright, and she would cry out. They hurt her head. Her vision. Her life. Everything hurt. Life had become an endless string of groggy awakenings into pain and confusion, then drifts back into dark dream-filled sleep sessions that would last upwards of sixteen hours. There never seemed to be any relief from the repetitious cycle. Waking wasn't worth doing. Sleeping was too frightful to treat as a refuge. Why was she even still alive? Was this to be her life from here out? If so, she didn't want any part of it. This was surely worse than the hell she had used to fear as a child. There was plenty of burning in her stomach and loins during those short dances with wakefulness. There were voices sometimes, but never ones she recognized. Dark silhouettes in her vision, uncomfortable pressures and pinches in parts of her body she could not identify. Loud humming. That was one thing that seemed to be persistent. A humming that sounded like an engine running in the next room. Idling steadily with no other purpose than to annoy. To upset. To cause discomfort.

She didn't know how long any of this lasted. There was no way to tell time in this umbra. This foggy netherworld of unreality had no clocks. No phones. No alarms. No comfort of any kind. Did she not have friends? She felt like she was in a purgatory. A limbo comprised of shadows and spots and muted noises. And that humming.

One time, she had been a woman. She had experienced the wants and desires, the needs of a woman. The carnal urges. The hungers a human faced. The thirsts. Now, though, there was none of that. She could not remember eating or drinking anything. She knew it had not happened since before she had left the hotel that morning with Cynda. Cynda! Where was Cynda? Was she real? Callie might have been imagining her. Just like this damned trip that seemed so real in her memory — what parts of it she could discern from the nightmares of this new reality, anyway. Something had happened somewhere. She had wanted to believe she had made a trip to another planet or something. But that was obviously nonsense. These weird hallucinations were so realistic and believable that she worried she might be replacing real memory — real *reality* — with these high-tech simulacrums.

She wanted someone to hold her. To hold her sweaty head in his lap and brush the sweaty hair back. A kiss on the cheek would be nice. If it were Walter, then a kiss on the lips would be acceptable too. Of course, she couldn't expect anyone to love her like this. Not anymore. She probably looked terrible. Wherever she was, she had not been able to take care of herself. She knew she wasn't clean. She wanted to brush her teeth. To wash her face. To make herself presentable. She prayed that no one would see her like this. That she would either die before someone saw her, or get a chance to recover and clean up. She had the wherewithal to know she was in a place of recovery, likely a hospital – though she had no tangible evidence to support the theory. Nothing was tangible anymore. Otherwise she would be able to understand some of the mumblings she sometimes thought she heard – those sounds that she thought of as the voices of strangers. Just muted tones, really. No one would love her if they saw her like this. She did remember a bloody nose at some point in her past. And she knew she had never had a chance to clean that up. To wash her face with soap and water. So she probably still had blood on her upper lip. Crusting around the nostrils. There was no way anyone would want her like this. If she still had hair, it was probably a wreck. No one loved anyone like this.

She realized that in all her thoughts, she had never thought of herself as a person since whatever event had transpired to bring her here to this place – this holding cell on the balcony of reality. She couldn't even remember her name. Maybe she didn't have one. Maybe she had been here all along. Maybe this had been her life. Nothing seemed real anymore. She tried to focus on the bright light coming through her eyelids. Could she not just open her eyes? Accept the blindness that would befall her for a while, then trade it for a smudge of vision that would creep in, eventually replacing the dark red spots? She tried, but to no avail. She had no control of anything, apparently. Maybe there *was* nothing. Maybe there was nothing to control. She tried to latch onto this thought for a moment, but felt herself falling. Falling backward. Back into a hole. The darkness came in around her as if she were backing down a tunnel at a high rate of speed. The light grew smaller and smaller. And then there was nothing.

Two people, a man and a woman, danced in the middle of an impossibly bright floor. It might have been ice. They might have been on ice skates. The music swelled so loud it almost hurt the ears, but it was so beautiful it brought tears to her eyes. There would have been a full-on cry if she had been alone. Back at home on the couch with no one there to judge her. But here, there were a hundred thousand people staring down from the stadium seats, watching the couple on the floor, so far below. The spotlight formed a cone around the couple as they spun and twisted on the ice, an abstract but vivid exercise in elegance. But even the rink outside of the spotlight seemed exquisitely bright. The crowd was completely quiet. She could not look at them directly. When she tried to turn her head, she saw nothing but blurs around her in the darkness. She was so many rows up in the stands that she could barely see the couple on the floor below already. The tears in her eyes only exacerbated the problem. They were twinkling fairy-tale figures swimming in the ice-water of her spilling eyes. But it was beautiful. She never wanted it to end. As it was coming to an end, and she knew this with a certainty, she latched instead, onto the music itself. It was a gorgeous classical score with swells in all the right places. But even it faded after a while. It seemed nothing could be held any longer. Everything was precious. Everything was on a timer. Under duress. Fleeting. *Temporary.*

And then she was gone.

One morning, everything was different. Callie woke up. The light was soft and pleasant now. It was coming through a window in the side of the room. The hospital room. There were no lights above her. The room itself exuded a coolness

– a crispness – that she couldn't put her finger on. But it was very much there. The curtains had been pulled to allow the morning sunlight to stream in, touching the whole room with its magnificence. All she could see out the window was the tops of trees. This tickled her memory, but she couldn't pinpoint it. Not now, at least. She felt like that might come later though. Everything seemed real now. *My name is Callie Simmons. And I'm awake. Welcome back, world.*

She was alone in the room, and lay there staring out the window, basking in the peace she felt. The IV tube stretched up past her shoulder where it attached to the bottom of a clear bag. Fine. Her forehead felt cool. She lifted her arm to touch it with the back of her hand and was rewarded not only with the ability to do so, but the ability to tell she was not sweating. Her hair felt like it had been combed too. Quickly, she moved her hand to her nose. It wasn't even sore. There was no crusted blood beneath it. Nor on her lip. Maybe that had all been part of the weird dream. She became aware of a thick remote control by her hip when she put her hand back down by her side. Callie realized this meant she could call for the nurse. Let the world know she was back. Back on the planet. Back in what felt like a stable reality. A *real* reality. But she wasn't ready for that yet. This was nice. This was pleasant. She felt a peace right now she had not often felt in her life.

There was no boss calling her to work. No one calling her to come do anything for them. Nothing to do. Nothing to get done. No bad guys to bring down. No phone calls to make, parties to attend, friends to visit, dishes to do or beds to make. She felt light. There was nothing in the world right now that needed her attention. Why shouldn't she lie here and savor this calm? This wonderful relief from all the callings of a lifetime of responsibilities and demands... Callie knew they would all be back. And probably sooner rather than later. But for now, she was free of all the burdens. She would enjoy this for as long as she could.

Callie smiled lightly as she stared at the window. She wondered what it felt like out there. Was it cool and crisp, like it was in here? Or was it warm and muggy? Probably the former. She didn't try to bother with coming up with a scenario that explained where she had been. She knew short-term, she had been unconscious at the least for a time. But before that, she knew an event of possibly earth-shattering hugeness had taken place. She didn't want to bother trying to remember that right now. It would all come in due time. Someone would fill her in. For now, she had time to reflect on her new friends again.

Cynda. Cardna. Codi. F sake, there were a lot of C-names. Callie smirked at that. At least she was one of them. And of course, Walter. He was not new. But a new side of him had been given to her in recent times. Callie closed her eyes, smiling peacefully, and let sleep wash over her. This was an enjoyable surrender to a nice late-morning nap. Well deserved. Welcome and refreshing.

When she woke this time, a nurse was in the room. As soon as Callie's eyes popped open, the nurse turned and put her hands on her hips. "You back with us, girlfriend?"

Callie smiled. Then she nodded. The smile that spread across the nurse's face was so rich and genuine that Callie was almost overtaken by the need to laugh. A soul-spilling laugh of happiness. Then the woman said, "Oh, glory hallelujah!" and grasped Callie's hand with both of her own. "Welcome back, precious! You fought through it. By God, you made it back."

Callie was still smiling, not wanting to let the confusion of her statements take the lead in her mind yet. She would know all in good time.

"I'm gonna go let the others know," the woman said. "Who would you like to see first?"

Callie's eyes widened. "Who all is here?" she said with a husky voice. She realized this was likely the first words she had said in a very long time. Maybe days.

"Honey, everyone is here."

Callie's heart felt hot with fiery love and joy. Her cheeks felt bright with it. Her eyes welled up with tears and she gasped out the beginnings of laughter. "Oh, my!" She wiped away her tears and then said, "I would like to see Walter if he's here."

The nurse squeezed her hand. "I think he's gonna be real happy you said that."

Callie was alone again for a time. She lay there smiling, thinking about what the woman had meant by 'everyone'. She was staring at the door, which the nurse had left ajar. She wiped tears away again. She couldn't remember the last time she had felt so happy. And then the door swung open and she got happier.

Walter sat on the edge of the bed, his hands clasping Callie's own. She had sat up when he came in, screaming his name, and wrapped her arms around his neck. She barely noticed the flare of pain this had caused in her stomach. She had obviously been lying on her back too long. Maybe a gas bubble had formed or something. But she had ignored it, and it had quickly gone away. He had held her like that for a long while, kissing her neck and cheek, her earlobe, the side of her head. Walter had one hand on the back of her head. A big, strong, man's hand that was big enough to cup most of the back of her skull. The feelings this gave her were thick and plenty, and covered plenty of areas of her body. Then he had pulled back and put his hands on her cheeks, staring at her in the eyes. He kissed her hard on the lips, and for a long few seconds. That had been refreshing to Callie in ways she would rather not have shared, were she asked. There had been thoughts that no one would want her anymore. She probably looked hospitalized. When one stayed in a place for a few days, they became the embodiment of the place. Surely she fit the bill.

Now he sat on the edge, holding her hands. "Your doctor says I'm not supposed to tell you anything that happened yet. He wants it to come back to you organically. Whatever that means."

Callie tilted her head and smiled. "Thank you for staying, Walter. How long have I been here? Can you tell me that? I probably ruined your week."

Walter's smile staggered momentarily. He squeezed her hands. "Callie, you've been in a coma."

Her heart skipped a beat. She felt the bottom nearly fall out of her reality. "What? Are you serious?"

Walter nodded.

"How long, Walter? Oh my God, what have I missed?" She pulled one of her hands away and covered her mouth with it. She could have pulled the other away to wipe the new tears, but opted instead for the comfort his hand was providing. No time to worry about the shame of a few tears.

Walter swallowed then breathed in deeply. "Three months, Callie. Eighty-eight days, to be exact."

Callie yelped. It felt like she had been physically pushed. She felt empty. Like she had missed out on so much life – so much action – that she was now useless. "Oh my God. Oh my God, Walter!" she said, and this time did pull her other hand free. She was now covering the bottom half of her face with both hands.

"Callie, you're okay. You're back with us. Let's take joy in that."

She was nodding, but the tears were coming fast. She was trying to say okay. To say, yes, I will. But she couldn't get any words out. She agreed with him in principle, but had no way to express to him her feelings right now. She was overwhelmed with this new emotion. Somehow, Callie Simmons had skipped out on a quarter-year of life, just existing. Kept alive by tubes and technology. She felt sick and angry at the same time.

Walter sat forward and took her in his arms. She buried her face in his shoulder and cried. She cried until she had no more tears to spill.

When Callie had finally calmed enough to ask Walter what had happened – what had put her in the hospital, or the coma to begin with – he had resisted at first. Still confused between dream and reality, Callie had not yet tried to dig into how much of her memory could be trusted. But she didn't feel like knowing what had brought her here could be detrimental in any way. She had finally had to talk tough to Walter. And he had finally relented.

"Callie, you got shot in the stomach."

She had opened her eyes wide and stared at him for a long moment – a flash of memory banging forward in her mind. Lying on a strange gray floor, kicking and squirming in hot pain… Then she had lifted her hospital gown to reveal her stomach. The pale flesh of her belly was covered in a large white bandage. There was no blood seeping through. So obviously it had scabbed and healed long ago. She wondered why she should need the bandage in that case. She began peeling it up at the top corner against Walter's objections. "Callie, no!" he shouted. But she ignored him. She had to see the wound. When the bandage was off, she stared in disbelief at the ugliest scar she had ever seen. She would never again feel comfortable in a bikini. It didn't look like she had imagined. A nice, neat, clean little circle of redness. No. It was a jagged line, puffy and red with tiny red dots along the edges where the stitches had been. She gasped as she gaped at it. Walter told her the doctor had assured him the redness would eventually fade, and it might even blend in with her skin eventually. She asked him why it was so large and he told her how much damage it had done to her organs. They had had to perform emergency surgery. "Most people don't live through that shot, Callie," Walter said.

It was Cardna who gave up the ghost. She hadn't the same sense of propriety that Walter had exercised, in following orders not to tell her what happened. Maybe Cardna had not been briefed. Either way, she came into the room all smiles and excitement, spreading her arms wide as she came in for a hug, and saying, "You did it, girl! You really did it!"

Callie laughed out loud, but didn't know what she was laughing at. It felt more like another of those happy laughs. Like the laughter that overcame a woman when she heard she had just delivered a healthy baby boy. The tear-filled excited laughter she associated with the best events in her life. Seeing this woman, *this* woman, come into her room smiling and offering hugs, made Callie feel that excitement. She couldn't quite say why, but she had been taken by Cardna's friendship. It had been a powerful drug somehow. Like she had befriended a rock star. Maybe it was because she had gone through that phase of suspected enemyship with her.

After their hug, Cardna sat in the same position Walter had sat in before she finally kicked him out, saying he would get to see her again later, but that she had to make her rounds. Cardna didn't stop smiling, either. Callie asked her what she had meant. "I did what?"

"You won! You beat that son of a bitch!" she said. She was shaking her head and staring out the window, as if to relive the events for a moment. "You and Walter brought him down."

Bradley! Brian Bradley! Callie thought, and it all came flooding back to her. All at once, everything she could remember came pouring in like a tidal wave. And she almost drowned in it. She stared at her hands as the memories of the events had washed over her. I guess this is what they meant by organic. And here it was.

"Weren't there some women in there?" Callie said.

Cardna returned her gaze to to Callie and nodded. She squeezed Callie's hand at the same time. Callie guessed everyone had the same routine for bringing comfort to her. Maybe it was a human thing. Every human instinctively knew to do these things. "There was one. Kenna. We got her out. You got her out, I should say. Well, technically, Walter did. But who's arguing that? You were brave enough to go in with him."

Callie stared into Cardna's green eyes, trying to use them as little looking glasses that would take her back to the inside of that airlock. That insane alien room she had been in that day. "Was I really there, Cardna?" she said, leaning her head forward and looking seriously at the other woman. "You know. There?" Callie nodded toward the window, not wanting to say something so kooky-sounding as 'Mars' or 'another planet' – just in case she was wrong. There was obviously a lot she would have to dissect in the coming days and weeks. Sort through memory and thought, trying to weed out what wasn't real. Most of what she knew to be real was foggy at best, anyway. She remembered being very sick during her stay on the Red Planet. It would not go down in her memory as a stay worth filing next to the five-star hotels she had been in. Though there was a small part of her that filled with regret every time she thought of it. She wished she had gotten to revel in the wonder and the amazement that came with visiting another planet. Callie had walked on an alien planet. That was so fascinating. So rare. So exquisitely and insanely wonderful that she could almost not come up with the words. And it had been ruined by transition sickness. She shook her head and refocused. She was still looking at Cardna. Cardna had remained silent, realizing Callie needed to sort some things out in her head.

"Why are you all here?"

"We all just came by to visit today. We come by every couple of weeks to check in with Walter and see if he needs anything. You know. Provide whatever support we can."

Callie squeezed Cardna's hand. "Thank you. You're wonderful."

Cardna scoffed. "Nah. Just being a friend." She pulled her in for a hug and squeezed Callie's shoulders.

It was a few days later that the doctor finally cleared Callie to be discharged. The worries of responsibilities and duties began to come back to Callie, but they were fought off pretty readily with the soothing words of Cynda Lohm, who told her that they had checked her out of the motel she had been in for the night she had arrived in Fiji. They had turned in the rental car for her. She had taken all of Callie's things to her own apartment for safekeeping. It was to Cynda's apartment they went when they left the hospital. Walter rode with Cardna, realizing that all of them wouldn't fit in Cynda's little two-seater.

Callie and Walter spent most of the day there, getting things in order for the return flight to the States. Callie wanted to drink coffee, but was too scared to try it yet. The doctor had said she could slowly introduce spicy things and drinks with caffeine back into her diet. Just to use her best judgment when it came to whether or not she was going to tolerate it. Well, she was too scared just yet to try it. And wasn't about to water it down. So instead she had drunk iced tea from a can. They sat around the small table in what passed for Cynda's dining area and Callie found herself a little jealous of the freedom that came with living in such a small space. It meant no landscape bills. It meant less responsibilities. More freedom. The freedom of being young again.

Callie had decided she really liked the woman. They had made promises to keep in touch. And Cynda had family who lived in Chicago, so she would be coming to the states at least once a year to see them. It wouldn't be too tall an order for her to swing by New Jersey on the way out and spend some time with Callie.

And Walter.

Callie had a big house. And so did Walter. And there had to be a point at which one or both of them would finally acknowledge the big horse in the room: they would likely need to get rid of one of them at some point. It did seem plausible that they were going to end up together. Callie had insisted she could see that in their future. And that Walter had better prepare himself to get used to seeing her face every morning when he woke up. Walter had smiled and nodded at that, saying he couldn't think of anything in the world he would like to see more than her beautiful face. That didn't do anything to push her away from the idea. Walter had been saying a whole bunch of the right things.

When they finally said their goodbyes, Cardna had come by to get them. It was late on a Tuesday evening and she had come straight from work to drive them to the airport. There were some tears and some laughter and a bunch of hugs. Callie felt closer to these two women than she had felt to anyone else in years. Even Rebecca. It was too bad they lived on the opposite side of the globe. When they had the technology to step through a ring onto another planet, it sure seemed preposterously slow to have to travel by plane. And the return trip to Newark would be close to thirty hours. *God. Do we even have to go?*

Neither Walter nor she actually had a job at the moment. It sure seemed a legitimate option to just stay in Fiji. But Walter reminded her they had houses and friends back home who eagerly awaited their return to the states. Walter looked forward to sitting in his Adirondack, listening to the Stones with his feet up on the fire pit stones, a glass of bourbon in one hand and a fat cigar in the other.

He had arranged with Rebecca to take care of their places while they were away. Codi and Sam had actually ended up staying in Callie's house for her. And Rebecca visited Walter's every few days just to make sure everything was holding up. Callie had been happy to hear that news, knowing that her bathtub would be getting some use while she was gone. She couldn't imagine a world where her bathtub sat getting dusty. That wasn't a world she wanted to live in. And she looked forward with great enthusiasm to the night she got home that she could sit in it and soak herself for a couple of hours. Walter had his fire pit, Callie had her tub.

On the three-hour drive to the airport, Cardna filled Callie in on all the happenings at the company. Several people suspected of allowing the leak had been fired. No one had any idea it was a girl who never even worked for them who had precipitated the fallout. And through most of it, very little was ever said about Brian Bradley's involvement. It had ended up looking like a complete circus, Cardna said. "A fucking circus."

They seemingly fired several people at random and acted like they had cleaned up the whole thing. Callie sat with her elbow on the door handle, staring out the window at the fast-passing landscape in the darkness. She had opted for the back seat, thinking she might need to stretch out across the whole bench, but had been able to stay upright after all.

"I'm ready to hear what happened out there," Callie finally said.

Walter and Cardna had looked at each other. Callie, sitting right behind Walter, couldn't see the face he had made, but she had seen Cardna raise an eyebrow. That could have meant many things. One being, *what, you haven't told her yet?* Another could have been *how does she not already know?* Either way, Walter turned and spoke from the side of his mouth, unable to come completely around to facing her in the front seat.

"Bradley is dead."

Callie nodded. Not as surprised as she was relieved. That meant nothing would come up again. Nothing would ever require her to go on this mission again. She had done it. She had brought him down. Death had not necessarily been the answer she had hoped for. But had it been on a list of acceptable choices, she would have checked the box next to it, all the same.

"I uh," Walter started, then cleared his throat, looking back at Cardna. "I had to fight with him after the gun went off the first time. That was the shot that hit you, Cal."

Callie was shaking her head. She had no idea how it had come to be that a gun pointed at another woman's head had fired its deadly projectile at her instead. She was glad, in the end, that it had, though. Because it meant Kenna Sharling was still alive. And since Callie had ended up making it too, well, she guessed that was just fine. A little pain, a few months of lost time, but at least the other woman was alive.

"I ended up getting the best of him. They'll uh…" he said, again looking at Cardna. She looked back at him, then back at the road. "They'll never find his body," he finished. Unless maybe the Rover comes across his bones someday."

"God, Walter," Callie said, shaking her head. "What did you do?"

"I dragged him out into the middle of nowhere, as far as I could go on one suit-worth of oxygen, and left him in the dirt."

Callie realized she had not heard about the woman who had been in there. It had come to her mind a few times while she was in the hospital, but something else had always come up, replacing the thought with something more urgent. And thus, she had no idea the fate of the mysterious woman kept against her will, apparently for years, on another planet. She shivered with the thought of such a horror.

"How is the woman?"

Cardna looked back at her, then glanced at Walter, who turned in his seat. "Woman?" he asked.

"Yeah. The woman who was in the place."

"Ah. Yeah. Kenna came to the hospital a couple of times in the beginning. She came to check on you. After a few times, she just stopped showing up. She said she was doing well. She was in therapy, and on a recovery diet. After the first few weeks, she looked like a new person. She had been pretty gaunt. Anorexic-like." Walter paused. "She was the one you saw when you went in."

Callie nodded, returning her gaze to the landscape out the side window. She had confirmed on the way out to the car that the weather she had seen through the hospital window had indeed been cold and crisp. Just like she had hoped. It completed the picture of serenity in her mind. Of beauty. Fiji, now a place of things at rest, was also alluring in its own mysterious aura. It held the terrifying reality of the teleportation ring, which Walter had already told her he had destroyed. When they were all out, he had begun shattering the capsules. After the second one, he said he could walk through the ring and still be in the same hallway. He had been able to touch the brick wall on the other side. The science had been broken. It no longer connected to an entangled partner millions of miles away.

The lights of the airport finally became visible in the windshield ahead. Callie felt a peace, but it was tinged with a sadness as well. Knowing a chapter of her life was coming to a close. A chapter she had been writing for many years now. About a quarter of her life, in fact. What would she do now? There were no more ghosts to hunt. She smiled at that. Then put her hands in her coat pockets.

Her left hand met some resistance. Callie frowned as her fingers closed around a small box. She pulled it out and examined it in the darkness of the backseat of Cardna Darwyn's car. By the lights brushing by on the side of the highway, Callie could see enough to discern that it was the small box Mr. Lancey's assistant had given her. *He wanted you to have this.*

Callie chuckled. How the heck had it made it this long and still stayed in her pocket? Shaking her head, she pulled the tiny cord that made a perfect bow on top. It unraveled and fell away. Then she picked at the perfect lines of invisible tape on the back of the paper-wrapped package until she finally had a good edge. She pulled the paper open, flipping the box in her hand. She removed the lid, then lifted out the object that sat inside, on a bed of thin cotton. As Callie felt the weight of it in her palm, a huge smile crossed her face. *Well, I'll be damned.*

EPILOGUE

Callie stood under the latticework of lights and flowers with her hands clasped together, calmly breathing, but her left foot continued to bounce, belying that calm with its intensity. The butterflies in her stomach had set to flight this morning, and had just never landed yet. She hadn't eaten a thing all day, afraid she would be too nervous to keep it down. The dress she had picked out for the occasion was slender and sexy without giving up its class. And while it had fit perfectly last month, it was actually snug against her belly today. She had opted for zero makeup and a low-maintenance hairstyle. It hung down past her shoulders for the first time in her life. She had straightened it this morning.

Callie had always hated other people's weddings. She also hated the photo albums that came from them. So many people on the planet had photo albums with the same damned pictures in them. Every combination of people with the bride, then with the groom, all so little creativity. *BoRing*. She didn't waste money on a cake, a photographer or a rental bill for rows of candles. She wasn't one to waste money on a one-time *anything*. Nor did she expect her friends to all go buy matching dresses. She told them to wear what they wanted. What she had spent the money on was the bar. Callie had opened a tab for all her guests. She would be funding their eats and drinks for the night. That was her idea for an expensive wedding.

She had also bought the dress though. That's one thing she had not skimped on. It wasn't a traditional wedding dress. She bought a gorgeous trumpet dress the color of lemonade, and spared no expense. And the best part about it was that she would wear it again and again.

She had phoned ahead a few weeks back to make sure the back patio would be available. So here they stood, on the covered patio of the Broken Anchor. The sun was starting to set. A breeze blew in from the bay, which the patio overlooked. There were a few boats creeping through the bay, and music could be heard coming from some of the boat slips across the water. A nice breeze carried it, along with the smell of the sea. They had been coming to this place since they had all moved to Neptune City so many years ago, and were on a first-name basis with the owners and staff. They had been delighted to reserve the ocean view for her and her party.

Callie stood, waiting for the man of the hour. They were breaking every wedding tradition she could think of, and this was one. She would stand on the rug up on the band stage and wait for her groom to walk down the aisle. Her five friends stood beside her. Rebecca, Shanna, Codi, Cardna and Cynda. Walter's friends stood across the rug, all wearing jeans and shirtsleeves. They were Sam, Aaron, Dwayne, Pierce and Kevin. Callie made eyes at each of them, trying to size them up, and realizing she was going to have to spend some time getting to know them. She had barely met most of them. Matt Minus stood directly to her right, all dressed up in linen pants and a Hawaiian shirt unbuttoned down to his chest. His thick gold chain stood out against the black forest of hair on his chest. He had a cigar in his mouth and a glass of scotch in his right hand. Callie put her hand on his shoulder and whispered something in his ear. He laughed out loud. She had at the same time used the gesture to adjust her heel, which had begun to hurt her foot. She had not worn high heels in years. She worried she might fall if she let go of him too soon.

She turned to assess the line of women behind her, dressed in a mixture of tight jeans, skirts, or in the case of Codi, a stretchy nylon dress that hugged her body like a layer of paint. Rebecca was first, looking stunning in a sparkling purple dress that also hugged her body, but went to the floor. There was a split that came all the way up her thigh. She was looking at Callie with eyes that said she knew something. She winked and Callie winked back. Shanna raised her eyebrows and showed her teeth, then blew Callie a kiss. It was nice to have Cardna and Cynda in town as well. She had not seen them for a few months. Callie turned back to Minus, who was standing there rocking back and forth like a man ready to be free to drink. Callie wiped the sweat off his forehead for him, then kissed him on the cheek. "Thank you for doing this, Matt."

"Sure thing, darlin'," he said, taking a drink of his scotch. "You say free drinks, I do pretty much anything you ask." Callie giggled at that. Then Minus said, "Oh, hey, here's the man!"

Walter came down the aisle shaking hands and clapping backs. He even got full-stopped about halfway up the aisle by a short man who looked like Danny DeVito. When the man finished speaking secrets in Walter's ear, they quit the hug and Walter looked up at Callie, grinning as he made the last few yards of the walk. He mouthed the word *wow* at her, then stepped up on the tiny band stage and grasped Callie by the hands. He leaned in to kiss her and Matt Minus shouted, "Hey, hold your horses, jerky!" and whacked him on the head with the hand holding a cigar. Ash went everywhere and the crowd erupted in laughter. That took the tension straight out of Callie's belly. She was giggling as Walter took his place trying to look ashamed and hurt, and failing miserably.

He finally smiled and turned to address the crowd. "Hey, everyone. Thank you so much for coming out today. This means a lot to me. And I know it means a lot to Callie here. Who, as soon as this asshole says it's okay, will be my wife."

There was more laughter. Minus nodded, taking a pull from the cigar, looking at Walter like he was going to sock him one when this was done.

"But seriously. It seems like maybe this has been coming for twenty or so years. I'm not sure why we were both blinded to it until recently. Anyway, carry on, Mr. Minus. And thanks again, everyone."

Everyone clapped briefly, then Minus silenced them all. "All seriousness aside, ladies and gentlemen, I've been asked to stand up here and perform a wedding because I'm so good at them. I've never been in one myself, but that doesn't mean I don't know how they're supposed to go." He let the laughter die down, then said, "Actually, I guess I don't know shit about them, because I thought the groom was supposed to wait up here while the bride walked the aisle. Either these people are backwards, or I haven't attended a wedding in too long." The crowd was very loud for a long few seconds.

"Actually, I've never been to a wedding. Good reason for that. But here's the thing. I know love when I see it. I've been asking these two knuckleheads when they were going to quit playing silly games and marry each other for about eighteen of these last twenty years. And now here we are, finally."

He waited for general silence again, then said, "Callie, do you take this guy to be your man? Every bit of him for every bit of the rest of your life?"

"I do!" Callie said, to peals of screaming and hollering. Applause and shouts of '*You go, girl!*' ran out for almost a minute. Callie felt her cheeks burning from smiling so hard. She couldn't remember the last time she had smiled this hard, and for this long. The general consensus in the crowd was in agreement with Minus, that this wedding should have happened many years ago. So the excitement level was incredibly high, for all these people were finally getting what they wanted. Some of them likely collecting on old wagers. *Told ya it would happen one day!*

"Well, all right, all right, all right!" Minus said. "Walter, do you take this woman over here to be your sweet wife? Including all her crazy projects and ideas? For ever and ever, every bit of her?"

"Minus," Walter said, looking at the man, putting a hand on his shoulder. "I take her like I take my bourbon. As much as I can get!"

The crowd went wild. Walter's guys were slapping him on the back and shouting, raising fists in the air. Callie was bent over at the waist, laughing so hard her eyes were watering. The girls behind her were clapping and dancing, snapping fingers and shaking their hips. Callie loved every bit of it. The perfect wedding, in her mind, was one that didn't waste people's time or money. They didn't need gifts. They didn't need tradition. They needed a party. Callie felt like time and money were spent on better things than weddings. Like, say, the marriage. They had sneaked away a few days ago and gotten married at the JP, where they said a prayer and took the vows all the way through. This was just for fun. Just to give everyone the show and the party.

After the scotch-riddled vows, Walter bent Callie over backwards and kissed her long and deep, to the shouts and roar of the crowd. Then he stood her up and raised her hand up in the air, like a boxer being declared winner by knockout. The crowd was on their feet, rushing the stage. Everyone wanted to be the first to offer hugs and kisses, handshakes and well-wishes. It lasted for well over five minutes. Minus didn't even get to pronounce it. After several minutes, he had waved a hand at the whole thing and stepped down off the stage to go get another drink. This brought another roar of laughter from the guys. And within the minute, the music came to life. Loud, punchy beats coming from the house audio system typically reserved for live bands. Restaurant employees and men in the crowd began folding up the chairs and moving them out of the way, leaning them against walls and putting them on carts. The party turned to a dance very quickly. The lights went down and the sun finally dipped into the water way in the west, in perfect timing. It was most serendipitous, Callie thought.

As she made her way through the crowd handing out hugs and accepting congratulations, she began to feel the tightness in her back. Too much bending over! Too much squatting! Everyone was shorter than her in these damn heels. She finally turned and locked eyes with Cynda, who was looking at her expectantly. "Will you go get my slip-ons?" Cynda nodded and disappeared. In a few minutes though, she was back, bending over and putting them on the ground in front of Callie's feet. Callie kicked off the heels and slipped into the flats, stepping down a good five inches. It had been fun being six feet, but now it was time to dance. She pulled Cynda in for a hug, thanked her and kissed her on the cheek, then watched her slip away in the crowd again, carrying the heels. Callie felt a hand on her shoulder, and turned, smiling, to see a new face in the crowd. The smile fell from her lips as she realized who it was.

"Thevi? Oh my God!" Callie said, unsure whether to smile or freak the hell out.

Thevi pulled her in for a hug. She hugged her long and hard. Then she spoke in Callie's ear, pressing it closed so she'd be able to hear her. "Callie, I'm sorry. I'm very happy for you and Walt. You two were crazy for waiting so long to get together. I was just lucky to get to interrupt your dance for a few years." She pulled away, holding Callie by the upper arms and looking in her eyes. "It should have been you all along," Thevi said, smiling richly. Callie pulled her back in and hugged her again.

"Thank you, Tev. Thank you so much for coming, and for saying that. I love you, friend."

"I love you too, Callie. Always."

Callie didn't see whether Thevi had made her way to Walter or not, but assumed she had. She had enough class to do so. Callie's eyes had filled with tears, so she now stood wiping them, but she was smiling, too. Natalie came straight up to her, smiling as she closed the few meters between them. Callie welcomed her in with a hug, stood there twisting back and forth.

"Dommie! I'm so happy you're here!" she said.

"You know I wouldn't miss it, big sis. I love you guys. So happy you're in my life now," said Natalie. She leaned in, standing on her tiptoes and kissed Callie on the lips.

Then it was Minus. He stood there nodding, twisting his mouth. "Well, Calculator, you've finally done it. Good job," he said, slow-clapping. Callie did a twist and a small curtsy, looking up at the ceiling with a fake smile.

"Thank you Matt," she said, and stepped in to hug him. Matt Minus was known not to be a hugger, but Callie wasn't taking no for an answer. He managed to lift one hand high enough to pat her on the lower back a couple of times, then backed up a step giggling uncomfortably. He took a drag from his cigar.

"So you're not having champagne, wedding girl?"

Callie furled her lips and framed her belly with her hands, pointing her elbows out dramatically. "I'm with child, Mr. Minus!"

"Uh oh," he said, taking another drag, smiling around the smoke. "Katie, bar the door!"

Callie's face fell a little. "What the heck does that mean?" she said, looking around for a door. He waved the smoke at her, then called her in with two fat fingers. She leaned over and he kissed her on the cheek. She patted his cheek as he did so, then he, too, disappeared into the crowd.

It turned out that the man who looked like Danny DeVito was, in fact, Danny DeVito. He introduced himself to Callie and kissed her hand as she smiled down at him. She would have to remember to ask Walter later how the heck he knew him. "That was a very lovely wedding, Mrs.

Watson. I wish you all the bountiful blessings the universe can bring," he said, turning and lifting a hand for effect. Callie thanked him and shook his hand, then he bowed, turning away.

Callie stood bouncing on her toes, smiling and assessing the crowd. She had hugged almost everyone in the place, and some people several times. Natalie's younger brother, for instance, had come in to congratulate her at least four times. He was twelve years old, and all five feet of him were excited by the hugs he kept stealing from her, which put his face right against her breasts. Callie giggled each time, and rubbed his head for him.

When Walter finally approached her and asked her to dance, a slow song had come on the speakers. It was a song Walter and she had danced to many times in his den, very clearly requested for this event. She noticed the whole crowd settled a little. The lights went down a notch. The DJ stood in the booth in the corner, nodding to the beat. A classy, sexy beat. Callie wrapped her arms around her new husband's neck. Holy cow, it would take a while to get used to hearing that. Saying it. She swayed back and forth with him, staring into his eyes. A permanent smile had found its way onto her face. She shook her head and sang along with the hook. *What if forever isn't long enough?* Walter nodded, chuckling silently. He took a sip from his whiskey, then leaned in and kissed her on the lips. She pulled his head close and whispered in his ear. "Thank you for marrying me, Walter Wayne Watson. I'm happy to be your wife," she said. When he pulled away smiling, he put a thumb up in the air, and she said, "Fucking finally!"

He laughed out loud and kissed her again. Then they got real close and danced.

She saw the long, tall Rebecca with her dress slit all the way up to the thigh, moving sexily with her body pressed tightly up against Natalie's. Callie smiled at them, but they were too busy in each other's embrace to see her. Codi stood with her toes on Sam's, swaying to the beat, resting her pretty head against his chest. He held it there tightly with his big strong hand. He wasn't much of a dancer like Codi was, but the girl loved him anyway. It was wonderful to see.

Everything was wonderful.

A light rain danced on the dark water. It made the lights of the nearby boathouses twinkle on the surface of the lake. It could be heard just above the music, pattering down on the tin roof above them. The breeze blew some of the mist in, cooling those close to the railing. And that was wonderful, too.

Callie met Walter's eyes again. He mouthed three words at her. She smiled peacefully, nodding. She blew him an exaggerated kiss and squeezed his shoulders. Then she buried her head in his chest. *I hope forever will be long enough.* She closed her eyes.

And danced.

Author's Note

Callie came to me in a dream in the mid-nineties. There was nothing untoward about it. She just appeared as a powerful female character. I had this idea that she would be this chaste, highly intelligent woman who was always on the right side of the law, but sometimes the wrong side of the 8-ball.

It would be almost a decade later that I would have my first child. I named her Callie. But I maintain to this day that the character was named after the daughter I knew I would have someday.

It was the character Callie's demeanor and attitude that carried me through my first three novels: *Midnight's Park*, *Resurrecting Mars* and *Into the Darkness*, but a separation happened somewhere in there. I let go of the chaste and pure angel I had created on paper so long ago. I let Callie Simmons grow up. If you've read the books, you've seen it. She adopted a foul mouth. She let the world get to her. She finally let it happen with Walter...

I felt like this made sense. She had known the guy for twenty years and had maintained her purity until she was nearly forty. It was time to let go of that slightly silly tenet.

But I had so much fun writing Callie and Walter. They just came alive on the page for me during my sessions. I hope you found that to be the case as you read them. And after four books with Callie playing the lead role, I feel like it's finally time to put them to rest. This will be the last Callie and Walter novel.

My newest work, a novel called *A Flutter in the Window*, introduces a new character set. My lead, again a strong female, is called Marcy Stedwin, though she goes by her middle name, Shawn. Her love interest is Cory Klein. Will they be my new Callie and Walter? I don't know. But I can tell you this: I'm already more excited to write Shawn than I was in writing Callie. A lot of that comes from having started the C&W series so long ago. That seems like another life now. It was time for something new. I'm probably a little more mature as a writer now as well. One can hope, anyway.

If you're reading these in order, then you have stuck with me through this journey full of ridiculous temporal contradictions and all other sorts of continuity issues I was probably too lazy to catch or correct. Thank you for that. I've learned a lot through the first five novels. These include the three mentioned above, plus *Shedding Sadness*, a standalone book, and this one.

My next to hit the shelf will be another standalone, called *Chasing Comets*, in which you will learn who Tanis Ransom is and all about her rise to fame. *Flutter* will come after that. I hope you'll stick around for these. I think it's just going to get better from here.

It's been a fun twenty-five years getting from *Midnight's Park* to *Red Bell*. I only hope it doesn't take me that long to write the next five.

\- brandon spacey
Garland, TX

www.ingramcontent.com/pod-product-compliance
Lightning Source LLC
Chambersburg PA
CBHW031235310726
48971CB00004B/1017